CW01369857

TRUTH SEER PROPHESY

Book One of "The Legacy"

by
Dean Butler

authorHOUSE®

AuthorHouse™ UK Ltd.
500 Avebury Boulevard
Central Milton Keynes, MK9 2BE
www.authorhouse.co.uk
Phone: 08001974150

© 2008 Dean Butler. All rights reserved.

No part of this book may be reproduced, stored in a retrieval system, or transmitted by any means without the written permission of the author.

First published by AuthorHouse 11/4/2008

ISBN: 978-1-4389-1907-2 (sc)

Printed in the United States of America
Bloomington, Indiana

This book is printed on acid-free paper.

*For the mother I loved but lost too
early in life.*

*For the mother I have now
and wouldn't be without.*

*And in remembrance of the father I loved
and miss.*

Chapter One

Number seven, Alexander Crescent was just a normal; ordinary looking, three bedroom house like any other in the street. It was the fourth house along in a street that had originally been reserved for the pit workers of the local coal mine, but was now generally available for anyone requiring a council property to rent. There were many such streets in the small but thriving mining town of Featherstone in the West Riding of Yorkshire, but unlike the rest of the houses in this particular street, number seven stood out for looking a little drab and a little gloomy, a little neglected one might say.

There were no colourful displays of flowers or neatly trimmed bushes in the front garden to look at as you passed by, just a dark plethora of weeds and a dull tangle of distorted shrubs. The wooden fence that topped a small two foot wall surrounding the front garden was looking decidedly rickety. A couple of the fence's slats had obviously been broken quite a while ago and now was in desperate need of repair. The metal gate at the end of the fence had once been coated in a black metallic paint, but it had long since begun to fade and flake; the metal rusted and browning beneath. The hinges were also rusted and from the dreadful and unnerving screeching sound the gate made as it banged open and closed in the brisk wind, it was in dire need of a bit of lubrication. The short narrow path that led from the street into the garden split in two, the left side leading to the front blue door. The door's paint was faded and flaking but the brass number plate above the brass letter box shone brightly in the evening moonlight as if it had just been polished; a deafening contrast of care and neglect. The right path led to the back garden and to the rear entrance of the house. A large piece of warped plywood had been attached to the remnants of a dilapidated fence and was propped against the wall of the coal house to act as a make-shift gate. If it was supposed to be some kind of deterrent against would-be intruders, it was a pitiful excuse. The rear garden had once hosted a majestic coronation of vegetables and cocktail of salad ingredients. Now, only the remnants of unused vegetables could be seen decomposing in rank and file of once cared-for rows as the garden grieved for its lost splendour. The house itself was small but comfortable; like the rest of the other three bedroom houses in the street. The third bedroom was a little small; more of a box room than anything else, but on a whole the house was big enough for the family living there at the moment.

Number seven, Alexander Crescent was home to widow, Mrs. Annabel Barnes and her three children, Jennifer, David and Christopher. They were just an ordinary family, living in an ordinary looking house, in an ordinary looking street of a small Yorkshire mining town.

But, as the autumn wind blew the fallen leaves from the next door neighbour's garden, there was an ominous and foreboding feel to it. It was a wind of change and like it or not, that change would affect the Barnes family like no other.

"Come on Dave; carry on with the story," Christopher beseeched his brother, "pleeease."

"I'm too tired Chris and mam will only tell us off, we should be asleep by now," David replied, "I'll tell you a bit more tomorrow!" David was sick of his brother bothering him all the time; all he wanted was stories of bloodthirsty pirates and magical adventures, he hated sharing their bedroom sometimes, especially at times like this when Christopher wouldn't stop nagging at him.

"Come on Dave." Christopher asked him again.

Why me? David thought as he looked at the persistent and somewhat infuriating gaze his brother was giving him. He normally wouldn't mind telling his brother a story, but he hadn't been sleeping too well of late; finding it increasingly difficult to wake up without feeling frightened, exhausted and in a cold sweat.

"Just go to sleep will you!" David shouted at his brother, showing his annoyance by raising his voice to his brother's incessant whining.

"Right you two, time to go to sleep now, I hope I don't have to tell you again? David, you have to get up early tomorrow, so straight to sleep now!" The boys' mother shouted from the bottom of the stairs.

"Now look what you've gone and done," David berated his brother with a stern look on his face. To his mother he shouted, "Ok mam, we're going to sleep now." David said, staring purposefully at his brother to emphasise the remark.

"Ok, goodnight love," she paused momentarily, listening for the expected whispers.

"But Dave..." Christopher began.

She wasn't disappointed and shouted back up the stairs, "goodnight Christopher."

"Goodnight mum." Christopher shouted back glumly; knowing his brother definitely wouldn't be telling him the rest of the story this night.

"Right you heard her, go to sleep now." David said quietly to his brother.

"Ok, no need to get in a mood about it." Christopher replied just as quietly then rolled over and went to sleep.

Mrs. Annabel Barnes stood at the bottom of the stairs and looked at her reflection in the mirror on the wall opposite. She was only 35, and still a beautiful woman, but the last year had taken its toll on her and as she pushed a couple of loose, long blonde strands of hair behind her ears, she realised she was looking tired. When her husband Tom was still alive she had been vibrant and alive, full of life. Now, well, she just looked like the worn out, tired and middle aged woman she thought she had become. She had been happy then she recalled; and who wouldn't have been. She had everything she could ever dream of; a loving husband, three wonderful children, a nice home, and a job she enjoyed. But that had all changed the previous year when her husband was taken away from her and their children, and literally overnight their lives had changed forever. She knew there was nothing she could do about the circumstances surrounding her husband's death, but that didn't stop her from feeling cheated and bitter. Cheated that her husband could not be with her and their three children anymore and bitter because he shouldn't have died the way he did. They should have grown old together and watched their children grow, watched their grandchildren play, everyone happy, living life to the full. But life wasn't that easy, you had to work with the cards you were given in life, she understood that. She knew the circumstances were beyond anyone's control and nothing could bring her lovely husband back to her and there was no point wishing things were different, they weren't. She just had to accept what happened and try to get on with the rest of her life, their lives. His death had devastated the family, like a bolt lightning it had pierced the very heart of everything they held dear. The children missed their father with each passing day, and nothing seemed to alleviate the pain of that loss. Oh, they tried to be strong for her sake; she knew, as she was striving to be strong for them. But at night, when she would lay in bed alone in the dark, she would hear them crying and calling for their father; to her surprise it had been her eldest son David that seemed to feel his loss the worse. She missed her husband, she had loved him since she was fifteen years old, and not a day went by, when she wouldn't see or hear some reminder of him.

They had met at a school disco and as she gazed into the mirror to see the reflection of that pretty, fun-loving girl she used to be, she remembered that wonderful occasion as if it happened only yesterday.

Thomas Barnes was a handsome boy; everybody said so, he was tall, athletic and had a likeable and approachable personality that suited everybody at school, whether they were pupils or teachers. He was kind and polite to everyone, although he had a tendency to be a little shy with people he didn't know. This never hindered him, as he made friends quickly and generally had a ready smile for anyone and everyone. Annabel Drake; as she was then was surprised when he walked up to her and asked her for a dance. She had only recently moved to the school; and to the area and didn't think he had even noticed her. The few friends she had made so far gave her encouraging nods and smiles as she was almost physically pushed towards the handsome young man. They giggled constantly as he escorted Annabel on to the dance floor. Annabel knew that from that moment; as he took her hand in his and gracefully, albeit a little nervously, began to dance, that she had been hooked. They laughed and danced the rest of the evening; without a thought for anyone, except each other. As they talked without pause throughout the evening she realised that he had totally and utterly captivated her, and all she could do was accept the fact that she didn't want the evening to end. She had never looked at anyone else from that moment, she had never wanted to. Annabel's father had liked the boy from the first moment they met, so when Tom had asked him four years later for his daughter's hand in marriage, he couldn't have been more pleased. Annabel had been thrilled when he went on bended knee and proposed to her later that same day, and they were married within two months. They were both young and in love, a little crazy perhaps for rushing the wedding, but everyone agreed that they looked fantastic together; a match made in heaven, they said.

A tear dropped onto her cheek as she looked at her reflection in the mirror once more, remembering her one true love, she wiped it away with the forefinger of her right hand.

"Pull yourself together Annie." She said. She knew she didn't have time to feel sorry for herself.

Yes, she was tired, and yes she looked it, but she had three children to support and a home to look after, which was why she was working two jobs now. The National Union of Mineworkers was still trying to sort out some compensation for the family, but red tape was stopping the money from being paid.

Life was getting exceedingly harder for the Barnes family, but she refused to bow down to the pressure she was under, she was a fighter and she knew it. She had to be strong for her children and she intended to be.

She sighed as she walked back into the living room and tried to get comfortable on the sofa, in front of the television. She fidgeted about for a few moments trying to find the most comfortable position; but the springs had recently gone; another thing she had to see to, she noted. She was just too tired to care, she realised. With the death of her husband, money coming into the household was scarce, and until the compensation came through she had to continue with the two jobs she was now working. Alan Barnes; her husband's younger brother had been helping them out, but he had a new wife and a baby on the way. She knew that he couldn't help them for much longer; not with a new family. Her children were the most important thing in her life and she was determined to provide for them, to care and watch over them, giving them what little protection she could. She gradually pulled herself off the uncomfortable sofa and made her way to her own bedroom. Sleep came slowly as she thought about her future and the troubles that lay ahead, but it did come, and with it, her dreams turned to her husband; her love, her life, her wonderful man and as she slept, a smile came to her lips and a tear ran down her cheek.

He was walking down a brightly lit corridor; its whiteness blinding but there was an odour of rotten flesh that seemed to permeate the atmosphere; the smell strong and nauseating, burning his nostrils with its putrid breath. A dense misty fog crawled along the floor and around his feet, but he wasn't interested in the fog or the smell for that matter; his gaze was focused on the obscure, indeterminate figure before him. He was walking toward that figure now; although he felt as if he was actually floating on the mist rather than walking, the dark figure watched silently as it awaited his arrival. He felt frightened as he drew closer, the figure had yet to raise its head as he glided toward it, but somehow he knew the face it would reveal would be cruel and hideous.

*He could feel the beads of sweating dripping down his neck and down his back, making him shiver as he moved closer to the waiting apparition. His stomach began to constrict in fear and although he didn't want to move forwards, he knew he didn't have the power to turn away. Closer and closer he moved until finally he was **standing** before the figure. He wanted to scream for help; he knew that if he* *could only make a sound, someone would come to help him, but he had no voice, and no will to make a sound, he was powerless, helpless as a new born baby. Petrified as he now was, he couldn't help but notice the faint sound of footsteps behind him, but all thoughts of rescue and deliverance were instantly gone from his mind as he realised the dark figure began to raise its hooded head towards him. As he gazed upon the face he screamed!*

David's alarm clock woke him at half past six in the morning; just as the pale autumn light began to filter through the dark blue curtains of the bedroom he shared with his brother. He stretched over to the bedside table and pushed the button down on the old sliver metal clock. As he turned his alarm off he quickly looked over to where his brother slept, but Christopher only stirred briefly, mumbling sleepily to himself before turning over. David looked at his alarm clock then, the same clock he had used for the last three years, and his thoughts immediately went to his father. His father had given him the clock as a present when he was eleven years old on obtaining his paper round. His father told him he needed the clock for his own independence. He treasured the gift, even more so since his father had died. Pulling himself gradually from his bed with a slight groan he quietly got dressed. He had a pair of fairly clean faded blue jeans; he'd only worn them two days so far, so that was ok, and a faded white Levi T-shirt. A thick brown woollen jumper his mother had bought him a few months ago from a charity shop in town was folded neatly on a chair, so he quickly put that on. He had put clean socks in his training shoes under the bed the previous night, so now they were easily retrievable, and ready to be put on. He liked everything ready for when he woke up on a morning, all his clothes laid out so he didn't have to rush around trying to find something to wear, everything in its place, that's how he liked it. Besides, he didn't want to make too much noise on a morning, if he woke his brother and especially his sister up too early, they would be in a foul mood for the rest of the day, something he tried to avoid as much as possible. So, quickly and quietly he got dressed and then walked over to the wardrobe just to check on his uniform; making sure his trousers and shirt hadn't fallen off their hangers; for some unknown reason they did that sometimes. They were hung up on the left hand side of the rail, ironed and ready to put on, just as he had left them. His brother's uniform was hung up on the right hand side; everything in its place, just as it should be. He liked the order and the uniformity of it; it was something he had shared with his father. Tom Barnes had told his son one day, that if you didn't have order, you would have chaos, and no one wanted chaos. David had listened intently to everything his father told him, but he hadn't a clue what he was talking about when he talked about chaos. Even so, he always tidied his things away when he had finished with them and always had his clothes laid out and ready for the following day.

Having dressed quickly, David rushed down the stairs, jumping the last three steps as he did so. It was a ritual he did every day, like putting his clothes out every night; it was just another thing that helped him get through the day. He would have a wash and brush his teeth later, before putting on his school uniform, but first he had newspapers to deliver. He quickly grabbed his duffle coat from the rack at the bottom of the stairs and ran out of the house to Harkin's Newsagents. It didn't take him more than a few minutes to get to the shop; it was just around the corner from his street, quite handy really. He knew his bright orange paper bag would be filled and waiting for him when he arrived; it always was. He had been delivering papers now for just over three years, it was a local round and he did it every morning except Sundays. However, he had already spoken with Mr Harkin; the owner, about obtaining a Sunday round that was about to become available. Alan Robertson was sixteen and having left school, he was now looking for an apprenticeship somewhere; the last thing he wanted to do was carry on with his paper round. Alan had bragged to everyone prior to leaving school that he would be working with his father down the mine, unfortunately for Alan; his father had different ideas and told his son that he worked down the mine so his son wouldn't have to. He didn't want his son to be a miner; he wanted something better; something safer for him, he wanted him to have a comfortable job in an office, or such like, anything but working down the pit. Disappointed, Alan had agreed with his father and after a few months of searching for the ideal job to make his father proud, he had obtained an apprenticeship with an electrician. David was envious, he would love to leave school and start looking for a job, but he was only fourteen and still had two more years at school to go, for now, he was resigned to being a paperboy. David was hopeful that Mr. Harkin would give him the job, but there were a couple of other boys interested in the same one. He gave his mother most of his money from the weekly round already but he knew the additional money would come in handy. He didn't begrudge the money either, he enjoyed his paper round and he was happy to be able to contribute a few pounds to the family pot. It wasn't a lot of money, but it was better than nothing, every little helped.

He was lucky with his paper round; he only had his estate and the one next to it to deliver to, which would generally only take him about thirty minutes to complete. He had timed himself on a few occasions to see how quickly he could finish it, but he was happy with thirty minutes, it meant he could plan his morning effectively. He also liked the fact that he was usually the only person up and about in the morning. He liked that feeling of solitude, where he could walk the streets, just him and his thoughts without being disturbed or distracted. The Sunday paper round however; if he could get it, centred in the new private estate adjacent to his own, and he had only managed a peak at it, but it was enough to impress him. The houses there had only recently been built. They were large and expensive looking with beautiful landscaped gardens, big driveways and a new red brick road leading into the estate itself. It was definitely not a council estate by any stretch of the imagination. Some of the kids he had seen around there went to his school, but he didn't know them, he didn't think they wanted to be known. When they came home from school, they tended to stay on their own estate, turning their prim and proper noses up at the rest of the kids in the area. He knew that wouldn't last long as some of them had already had those prim and proper noses put out of joint by some kids at school. You didn't last long at South Featherstone High School with an "I'm better than you" attitude; that was one thing for certain.

He arrived at the newsagents a few moments later.

"Hey up lad." Mr Harkin greeted him as he walked into the shop. Mr Harkin had the broadest Yorkshire accent David had ever heard, though he claimed to have been born and brought up in the area, it had a Barnsley twang to it.

"Morning Mr Harkin, bag ready?" He replied but knowing it would be he looked on the floor for his number; number seven, his lucky number and the number of his house.

"Aye lad, as always." Mr harking replied, pointing to a bag nearest the shop window.

David grabbed the bag. "Ok, see you later then." He said waving his hand and turning back to the door.

"Hang on David; I've got some news for thee." Mr. Harkin said as he smiled at the expectant expression on David's face and walked round the shop counter toward the boy.

"Oh?" David asked, trying to remain calm, he knew it must be about the Sunday paper round, but he just waited patiently as Mr. Harkin approached him.

"I'm giving thee Alan's job, if thy still wants it, that is." He replied after a brief moment, a slow smile coming to his face.

"Yes please Mr. Harkin, that's just great, thanks." David said happily and ran out the shop.

Mr. Harkin walked over to the shop window and watched as David excitedly left the shop, leaving the door ajar. He walked over to close it and a sad smile came to his lips as he peered outside. He had grown up with David's father and missed the friendship they had shared. He also knew that the family was finding things very difficult at the moment. He had been in the pub one night and a friend had told him things were that tight that David was giving his paper round money to his mother. He was just like his father, Frank Harkin thought, always kind and considerate to others. Which was more than what could be said for some other members of the Barnes family, he thought, thinking darkly of at least one family member he had never gotten along with. The thought was quickly pushed to the back of his mind and he returned his attention on the happy boy leaving his shop. He smiled then as he said, "That's alright lad, owt to help." Then he turned around and went back to the counter to sort the rest of the morning's papers out, the boy and his old memories forgotten as he busily worked away.

David left the shop in high spirits, as he put the last paper through the letter box he looked at his watch but was surprised to note that he was running a couple of minutes later than normal. "Strange", he thought, but he was obviously still tired from the sleepless night he had last night. He hadn't been sleeping well for a long time now he realised, his dreams generally focused on his father, but he knew he hadn't been dreaming of him for a while now and that worried him a little, especially as he had only passed away the year before. Was he forgetting him so soon, would his face fade from his memory and all he would have to remind him of that wonderful man would be the few photos that were scattered around his home. What made it worse was the fact that he couldn't even remember anything of the dreams he had. He usually remembered all his dreams; and could even relate them back in vivid detail when he concentrated, but not the ones he had been having recently for some reason. In fact the only thing he could remember was being scared and the faint sound of footsteps behind him, everything else was just a blur. He was concentrating on trying to remember the details of the dream he had last night when a sound finally registered in his brain. Footsteps, he could hear faint footsteps behind him. He turned quickly round to see who was making them, but there was no one there, the street was empty. He realised those footsteps had been with him for a good while, probably from when he began to think about his dream. He must have imagined them, some sort of manifestation brought on by his thoughts, because there was definitely no one behind him now. He stood still for a moment to consider whether or not he had just imagined the footsteps, or if there had been someone behind him. With all the houses in the street, it wouldn't be unusual for someone else to be up this early and walk their dog, or collect a newspaper for instance. But David felt it was something more, it was the feeling someone got when they thought they were being followed; the hairs on the back on their necks standing up. A little nervously, David looked all around, searching for any signs of life, and then a moment later, he gave a weak laugh and rather annoyed with himself for standing in the street like a prize cucumber; he quickly turned away and headed for home.

He arrived home a few minutes later and threw his coat onto the chair in the kitchen before making his way into the living room, where he set about making the fire, the footsteps and his unease soon forgotten. It was his daily chore to make the fire, all the Barnes children had jobs to do, but only David was responsible for preparing and lighting the fire on a morning.

David Barnes was the middle child of three, and at fourteen he had already inherited his father's athletic build. He was tall, although slightly skinny, with dark brown hair and bright blue eyes. Like his father, he was pleasant and well like by everyone, but he had been told that he had inherited his father's shyness, but unlike his father, he still hadn't overcome it. Since his father's death, his family and friends had noticed that David had become even quieter, keeping his thoughts and feelings locked away. He hadn't been one for showing his feelings before his father's death, but recently he had showed very little at all, becoming more withdrawn as the months passed by. For some reason it had hit him the hardest and although all three children felt their father's loss, it was David that was struggling to come to terms with what had happened, as if he couldn't quite accept it. Everyone was being sympathetic and supportive, but as the time ticked by, he was becoming more withdrawn, and his mother in particular was worried about him. For David, it seemed like only yesterday when he had been given the news that his father was dead. At a time when everyone in the world still seemed to be mourning the death of the "King of Rock and Roll", Elvis Presley; who had died the month before, David had lost his father. The loss had almost been too great to bear and he constantly thought about him, he missed him so much. Every time he heard Elvis's name, he was reminded of the times when he and his father would sit together and watch his films, singing along to the songs. His mother had given him chores to keep him occupied and reminded him that he was now the man of the house and she relied on him to keep everyone strong and safe. David knew what she was trying to do, and although he often didn't feel up to the task, he didn't shirk his responsibilities. He had no problems with his brother, but he realised quite quickly that he couldn't make his sister Jennifer, do anything she didn't want to do. She constantly reminded him that she was the eldest and she would do whatever she damn well pleased. They would argue and he would walk away in the end, in case he did something he might regret. The last thing their mother needed right now was for her children to be at each others throats and he deemed this to be the best response; which as it so happened, infuriated his sister and made him smile once he realised it. David realised quickly how to wind his sister up; just as she knew how to wind him up, and it was a constant battle of wills to see who would win each day. They both tried hard not to argue in front of their mother; they didn't want her to be more upset than she already was, so they made a pact to try and spare her from their childish wrangling. A pact, they had managed to adhere to so far; albeit with a little difficulty.

David looked at his watch again and for the second time that morning he realised he was running late. He had to get a move on if he was to finish his chores and not be late for school. He normally allowed himself plenty of time to complete his paper round, finish his chores and get breakfast before getting ready for school, but not toady for some reason. He quickly walked into the living room and set about preparing the fire. He began by cleaning out the grate, putting most of yesterday's ashes into a bucket and sweeping the remainder back into the fireplace. A bit of excess ash wouldn't cause too many problems and he thought he could dedicate more time to the task tomorrow morning, but for now, time was ticking by. He folded sheets of yesterday's newspaper into knots; this allowed the paper to burn longer, and then placed the sticks of firewood on top. He sprang to his feet and walked from the living room through the kitchen to the coal shed, where he filled a bucket full to the brim with bricks of coal. Taking it back through the kitchen and into the living room, he placed the bucket next to the hearth and carefully placed a few pieces of coal on top of the wood. He was just adding a few more to finish off before lighting the now complete fire when the grate moved slightly toward him of its own volition, toppling the couple of pieces of coal he had just laid, onto the hearth. He looked at the grate in astonishment and watched in amazement as it moved again. He moved away from the fireplace involuntary; more from surprise than anything else. As the grate moved, more coal fell from the top and landed on the hearth, and he couldn't do anything but stare in shock. He eventually gathered enough courage to investigate and knelt closer to the fireplace, looking under the grate to see if there was something pushing it forward, although he couldn't think what that something could be. As he stared at the back of the fireplace he noticed a brick had become dislodged somehow from the back. He wondered how that could have happened and thought maybe something had become stuck there, it sounded absurd but he didn't know how the grate could move forward like that without being pushed or pulled, and there didn't seem to be anything doing either. On closer inspection he noticed that the brick had actually come away from the back of the fireplace now by a couple of inches.

David reached his hand under the grate to try and feel if there was anything behind it or at least push the brick back, but as he touched the brick, he was astounded to feel a strange sensation and then shocked to see his finger tips fade to transparency.

"What the..." He exclaimed, snatching his hand back from the brick, scraping the top of his hand on the underneath of the grate. His fingers had returned to normal as soon as he moved them away from the brick, but now he had a nasty red scratch on the top of his hand. He held the now injured hand in his good one and brought it up to his face to have a good look. He wiggled his fingers and then gently touched them with his other hand, almost expecting them to disappear.

Realising that he still had his hand; and intact, he used his other hand to reach out and touch the protruding brick once more. He felt the same strange sensation once more when his fingers touched the brick and watched in wonder as they began to fade. He pulled his hand back; carefully this time and his fingers returned to normal, as before. He sat there a few moments watching the brick with suspicion, trying to determine why and how the brick acted this way and what he was going to do about it. He couldn't decide if he was dreaming or having hallucinations, but he couldn't have this sort of thing happening in his fireplace.

"This is just too weird," he said out loud, "I don't know what's happening here, but I don't like it."

Composing himself, David decided to see how far his hand could go and how much would fade. Reaching for the brick, and preparing himself for the worse, he said. "Ok, let's see what you do now?" And closed his eyes, as if by doing so, he could stop whatever trickery was happening to him.

"Who does what?" Christopher asked as he entered the living room.

David jumped at the sound of his brother's voice, he hadn't heard his brother step into the room, and he scraped his other hand on the grate knocking the coal, the wood and the pieces of paper on to the hearth.

"Shit!" He exclaimed, "Now look what you've made me go and do Chris." David berated his brother.

"Me, I didn't do owt," Christopher replied in amazement. "It was you talking to yourself and I think you'll find it was you that tipped that lot up". Christopher retorted pointing to the mess.

David quickly glanced from his brother and back to the fireplace, and to his surprise he noticed that the brick that had been protruding out from the back of the fireplace was back where it should be. David stared in disbelief.

He looked back at his brother, who was frowning down at him from the doorway. Christopher Martin Barnes was large for his age, not excessively tall, but definitely stocky. David was tall and athletic, but Christopher was slightly shorter and a lot bulkier. He also acted older than his twelve years; but that could be due to the fact that he hung around his brother all the time. As he stood there in the doorway, an expression of concern on his face, David knew he was only angry with his brother because he had made him jump and changed the angry expression on his face.

"Sorry Chris," he smiled weakly at his brother, "I think I must have been day-dreaming." he said as he stared back at the fireplace.

"You ok Dave?" Christopher asked as he looked at his brother's glazed expression.

"Yeah fine, just a little tired I suppose, I didn't sleep too well again last night." He replied shaking his head, trying to convince himself that was why he was now seeing things, although he didn't really believe that.

"Well, tired or not, you best get a move on, Jen is making breakfast and she's in a foul mood."

So much for trying to be quiet this morning then, David thought.

"Ok Chris, tell the witch I'm on my way." David smiled faintly at his brother who walked back into the kitchen laughing.

David smiled as he heard Christopher telling their sister that he was on his way, but didn't mention that he had called her a witch, thankfully he thought.

"You took your time." Jennifer said to David as he walked into the kitchen and sat down beside his brother. She scowled at Christopher when she noticed him smile at David. "I'm not here to be your slave you know." She moaned as she put his bowl of cereal in front of him with a mug of tea.

David decided to keep quiet, he didn't feel like getting into an argument with his sister this morning and especially as she seemed to be in the mood for one.

Realising David wasn't going to say anything to her comments she turned away from her brothers and began clearing away Christopher's plate and mug, mumbling to herself as she did so.

Jennifer Barnes was the eldest Barnes child, she was fifteen going on thirty, and didn't everyone know it. But she was the spitting image of their mother, they were both tall and slender and before their mother cut her hair short, she use to have long wavy blonde hair with natural ringlets that cascaded down her back almost reaching her bottom, like Jennifer had now. Jennifer was a girl of natural beauty, she didn't need to apply make-up like a lot of girls her age did, and everyone thought that "butter wouldn't melt". But Jennifer had a temper; unlike her mother, and the boys had seen it manifest itself on more than one occasion and generally in their direction. Luckily for her brothers there were tell tale signs when she was getting angry; like her nose scrunching up and her brows knitting together. They would soon make themselves scarce when they saw those signs.

She looked over at her brother as he sat at the kitchen table eating his breakfast, Christopher chattering beside him. She could feel the anger boiling up inside of her, but she didn't know why she was angry all the time these days, she just was.

"Hurry up you two, you still need to get washed and ready for school." She said as she looked at the clock on the wall above the table, "And look at the time." She continued as she put her empty bowl into the sink and quickly left the kitchen to go up stairs to get ready for school herself.

"Is she ok Dave?" Christopher asked his brother.

"She's fine Chris; she's just not a morning person."

Finishing his bowl of Rice Krispies, David said. "Come on Chris, we'd best go and get ready.

Chapter Two

Jennifer and David Barnes went to the same school; South Featherstone High School, but they never went to school together. Jennifer was in the fifth and final year, where as David was in the fourth year. He wasn't sure why they called it the "fourth year", because it was only his second year in the school, the second of three to be exact. His first year at the school had been terrible and not only because his father had died in the summer. He just didn't feel as though he really fitted in, and although this term had started off a little better, he knew it wasn't because of something he had done, but more to the fact that his father had died and everyone felt sorry for him. He was still getting the odd look of pity from some of the teachers, and even the students; when they didn't think he was looking, but thankfully not as often any more. Although, he did think that maybe he had finally got use to seeing that particular look, and didn't really notice it anymore.

David walked to school with a group of friends he had known most of his life. They would all meet at a pre-determined time and place so they could make school with sufficient time to play a game of football. He would meet Ian Cavendish first, who lived opposite his house at number 8. He had known Ian the longest but he was a bit of a know it all and constantly got on everyone's nerves with his constant nonsensical chattering; including David's, though he never said anything. The pair of them would walk to the end of the street where they would meet up with Robert "Robbo" Hanson; he lived at number 6 Alexander Road. Robbo had the girls swooning at his feet. He not only had the looks but was an athlete to boot. He was that fast and skilful that he was the only fourth year pupil allowed to play in the school senior rugby team and had already been spotted by the Featherstone Rovers coach. Charles "Gos" Gosforth normally called for Adam Ping at the Chinese takeaway; "The Golden Bowl", before meeting everyone else at Cresses Corner; which was just off Featherstone Lane. Ping; as he was referred to had only moved into the area the previous year, and around the same time David's father had died. Ping fitted in right away with the rest of the boys and they all soon became friends. The five boys would meet up and then cut across the fields to walk the one and a half miles to school. The journey took them from their final meeting point to the railway crossing by the cricket ground and across the farmer's fields. The only problem with the route was that sometimes the farmer would be waiting for the boys to try it. David wasn't sure why, but the farmer had been chasing boys across his fields for years and now it had become a bit of a competition to see who could get closest to the tractor without the farmer actually catching them. There was an alternative route, which took them around the fields and past the ground used by the Featherstone Rovers Rugby League team, but it added an extra fifteen to twenty minutes onto the journey and to be honest, wasn't as much fun. All the boys enjoyed the thrill of the chase and would always laugh about their close calls, once they by-passed the irate farmer. Besides, if they decided to take the indirect route they wouldn't have time for a game of football when they arrived; so no choice really, football won every time.

Quite a few kids turned up early for the game prior to the bell going for the start of the day, which was surprising really as probably most of the school's four hundred pupils didn't really want to be there. Unfortunately, attendance wasn't an option, and although it was relatively easy to get out of the school without being seen, the punishment for being caught wasn't exactly worth the crime. Letters had been sent out to all the parents with the start of the new term to reiterate that all pupils caught out of school grounds in school time would be punished. Those letters had been duly signed by the caring parents to agree with any punishment imposed by the school, which ensured their beloved children remained there or face the consequences. Caning was still the preferred method of punishment by many of the teachers; although a couple used an old trainer on a bare backside. Not all of the parents had agreed with the methods of punishment, but most had and the same punishment had to be administered to all the pupils or none, so suffice to say the majority won and truancy wasn't a real problem at the school any more.

Mr. Brubeck was the head teacher for the Fourth Year pupils at the school and it was his responsibility to administer all punishments for his particular year group. The only problem was, Mr Bill Brubeck, was the nicest teacher in the whole school and anyone who had been punished by him would often say afterwards that it wasn't the punishment that had hurt them as much as the look of disappointment on his face as he thrashed them. Bill Brubeck wasn't always portrayed as a nice man though. In his youth he had been picked to play rugby for Wakefield, but a bad knee injury had ended his dream. He was a big man, possessed of incredible speed for someone his size and weight, and the fact that he couldn't play rugby again had really hit him hard. Having been told he couldn't play his beloved game anymore he literally went off the rails. He became a bouncer at the local night spot for a while; gaining a terrible reputation, beating up the customers for laughs and causing trouble in general. This carried on for about six months or so until it was David's father, who finally had a word with him. Bill left his job that day and never went back to the club. A few weeks later, Tom Barnes had got him a job at the school as a PE teacher, where he coached the under elevens rugby team. To everyone's surprise; Bill's included, he found he not only enjoyed it, but he was good at it. He realised he had found his vocation in life and decided to make teaching a full time occupation. This eventually led him to find a placement at the school. After only a couple of years he had been promoted to head teacher after displaying a natural ability to establish a rapour with the kids he taught. His earlier exploits had been forgotten and he was considered to be more of a gentle giant than anything else. He became respected by the teachers and especially his pupils. As to his conversation with Tom Barnes; there was a lot of speculation, but neither man had spoken of it to anyone. At the end of the day, the conversation had the desired effect and now Bill Brubeck was the most popular and best teacher at the school.

After Tom's death it had been Bill's unenviable task of telling David and Jennifer about their father's accident, as their mother was too distraught at the time. He had called them both into his office and given them the details of the accident. They were told that their father had gone into work on his day off to sort out a conveyor belt problem in the main shaft. The details appeared a bit hazy, but there was a fault with a piece of machinery and their father had died as a result.

Bill had tried to comfort them, but they were beyond consoling, so he drove them home and waited there for the rest of the day until their uncle Alan brought their mother home from seeing their father's body. He offered his sincere commiserations and then left the family to grieve together. Since that fateful day, he had watched out for the two children, always offering them encouragement in everything they did, and offering his assistance whenever he thought they might need it.

David Barnes was watching Bill Brubeck now as he taught his English class, and all the memories of that terrible day came flooding back. He looked out of the window next to him to try and banish the images that had come into his head and was surprised to see a dark figure standing next to the bicycle shed. He thought it couldn't be a pupil as everyone should be in lessons now, and with them the teachers, so he wasn't sure who it could be. Then the figure seemed to fade into the trees behind it, until it eventually disappeared. David stared in the same direction a little longer, straining to see where the figure had disappeared to, that was until his attention was brought back to the class by a loud cough from the teacher. All the children began to laugh until the teacher stared them into silence and then told them to get on with their work.

Bill Brubeck walked over to David a few moments later once he was satisfied the children were working and whispered as he walked past him. "You ok David?"

Just as quietly he whispered back. "Yes sir, sorry!"

The teacher smiled briefly and winked at him as he walked back to the front of the class, no one had noticed or heard the exchange, but David felt as if someone was staring at him, the hairs on the back of his neck stood on end. He looked around the classroom, but couldn't tell if anyone was looking at him or not, but the sensation stayed with him for a few moments longer before it eventually disappeared.

Mr. Watson was the Math teacher at South Featherstone High School; he was a short, stick-like man of about forty years. He had thin wispy brown hair, a long, thin face and an Errol Flynn style moustache. Mr. Watson tried hard to make his lessons interesting and enjoyable, but he had a small problem, which stopped everyone from concentrating on what he was teaching. Mr. Bernard Watson had the most nauseating, high pitched, screech of a voice anyone had ever heard in their lives. It grated on everyone's nerves; including the other teachers, and to make matters worse, every time the man got annoyed or angry, his screech resonated tenfold. A couple of boys in the class found this extremely amusing, and found every opportunity to disrupt his lessons; just to watch him lose his composure and laugh at the poor man.

David sat in Mr. Watson's class, and as he listened to him drone on about equilateral triangles his attention began to wander. Ian was sat next to him and was trying to tell him about some girl that fancied Robbo. David had heard it all before though, and had heard the whispers and giggles as he and Robbo walked by the girls in the corridor, though Robbo seemed oblivious most of the time.

Glancing out of the window, his gaze was drawn to a dark figure shadowed in the corner of the building where the entrance to the gymnasium was located. It couldn't be coincidence he thought, this looked like the same figure he had seen only half an hour earlier in his English class. The distance from the window to where the figure was standing couldn't have been more than twenty yards but David couldn't make out any details, though he leaned toward the window trying to get a better look. The figure appeared to be about six feet tall, but any other distinguishing features were obscured by the shadows. He could tell though, that the figure was facing his direction, which was quite disconcerting to David, though he didn't know why.

"Wonder what he's doing?" David said quietly, but to no-one in particular.

"Who?" Ian said, leaning over David toward the window for a nosey.

"Ow!" Simon Aston shouted turning to look behind him.

"Stop that Alan!" Mr. Watson screeched at a boy to the left of David and two rows up. The teacher walked over to the boy and began to berate him.

The two boys looked over at the commotion, the stranger forgotten.

Alan Saunders had thrown a paper aeroplane at the boy in front, Simon Aston. Simon was rubbing his neck, where a red mark had been made by the offending plane and turned to glare at Alan as the teacher stood in front of the boy and told him off for his disruptive behaviour. Alan smiled at the teacher, fully aware that he wouldn't actually do anything to him except bump his gums for a few seconds. Alan Saunders was a trouble-maker and considered to be one of the toughest boys in school. His family was notorious for causing bother in the town, but nothing was ever done about it, and it looked like Alan was continuing with the family tradition. The other pupils in the class just smiled back as Alan smirked at the teacher and looked round the classroom to ensure everyone was watching him; he was a bit of an exhibitionist. They didn't smile because they thought it was funny though, they smiled because the alternative would be painful. If they didn't show Alan they were enjoying the spectacle, that would make him angry, and when he got angry, it normally resulted in someone getting hurt. None of the pupils wanted that someone to be them. Simon wasn't stupid either; he turned away from Alan and just sat there quietly as the teacher continued to berate his tormentor.

Alan would probably call him a baby for shouting out in the first place; when they left class, but hopefully that would be all. When Simon looked in his direction, David gave him a weak smile of commiseration; they both knew that Alan would probably torment him for a few days at least, for calling out.

The entire classroom watched avidly as Alan sat at his desk and smiled at the teacher. Trying to present a face of innocence and raising his hands to emphasise the point, much to the teacher's exasperation.

David soon lost interest in the proceedings and looked back towards the entrance to the gymnasium, the figure; if it had been there at all, had definitely disappeared now. He quickly scanned the area again but there was no one present anywhere. He turned back to watch Mr Watson lose his control when Alan continued to smile innocently and his voice began to screech, as everyone knew it would. David's attention was still focused on the teacher and pupil exchange when he glimpsed something in the corner of his eye. He turned his head to see what it was, and almost jumped out of his skin.

"Shit!" He exclaimed, as he looked out of the window to see the figure standing right in front of him on the other side of the window.

David looked toward Ian; who incredibly was still chattering away about nothing; while he watched the teacher and pupil exchange, as if he hadn't even noticed anything unusual. David turned toward the window again in amazement and confusion.

The face was still there and looking straight back at him, it was a pale face of a twenty something man, with snake-like blue eyes and matted wispy white hair, which could just be seen in the darkness of a hood that covered most of the man's face in shadow. The man was wearing a long dark habit, like that used by a priest or monk, which was fastened at the waist with a brown leather belt; a sheath and dagger were attached to the belt. As he looked into the man's eyes, they seemed to bore into his very soul. Captivating him, he found he couldn't concentrate, his thoughts flitting from one thing to another in an instant, he tried to think about something that would break the spell, to stop his thoughts from wandering, but to no avail. It seemed like magic; as if the strange man was trying to tear every thought he ever had from inside his mind. David tried to concentrate harder, to will himself to turn away from the man's piercing eyes before he lost his mind. Then an image of his father was in his mind and the stranger's eyes lost their intensity and David managed to focus his thoughts once more. Once the spell had been broken, the stranger appeared to gasp in disbelief and then he tried to speak. When no words came from his mouth, the stranger seemed surprised and annoyed at the same time. The annoyance became frustration when his brows creased together and his concentration on getting the words from his mouth failed. Then suddenly, the man's exprsion changed to one of panic as he slow gan to fade to nothing.

David jumped again at the si strange man as he began to dis

his eyes. He quickly moved toward the window to try and get a better look outside, placing his hands on the window he looked all around, but there was no one there.

"Yes David?" Asked Mr Watson.

David swivelled his head around to look at the teacher; who was once more standing in front of the Blackboard. "Sorry sir, nothing." David stammered disorientated. Something wasn't right; he thought, something was different, he couldn't put his finger on it, but something was definitely different about the classroom.

"Well sit back down then." He waved at him and returned to scribbling something on the blackboard.

"You ok Dave," Ian asked, concerned for his friend.

"Yeah fine." He whispered back, not sure what to say.

He sat down, shaken, but still thinking something wasn't quite right, he also continued to look outside in case he could see the strange man again. He wasn't sure if he was day dreaming or not, but everything in the classroom appeared to be normal, so why did he feel that it wasn't right, he wondered.

Maybe he had just nodded off for a few moments and had dreamed the entire incident, he thought to himself, and tried to concentrate on the rest of the lesson.

He tried to concentrate but it was almost impossible, his thoughts kept returning to the stranger and the effect he had on him. He still felt that something was wrong in the class but he still couldn't put his finger on it. Everything was how it should be; no one else had noticed anything unusual from what he could gather, but he was sure something inexplicable was going on. He began to think about the incidents of the morning, from the fireplace to the appearance of the strange man, nothing seemed real. The man had seemed real enough at first, flesh and blood, like himself, but how had he just disappeared like that? Was he losing his mind? He thought he must be. He decided to try and not think about it any more.

Then Ian began to babble about some girl that fancied Robbo, and that struck David as being a bit odd, as he was certain that Ian had already told David about the girl a little earlier. Why was he going on about the same thing? As he listened though, David realised that not only was Ian talking about the same topic, but he was repeating the same words, exactly the same words.

"Ow!" Simon shouted.

"Stop that, Alan!" Mr. Watson screeched at him.

David sat up, alert and in shock as the events he had just witnessed moments before between his teacher and Alan Saunders happened again. He quickly looked outside his window to see if the stranger had reappeared too, but there was no one there. He couldn't believe what he was seeing, everything happened again in every detail, everything that is, except the presence of the stranger at his window.

David could think of nothing else for the rest of the day. His mind was lost in thoughts of strange men with piercing blue eyes who were shrouded in dark monk-like robes. He could not shake the feeling that someone was watching him either, as he walked the mile and half route back home with his friends. It was an uneasy feeling, a feeling which in the end forced him to say goodbye to them, saying he had to hurry and get home on some pretence of doing some jobs for his mother. He ran the last half mile home. He wasn't frightened; he thought to himself, but he was uneasy and didn't particularly like the feeling.

He arrived home a while later breathing hard and sweating from the exertion, the feeling still persisted and made him sprint the last two hundred meters or so. Christopher was sitting at the kitchen table; still dressed in his school uniform when he rushed into the room, closing the door firmly behind him. It was only then, with the door closed and him leaning against it that the feeling finally subsided. David looked up at his brother trying to gather his breath and noticed the bemused look his brother was giving him.

"You ok Dave?" He asked.

"I am now," he said smiling at his brother. "Just ran up the street."

"Why?" Christopher asked his brother, shaking his head.

"Why? What?" David replied still trying to catch his breath.

"Why did you run up the street? Were you being chased?" Christopher asked suspiciously.

"No, nothing like that," he replied sheepishly. "Just wanted to get home quickly, that's all."

"Oh, what for?" He said unconvinced, but interested never the less.

"Well, nothing really." David replied trying to think of something but failing miserably.

"So let me get this right, you ran up the street to get here quickly, but now your home you haven't got anything particular to do." Christopher surmised.

David was getting annoyed, he knew it sounded stupid but he didn't want to tell Christopher everything he had witnessed today; he would think he was mad, especially if he mentioned the strange disappearing monk. So he turned to the sink and grabbing a glass from the draining board, he poured himself a glass of water.

"Council pop Dave, now I know you're not feeling ok!" His brother said to him, smiling. That's what they both called the water from the tap; David rarely drank it, preferring fizzy pop; and especially Dandelion and Burdock, although Caribbean Crush was just as nice.

"I'm ok, just a bit thirsty." He replied as he quickly guzzled the last of the water in the glass. He turned to his brother and said, "Think we best go and get changed out of these uniforms before misery guts gets home from school."

"God she was in a bad mood this morning, wasn't she?" Christopher replied still smiling.

"Yeah, and I don't feel like having an argument with her today, so come on."

The two boys walked from the kitchen into the hall and upstairs to their bedroom, and were just at the top of the stairs when they heard the back door open, then close.

"You two home yet?" Jennifer shouted as she walked into the kitchen.

"Yeah," David shouted down the stairs. "We're just getting changed."

Jennifer looked at the sink full of plates and cups and sighed before shouting back. "Well don't take all day, we have to make tea."

"I think she's still in a mood?" Christopher said quietly to his brother as they both changed out of their uniforms and into their scruffs.

"Isn't she always lately?" David replied with a smile.

Chapter Three

He was walking down a brightly lit corridor; its whiteness blinding but there was an odour of rotten flesh that seemed to permeate the atmosphere; the smell strong and nauseating, burning his nostrils with its putrid breath. A dense misty fog crawled along the floor and around his feet, but he wasn't interested in the fog or the smell for that matter; his gaze was focused on the obscure, indeterminate figure before him. He was walking toward that figure now; although he felt as if he was actually floating on the mist rather than walking, the dark figure watched silently as he awaited his arrival. He felt frightened as he drew closer, the figure had yet to raise its head as he glided toward it, but somehow he knew the face it would reveal would be cruel and hideous.

He could feel the beads of sweating dripping down his neck and down his back, making him shiver as he moved closer to the waiting apparition. His stomach began to constrict in fear and although he didn't want to move forwards, he knew he didn't have the power to turn away. Closer and closer he moved until finally he was standing before the figure in the monk's habit, the figures face obscured by an overlarge hood. He wanted to scream for help; he knew that if he could only make a sound, someone would come to help him, but he had no voice, and no will to make a sound, he was powerless, helpless as a new born baby. Petrified as he now was, he couldn't help but notice the faint sound of footsteps behind him. Faint they might be, but he was positive they were heading in his direction. His body began to stop shivering and he began to relax as the footsteps grew stronger. Then he realised the figure was raising his head and all thoughts of salvation and deliverance diminished as he gazed upon the face. He screamed!

David woke with a start; he could feel the clamminess of his body where the sweat had soaked him through, his sheets damp and crumpled uncomfortably beneath him. Still half-asleep, he groggily got out of bed and made his way down the stairs to the kitchen. The stairs were cold and the pale blue light of the moon crept in through the landing window. He felt the night's cold air on his breath as he walked into the kitchen and filled a glass with water from the tap. He was conscious of the fact that he was drinking a lot of water lately; he didn't know why, but he seemed to be constantly thirsty. He took a generous gulp before refilling the glass and then he made his way into the living room. The room was still relatively warm, he thought as he made his way across the room to sit on the sofa opposite the fireplace. He sat there silently and shivered as he watched the last remnants of the days fire burn itself out. He took another swig from his glass and noticed a faint plume of smoke wafting up the chimney breast; he watch it as it snaked its way upwards, trailing out of sight until it disappeared altogether. He put the glass of water to his lips and was just about to drink that last few drops of water when he heard a faint tapping sound. He quickly got to his feet and instinctively moved toward the window. The tapping sound was made by something or someone tapping on the window pane. The curtains were closed, but David didn't hesitate as he threw them open. He let out a weak gasp of surprise and took an involuntary step backwards as he looked at the mysterious stranger tapping on the window. David still clung to the curtains and squeezed them tighter as the figure on the other side of the window smiled at him.

The tapping sound began again, and David realised that his mind had wondered, when he saw the frustrated look on the stranger's face. He was trying to say something, trying to tell David something important, but David couldn't hear any words or even read his lips, like some people could. Frustrated, the man began to point vigorously at the fireplace, nodding his head at the same time as if to indicate that's where David should go.

David turned his head toward the fireplace briefly, taking a hesitant step towards it; he turned to see the man smile encouragingly at him. David slowly walked toward the fireplace and bent down before it, he quickly looked toward the man at the window again, and he was still there and still pointing at the fireplace, his smile wider than before.

David reached his hand out toward the grate, but fearing it still might be hot he reached for the poker on the hearth and used it to lever the grate out of the way. Again he looked toward the man, who was still smiling and nodding encouragingly at him.

When David looked back at the grate he ticed the brick had become lose again pushed the grate forward.

David looked back toward the window but the stranger had disappeared. Had the stranger wanted him to touch the brick? He wasn't sure, but he knew what would happen if he did, he would feel that strange tingling sensation, but what then? He wondered if the man had witnessed him touching the brick earlier or if the man had actually caused the brick to make his hand disappear in the first place. If the man could make himself disappear, what else was he capable of, he wondered!

He didn't give himself time to consider the repercussions of his actions; he just reached out his hand toward the brick and waited for the inevitable to happen. He was a little surprised by what happened. He had expected the tingling sensation he had experienced before, but this time the brick was solid, it just came away from the back of the fireplace as his hand reached out to touch it. He pulled it free, removing it from the fireplace and was almost blinded by a bright white light that emanated from the hole he had made. The light was so intense that it illuminated the entire room as if someone had turned on the light.

"I wasn't expecting that!" He said to himself as he put the brick to one side. He then leaned closer to inspect the hole and had to move the grate out of the way before he could manoeuvre his head in enough to make anything out. David couldn't believe his eyes, through the hole he was amazed to see a vast room, empty except for a large winding slide that appeared to start from the very point where his hole was. At the end of the slide was a large wooden door, the room was empty of anything else. He was just about to pull back; thinking he must still be dreaming when the stranger materialised out of nowhere. He was standing at the end of the slide in front of the door, as if waiting for something or somebody. David pulled his head back and looked toward the window, expecting the stranger to return, but there was no one there. He peered back into the hole and the strange man was now looking directly upwards at the hole and at David.

"David," the man whispered, "David." He repeated more urgently as he realised he had a voice.

David banged his head on the side of the fireplace as he pulled it back in shock. The man had finally found his voice; though it was a whisper. The strange man knew his name and he was calling for him.

David scrambled back from the fireplace and sat with his back against the sofa as he stared at the hole with the light still emanating from it.

He was scared, he was more than scared, he was extremely scared, too scared to think about getting himself drawn into a strange room by a strange man who was calling his name. He stared at the fireplace for a long time, and didn't realise for a while that the light had gone out. How could he not know the light had gone out, he thought to himself, once he realised what had happened. It had illuminated the room; he should have noticed when it went out, surely? He sat there in silent contemplation, waiting and wondering what would happen next. He waited a few minutes, and then he waited a few more, but nothing happened except that the room was beginning to get decidedly colder. He could see his breath in the dim moonlight and he shivered once more.

Finding a small element of courage from deep within himself, David approached the fireplace and slowly, cautiously looked into the hole. There was nothing to see but the hole where the brick had come from. He decided to replace the brick and see what happened, but when he did so the brick just became part of the fireplace again and he couldn't remove it.

He felt all around the brick and nothing happened. Thinking he was trying to grab the wrong brick, he tried the others but still nothing happened. He sat back on his haunches and gazed at the fireplace and wondered what was happening to him. He tried again a few moments later but still nothing happened. He went to the window looking for the strange man but he wasn't there either. He sat for a few minutes more before deciding there was nothing else he could do. The temperature had dropped quite considerably now and so he decided he would be better off going back to bed. Maybe this was just some crazy dream and he would wake up and laugh at it all. Deciding, that was probably the case, but knowing he had no choice but to let the dream sequence follow its path, he made his way back to his room.

Christopher was still fast asleep as he jumped into bed; he could see his chest rising and falling as he breathed a peaceful sleep. David watched his younger brother with envy; he didn't think he had had a good nights sleep for quite a while, and wasn't sure if he was truly awake or asleep now.

Never the less, he lay awake for a good hour; watching the moments slowly tick by on his clock, thinking of everything that had happened to him throughout the day. He tried to think of a logical explanation for the strange events, but couldn't think of anything that could explain what had happened. He wasn't sure if they were dreams, hallucinations or if he was just going crazy; but he didn't like what he couldn't understand. He struggled to get back to sleep, worried what was going to happen when he woke in the morning. This latest incident had frightened him; he hadn't been scared of the day dreams or whatever they were, during the day time, but night time was different, night time was when all the stories you had heard about, fired the imagination. David had a very vivid imagination, and as he watched the minutes slowly, ever so slowly tick by, his imagination worked overtime. Every little noise made him jump and his mind made shadows appear out of nowhere to mock him. He was frightened, not by what had happened he realised, but by his own imagination, his mind was making the situation worse than it actually was. He wondered what his father would have made of all this, and with the thought of his father clear in his mind, he began to relax. He realised he had never been frightened once when his father was alive. But he wasn't alive any more, and now he was alone, he had no choice but to face his fears, he had to be strong, not only for himself, but for his family. He forced his head out of the covers and looked around the bedroom. There were no evil shadows waiting for him to appear, no monsters or goblins from the scary stories he had heard tell; only Christopher peacefully asleep in the bed opposite. Realising that one fact made him want to laugh at himself, he had let his imagination get the better of him; but no more, he thought. He knew he must be imagining everything and it was time for him to put a stop to it and regain control. Thinking how ridiculous it all sounded, and how disappointed his father would be to think that David couldn't overcome these childish fears, David finally fell asleep.

It was 6:30am when his alarm clock woke him from a restless night full of dreams of the mysterious robed stranger and a house made of magical bricks. With his thoughts still on the events of the night, he rushed down the stairs and walked into the living room; somewhat apprehensively. He couldn't remember putting the grate back, or putting away the poker, but everything seemed to be back in their original places. Had he in fact dreamt everything about the previous night, he wondered?

He would have been content with that explanation, but as he headed back up to his bedroom he saw his reflection in the mirror at the bottom of the stairs. The reflection of a boy with a sooty face and a small round bump on the top side of his head. He touched it gently; it was a little tender but realised he hadn't even noticed it in the night. He looked at his reflection in the mirror; saw his own eyes staring back at him and began to wonder if he wasn't just going crazy after all. He sighed as he stared at his reflection. What did this all mean, he thought to himself once more? What was happening, and why him? He got no answers or sympathy from his reflection, only a frown, his frown. He wasn't sure what to believe anymore, but something inside his head told him that whatever was happening wasn't just a dream, it was real, and it was happening to him for a reason. But, when he posed that question to that something in his head, there was no answer. Maybe today would be different; maybe there wouldn't be any more strange events? And maybe he could get on with his life. But as he looked at his dirty face, he knew it wouldn't be the end, in fact he knew, somehow, that this was just the beginning and he shuddered involuntarily.

He wondered if he could just hide away and let whatever was happening to him, just pass him by. But he was sure that wouldn't be possible. He either had to fight it; which seemed impossible, or go with the flow and see where it took him. He wasn't a brave boy, he knew that and it didn't really bother him. But he hated not knowing things; especially things that affected him. So, really he had no choice, he had to find out why he was seeing strange inexplicable things. With that in mind he quickly climbed the stairs and made his way to the bathroom, and washing quickly, he wasted no time in returning to his bedroom to get dressed. A few moments later; and carrying his trainers, he went down the stairs; jumping the last three as normal, because some things never changed, no matter what! He then walked into the living room and sat on the sofa and began to put his trainers on. He occasionally looked toward the fireplace; almost expecting something unusual to happen, but it didn't. Taking a deep breath, he peered reluctantly at the fireplace; hoping nothing strange would happen. He waited for a few seconds; satisfied all was ok, he forced himself through the door and out in to the brisk morning air, running to collect his bag of papers.

His paper round went without incident and he finished it in his usual time, just happy and relieved that nothing out of the ordinary happened. There were no strangers, no footsteps, nothing unusual at all and he was thankful for that. He arrived home and confidently walked into the living room and was beginning to feel quite relieved about the situation that he didn't even give the fireplace a second glance.

He didn't notice the brick had moved again until he was emptying the ashes from beneath the grate into the bucket. He just stared at the brick in disbelieve; not wanting to acknowledge that it had moved at all. He continued to empty the ashes and then he placed the paper and wood on top of the grate. The brick moved again knocking the firewood off the paper and onto the hearth.

"Stop it!" He whispered angrily at the brick. But the brick replied by nudging forward once more.

"I mean it, just stop whatever you're doing and leave me alone!" He said angrily.

The brick stopped.

Hesitantly and cautiously, he moved the grate out of the way and after staring at the brick for a few moments he reached his hand out towards it. He couldn't help it, he was drawn to it and as he touched it, he realised that he was experiencing a different sensation. It was like pins and needles, and before he knew what

Truth Seer Prohesy, Book One of The Legacy

was happening, that sensation was rushing up his arm. He noticed his fingers begin to fade again, just as before. The sensation was growing stronger, more intense and he tried in vain to pull his hand back from the brick, but it wouldn't come. He began to panic and leaned away from the fireplace, trying desperately to pull his hand free, but it wouldn't come. He thought about shouting for help; but couldn't bring himself to do it. He got himself into this situation, it was up to him to get himself out of it, and besides, who could help him? His body began to tingle all over as whatever force that held on to his arm began to pull him into the fireplace. He struggled briefly and felt tears of anger and frustration run down his cheeks, when he realised his resistance was useless and then his body disappeared into the fire.

A moment later he was through the fireplace and whizzing down the slide he had seen the night before. He knew he would have laughed in delight at sliding down it, if it wasn't for the fact that he wasn't in control and he mind was reeling from the shock of being in the room in the first place.

Seconds later he was splayed out on the floor in front of the large wooden door.

He stood up quickly and looked around nervously. He couldn't believe where he was, it was the same room he had seen the stranger in, and he stood in the exact same place now; in front of the large wooden door. The room was empty except the slide and the door, but as he looked up at where the slide began, he could see the fireplace, and the living room beyond it.

He tried to climb back up the slide, but however much effort he put in, he just couldn't seem to get a good enough grip, and only ended up tumbling down the slide again.

Defeated he faced the large wooden door and tried to sum up enough courage to open it. A fountain of thoughts came to mind as he contemplated what would be behind the door before him, but none of them were good. In fact some of them were downright scary; but that was his imagination kicking in again, he knew.

He noticed a little dust on the large brass doorknob, that dulled its reflection and he thought that strange, because it looked to him last night, as if the stranger had tried to open the door. Beneath the doorknob was a steel padlock; which looked fairly new, it was barely closed, as if someone had hastily put the lock in place. The door held no keyhole; so the only way to lock the door was to use the padlock and for some reason it looked out of place, as if it was a late addition.

Slowly and carefully, he removed the padlock and put it on the floor and then put his hand on the large brass doorknob. Turning the doorknob gently; without a sound he pulled the door open. He really hadn't expected it to open so easily and was a little surprised at the ease in which it did. The door opened a fraction and David cautiously moved his head close to the gap and peeked round it. He wasn't sure what to expect; maybe the stranger would be there or something more sinister, but there was no time to think about that now as he had made the decision to go forward. Pulling the door open a little further; enough to fit his head through, he could see that he was actually peering in to what could only be described as a long wide corridor. It seemed familiar to him somehow, but he couldn't recall where he had seen one like it before. It appeared to be quite long and was quite deceiving in its design; whether by purpose or not, he didn't know, but the bright white walls and the gleaming white ceiling and floor seemed to merge as one. David could see that the corridor in both directions seemed to turn out of sight; probably to form a circle or at least a semi circle, he didn't know which, but it seemed a reasonable assumption. The source of the light that filled the corridor couldn't be seen, but then David realised that he was reminded of a clean, white, sterile hospital corridor. David could see from his vantage point another two doors along the corridor; one in either direction on the opposite side of the wall to his door, where those doors led to, he couldn't guess. He summed up enough courage to enter the corridor; one careful step at a time, he walked into the middle of the floor, tentatively looking in one direction and then the other.

At first he felt small and inconsequential; like an ant crawling along the chalk line of a football pitch. But then, it was as if the corridor had sensed his presence and it began calling to him; as if greeting an old friend and suddenly he felt more alive than he had ever done before. He felt infused with a power so strong that he staggered for a moment and found himself leaning on the wall of the corridor. The power abated as quickly as it had arrived and he stood once more looking down the corridor. There wasn't much to see except the two doors and in the distance what appeared to be two more doors on the side of the wall where his door was.

He turned on shaking legs to his left and started to walk along the corridor and toward the nearest door; excited but still a little frightened, constantly turning around to see if he was being followed, though he didn't know why he would think that. He felt uneasy; thoughts of the mysterious stranger entering his mind. He realised that he expected to see the man emerge out of thin air and call his name. So it was with trepidation that he walked along the corridor, step by careful step. He continued to walk towards the intended door but he wasn't sure if he was getting any closer. It hadn't seemed that far away at first, but as he looked to his own open door behind him, he realised that he had walked at least a hundred yards or so. He stopped to ponder the situation and he realised a light mist had entered the corridor; from where he didn't know, but its presence wasn't unexpected and it didn't bother him, he realised. The corridor and the mist somehow seemed to go together, and they almost felt familiar to him, though he didn't know why. He tried to forget about the mist and concentrate on reaching the doorway just ahead. But his mind became clouded and he found it difficult to concentrate on anything. He looked from the door to his own door and back again, trying to figure out what he should do. Maybe this corridor was playing tricks on him, he thought then. He had to make a decision; he couldn't just stand in this strange corridor and do nothing.

It was the footsteps that now entered his consciousness that made his decision for him, that and the foul smell that began to burn his nostrils. Both the sound and the smell appeared to be coming from the direction he was now facing, and instantly, a feeling of immense dread overcame him. He quickly turned on his heels and headed back to his own door. The decision made so quickly that he didn't even have time to contemplate what he was doing. He just needed to get away from those footsteps and get back to the safety of his own door. He began to run, first nothing more than a jog, but it wasn't long before he was running as fast as he could. As he ran, he could hear that the footsteps had increased in speed to match his own. He stopped suddenly and as he tried to regain his breath, he looked both ways along the corridor. The footsteps hadn't stopped though, they were still coming, and were now growing even louder and worryingly closer. David once again began to run, panic was forcing him to run faster and faster towards his door, towards safety. He really hadn't realised how far he had come, but relief washed over him as he eventually reached his door; sweating from the exertion, or from the frightening thoughts his imagination was conjuring up, he didn't care as he put his clammy hand on the doorknob and stepped back into the room, and back to safety. He quickly scanned the corridor in both directions for signs of any pursuit before he firmly closed the door behind him. With his back to the now closed door, the uneasy feeling of being pursued vanished. His mind wandered to thoughts of what could be in the corridor when he looked down and saw the padlock.

"Shit!" He cried, and quickly bent down to retrieve the lock and clamped it in place. He didn't want to take the chance that whoever was making those footsteps would reach the door and open it to find him there alone. He didn't know why those footsteps made him feel so uneasy, so frightened, but he didn't like the feeling, and he didn't think he would like to meet the person that made them, especially as the smell that accompanied the footsteps was so putrid and made him feel so nauseous.

David moved away from the door and was just contemplating his next move when he felt the now familiar tingling sensation in his body; the same sensation he had felt before and then he felt the invisible force pulling him back into the fireplace. He closed his eyes and managed to take a quick gulp of breath as he felt his body being pulled back up the slide. He opened his eyes just as he tumbled out of the fireplace and landed in front of the sofa in his living room.

He smiled at the fireplace and sighed in relief as he brushed himself off and sat on the sofa, shocked but relieved to be back home.

"You ok Dave?" Christopher asked from the open doorway. He was still in his pyjamas; his left hand had moved up to his face and he began to rub the sleep from his eye.

David jumped in surprise. "What?" He said, startled by his brother's voice.

"You ok?" He said again as he released the door handle and stepped into the living room.

"Yeah, I am now." he said in relief. "I wasn't sure I could get back!" He said, his voice echoing relief but tempered with a little excitement.

"Get back? Get back from where?" A confused Christopher asked.

"Chris, sit down. I've got something to tell you, something you probably won't believe but I have to tell someone." He said, gesturing for his brother to sit down beside him. Once seated, David began to tell him everything that had happened, from the footsteps and the mysterious strange man dressed like a monk to the magical fireplace, the secret room and the incredible hospital-like corridor.

Christopher sat quietly, and listened intently as David related the events of the last couple of days. When David finished, he stared at the fireplace and scrunched his face in thought and then a confused expression appeared on his face.

"Well?" David asked. "What do you think to all that?" He finished expectantly.

"Why didn't you wait and see who the person was making those footsteps? I bet it was that monk. He's the one that has been trying to tell you something and he was the one pointing to the fireplace. I reckon he knew you were in the corridor and he wanted to talk to you. What do you think?" He asked in return.

David turned crimson and looked away from his brother's penetrating gaze. He didn't know what to say to that; he had been frightened by those footsteps, more frightened than any other time in his life, but how could he tell his younger brother that.

"Well," he paused. "It could have been him I suppose," he agreed reluctantly, "but it could've just as easily been anyone, and I wasn't about to hang around and find out."

Christopher guessed his brother must have been scared, he could always tell by the look that came on his face, but he didn't say anything.

"So you didn't get to see what was behind the other doors then?" He asked quickly, trying to alleviate his brother's discomfort.

"No, it was a bit weird, "David said, grateful that Christopher had changed the subject, "I got further and further away from my door, but never really seemed to get closer to the intended one."

"Sounds like you were in some sort of dream really." Christopher offered as an explanation after a moments thought.

"It was real Chris as you're right there before me, it was all real." David stated quietly, thinking about everything that had happened.

"Oh I believe you, I just thought it was a shame that you didn't reach the door and see what was behind it." Christopher placated his brother down. Christopher stared at the fireplace with a wistful expression on his face; it was a look that said "why couldn't it happen to me".

"Chris, I was stranded in a magical corridor with someone chasing me, I wasn't sure if I could get home and you're wandering if there was anything behind those doors?" He said incredulous. Sometimes David worried about his brother; he had a strange way of looking at things, which really worried him.

"Yeah sorry Dave," he replied, "but you were obviously there for a reason and maybe that was to open one of those doors." He offered as he continued to stare at the fireplace.

David stared at the fireplace as well and realised that it did make sense; well a little anyway. Maybe he was suppose to open one of the doors, but if that was true, how come he never seemed to get any closer?

"You could be right," he conceded after a while, "but to be honest, those footsteps made me want to leave that place as soon and as fast as possible."

Christopher looked across at his brother staring at the fireplace, he wouldn't normally tell him when he was scared, and he realised David must have been very scared to divulge that to him.

"Well that's not surprising really; I wouldn't like to think someone was following me especially after everything you've seen, I'd have run too." Christopher smiled reassuringly at his brother.

David smiled back, realising that Christopher always found a way of making him feel at ease. He knew Christopher was very perceptive and he appreciated what he was saying, but he still thought he was a bit strange; even if he was his brother.

"I wander if it would suck me up too?" Christopher asked as he slid off the sofa and peered into the back of the fireplace.

David slid off the sofa and sat next to his brother. "I don't know Chris, but you should be careful."

"What a load of rubbish." Jennifer Barnes said as she pushed opened the door and stepped into the living room. "You definitely know how to tell a good story Dave." She laughed at him.

Jennifer had obviously been listening at the door and dismissed the tale as a load of rubbish. "And did you see Robin Hood on your journey when you met with your robed friend, Friar Tuck?" She asked mocking her brother.

David glared at his sister, trying not to show her that her words were upsetting him, even if they were. She must have been listening from the beginning, as she continued to taunt him with his own words.

"Leave him alone, Jen." Christopher said, sticking up for his brother.

"Leave him alone, Jen." She mimicked. "He can stick up for himself, can't he?"

Jennifer continued to harass her brother, pulling faces as she laughed at various portions of his story.

It was too much, he couldn't stand it any longer, his temper was rising and he could feel the blood rushing to his face. He got up and walked over to Jennifer as she continued to taunt him. As he glowered at her he didn't feel in control, he could see his hand rising in slow motion but he had no control over it, it was as if he was possessed, because just at that moment; with blinding speed, he slapped her face. She stopped laughing and stood there staring at him, tears coming to her eyes.

The slap stung his hand, but his body seemed to act on its own accord. It was as if he was stood to one side and someone else had slapped his sister. She had taunted him on numerous occasions before, but he had never hit her, so what was so different about this time. He had just seen red and then his body had a mind of its own. What the hell was happening to him? He thought.

Jennifer's hand instinctively went to her face. It wasn't a very hard slap; she had experienced worse at school, but it hurt more by the fact that it was her brother that had done the slapping. It just took her by surprise. She knew he was angry and upset by her taunting, but she never expected him to hit her. She stood there looking at her brother as he looked at his hand mesmerised, it was as if he was in shock as well. His eyes slowly rose to look at her and she could see the disbelief and an apology in them.

Without a word, David turned away from the hurtful look in his sister's eyes and sat down on the sofa and whispered, "It's all true, I didn't make it up."

Christopher rose from the floor and stood looking at his brother and sister, not knowing what to do or say. He too seemed surprised by what had just happened, and although he thought his sister had gone too far, he also thought that she didn't deserve to be slapped.

Jennifer's own anger began to rise, she had just been slapped by her brother and all Christopher could do was to stand there gawping at them both.

Jennifer realised she had to say something, she couldn't let her brother get away with this. "You always had a good imagination Dave, telling stupid, childish stories to keep the kids entertained. It's pathetic!"

"Ay!" Chris retorted.

David couldn't bring himself to respond. He couldn't understand what had come over him. "It's true." Was all he could say.

"Whatever." She replied, laughing weakly and somewhat cautiously.

She walked over to the fireplace and knelt before it. She knew they were both watching her as she knelt down and peered into the fireplace. She was going to make David pay for hitting her, she was going to make his life hell from now on, she decided.

"Don't listen to her Dave," Christopher whispered, "She's just a silly girl." He said trying to console his brother.

Jennifer stuck her tongue out, but Christopher just looked away, disgusted by her childish behaviour. She didn't care, David had upset her too much; she wanted revenge, though she didn't know how to get it just at the moment. Then she looked toward the fireplace and a small smile appeared on her lips as she moved towards it.

"Oh my God, look at this!" She exclaimed pointing to something in the fire.

Instantly the boys were on their feet. "What? What is it?" David said as they both rushed over, both trying to focus on what she was pointing at.

She turned her head slowly to look David in the eyes, a wide grin splitting her face; she shrugged her shoulders and added. "Oh sorry, I thought I saw a goblin poking his head out of the fire."

David knew he deserved that for hitting her and couldn't bring himself to say anything in response.

"Very funny Jen." Christopher said, giving her one of his coldest looks.

David moved away from the pair of them and sat back down on the sofa. His body felt his own now, the feeling of self-control re-asserting itself. He couldn't stop himself from slapping her, but he knew she wouldn't believe him, so he just kept quiet. He also knew that Jennifer would make his life a misery from now on, until she believed she had got her revenge. He would take whatever she threw at him; he deserved it.

Jennifer walked over to the door; rubbing her cheek gingerly to make a point. As she opened the door she turned to them and said, "I think you should grow up and stop telling these stupid stories, someone will get hurt and I promise you this, it won't be me again."

David had his head down and was looking at his feet obviously ashamed and she felt a pang of guilt herself. "Go and get your breakfast, its on the table, I've got to get ready for school." She said softly.

As she moved around the door she noticed a shape in the corner of her eye. She turned her head and almost fainted in shock; a weak gasp of surprise managed to escape her lips. She quickly grabbed hold of the door handle with her right hand to steady herself, and although she couldn't find the words to express her shock, she was able to point to the window with her left hand.

David raised his head at her gasp, but wasn't prepared to look to where his sister was pointing.

"I get the point Jen." He said. "I know my life is going to be hell now, but I'm not falling for that one again."

Christopher had instinctively looked to where Jennifer pointed and his mouth opened in surprise. "Dave." He managed to stammer as he pointed towards the window.

David realised something was wrong and quickly turned his head towards the window, and was amazed to see the appearance of the mysterious stranger. Now they had to believe him. They could all see him and they would have to believe everything he told them. He couldn't help but smile as he looked at the strange man looking through the window at them.

"Good morning kids!" Annabel Barnes said as she gently placed her hand on Jennifer's shoulder as she walked into the living room.

Jennifer screamed; a loud, high pitched, hysterical scream, that reverberated around the tiny living room.

Annabel Barnes quickly removed her hand from Jennifer's shoulder, jumping in shock at her daughter's reaction.

"What's wrong love?" She asked, concern creasing her face as she looked from Jennifer to the boys, who had also jumped at her appearance.

Jennifer couldn't speak, the shock of seeing the stranger and then feeling her mother's hand on her shoulder almost made her jump out of her skin.

"What's happening? Their mother asked, clearly worried now by the reaction from all her children, "Is everyone ok?" she said glancing swiftly from one to the other, trying to get some reaction.

All three children had been distracted by the arrival of their mother that when they turned back to the window the stranger had disappeared. They all rushed over to the window, each looking through it to try and see if the stranger was still there or not.

"What's going on?" She asked her children, worried that something bad was about to happen.

David recovered first, "Nothing, mam." David replied. "We just thought we, err."

Christopher finished the sentence for him, "we thought we saw a squirrel in the garden." He said smiling innocently at his mother.

Jennifer and David stared at their brother as he explained to their mother that they had just noticed the squirrel and were just telling Jennifer about it when she had walked in.

Their mother sighed in relief, "Good, I thought something terrible had happened. Anyway come and get your breakfast, it's getting late." She said as she walked out of the room. "Jenny, make sure you come straight home from school today, because I think I may be a bit late getting back from work today."

"Yes mam." Jennifer whispered in response.

David put his finger to his lips and waited for their mother to close the door. He listened for her footsteps moving away before speaking to his siblings.

"Right you two, we've got to keep this to ourselves, ok?" He told them hurriedly.

"Why don't we tell mam, Dave?" Christopher asked his brother.

"I can't believe he's real, that it's all real." Jennifer said, still trying to comprehend what she had just seen.

"Because she wouldn't believe us for one thing, Chris." David said.

"She might." Christopher said unconvincingly.

"No Chris she wouldn't, and who could blame her, you two didn't believe me either until the stranger appeared."

"I believed you Dave." Christopher replied weakly.

David looked at his brother and conceded "Maybe Chris, but you saw how Jennifer reacted. Do you honestly believe that mam will believe me?"

"She might." Christopher said shrugging his shoulders.

David knew that no one would believe it unless they witnessed what he had seen or they saw the stranger, and who could blame them. He was finding it difficult to believe himself and thought it was all in his imagination, until this morning.

"She wouldn't Chris, so I think we should keep quiet for now, ok?" He asked them.

Jennifer was staring out of the window, her gaze taking in the full view of the garden. She scanned it looking for the stranger, but he had disappeared. She turned slowly to her brother and held his gaze for a few seconds before nodding slowly, not saying a word.

"Good, now that's settled, let's get some breakfast before mam comes looking for us. We can talk about what we're going to do about this when we get back from school." David said as he ushered his brother and sister out of the living room into the kitchen.

Chapter Four

David met with his friends as usual and wanted to tell them everything that had happened, but somehow he felt it wasn't the right thing to do. He wasn't sure if they would believe him for one thing, though on reflection they probably would; he wasn't known to exaggerate things. Strange things were happening to his family, and he didn't think that his friends needed to be involved at the moment, if ever. His family were the only ones that this affected, and they were the only ones that had to figure out exactly what was happening and why.

"You ok Dave, you're pretty quiet?" Ping asked him as they walked past the cricket pavilion.

"Yeah fine Ping." He answered, but didn't meet his friend's look.

"He was acting a bit weird yesterday." Ian said out loud but to no-one in particular.

"No I wasn't." David retorted, annoyed.

"Well you weren't very talkative."

"Who gets a chance when your there?" Ping said smiling at everyone at once.

"Yeah, right enough." Robbo agreed.

"It's not my fault I like to talk; it's to hide my nervous disposition." Ian said smiling, along with everyone else.

"Who told you that load of crap?" Gos asked, "You talk rubbish because you want to."

"No, my mum told my dad that I have a nervous disposition and that's why I talk so much." Ian said affronted.

"Whatever." Gos said, raising his eyebrows and pulling a face, making everyone else laugh.

David continued to walk along, not really joining in the rest of the conversation but nodding and smiling when the need arose. He couldn't get the strange occurrences out of his mind, or the strange man.

All day long, David sat through his lessons in a dream-like state, anticipation tingling down his spine. He wasn't losing his mind; he kept thinking to himself, relieved at least for that. Both Jennifer and Christopher had now seen the robed stranger, so maybe everything else was real, but if that was true, what did it all mean? He had said to his brother and sister that they would talk about the stranger and what they were going to do about him when they got home from school, but he hadn't a clue what they were going to do. Somehow he had become in charge of the situation; even Jennifer had agreed with what he said and hadn't tried to say anything else about the subject; which wasn't like her at all. David could hardly contain his excitement throughout the day, each time he looked out of the window he expected to see the strange man staring back at him. But as the seconds dragged into minutes and the minutes into hours, he was resigned to the fact that he wasn't going to see the stranger again this day and tried to relax.

As he was changing classrooms for his next lesson, Jennifer brushed past him in the corridor, just before lunch.

"Anything?" She quietly asked as she walked by.

"No, nothing." He whispered back.

He didn't get the opportunity to see her again during the remainder of the day, but there was nothing to say; even if he did, the stranger hadn't reappeared and nothing unusual had happened.

Jennifer was eager to get home as she sat in the classroom and peered out of the window. The appearance of the strange robed man described by her brother had shocked her beyond belief. How could he have just appeared like that and then disappeared a moment later. She didn't know who the man was or what he wanted but she had a strange feeling of foreboding. She stared at the green fields outside her classroom window and pictured the face of the stranger and a cold shiver ran down her back. The man had been dressed in a monk's habit; as David described him, and looked unusual to say the least, but it wasn't what he was wearing that concerned Jennifer, it was something in his eyes, she realised. She wanted answers to lots of questions that were forming in her mind and the only person that could potentially answer those questions were her brother.

She also felt guilty about laughing at David's story now, though she still felt the sting of the slap on her face. She didn't know what had gotten into her brother, but she realised she had gone too far.

She was just contemplating what she was going to say to her brother when the bell rang for the end of the lesson. Finally! She thought, as she collected her books and utensils and quickly put them in her bag. She had already decided she was going to skip the last lesson of the day; maths. A temp was standing in for Mr. Watson while he was attending some sort of lecture at the catholic school, St. Michaels; a few miles away.

"Don't forget everyone, homework to be in, first thing in the morning." Mrs. Emerson the geography teacher shouted as her pupils began to file out of the classroom.

"Yes miss." Jennifer answered automatically, like the rest of the class and left the room.

She didn't waste any time in leaving the school grounds; using the hole in the fence behind the incinerator to make her escape; a hole that none of the teachers had found yet. She rushed across the road on the other side and then ran through the ginnel, not stopping until she reached the bus stop opposite the main school gate. No one ever left the school grounds early unless they were bunking off, so she wasn't bothered by anyone seeing her. As she walked home she thought about everything that had happened earlier that morning. While she had been listening to David tell Christopher about the fireplace and the events he had experienced she felt as if she was there with him. She marvelled at his ability to bring his stories to life, she could get so engrossed in them that all her troubles and fears were washed away, but for some reason she could never tell him that his stories brought her comfort, she could never do that. She often sneaked out of her bed at night and listened outside their bedroom door as he told Christopher numerous stories about pirates or soldiers in great battles, fights between the forces of good and evil. He told many stories but she realised that none of them had captivated her as much as the one he told earlier today, a story so unbelievable that she couldn't get it out of her mind, even now. But it had become even more enthralling with the appearance of the robed stranger.

This time David's story was different, it wasn't an ordinary story. This time it was real, and what frightened her was that they were all caught up in it in someway. David's story hadn't been a story at all, it had been a series of true events; and as hard as it was to believe in magical fireplaces and secret rooms, there was no hiding the appearance of the strange robed man he had described.

It didn't take her long to get home, her thoughts of the strange man and the story David had told kept her mind busy, and it was a bit of a shock when she suddenly realised she was putting the key into the door of her home.

She walked straight upstairs to her bedroom, changing her school uniform of grey skirt, jumper, white shirt and white socks for a pale blue dress, before she went back down stairs. She made herself a cup of tea and sat down on a chair at the kitchen table waiting for her brothers to come home, and contemplated what she was going to say to her brother yet again. She knew she had to try and stay calm; knowing her brother would only clam up if she pushed too hard. Both her brothers annoyed her at times and she would lose her temper, but this was one of those time to remain calm, otherwise David wouldn't tell her anything, and she needed answers.

When the bell finally rang at the end of the day, David quickly rushed from the classroom, wanting to be away as quick as possible and didn't even hear Ping shouting him, until he caught him up as he was leaving the school grounds.

"What's wrong with you Dave?" He asked worriedly. "Didn't you hear me calling you?"

"Sorry mate, I didn't." David replied, surprised by the appearance of his friend.

"You have been acting a little weird the last few days, are you sure you're ok?" Ping asked him in concern.

"Fine, but I do need to get home." David said, looking around nervously.

"What you doing later?" Ping asked, also looking around to see what his friend was interested in.

"Nothing much, just going to do my homework and watch a bit of TV." David replied.

"Well, do you fancy coming round mine for a bit later?" Ping invited.

"Thanks Ping, but I'm not sure, depends what time my mam gets home."

"Ok, no problem, just come round if you can." Ping said. He knew that things were difficult at home for David and left the invitation open.

David just nodded and smiled and then he said, "Come on, I'll race you home." Then he set of running.

Ping watched his friend as he took flight and after a few moments he shouted after him, "Hey, wait for me." Laughing, he quickly gave chase.

"You took your time, where have you been?" Jennifer greeted David as he walked in to the kitchen through the back door.

Jennifer was sat at the kitchen table, already changed and out of her school uniform David noticed and was deliberately tapping the table in an annoying manner, full of impatience.

He gave his sister a look of warning as Ping walked into the kitchen after him.

"Hi Jen." He said as he smiled at her.

"Hello Ping," Jennifer said and gave him a small smile in return. Jennifer liked Ping and knew he fancied her, but she wasn't interested in any of David's friends. It would have been frowned upon by her friends if she entertained the thought of going out with a boy younger than herself; even if she did find this particular one attractive.

David gave his sister a stern look and then walked into the pantry to retrieve a bottle of Dandelion and Burdock, which he poured into two glasses that were sitting on the draining board by the kitchen sink. He handed one to his friend before taking a big gulp from his own glass. He put his glass on the table and returned the bottle to the pantry.

Ping wrenched his attention from Jennifer and asked David, "You coming over later then, we could even have a quick game of footy?"

They usually played a game before it got too dark, but David wasn't really in the mood for football today and said so to Ping.

"I don't think so Ping, but if I change my mind I'll see you there, ok?" David said to his friend.

"Come on Dave, it'll be a laugh," Ping persisted.

"Maybe, maybe later."

"Ok, well, maybe see you later then," he turned to Jennifer, "bye Jen." He said smiling again; the biggest smile he could manage.

"Bye Ping." Jennifer said smiling back, a half laugh almost escaping her lips at her brother's friend.

"You got home quickly." David said as he saw his friend out of the door.

"Yes, yes." She said impatiently, the almost laugh and smile vanishing. "Well?" She asked, still tapping her fingers on the table.

"Can't you stop that? It's very annoying." He said as he tried to collect his thoughts. What the hell was she doing here so soon, he thought? He needed time to think before he could say anything, but it didn't look like he was going to get it.

Jennifer stopped, getting up she walked over to the back door and opened it.

Christopher stumbled into the kitchen out of breath; probably from running all the way home from school, by the look of him. He didn't like to miss anything, but today, it seemed, there was no way on earth he was going to miss the conversation about the stranger.

David stared at his sister, a confused look on his face. "Jen, how did you know Christopher was at the door?" He asked. He hadn't heard a sound and wouldn't have known someone was outside if she hadn't opened the door just as Christopher had arrived.

"I, erm." She began, she hadn't a clue how she knew he was there, but thought she must have heard his footsteps, how else could she know he was about to walk in. "I don't know I must have heard him running down the path obviously." She replied, but didn't appear convinced herself.

"I doubt that." He said with an element of scepticism. "But anyway, I want to get changed out of my uniform before I discuss anything, ok?" David said as he walked towards the stairs.

Jennifer was still puzzling over how she knew about Christopher being at the door but quickly turned her thoughts and attention to what David said. "No David!" She replied, "I have some questions that need answers, and I want those answers now." She demanded, trying to suppress the anger that was rising inside her.

David knew she was upset; she never called him David unless she was really upset, but he was not prepared to discuss anything until he was ready.

"That's just too bad then Jen, because I'm going to get changed." He replied determinedly. "I'm sure you can wait a few minutes." He said before turning to his brother; who was silently watching the exchange, whilst trying to catch his breath, "You coming?" He asked.

Christopher just nodded and the two left their sister standing in the kitchen with her hands on her hips and her lips pressed tight, her face furrowed in a frown of annoyance and one foot tapping on the kitchen floor. Christopher turned to see the scowl on his sister's face but quickly turned and followed his brother up the stairs to their bedroom.

As David climbed the stairs his mind returned to the question he'd asked his sister. How had she known Christopher was at the door? She couldn't have heard his footsteps from the kitchen, with the kitchen door closed and the main back door beyond it closed also, it was just impossible. As he changed out of his uniform into a pair of old blue jeans and white Levi T-shirt, the more he thought about it, the more the elusive answer to that question intrigued him. There were a lot of strange occurrences at the moment, was this just one more thing to add to the list? Were there more things? Unusual things that she hadn't told him about, he wondered?

He would bring this up when he got back down stairs; she wasn't the only one that wanted some answers.

It was a short while later that David and Christopher walked down the stairs; David looked over the banister and could see Jennifer's legs; her foot still tapping as it had been minutes earlier. He jumped the last three steps and turned to see Jennifer still in the exact same position she had been before he and Christopher had gone to get changed.

Jennifer's face was now bright red; he could almost see the steam coming from her ears he thought as he entered the kitchen with Christopher hot on his heels, but keeping aware from Jennifer's view.

"Right, are we ready now? We need to discuss what's been happening." She very nearly spat at him as he took one of the chairs and sat in it.

"Let's all just sit down and I will tell you what I know." David sighed and pulled the chair up toward the table; placing his hands face down on the top trying to look composed, but really feeling terrified by his sister's anger.

Christopher followed his brother's lead and pulled another chair out to sit down beside him. The two of them waited as Jennifer continued to tap her foot on the floor, she was staring at each of them in turn, and looked to be pondering what to do next. She finally came to a decision because a moment later she was seated at the kitchen table with her arms folded, her chin thrusting out and that expression on her face that said in no uncertain terms, "Well, get on with it, I'm waiting."

David sighed before re-telling his story once more. He slowly and carefully went though everything that had happened. He didn't mention the strange dreams; but he couldn't really remember them anyway, and he didn't reveal the feelings the corridor had awoken in him, but everything else was mentioned. Jennifer and Christopher sat in silence as he recalled every detail he could remember, not daring to interrupt him in case he missed something.

When he had finally finished, he sat perfectly still and waited for one of them to say something. His throat was dry and he really needed a drink but he didn't want to get up from his chair until one of them said something, anything. After a few moments he couldn't stand it any long and he went to the sink to pour himself a glass of water. He drank the water greedily and poured himself another glass before returning to his chair and then he just waited quietly, looking occasionally at each of them for some kind of response.

It was Christopher who broke the silence first.

"Well, we all saw the stranger in the window, and he was just as David described." He said to Jennifer.

Jennifer was trying desperately to think of some logical explanation for everything that had happened to her brother, but couldn't think of anything. The strange man had been there, she had seen him, and he had disappeared just as quickly; she had also seen that. But this couldn't be real, it must be just some stupid story David had made up to entertain their brother. The only problem was; though she didn't know why! She knew he was telling the truth, and that scared her. But if she knew he was telling the truth, what did that mean? It frightened her that they may have magical and mysterious rooms in their house and even more that a strange man could enter those rooms willy-nilly. Impossible and inexplicable things had happened to her brother, and with the appearance of the strange robed man, they now seemed to be happening to her, and her other brother Christopher as well. She just didn't know what it all meant, she had no answers, but she knew there would be trouble heading their way.

"Say something Jen." David asked her impatiently.

She looked into her brother's eyes and could see confusion, shock and worry looking back. He looked at her as if he had all the cares of the world upon his shoulders and it made her breath catch in her throat as she realised he needed her to say she believed him and everything was going to be ok.

As much as she disliked him sometimes, he was her brother and she did love him. She couldn't let him go through whatever was happening to him, alone. "As strange as it all sounds," she said to him. "I believe you."

David smiled and the tension and worry she had seen a moment before had been replaced quickly with relief as he sighed and nodded his thanks.

"The question is," she remarked, "what are we going to do about it?" she asked.

"I don't know," David replied. "But we've all seen the strange man now. I believe he is the key to all this and the fact that we have all seen him makes me think whatever happens in the future will affect us all." He finished solemnly.

"You really think so?" Christopher beamed with unbridled enthusiasm.

"I think your right Dave, but I don't like the idea of a strange man coming to our house or the thought of magical rooms and enchanted fireplaces." She replied.

"Well I think it's just great." Christopher laughed. "What an adventure, just think of it Dave, what fun we'll have, I can't wait." He said as he stood up and paced up and down the kitchen, an excited twinkle in his eyes.

David looked toward Jennifer to see her reaction and she had a look of trepidation that he himself was feeling. He didn't think this was going to be as much fun as Christopher believed and he was feeling rather apprehensive about the entire situation. Jennifer shrugged her shoulders and gave him a tight lipped smile as she watched Christopher pace up and down the kitchen with excitement.

David, Jennifer and Christopher were sitting in the living room when their mother came home from Green's Butchers, about half an hour later. Mrs. Barnes walked into the living room to see her three children sitting huddled together discussing something in quiet tones. She knew instinctively that there was something wrong; the tell-tale signs were all there; like the television wasn't switched on for a start and they weren't arguing with each other for another. She didn't know what to do or say, so she just walked over to the single chair and sat down, looking at the three of them as if they had all grown two heads.

"You ok mam?" David said as he watched his mother sit down and looked at them with a curious expression on her face.

"Yes I think so," she replied, "everything ok kids?" She asked suspiciously, looking at each of them in turn for any giveaway signs of what was happening.

"Yeah fine mam." Jennifer replied nervously looking at her two brothers who were now sat with guilty expressions on their faces.

"Just chatting." Christopher answered.

Mrs. Barnes gave her youngest child a tight lipped smile; as if to say "Yeah right, and I'm supposed to believe that." But said, "Ok, well behave yourselves while I run myself a bath." She really was too tired to worry about the children being nice to each other, besides, she knew it wouldn't last; they would probably be at each others throats before she got half way up the stairs.

"Do you want me to make you a cup of tea mam?" Jennifer asked.

"No I'm ok, but thanks." She said as she went to open the door. She shook her head as she turned to look at her children huddled together again. They were good kids she knew, but not normally this good. Then she left the room and walked up the stairs to run her well deserved, hot and foaming bath.

Jennifer rushed to the door to make sure their mother had gone upstairs and then turned to her brothers. "Just chatting?" She mimicked.

"Stop it Jen." David said before Christopher could respond or react.

Jennifer stared at her brother but didn't say anything.

Surprised that his sister didn't start arguing, he quickly told them to keep their voices low and sit closer to him on the sofa. To his surprise, they did just that and waited for him to start talking. He wasn't sure why they had started taking orders from him, maybe because he had seen the stranger first, he wasn't sure, but he wasn't complaining.

"Ok, there's something I need to ask the pair of you." He said just above a whisper.

"What?" Christopher asked just as quietly.

"Did either of you experience anything unusual today?" He asked expectantly.

"Not me." Christopher replied immediately.

Jennifer paused, and then shook her head.

"Are you sure? What about day-dreams or even weird dreams at night, anything like that?" He asked, hoping he wasn't alone in these weird occurrences.

They both shook their heads again to his disappointment. He had been expecting at least one of them to be experiencing some strange dreams, since they had seen the stranger as well, but they obviously hadn't.

"There was one strange thing." He said after a slight pause. He turned to look at his sister and waited for her to say something, she didn't.

"What? What strange thing?" Christopher asked, looking from his brother to sister and back again, annoyed that they both seemed to know what David was referring to and he didn't.

He addressed the next question to Jennifer. "Jen, how did you know Chris was at the back door earlier?"

Jennifer just knew David was going to ask that particular question, but she didn't have an answer. She didn't know how she knew he would be there, she just did.

"I don't know Dave." She replied honestly.

David looked at his sister's face and could see a slight frown of annoyance there. He understood how she felt, he was experiencing lots of strange things himself, and it was the not knowing that he hated the most.

"Well, it looks like there are a lot of things that are happening here and none of them have an explanation that I can see". He said.

"What about this stranger? What do you think he wants?" Christopher asked.

"I don't know Chris, but I don't think he means any harm."

"How do you come to that conclusion?" Jennifer asked.

David pondered the question for a moment before answering. "Well, I've seen him a few times and each time, I get the impression he is trying to tell me something. Something important I think, but he just can't seem to get the words out. Besides, he hasn't tried to hurt me or anything like that, so that's why!" He replied.

"That doesn't mean that he won't though." Jennifer said remembering how she felt when she saw the man for the first time.

"You're right, but I get the feeling he is after my help and someone who is after help isn't going to hurt you, is he?" David surmised.

"Maybe?" She agreed reluctantly.

"I didn't even think he was real at first." David whispered.

"Well now you know he is Dave," Christopher said. "We've all seen him now."

"True." David agreed. "But he just appears then disappears all the time and let's not forget the fact that I saw him on the other side of the fireplace, in the room with the slide, in a room that shouldn't exist."

"You're not suggesting he's some kind of ghost are you?" Jennifer laughed and then stopped as quickly as she started, the impact of what she had just said making her nervous.

"I don't know what or who he is. I can't explain any of this, I wish I could, but I can't." David said as his brow furrowed in concentration. "Even his clothes are strange, he looks like a monk or friar, but somehow different to the ones I've seen in books or on television."

"Yes, there was something different about him now you come to mention it," Jennifer said, she had no intention of saying that the stranger frightened her, but there was something not quite right about this monk.

"Could it be the dagger he was wearing, that looked a little strange?" Christopher asked trying to help. His eyes had been drawn to the dagger in the monk's belt at the time, though he didn't know why. It came to mind now, however, so he thought he would ask.

"What?" David and Jennifer said together.

"The dagger, he had a dagger, surely monks wouldn't normally carry a dagger on their person, would they?" He asked defensively.

"Your right Chris, I think you have it there, a monk wouldn't. So if he's not a monk, what is he then? David asked out loud.

"I don't think we will find the answer to that question until he either shows himself again." Jennifer said thoughtfully.

"What are we going to do then Dave?" Christopher asked.

David looked toward his brother; waiting for him to make a decision and tell him what to do. He looked at Jennifer; she too was waiting for him to say something. They were both waiting for him to take control, to let them know, he knew what to do about the situation and make everything ok. He was both elated and repulsed by the idea. He didn't know what to do, how to act or how to react to the situation. Why was this happening to him? To them? He didn't want the responsibility; he didn't want to make the decisions. All these thoughts rushed through his mind at once and he almost wanted to cry when he saw the expectant looks on the faces of his brother and sister. It was then that an image of the corridor came to his mind, an image that brought with it strength and control. Then he knew he could control the events around them, he would find the answers, if only he had the courage to try. The more he thought about the corridor, the stronger the feelings became, he could almost hear it calling to him and he drew strength from that. Jennifer and Christopher were still waiting patiently, still waiting for him to take the lead and tell them what to do. He still retained an element of doubt about what he was doing, but now he felt empowered; the corridor seemed to give him a strength he didn't know he had and willed him to speak.

"Let's just keep everything to ourselves for now and see if anything else happens. We have to keep our eyes open and be ready for anything, if the stranger shows himself again, we try to speak with him and find out what he wants, ok?"

"Ok." They both agreed, nodding as he spoke.

He was surprised by their ready response; he had expected at least some resistance, or a difference in opinion, anything but agreement. But they just nodded and agreed that was the best thing to do under the circumstances. They even agreed that telling anyone else would just be foolish, as they couldn't prove anything and no one else but they, had seen the stranger. With their agreement so forth coming, he felt the control and power the corridor supplied him slowly ebb away, allowing his doubts and fears to resurface. He wondered how he had suddenly become the person in-charge; he didn't want to be in charge of anyone.

"You ok Dave?" Christopher asked his brother.

"Yeah fine, was just wondering if we shouldn't tell a grown up about what has been happening." He replied.

"But you just said." Christopher began.

"It's ok; I was only thinking about it again, I think we made the right decision not to tell anyone." He said hurriedly.

David may have been given command of the situation for a short while, whether he wanted it or not, but as he watched his sister muse over everything that had happened, he knew it was only a matter of time before she would take control. Jennifer wouldn't be able to help herself, and he was more than happy for her to do so, the sooner the better as far as he was concerned. He began to smile at the thought and it was as if a weight had been lifted from his shoulders.

Chapter Five

He was walking down a brightly lit corridor; its whiteness blinding but there was an odour of rotten flesh that seemed to permeate the atmosphere; the smell strong and nauseating, burning his nostrils with its putrid breath. A dense misty fog crawled along the floor and around his feet, but he wasn't interested in the fog or the smell for that matter; his gaze was focused on the obscure, indeterminate figure before him. He was walking toward that figure now; although he felt as if he was actually floating on the mist rather than walking, the dark figure watched silently as he awaited his arrival. He felt frightened as he drew closer, the figure had yet to raise its head as he glided toward it, but somehow he knew the face it would reveal would be cruel and hideous.

He could feel the beads of sweating dripping down his neck and down his back, making him shiver as he moved closer to the waiting apparition. His stomach began to constrict in fear and although he didn't want to move forwards, he knew he didn't have the power to turn away. Closer and closer he moved until finally he was standing before the figure in the monk's habit, the figures face obscured by an overlarge hood. He wanted to scream for help; he knew that if he could only make a sound, someone would come to his aid, but he had no voice, and no will to make a sound, he was powerless, helpless as a new born baby. Petrified as he now was, he couldn't help but notice the faint sound of footsteps behind him. Faint they might be, but he was positive they were heading in his direction. His body began to stop shivering and he began to relax as the footsteps grew stronger, grew closer. Then he realised the figure was raising his head and all thoughts of salvation and deliverance diminished as he gazed upon the face hidden beneath the cowl. He screamed!

The sun hadn't even decided whether or not it was going to rise when David woke groggily from a restless sleep and tried to dress quickly and quietly before making his way down the stairs. He wasted no time as he quickly put on his coat and headed out the door to the cool crisp autumn air and ran all the way to the newsagents. His paper round ended without incident yet again and it wasn't long before he was sat in front of the fireplace watching and waiting for something to happen. He was warily watching the grate for any movement as he began to take off his coat and put it on the sofa. It had been bitterly cold outside; although his body hadn't registered the fact until he was half way through his paper round. He had a lot on his mind and it was only when he saw the cold air being exhaled from his mouth that he realised it was colder than usual; winter was obviously on its way. He was relieved at first that the grate hadn't moved and there was nothing to see, but he realised that he was also a little disappointed. He found that he wanted to visit the corridor again; he wanted to feel the power the corridor offered him. Even the thought of someone patrolling the corridor didn't diminish the rush of adrenalin he felt as he thought about it. He had even remembered that there was a corridor in the dreams he couldn't quite remember. He wondered if the two were connected in some way, but then again probably not. If he could only remember, maybe he would have some answers. He knew somehow that his forgotten dreams held some key to the mystery, something significant, but he didn't know what. He had experienced a few dreams in the past that had scared him and he'd told his father. His father told him to change the dreams if they frightened him, to think of nicer ones. He thought that sounded ridiculous at first, but had been surprised one night when he did just that. When he found himself conscious after his mind had forced him out of a bad dream he instantly dived back in and to his utter surprise and delight he managed to change certain aspects of the dream. His father had asked him the morning after he had changed his first dream, if he was still having any problems with them. David told him what he had done, but he felt that his father already knew, though he didn't know how. Neither he nor his father ever said anything about the dreams again and David hadn't really experienced any problems with them since, but something had changed recently and David had no control over what that something was. Now he hardly remembered his dreams at all, and that also scared him. He just felt as if something bad must have happened, so bad that he couldn't do anything to change it and now he was feeling tired; the sort of tired you feel after a sleepless night.

So, here he was again, staring at the fireplace, hoping to see something out of the ordinary, but seeing nothing. The moments ticked by as he patiently watched the fireplace. Eventually, he decided he couldn't waste any more time waiting and began to prepare the fire as usual. He ritually removed the grate so he could brush the ashes from the back of the fireplace, replacing it when he had done so. Nothing unusual happened but he looked toward the window on impulse. There was no one there. He returned to the job at hand and began to fold the newspaper to put on the grate. It happened when he reached for the pieces of wood to put on top of the newspaper. The grate suddenly lurched forward; not much, but enough to make David jump in surprise.

He instinctively reached out to touch it, and then paused. He knew that if he actually touched the brick, he would find himself back in the strange room. Did he really want to do this? Did he really want to find himself back in the corridor? Just thinking about the corridor made him think he could hear it calling to him, promising him strength and power, power to do great things. It was mesmerising, entrancing, but he forced himself to concentrate and think about the consequences of any actions he were to take now. Did he really want to do this, he thought again? The corridor had some sort of hypnotic influence over him that made him promises of power. But could he put his trust in those promises and did he really want power? No, he didn't want power, but he did want answers and in the corridor, he knew he could get those answers. Now, even though he knew he had the opportunity to visit the corridor and find those answers, he didn't know if he had the courage to do it. He wasn't sure if he was the one who should be going in the first place. He could feel something or someone calling him, but was it just his imagination or was he destined to do something. All these questions ran through his mind as he looked at the fireplace before him.

He sat on his heels; staring at it but not really seeing it, the grate had moved and with that movement came the promise of an adventure. The problem was David wasn't sure if he was ready for this, since his father had died he wasn't sure if he wanted to do anything. But now it seemed he was to be given a choice, he could ignore this opportunity and let life carry on as normal or he could take a chance and see what happens. He knew as soon as he had identified the choices that he couldn't just sit by and do nothing. He had promised Jennifer and Christopher that if anything unusual happened again he would tell them, but there wasn't time for that now. If he was going to do this, he had to do it now. The fireplace could just as quickly return to normal and the opportunity would be missed. Besides, he thought, the stranger had come to him first, had tried to speak to him, not them. The stranger wanted him for a reason, some purpose, and he wanted to know what that was. Here and now was the opportunity to find answers to those questions, he had made his decision, as Elvis once put it, "It's now or never."

"Come on David," he said to himself, "Be courageous for once in your life and take a chance."

He paused a moment longer, and then decided he didn't really have a choice at all, if he wanted answers he had to take the plunge and see where this journey would take him. He reached out toward the grate; fearful but excited at the same time, and he made contact.

The living room door swung open and Christopher rushed in.

"Dave, stop!" He yelled.

But it was too late, David had already begun to fade before Christopher's eyes and now he was being pulled into the fireplace.

Christopher rushed forward and dove for the vanishing figure that was his brother before he disappeared altogether. He just managed to touch his foot, but as he did so he instantly felt the tingling sensation his brother had described. It started along his arm, but soon spread throughout his body like an electric shock, his body seemed to spark with energy, but all thoughts were lost as he too disappeared into the fire.

Christopher was dazed and confused for just a moment as he passed through the fireplace, but then he was riding the slide his brother had told him about; it had appeared from nowhere and now he was heading down it and towards David; who had just tumbled from it a moment before to land before the door. Christopher couldn't help but whoop with delight as he collapsed at his brother's feet with an enormous grin on his face.

"You ok Chris?" He asked, but knew he was fine when he saw the expression of pure pleasure on his brother's face when he stood up.

"Yeah, that was great." He replied.

David began to shake his head in amazement and was just about to ask his brother how he managed to follow him when they both turned as they heard a shrill scream coming from the direction of the fireplace. David couldn't believe his eyes as he watched his sister; her face full of terror, tumbling down the slide toward them.

He quickly pushed Christopher out of the way as Jennifer crashed at his feet, almost knocking him to the ground in the process.

Jennifer didn't move as she fell from the slide, but a moment later both David and Christopher had taken hold of an arm each and were trying to pull her to her feet.

"Get off me, let go." She screeched at them.

"You ok Jen?" David asked in concern as he released his grip on her arm.

"Yes, yes!" She replied curtly as she tried to stand.

Her legs almost gave way and David grabbed hold of her again to steady her.

She accepted his assistance this time and once she was firmly on her feet she began to look around the room.

"This is it, isn't it?" She demanded as she looked at the slide, to the big wooden door and then to her two brothers, who were grinning from ear to ear.

"This is it Jen." David replied still smiling.

"This is totally unbelievable, I must be dreaming." She exclaimed.

"Maybe, but if your dreaming, we're dreaming as well."

Christopher pinched her arm. "Ow, what was that for?" She cried.

He laughed as he replied. "You're not dreaming then."

Jennifer scowled at Christopher as she rubbed her arm. "Obviously," then she laughed too; amazed that she was actually in the magic room behind the fireplace.

"How did you get down here?" David asked soberly, "I think I saw the living room door open as I was going through the fireplace and that was obviously Chris, but you came through a little later."

She turned slowly toward her brother, amazement and disbelief still evident on her face, but with a slight twinkle of excitement in her eyes she explained that she had witnessed Christopher being pulled into the fireplace and without thinking had tried to grab hold of him, much the same as Christopher had done with David. She hadn't actually managed to touch Christopher, but to her utter amazement, she had felt the tingling sensation and found herself being pulled into the fireplace. The next thing she knew she was riding down the slide heading straight for the two of them; she grimaced at the reminder. Jennifer never liked going on the slides in the playground, she never went on any rides; truth be known, even when the fair came to town. The town held a Gala every year in July and with it, came the fair, which was full of rides; such as the Waltzers and Dodgems, Jennifer hated it. So it wasn't surprising that she had hated the trip from the fireplace so much.

"Any way, I couldn't very well let Chris get pulled into the fireplace without trying to save him, could I?" She said. "I didn't know you were here already, but I had to do something."

"It's ok Jen, I'm glad you're here, I'm glad we're all here together." David said.

Christopher stood there smiling at the pair of them with a big wide grin spread across his face.

"Why do you look like the cat that's got the cream?" Jennifer asked him.

"I'm not, I'm just happy that we're all here like Dave said, the three of us, like the three Musketeers." He said still smiling.

"Well it looks like you're going to get your adventure after all Chris." David said, a smile appearing on his face too.

"Let's go through the door Dave." Christopher shouted excitedly, moving towards it and inspecting the large brass door handle.

"I think we should maybe go back for now," Jennifer said sternly as she looked at her brothers. "Now is not the best time to go off gallivanting, we don't know what's behind that door and we haven't made any plans or really prepared properly for this."

"I think Jen's right Chris," David agreed reluctantly. Now they were all there he had lost the drive and determination he had felt earlier, it probably would be better if they planned for the adventure a bit more before embarking on it. "We should probably try and get back, but at least we now know that we can all get here and not just me."

Christopher wasn't happy, he dropped his head sulkily knowing that he would have to do what his brother and sister agreed to do in the end, and he didn't like what they were about to agree on.

"But we could go on the adventure now Dave, it'll be great, I know it will." He said quietly, raising his eyes only to see if his words had made any difference to his brother's decision.

David smiled at his brother's excited face and just as he was about to say he agreed with their sister, he heard something, a strange sound. "Maybe we could have a look at the doors in the corridor Jen, we won't be long." David found himself saying. Something had changed; he didn't know what for certain, but it was something to do with the corridor. It seemed to be calling him; it wanted him to enter and it promised him the answers he was looking for.

"I don't know Dave; we don't know what's waiting for us." She said. "That strange man could be behind that door and we don't know what he wants."

"Well, there is one way to find out sis." Christopher replied, smiling his best smile at her.

David turned to the door and put his hand on it, he could feel the corridor beyond it, and it was still calling to him, promising him, if only he entered.

"Dave, you ok?"! Jennifer asked him.

"Fine." He replied absently as he stroked the door. Then it hit him like a thunder bolt, he didn't know where the idea had come from, but he knew instantly that he had to tell them what he had just realised.

"I think we may have a problem."

"What problem?" They both said together as they watched him slowly turn away from the door somewhat reluctantly and face them.

He paused momentarily trying to figure how best to tell them, but instead he decided to come straight out with it. "The problem of how we are going to get back. The last time I was here, you opened the door Chris. When you did, I was drawn back into the living room. How are we going to get back now, with all three of us down here?"

They both looked at him in shock as the predicament of their situation slowly registered on their faces. They looked as one at the slide and at the fireplace beyond, and each of them tried to think of a way back up there.

"Maybe when mam comes down, she'll open the door and we'll all be pulled back." Jennifer said hopefully after a pause.

"Yes, that'll work wouldn't it Dave?" Christopher clapped his hands in excitement.

"I'm not sure, but for some reason I don't think so. Don't look at me like that Jen," David said as his sister gave him a cold hard stare. "I don't know how I know, but I just do and I don't think that'll work." He said.

David watched them; he saw the excitement and enthusiasm disappear from Christopher's gaze and watched as Jennifer contemplated what to do about their situation.

"We could all try to push one another up the slide, form a sort of ladder; one climbing on the shoulders of the other and see if we can reach the top. That might work." He suggested.

Not convinced, but willing to try anything she agreed. "Ok, le's give it a go."

"And once we have proved we can get back up, can we come back down and have a look behind one of those doors in the corridor Dave? Christopher asked hopefully.

"What do you think Jen?" David asked his sister, "I don't have a problem with that."

"Ok, why not, but let's see if this works first, ok?" Jennifer said.

They approached the slide and were just discussing who would be better suited to start the climb first when the slide just vanished before their eyes. One moment it was there, the next it had gone, with no sign of it anywhere.

"No!" Jennifer screamed as she finally came to her senses and lunged for the place were the slide had been a moment before. She fell flat on her face as reached out her hands for the disappearing slide and landed on the now empty floor, a look of undisguised shock and trepidation on her face.

"Shit!" David exclaimed.

"What's just happened Dave?" Christopher cried in astonishment.

"I don't know," he said, visibly shaken, "It's never done that before."

The slide had definitely gone, and with it the only way back home, the room was now totally empty except of course the three of them.

David realised they had only two choices open to them now, they could wait and see if the slide came back or they could take a chance and see where the doors in the corridor led. Either choice was quite daunting, but they were the only two choices available. David wasn't sure how he knew, but he was sure the corridor had something to do with the slide's disappearance. He wasn't going to say anything to the others but he could still hear the corridor calling to him from the other side of the door.

"Well I can't see the point in waiting here." Christopher began. "I'm sure the slide will come back when it's good and ready, so we may as well go and have a look at what's behind there." He finished pointing at the large wooden door.

"I don't know Chris, there's something not quite right with all of this." Jennifer said quietly.

David could feel the pull of the corridor. "I think we might as well have a look, we could be waiting here all day for it to come back. We don't have to be long and let's face it, there's nothing else we can do for now." He said.

Jennifer stared at the pair of them for a long moment before deciding. "Ok, let's do it before I change my mind." She agreed.

David walked over to the door and pulled on the large brass door knob. The door creaked open slowly and bright white light poured through the gap.

The three children moved cautiously through that gap and into the corridor beyond. There were no lights to be seen, but the corridor was blindingly bright. The floor, the ceiling and the walls were all white and almost seamless. You could hardly differentiate between the walls, the ceiling or the floor, it was quite disconcerting.

The only other colour came from the rows of doors on either side of the corridor; their stark dark brown colour standing out like beacons.

Three heads looked right and then left in wonder. A feeling of utter joy enveloped David as he stepped into the corridor; it was as if it was singing to him, and glad of his presence there. He felt wonderful, as if he could achieve anything he ever wanted, and he began to smile as he embraced the feelings. It was the same welcoming presence he had felt before and it took him a moment to get use to the power that infused his body. He looked at his brother and sister to see if they too experienced the euphoria he himself was feeling, but he could see they didn't.

"You ok Dave?" Christopher asked a little shakily but smiling never the less.

David looked at his brother's smiling face, he could tell he was a little worried but he could also see the excitement and wonder that was hidden behind those eyes.

"Yeah fine Chris." He said as he continued to smile.

"Ok, we've had a look." Jennifer said nervously. "I think we should think about getting back now."

"You must be joking? We haven't seen anything yet, come on Dave." Christopher replied as he began to walk along the corridor. David shrugged his shoulders at his sister then followed on behind his brother.

David turned round to see a reluctant Jennifer following behind him, nervously turning round and looking in both directions with every step.

"I wonder what's behind these doors." Christopher asked as he moved along the corridor.

"Not sure I want to know?" Jennifer said quietly.

"We could open one." Christopher said eagerly, as he began to walk a little faster, moving towards one of the doors.

"We have no idea what's behind these doors Chris, I'm not sure we should take a risk and open one, let's just get back eh?" She almost pleaded.

"Ah come on, we may as well now we're here." Christopher argued.

"No, I think we should get back." She turned round looking for the door they had come through and stopped stunned. "I didn't think we had walked so far." She said in surprise.

The brothers turned round too, David had estimated they had walked about two hundred metres along the corridor.

"Me either." He replied. "The last time was different, but I didn't think we'd come this far." He said looking down the corridor.

Jennifer began to walk again but stopped suddenly and motioned for her brothers to be quiet. She cocked her head to one side as if listening to something. "Did you hear that?" She said.

"No, what?" Christopher replied.

Holding their breaths, they barely heard a faint sound that seemed far away, but was getting progressively stronger and closer.

"That." Jennifer said.

The three children stood motionless as they heard the faint noise get louder and louder. It appeared to be coming from somewhere behind them, from the direction they had just come from and it sounded familiar.

They were footsteps they realised at the same time, and they were getting increasingly faster and louder as the children stood there in shock.

"I don't like this." David said. "I think we should get back to our door, now."

"Yes." Jennifer agreed and turned round. "Come on Chris."

"It could be the stranger; the monk, maybe we should wait and see what he wants?" Christopher said hoping to change their minds about abandoning the adventure so early.

"Maybe it's not though Chris, what do we do then?" Jennifer retorted.

"I think we should head back just in case." David said an uneasy feeling descending down on him.

"Agreed!" Jennifer replied.

The three children began to walk back to their door slowly and cautiously at first, and then with a bit more urgency as the footsteps became louder. They increased their speed until finally they were running as fast as they could.

The reality of the situation hit them all squarely in the eyes. They weren't alone any more, someone else was in the corridor with them, and that someone was heading right towards them. It could be the strange robed man, but did they really want to wait and find out for sure? It could be anyone or anything and they weren't prepared at the moment to find out whom or what was making those footsteps. They needed to get out of the corridor, and they needed to do it now.

"Come on!" David yelled breathlessly. He didn't know why, but those footsteps frightened him every time he heard them and the closer they got, the more frightened he became. The feelings of power had deserted him and now all he felt was a simmering feeling of fear developing in his stomach.

Jennifer and Christopher were running beside him, but he didn't think the door appeared to be getting any closer and they were becoming exhausted.

He looked up and saw a shrouded figure emerging from around the corridor in front of them. He suddenly stopped running and stood transfixed by the image before him. Jennifer and Christopher; who were right behind him, almost bumped into him as they moved around him. They stopped too and tried to catch their breath. They were both huddled over with their hands on their knees trying to gulp in the air as they looked at their brother.

"What's up Dave?" Jennifer asked through laboured breath.

David couldn't keep his eyes off the figure as it moved towards them slowly. David couldn't even point; he had no control over any parts of his body as the figure moved closer.

Jennifer looked at Christopher worriedly and then they both looked in the direction their brother was fearfully looking at and they froze too.

David looked down the corridor and he began to feel a strange sensation, as if he was walking through the air as light as a feather, and as the figure moved along the corridor the light began to dim with its passing.

The figure before them exuded danger. It was wearing a black robe, similar to the one worn by the strange man, but nothing could be discernable about the person wearing the robe, and the face was totally hidden from view. But the apparition before them seemed to radiate a feeling of such loathing and hatred that the children were frightened to move. As if by staying still, the figure would pass them by and they couldn't be seen.

But the figure had seen them. The cowl lifted slightly towards them and the figure seemed to float ever closer, ever faster towards them.

He was walking down a brightly lit corridor; all white and clinical, an odour of rotten flesh seemed to permeate the atmosphere; the smell strong and nauseating, burning his nostrils with its putrid breath. A dense misty fog crawled along the floor and around his feet, but he wasn't interested in the fog or the smell for that matter; his gaze was focused on the obscure, indeterminate figure before him. He was walking toward that figure now; although he felt as if he was actually floating on the mist rather than walking, the dark figure watching and waiting for his arrival. Before he knew what was happening he was standing before the figure who was dressed in a monk's habit, its face obscured from view by an overlarge hood.

He knew he was shaking with fright, but he could do nothing about that, his body was no longer his own, he had no power of it anymore, the figure before him was now in control. Then he heard the footsteps behind him, faint but there nevertheless, and heading in his direction. His body began to stop shivering and he began to relax, that was until he realised the hooded figure was raising its head toward him. He screamed!

Jennifer slapped David's face. "Dave, David" She shouted, trying to stop her brother from screaming.

David's eyes began to focus and he managed to concentrate on the concerned face of his sister; with tears running down her face, she was almost hysterical with worry and fright.

David quickly regained some semblance of thought and shouted for Jennifer and Christopher to run, run as fast as their legs could carry them.

He grabbed hold of the pair of them and thrust them towards the way they had just come. His only thought was to get as far away from the robed figure as possible. A colour emerged in front of him as he propelled his siblings forward. It was a door, not their door, but a door none-of-the-less. He headed straight for it, still aware that the robed figure was following not far behind.

Without hesitation or a moment's thought of the consequences, he pushed open the door and the three children dived into the unknown.

Chapter Six

It was the intense heat that struck them first as they fell to the ground on the other side of the door. That is, the heat and the blinding bright light that shone mercilessly down on them from a bright blue, cloudless sky.

They had collapsed on what appeared to be a baking hot stone floor, a fact so quickly realised that they wasted no time in scrambling to their feet so they wouldn't burn themselves.

They looked around in wonder at their surroundings and couldn't believe their eyes. With their mouths wide open in amazement, the three Barnes children could only gawp at the incredible site before them.

They were standing on a large dark stoned plinth; at its centre stood a large stone obelisk; at least a hundred feet tall and approximately ten feet or so wide. The obelisk itself seemed to be made from the same stone material as the plinth, by the look of it. But most amazing of all was the fact that the plinth itself was situated in what could only be described as an immense and uncompromising, lifeless desert. Neither one of them could see anything other than mountainous ridges and seas of sand for miles, as the sun beat down from above. There seemed to be no vegetation in sight, and apparently no other structures; except the one they were standing next to. Christopher quickly walked around the plinth until he finally came back to stand with his brother and sister. They were still standing like statues, covering their eyes with their hands; they looked out at the vast emptiness before them.

All thoughts of the foul robed man had vanished as they stood there silently, trying to comprehend what had just happened to them.

Christopher was the first to break the silence. "Where are we?"

"I don't know Chris!" David replied a little harshly as he surveyed the vast empty desert before him.

"I was only asking." Christopher said quietly as he looked out at nothingness. "It's all around us you know." He said, scanning the dunes.

"What? What is?" David asked his brother.

"The sand." Christopher replied. "I've been all around this building, looking in every direction and there's nothing to see but sand."

"Well, I'm not staying here," Jennifer said. "Let's get back." She turned back to look for the door, but to her utter dismay it had disappeared, just like the slide. All that remained was the stone obelisk, its dark greyness, stark against the bright, unyielding sun.

She stood mesmerised by the disappearance of the doorway, the doorway was the only way she knew of, that could take her home and it had disappeared.

Sensing something was wrong; David looked at his sister as she stared at the point where the door should have been.

"What's wrong Jen?" He asked, and then he noticed what was missing, "Oh!"

"What?" Christopher asked, still not comprehending.

"What! What do you think?" Jennifer shouted at him.

Then it dawned on him, the door had disappeared. "It's gone."

"Faster than a speeding bullet, the light has finally been switched on at last." She said as she dropped to her knees, putting her head in her hands.

David moved toward his sister and put his hands on her shoulders only to have them shrugged off. He stood there looking at the obelisk, wondering where the door had disappeared to, but not finding an answer.

Christopher stared at Jennifer a moment before whispering to his brother. "I've had a good look round this stone thing and I didn't see any other doors Dave."

"Oh that's just great!" Jennifer wailed.

"Jen, pull yourself together, there must be a way out of here, so come on, get up and let's have a good look round." David said angrily as he stomped around the plinth, determined to find another doorway.

They searched the entire bottom part of the structure, searching for any indications of a doorway, a gap or anything that might appear to yield a way out of there, but found nothing.

"Ok, I'll admit it," Christopher began. "I'm a little freaked out by this." He said quietly as he moved closer to his brother, not wanting to upset his sister more than she already was. Sweat was dripping from his brow as he asked. "Any idea where we are?"

"I have no idea Chris; it's not as if I have been here before you know."

"It's a desert, and by the looks of it, quite a desolate one." Jennifer replied to Christopher's question as she sat down on the plinth out of the sun's bright burning light.

"Well, it's hot and there's plenty of sand, so yes, it's a desert alright, but that's all we can say." David agreed.

"Yep, stranded in a desert and our only way out of here has gone, there's no way home." Jennifer whispered totally dismayed.

"You don't know that Jen, there could be another way out of here." David retorted.

"Oh and where is this other way then?" She asked heatedly.

"I don't know, but we can't just give up, there must be a way out of here."

"Well let me know when you find it will you." She said as she looked out at the desert, tears beginning to run down her cheeks.

"I don't know what's happening, one minute we were being chased by that man, that thingy, whatever it was and the next minute we're thrust through a door and landed here, where ever here is." Christopher said. "Where the hell did this desert come from?"

"I don't know, I don't have the answers." David shouted, annoyed with himself as much as he was annoyed with Christopher for asking stupid questions.

"I know you don't, but I can't believe there is nothing here, only this desert, this strange structure and no way home." Christopher said as he began to look defeated.

"There must be a way home." David said again.

"Well find it then, you have to do something Dave." Jennifer shouted at him.

"Like what? What do you want be to do, simply produce a doorway out of thin air?" He said getting annoyed further.

"Well it disappeared into thin air, so why not?" She retorted.

"I can't make a door appear Jen, can you?"

"Don't be silly, but you have to do something, you got us into this mess." She spat at him venomously.

"I did what? I didn't ask you to follow me through the fireplace did I? I didn't ask you to do anything you didn't want to do, so don't blame me." He shouted back at her.

"It's someone's fault and if the cap fits!" She replied.

David took a deep breath, they had to stop arguing and start working together to find a way out of this. "Look," he said, "it's no ones fault, it just happened, but there is no point everyone falling out over this and blaming each other, we have to find a way out of here, a way home and we have to work together to do that, ok?" David said calmly.

Jennifer heard the sincerity in his voice and knew she was being too harsh.

"Ok, ok, I'm sorry, but this can't be happening." Jennifer said trying to overcome the sulkiness she heard in her own voice.

"Well it is, and like you said, we have to do something, so let's have another look around." David said as he marched off again to take a look around.

"There's nothing here Dave." Christopher shouted at him as he walked off.

"There's nothing here Jen." He said quietly to his sister.

"Listen Chris, there has to be something here, and someone, we'll find our way home don't worry."

"How do you know?" He asked.

"Well for one thing, somebody had to build this thing." She said as she patted the obelisk.

David returned. "Nothing here but desert, and more desert." He said as he approached the pair.

The three children looked at each other and then David and Christopher sat beside their sister silently and pondered what to do about their predicament.

"I'm sorry Jen," David said after a moment. "I've no idea where we are or how we got here, I just knew we had to get away from that thing in the corridor."

"I know what you mean, there was something about it wasn't there?" She said, shaking at the thought of the figure chasing them; forgetting her anger.

"Yes and I hope we don't get to meet it any time soon."

"What happened to you in the corridor Dave? One minute you were ok, and then you were just screaming." She asked him, concerned.

David remembered all too clearly the malevolent figure as it appeared round the corner in the corridor and he knew instinctively that it was the same figure he had seen in the recurring dream he had been having for the past few days, the one he could never quite remember. It had scared him half to death, and the robed figure in his dream now had a physical body and that frightened him even more. Not only that, but the figure had tried to get to him, to them, and he could sense that the figure's intention hadn't been friendly.

David told them what he could remember of his dreams and quite unashamedly told them of the fear he had experienced each time. It was as if he relived the fear every time he thought about it, but this was one secret he felt compelled to share, though he didn't know why. Once he had finished they just huddled down next to him to offer him what comfort they could. They stayed there huddled together and watched the sun as it began to lose its brilliance and fade behind a pyramid dune in the distance.

With the fading light, David at last got to his feet and looked around. "Ok!" He said, "We have to do something! We need to find a way out of here!"

"What do you have in mind?" Jennifer asked expectantly, looking up to her brother as he stood and began to pace up and down the plinth.

"I don't know, but we can't just sit here, we have to do something, there has to be a way out of here." He said as he smashed his left fist into his open right palm in frustration.

"I agree Dave, but we don't know where we are and we don't know how to get home." Christopher said as he too came to his feet.

"I know where you are, "Came a voice to their left from behind the structure. "You are at Junggar Shan, The Guardian's Stone." With the voice appeared the figure of a man, he was dressed in a long beige robe, which was tightly fitted around the waist with a beige sash and thick leather belt. Underneath the robe he was wearing a white loose-fitting cotton shirt and fitted cotton breeches; similar in colour to the robe; albeit slightly darker. Only his eyes were visible behind a dull yellow shemagh that was wrapped around his head; the robe's large hood was down. He had another two daggers in his belt next to his curved sword but they weren't his only weapons on view. His robe extended all the way down to the top of his soft leather boots; which also had a dagger in each, and he carried a short bow with a quiver of arrows, which was lazily slung over his right shoulder. The man raised his hand to part of the shemagh covering his face to reveal a bright white grin and a long slightly crooked nose as he looked the children up and down.

David moved quickly in front of his brother and sister; though if it was to protect them, he wouldn't be able to offer much against the man with all the weapons at his disposal. They rushed to their feet, all the same and stood close behind him.

David was reminded of a picture of an Arab Prince he had once seen in a book at school. That Prince had worn a turban like the stranger was wearing and also had a curved sword, and although he remembered that the Prince's sword was for ceremonial purposes only, he was certain the sword at this man's side wasn't.

"Who, who are you?" David stammered at the stranger who was still smiling at the three children before him.

The man leaned forward slightly in a bow, extending his right hand in a flourish, whilst never removing his gaze from the three of them as he introduced himself.

"I apologise for my rudeness, "he began, "I am Sukhoi Mikoyan of the Kavacha." The man said formally. "And, if I may be so bold, who are you?"

David looked nervously toward his brother and his sister as they stared at the apparition before them. David was surprised that Jennifer didn't really seemed surprised by his presence; he couldn't tell what the expression on her face indicated but it wasn't fear. Her head was cocked to the left-hand side as if listening to something; definitely not frightened at all, if anything it was more an expression of concentration. He was just wondering what she was concentrating on when she suddenly lost her balance and he reached out his arm to steady her.

Jennifer couldn't help but stare at the stranger but when she looked into the man called Sukhoi's eyes, she almost fainted. Her legs almost gave way and would have, if David hadn't at that moment reached out his arm for her to grab hold of and steady her. She realised instinctively somehow that this was a dangerous man, but even stranger was the knowledge that she knew this man could be trusted; trusted in fact with their lives. How she knew this, she had no idea, but it was as if she could almost read his deepest thoughts, and thereby know the man within.

David was talking to the stranger as Jennifer tried to concentrate on staying upright, she felt disorientated for some reason, but as she looked at the man she realised she could also sense other thoughts. She couldn't decipher them enough to know what they were saying; it was like trying to grab hold of a fish as it swam down river, she just wasn't quick enough to grab hold of it. She looked at her brothers and at the new arrival, but it wasn't their thoughts she was sensing. Again she didn't know how she knew it, she just did know it. When she concentrated on her brothers she could feel their fear and apprehension, but surprisingly she could also sense their curiosity and excitement of meeting someone else in this barren land. Then, quite unexpectedly she realised she could sense other thoughts and feelings. She didn't know exactly where they were coming from but she did know they were coming from two people in front of her, somewhere behind the stranger before them now. There didn't seem to be any malice in those feelings; just like the man before her, they too were curious and particularly cautious. Like them, they were surprised to see anyone else out in the middle of desert, and especially three children.

"I am David, "David was saying as she began to concentrate on what was happening right in front of her, "This is my sister Jennifer and my brother Christopher." Jennifer nodded in recognition of her name then turned to her brother and whispered in his ear.

"There are others out there directly behind the man Dave, be careful."

What did she mean by that? David thought. What was she on about, there are others out there? How many others? And out where exactly? And how did she know?

The man continued to smile as the introductions were given. His brow briefly bunched into a frown, but then instantly relaxed as he looked at each of them in turn.

"I hope I do not offend you when I say, these are strange names." He said as he pronounced each one in turn.

Christopher smiled up at the man, "Not half as strange as yours Sukhoi." He said.

Sukhoi looked toward the smaller boy and at his innocent face, and began to laugh; a full throaty laugh that you heard only when someone genuinely thought something was funny.

"Yes Christopher, yes, you are right of course." He said as he chortled.

"You can call be Chris Sukhoi, everyone else does." Christopher offered.

"Thank you, I will Chris." Sukhoi replied pleasantly.

Jennifer whispered the same thing into David's ear again.

"Ok, hang on a minute will you." He whispered back. What the hell was she on about David wondered annoyed, but now the strange man was looking at him.

Sukhoi raised his eyebrows expectantly but remained silent.

David gulped as he looked at his sister, who gave him a look of encouragement, and asked. "Sukhoi, are you alone or have you got some friends here with you?" He stammered, "It's just that my sister here seems to be under the impression you have some friends out there, hiding." He finished, looking beyond Sukhoi apprehensively.

Sukhoi's face went totally blank; devoid of any expression, even the smile had vanished in an instant as he stared first at David, and then at Jennifer, giving her a long, penetrating look.

David gulped again as the man stood rigid, not even the light breeze seemed to move his clothes, only his eyes moved at all and they focused on each one of them in turn. It was quite disconcerting for all of them, it was as if they were being scrutinised down to their very souls.

David didn't know what to do, what had his sister made him do? Here they were in a strange desert in the middle of nowhere, with a man that had appeared out of nowhere and now it looked like he had just offended him or something. What made it worse was the man had enough weapons on him to skewer all three of them and put them on a bar-b-que if he wanted, and they wouldn't be able to do anything about it.

Sukhoi gave a quick, sharp whistle through his lips and instantaneously two figures materialised from the sand dunes a few feet behind him.

The children stepped back in surprise as the two figures shook and brushed the sand from their garments. They were both slightly bigger in build to Sukhoi, and a lot more intimidating. They too were wearing a beige robe, but theirs was even more tightly fitted, their hoods were up and pulled tight around their heads; which was probably to keep the sand out of their faces. They had leather wrist bands buckled on each arm that extended almost to their elbows with daggers in each; as well as an array of daggers held in their belts. The only difference between the two men was the additional weapons they were carrying. The figure on the left had a twin bladed axe strapped on his back, while the figure on the right had two crossed swords on his. Neither of them carried a bow, but the looked frightening enough without them.

"Please accept my apologies, I mean no harm or subterfuge, but these are dangerous times, and I did not know if you were friends or foe." Sukhoi said solemnly, bowing to them respectfully, but still maintaining his gaze on them all as he did so. "I would like to introduce my companions; my Ruedin."

Sukhoi turned to his left. "This is Socata Matra of the Palana."

The figure nodded his head slowly towards the children; it was the only movement he made.

Sukhoi then turned to his right. "And this is Braduga Sikorsky of the Govena."

The figure known as Braduga also nodded slowly toward the children and made to step forward, but was quickly stopped by the raised hand of Sukhoi.

David had not believed his sister when she had whispered in his ear that the man before them was not alone. He couldn't see anyone else out in the desert, no movement or sound, nothing, but these figures had just materialised from beneath the sand, like a magician could pull a rabbit out of a hat. David didn't know how Jennifer had known about the others, maybe she had seen something he hadn't, but he must ask her about it, if they lived through this encounter.

David must have had a worried or frightful look on his face at this point because Sukhoi stepped closer toward him with his hands open palmed, to indicate he had nothing in them.

"Please do not be frightened, we mean you no harm." Sukhoi announced.

Jennifer whispered in David's ear. "I believe him."

David turned his head side-wards to look in his sister's eyes and he instinctively knew that she believed what she had just told him. It didn't make him feel anymore relaxed or comfortable about the situation, but he did believe her.

"How did you know my friends were there, Jennifer?" He turned towards the girl and asked politely.

It was Jennifer's turn to gulp, turning bright red as she became the focus of everyone's attention. "I think I saw them move, and well thought maybe there was someone else travelling with you." She stammered back. She couldn't tell them that she had heard some half thoughts in her head, not even her brothers would believe that, even if it was the truth. They would just lock her up and throw away the key if she told them that.

Sukhoi raised his left eyebrow in obvious disbelief but didn't press the matter; he simply motioned his companions forward and looked toward the obelisk.

"May I ask what you are doing here, The Guardian's Stone is a very ancient and sacred monument, and rarely visited. It is many miles from civilisation, in a hostile part of our land and it is not prudent to be alone here in the present climate." He said as his gaze moved from the obelisk to the children once more.

"We meant no harm Sukhoi." David said quickly. "We haven't done anything wrong have we?" He asked. The last thing they needed right now was to get into trouble for being somewhere they shouldn't and get locked up or worse killed for it; they were in enough trouble as it was.

Sukhoi smiled. "I believe you David and no, you have done nothing wrong." He said as he saw their faces change from worry to relief. "But could you tell me how you came to be at this place, at this time?" He asked "Unless of course you are Toureng? He asked as he raised one eyebrow as if to emphasise the question, but the look he gave them said he didn't believe them to be whatever this Toureng was meant to imply.

"Toureng? Is that bad or good?" Christopher asked.

He could tell from the puzzled looks on their faces that they had no idea what he was talking about, and he himself felt relieve at that. They hadn't seen any Toureng themselves so far but they had come across their tracks.

The worry returned to their faces as they looked quickly at each other.

"Toureng are our enemies Chris, so I suppose you could say that would be bad." Sukhoi said as he smiled disarmingly at the boy and then just stared at them all as if waiting for them to say something, raising the same eyebrow again.

"Well, we're not Toureng then." Christopher said with a smile.

"Tell him how we got here, tell him the truth." Jennifer whispered in David's ear.

"You tell him, why do I have to do all the talking?" David whispered back.

"You're the one in front." She replied in a tight lipped whisper, nudging him forward a little more.

David realised then that they had put him in charge of this meeting, whether he liked it or not. He just didn't know what to say, he never did when meeting anyone for the first time. It was alright Jennifer telling him to tell the strangers the truth, but they wouldn't believe him and they would probably chop his head off for lying to them.

How could he tell them about the fireplace and the corridor, magical things that happened in another place at another time, they just wouldn't believe him.

"We don't know how we got here." Christopher said into the silence. "One minute we're opening a door, "he paused, "the next minute we're here." He finished shrugging his shoulders for effect.

David and Jennifer both stared at their brother as he gave them a shrug of his shoulders as if to say, "Somebody had to say something."

"A door you say?" Sukhoi sounded intrigued, but David realised he showed no surprise, maybe this was a common occurrence. Maybe, just maybe, this happened all the time and they were used to strangers turning up willy-nilly. And maybe, just maybe, they knew of a way out of here and a way back home. His face brightened at this and a smile appeared on his face at the prospect of finding a way home.

"Yep." Christopher replied and Jennifer grabbed his arm, squeezed it and gave him one of her stern looks of disapproval.

As the smile appeared on his face he noticed that Sukhoi was looking at him curiously, again with that one raised eyebrow, which appeared to have lots of different meanings.

"Sukhoi," he said, "we don't actually have any idea of where we are, but more importantly we have no idea of how to get home," he paused for that to sink in a moment before asking the all important question, "We could do with some help."

He could feel the eyes of Jennifer and Christopher on him as well as the eyes of the three strangers, but what other option did they have, he had to say something and they needed help.

"It is not our way to leave children helpless and stranded from their homes David; we will help all we can." Sukhoi said as he smiled encouragingly at them.

Suddenly he turned quickly to look behind him as if he had just heard something unusual or some out-of-the-place sound, because he turned back to the children with real concern on his face and told them. "We must go and quickly!"

"Why? What's the matter?" David asked alarm and fear evident in his voice.

"David we must go, all of us, we have little time, we must hurry, our lives depend upon it." He replied hurriedly, "Please just come with us now and I will explain everything when we are safe, you have nothing to fear from us." He said as he turned around and started to walk away briskly.

Jennifer closed her eyes briefly and she felt something strange, she didn't know what it was but it frightened her. "Dave let's just do as he says, something is coming and I don't think it's anything good." Jennifer said as she started after the three moving figures.

David didn't understand how Jennifer seemed to know everything and was even more shocked to realise that he believed everything she said even though she didn't explain or provide any proof.

"Come on Chris, I'm not waiting to find out what everyone seems to be scared of." He said as he quickly grabbed hold of his brother's arm and pulled him along after himself.

"Ok, ok I'm coming, don't pull so hard." Christopher said as he ran a few steps to catch up with his brother, his feet sinking in the sand as he walked.

They had managed to walk about twenty minutes or so when they all heard a terrible whistling sound to their right. They stopped and everyone looked in that direction. In the distance they could see a vast cloud of something heading in their direction and it was coming fast.

It was still quite a way off but it was incredible, the cloud seemed to be coming from out of the sky itself. It covered an enormous area, seemingly stretching for miles and it was heading right for them.

"What is it?" Christopher asked as he stared in awe.

"Please keep moving we must hurry, it will be here in a few minutes." Sukhoi motioned with his hands to hurry and was clearly disturbed by the enormous menacingly looking cloud.

"How far Sukhoi?" The man called Socata asked as they quickened the pace.

"Another hundred metres, but we must hurry, I am not sure we will make it in time." He replied anxiously.

The three children had to try and run in the sand to keep up with the three men, which was extremely difficult as their feet just seemed to sink with each step. It was like trying to wade across river, the sand was forcing them to traverse the dunes instead of walking in a straight line, but they could all feel the urgency now, especially as the cloud seemed to be drawing ever closer at an incredible speed.

As David trudged along the dunes, he watched as the three men suddenly stopped. Sukhoi then knelt down and moved his arms about slowly for a few moments. The children were on top of the men in no time and David just managed to hear the word "Haram" before the cloud reached them and he found it difficult to hear or see anything. The sound was horrendous, piercing the eardrums and the sand that was swirling about them bit into their flesh on their faces and hands. The sand storm was about to hit them with its full force and intensity and they were stuck in the middle of the desert, without any protection.

That was until the ground suddenly erupted under their feet, the sand parting to expose a flat sheet of rock. The rock then slid to the side to reveal a hole, with steps leading down a dark tunnel.

"Quickly!" Sukhoi shouted over the whistling and howling sound of the sand storm. "Everyone inside, Brad you go first." He said.

Braduga nodded briefly to Sukhoi and then he leapt into the hole, quickly moving down the steps two at a time. Sukhoi grabbed hold of Jennifer and Christopher and pushed them after him. David peeked into the hole; he didn't like the look of the tunnel and really didn't want to enter it. His sister and brother were now out of sight, so he really had no choice but to enter it, he reasoned.

"David, we must go now and quickly!" Sukhoi shouted at him.

He stood there riveted until Socata grabbed hold of his arm and forcibly encouraged him to enter the tunnel. Sukhoi brought up the rear as the storm washed over them, just as he replaced the rock sheet, blocking the entrance to the tunnel and their only way out.

Chapter Seven

David realised he could see quite clearly as he walked down the steps of the tunnel. There were rows of glass orbs attached to the tunnel walls on either side that emitted a pale translucent light. He could see Jennifer and Christopher just ahead of him and heading toward a brighter white light at what must be the end of the tunnel. A few moments later he was standing beside them and all three of them were looking in wonder at the sight before them. They had entered a large cavern, the air inside was cool, but not cold, sweet smelling and fresh, as if it was somehow air-conditioned. What captivated the children was what the cavern contained. Inside was an array of various items that just wouldn't normally be associated with a cavern beneath the sand. At the centre stood a table full of pots and pans, on either side of the table were bright colourful cushions of various sizes. Behind and beyond the table was a relatively large pool of water with a waterfall of clear fresh water falling from the rocks above. Around the walls were the same glass orbs that lit the tunnel, but the light from these was stronger and brighter, there were also various weapons and instruments, furs and clothing lining the walls. It was an incredible sight and one the children hadn't expected to see when they first entered the tunnel a few minutes earlier

Sukhoi appeared from the tunnel that led into the cave and quickly walked over to his companions and whispered something to each of them. He then turned to the children and looked them all up and down.

"Everyone ok?" He asked in genuine concern.

"Yes, I think so Sukhoi, thank you." David replied.

"What was that Sukhoi, the sound was terrible and the sand, I could hardly breathe." Christopher asked shakily.

"That was Har Mattan," he replied, "It means; "to tear your breath apart", it is a terrible sand storm."

"Well it certainly lives up to its name." Jennifer said.

"Yes, many men have lost their lives to that cruel storm." He replied solemnly.

"But we're safe down here though, aren't we?" Christopher asked worriedly.

"Yes my friend, you are safe here." Sukhoi said as he ruffled the hair on Christopher's head.

"And where are we now?" David asked.

Sukhoi smiled. "This is a Haram."

"A Haram?" David asked. "I thought I heard you say that word earlier."

"Yes, it is a place of sanctuary; you will always be safe in a Haram, safe from all things."

The way Sukhoi described it, made David extremely nervous, though he didn't know why. What did three fully armed men need to be safe from, he wondered? There were things that you could be scared of in a desert he supposed, but what would frighten three men; especially with the amount of weapons each of them had. He would have to ponder that question another time, as he thought he just heard Sukhoi mention something about food, and he was ravenous.

"There is plenty of food and drink here so help yourselves and then, when you have finished, maybe we can have a talk." Sukhoi said as he walked over to the table in the centre of the room.

There was indeed plenty of food, Socata and Braduga; probably on orders from Sukhoi, were laying dried fruits, flat bread, various cheeses and strips of meats onto the dishes already on the table. Jugs were filled from the waterfall and brought over to the table.

"Please my friends, eat, eat all you want."

As the children, first tentatively, then hungrily ate the food before them, Sukhoi watched with mounting interest. Who were these strange children? Where had they come from? But more importantly, why were they at the Guardian's Stone on this day of all days? There were lots of questions he wanted to ask, but he was a patient man, and everything comes to he who waits, he thought.

As she ate her food, Jennifer felt the eyes of the men on them and she felt uneasy.

"They keep staring at us." She whispered to her brothers.

"Well let's be fair Jen, we do look a little strange to them, we're not exactly dressed for the desert, and they must be wondering what three strange kids are doing out here, especially all alone." David whispered back.

"There's something else, but I can't just put my finger on it at the moment."

"Forget it for now, you said we can trust them, so let's do just that and just finish this food, I didn't realise how hungry I was." He said putting another morsel of food into his mouth. "We can ask Sukhoi about getting home after, I'm sure he'll know of a way." David said convinced of the fact.

"Ok, Dave, you're probably right." Jennifer agreed, though she had an idea it wouldn't be as simple as that.

"Just let me do the talking, I don't want them to know everything." He said.

"Why not?" Asked Christopher.

"Well to be honest, I just don't think they will believe us, "he looked at his sister pointedly for any remarks and continued when she didn't say anything, "and besides, I don't know if we can really trust them fully, not yet anyway, ok?"

"They saved our lives Dave and their looking after us, why can't we trust them?" Christopher asked.

"I know that Chris, but we're strangers here and the only people I am going to trust for now, are you two, ok?"

Jennifer and Christopher nodded their agreement and the three children continued with their meal.

Sukhoi joined them at the table when he was sure they had enough to eat, while Braduga and Socata appeared to busy themselves in the cavern with one chore or another.

David realised that whatever chores they were doing, their attention wasn't entirely on their tasks as he found that they had moved closer to where the children were sat and well within earshot of any conversation that may arise.

Sukhoi sat down next to them and waited silently while the children put their empty plases to one side.

"Have you had enough to eat my friends?" He asked.

"Yes thank you, it was wonderful." Jennifer replied.

"Hmm." Christopher replied rubbing his belly.

"Good." Sukhoi said and then sat there again silently as if waiting for one of the children to speak, especially as he raised that eyebrow of his again.

David sat at the table, his brother and sister waiting for him to start talking first like they had agreed. Unfortunately, when it came down to it, David didn't really know what he should or could tell them. They had arrived in a desert earlier that day; God knows where, and through a door that had now disappeared. They didn't know where they were or how to get back home, what else was there to say. He looked towards Sukhoi but he just didn't have the confidence to say anything.

Sukhoi realised that his brother and sister were waiting for David to start the conversation off. He also realised that David was a little uneasy about doing that, so he decided to talk first, hoping he could establish a mutual conversation with these three young strangers.

"I told you earlier." Sukhoi began. "That I am of the Kavacha."

The three children nodded enthusiastically, David full of relief that he didn't have to say anything for the moment and Sukhoi continued.

"The Kavacha are known as the "Seekers".

"What are you seeking?" Christopher interrupted.

"Chris, be quiet and he'll tell us." David admonished his brother for interrupting.

Sukhoi smiled and then continued. "We search for the Nadym Varsk; the Truth Seer, who will fulfil an ancient prophecy and help us to defeat Nuba Driss, a terrible and powerful mage, an enemy of our land."

Sukhoi paused to see if there was any reaction to what he had told them so far, but to his surprise none on the names meant anything to them. These were indeed strange children not to know of Nuba Driss. His own curiosity was stimulated by this revelation, but he continued without asking his own questions.

"Each Kavacha is protected and accompanied by an honour guard; the Ruedin, Braduga and Socata are my Ruedin. We search together for the Nadym Varsk and have been together for a few years now."

"Are there many Kavacha?" David asked intrigued.

Sukhoi looked at David suspiciously, but couldn't tell if there was any ill intent on his part. He was still a little suspicious of the children, but his Kavacha instincts told him he could trust them. There were spies everywhere these days and it was always difficult to determine who to trust and who not to, but he had always trusted his own instincts and he saw no reason not to trust them now.

"There are quite a few, yes, though only the Keeper could give you an accurate number." He replied a little evasively. "The Keeper; to pre-empt your next question, looks after the Kavacha knowledge; a rare and powerful book, but I have said too much already."

"That's ok, I was just interested." David said smiling, but inwardly he thought that the reply was a little ambiguous.

"How can this Nadym Varsk help you defeat your enemy, Nuba..? Jennifer asked, changing the subject.

"Nuba Driss. We do not know. We only know that in order to defeat our enemy we need to find the one prophesised." Sukhoi replied.

"What does this Nadym Varsk look like?" David asked.

"Again, I do not know the answer to that either, but it is prophesised that the Nadym Varsk will arrive on a certain day"

"Why do you search then, when you know the day the Seer will show up?" Christopher asked.

"Good question Chris," Sukhoi said as he smiled at the youngest Barnes child, "We know the day, but unfortunately not the year."

"I can see that being a problem." Jennifer said, "Have you been searching a long time then?" She asked.

"I have been searching for twenty years, but the Kavacha as a whole have been searching and waiting for five hundred years."

"How long?" Jennifer asked amazed by this revelation

"Yes it has been a long time." Sukhoi said smiling again.

"Hang on a minute," David said as he frowned, trying to think things through, "you said that this Seer will help you get rid of this Nuba Driss right?" He asked.

"Yes." Sukhoi agreed.

"If that's true, and the Seekers have been searching for five hundred years, shouldn't this Nuba Driss be dead by now?"

Sukhoi was amazed at how quickly the boy came to that conclusion and was impressed. "That is right David, he should be dead; if he was an ordinary man, but Nuba Driss has powerful dark magic at his disposal. The prophesy states that the Nadym Varsk shall defeat him by revealing the truth."

"Reveal the truth, what else?" Jennifer asked, there must be more to it she supposed.

"That is all I know." Sukhoi conceded.

"Did you say magic? Real magic?" Christopher asked excitedly.

"Yes, is there another kind?" Sukhoi inquired.

"There are tricks that seem like magic." David offered. "We don't have proper magic where we come from."

"Where is that?" Sukhoi asked.

"Yorkshire, there's no real magic there." Christopher replied smiling to himself.

Jennifer gave him a stern look before turning back to Sukhoi.

"How do you know Nuba Driss is still alive after so many years?" David asked a little sceptically.

"The Guardian told us that Nuba Driss would not age in our land."

"What? How is that possible?" David asked incredulously.

"Who is the Guardian?" Jennifer asked at the same time.

"We do not know how this is possible, but my ancestors believed the Guardian, and so must we." Sukhoi replied, though it seemed he didn't actually believe that Nuba Driss could actually live that long, himself.

"And the Guardian?" Jennifer prompted.

"The Guardian came to our land shortly after Nuba Driss; it is not written where he came from, but it must have been a land far away, because it is written that his clothing and speech were different to ours in some way. He was a great wizard who taught our ancestors many things, but alas most of his teachings have been lost over the centuries. It was the Guardian that made the Haram and showed a chosen few how to protect the people of this land." Sukhoi told the inquisitive children.

"The chosen few being the Kavacha?" Jennifer asked, but she knew instinctively before Sukhoi even acknowledged the question that she was right.

"Yes, although they were not addressed as such then, they were merely a group of trusted warriors." He replied.

"So the Kavacha have a little magic then?" Jennifer asked expectantly.

"Yes, a little." Sukhoi answered surprised by Jennifer's questions.

"You can do magic?" Christopher asked in astonishment.

"A little, yes." Sukhoi said quietly. He had said too much now he realised, even if he did trust his instincts, these children were still strangers and he knew nothing about them really. Although for some reason he couldn't explain, he felt as if he could trust them with anything, and that really surprised him in the current climate. There had been rumours of sightings of the Toureng in the Gratishk Mountains and as far as the Konare Forest. Rumours that involved them trading with the Koutla Raiders; a band of outlaws and thieves that were becoming a real problem in Sakhalin as their numbers began to increase at an alarming rate. Sukhoi and his Ruedin had seen signs of the Toureng just recently; but had yet to find their hunting parties. They had seen far too many of the Koutla though. They still investigated all sightings and constantly made reports to the council of elders at Enkan Mys. Any movements involving the "Banished Ones", which was the name given to the Toureng, could only mean trouble, trouble of the Nuba Driss kind; the Council of Elders at Enkan Mys had warned. So most of the Kavacha had been sent out to every corner of the land to search out these rumours and find the truth. That was why he was here with his Ruedin, to find the truth and one more thing. To be at the Junggar Shan at dusk today, the day the Nadym Varsk was prophesised to appear.

"Was that how you knew that storm was coming?" David asked Sukhoi again, the man was obviously deep in thought but David was interested in the answer, so he posed the question again.

"What? Sorry, yes." Sukhoi said in surprise.

"You said earlier that Braduga was of the Govena and Socata of the Palana, what does that mean?" David asked.

"Another good question, especially from a stranger to our land." Sukhoi replied as he paused to consider the best way to explain.

Sukhoi hadn't intended to tell these children anything but somehow he wanted to share his knowledge with them and decided it couldn't do any harm to give them a bit of a history lesson.

"I think I must start at the very beginning, but I will try to keep it as brief as possible, ok?"

They all nodded and silently waited for Sukhoi to begin.

"This land of ours is called Sakhalin and there are four main tribes, the Ossora, Govena, Palana and the Toureng. We generally refer to the Toureng as the Banished Ones now, although I have heard from the Koutla that they refer to themselves as the Imazaghan, the "Free People".

"How do the Koutla fit in, you said there were only four tribes?" Christopher asked.

"Be quiet Chris, Sukhoi will tell us if you keep quiet." David admonished his brother. David hated it when his brother butted in on stories, which was one of the reasons he kept his own stories short, the boy couldn't help himself.

"Sorry." Christopher returned sheepishly.

"The Koutla Raiders; as they are referred to are outlaws and bandits that have been banished from the three tribes. They are the lowest people in our land, who prefer to steal and take what they want instead of working for it. Such people tend to come together over time and I suppose they have come to form their own tribe now; though I doubt they have any code or honour." Sukhoi explained. They will do anything for money and have lost all sense of decency as they moved from place to place.

"What about the Toureng, why are they called the Banished Ones?" Christopher asked.

"They betrayed you?" Jennifer said, more as a statement than a question.

"Yes, Jennifer," Sukhoi said surprised again by her insight, "Approximately five hundred years ago Nuba Driss appeared in Sakhalin and tried to conquer the four tribes; who were four separate entities back then. Each tribe had their own king and there were many wars and battles, although they never lasted long. The war with Nuba Driss united the tribes, but he used such unimaginable creatures to do his bidding; such creatures as the Gourtak and the Griffins, that he almost ripped the tribes apart."

The three children looked at each other, wondering if he was really speaking the truth. They had heard of Griffins before but they were creatures of mythology, and they had never heard of the Gourtak. David held his finger to his lips for silence as Sukhoi continued with his narration.

"He brought death and destruction in his wake and attacked everyone mercilessly, giving no quarter." Sukhoi continued. "All four tribes, having decided to unite under one banner tried desperately to defeat him and almost did. Until the treacherous Toureng king decided to turn his back on the rest of the tribes and joined his forces to that of Nuba.

"Why would they do that?" Jennifer asked astonished.

"It is believed that the King was promised sole dominion over the rest of the tribes once they were defeated, providing he bowed and scraped to Nuba Driss." Sukhoi recited with displeasure.

With the foul army of Nuba Driss combined with that of the Toureng, the three tribes had no chance of victory and would have been defeated if not for the arrival of the Guardian. The Guardian used his magic against Nuba Driss, his army of creatures and the Toureng, pushing them back beyond the Gratishk Mountains to our west. Even with his help it was a bloody battle; thousands died and thousands more were injured. The Guardian, himself was wounded but continued to fight for the three tribes until Nuba Driss retreated beyond the Amal Desert, where we are now. Nuba Driss escaped with the remnants of his army of foul creatures and what was left of the Toureng. The Guardian feared that he would one day return with a greater army and told the people to prepare for that day. He said he would have to leave, but in order to give the people some semblance of hope against such a formidable creature; should he re-emerge in the future, he taught a few chosen warriors some magic. All that magic is contained in a book and it has been taught to the Kavacha since that day. Before he departed to help other people in a far away land, he said that Nuba Driss will return, but if the Nadym Varsk could be found in time, the tribes may be victorious. The Prophesy of the Nadym Varsk is contained in the book and gives us clues as to when he will appear.

Sukhoi paused a moment before continuing. "The Kavacha have been waiting for five hundred years for Nuba Driss to bring his army; while everyone else believes the stories of his return are told to scare children. I believe; as do many others, that there has been a change in the wind and with it comes such darkness, that it will consume everything in its path. It appears the Gourtak and the Griffins are roaming the lands of Sakhalin once more, and where they tread, so will Nuba Driss. So we continue our search for the Nadym Varsk and we continue to look for signs of the Toureng Army, which could once more bring death and destruction to our land.

"How will you recognise this Nadym Varsk?" Jennifer asked.

Sukhoi paused before answering, "It is written that the Nadym Varsk will arrive on this day at the Guardian's Stone, when the need of the three tribes is at its greatest, then through revealing the truth will he be recognised."

"It doesn't give you a lot to go on, does it?" Christopher said after a moment's deliberation.

"No, I suppose not." Sukhoi said with a laugh.

David didn't know what they had got themselves into, but hopefully they wouldn't be around too much longer. It sounded to him that the three tribes were just sitting around waiting for a war to begin against this Nuba Driss, and he didn't want any part of it.

"Sukhoi, why are there only three of you?" Jennifer asked. "I would have thought there would be more, especially if you find any Toureng or these creatures you spoke of."

"Ah, let me explain." Sukhoi said as he smiled at her.

"As I said before, a Kavacha has a little magic, but his strength comes from his Ruedin. They are the force which protects the magic; a Kavacha from one tribe is given a warrior from each of the remaining tribes as his guard."

"Why is that?" David asked.

"So when we find the Nadym Varsk, each of the tribes can have a piece of the glory." Sukhoi replied.

"Makes sense." Jennifer said. "No one will fall out that way."

"That is so, Jennifer." Sukhoi agreed.

"So the Kavacha are the chosen few who have this knowledge you spoke of?" David asked, trying to understand.

"Yes, the Kavacha are chosen for their special ability they are born with. Once they are found, they go to Enkan Mys to be trained in the old lore, the Kavacha knowledge. When they are ready they must then pass certain tests. If successful, they will be escorted by the Ruedin and sent out into the world to search for the Truth Seer."

"How long do they train for?" David asked.

"It depends on the individual but it could take many years." Sukhoi divulged.

"How long did you train for?" David asked.

Sukhoi smiled and then answered proudly. "I was eighteen when I took the tests."

From the way he smiled, David assumed that wasn't very long and was about to ask when Christopher beat him to it.

"I take it, that's pretty good then?" Christopher asked.

Sukhoi realised this meant nothing to the three children but smiled at their lack of understanding. "Yes Chris, very good. Most Kavacha do not take the tests until they are in their late Twenties and then they may have to forego some of the tests, depending on their skills."

The astonishment on the children's faces made Sukhoi laugh. "I see I have impressed you at last." He said smiling.

"You must be what we call a child prodigy." Jennifer said.

"Yes, I suppose I must." He said and laughed again, which made the children join in and laugh with him in his modesty.

"What about the ones that are not found, the ones with the ability?" David asked suddenly.

Sukhoi paused for a moment before answering, "There are none, they are all found, the magic always finds a way to be seen."

"Oh." David said quietly as he thought about that. He wasn't sure how big Sakhalin was and how many people were in it, but could they really find every child that had the ability, he wondered.

Everyone seemed to be pondering this last bit of information when Jennifer asked. "What is that tattoo on your neck?"

Instantly Sukhoi was on his feet, his hand going to his neck to where Jennifer had pointed.

"What?" Sukhoi asked.

"What tattoo?" Christopher asked.

"What you talking about Jen?" David asked.

Sukhoi looked from Jennifer to David and Christopher, before returning his gaze back to Jennifer.

"The tattoo on your neck, it looks like a Chinese symbol, what does it mean?" She asked again.

"There isn't a tattoo there Jen." Christopher said.

Sukhoi stood up in shock as the three children argued about whether there was a tattoo on Sukhoi's neck or not. It appeared that Jennifer could see one but her brothers couldn't.

"I think everyone should calm down, maybe it is time to get some rest, it is getting quite late and I believe everyone is tired." Sukhoi announced.

"What about getting home?" David asked, everyone went silent, the argument momentarily forgotten.

"I think it is too late to think about getting home now, and besides the storm still rages outside." Sukhoi replied compassionately.

"Oh." David said, with the realisation that they would have to spend a night in this strange place.

Jennifer stood up and strolled away from the group, where she began to collect a gathering of cushions, pillows and furs to keep her warm.

"Ok Sukhoi, we will sleep over there with Jennifer." David said. "Sorry if Jen offended you in any way." He said as an afterthought. His mother always told him to polite, even if it wasn't him that had been rude.

"There is nothing to apologise for, we will be here if you need anything." Sukhoi said frowning at Jennifer as she was laying the cushions on the floor to make her bed.

David, followed by Christopher, went over to where Jennifer was settling down and tried in vain to engage her in conversation. She refused to even look at them, obviously annoyed that they thought she had been lying about the tattoo. David finally gave up in his attempt and the two boys set about collecting some more cushions for themselves. Sukhoi watched with interest as David sorted out Christopher's cushions and then his own. There was a uniformity about the process that intrigued him, as if the boy had done the same thing time and time again.

"Interesting." Sukhoi whispered to himself as he walked over to the pool of water and cupping his hands together he withdrew some to drink. If anyone had heard them, they would wonder if he said it because of the boy or the girl. Sukhoi sensed something about the boy that he couldn't put his finger on, but the girl had seen his Kavacha mark, which only those tested in the Kavacha lore could see.

"Socata?" Braduga whispered.

"Yes my friend." Replied Socata.

"Did you hear what the girl said?" He asked.

"Jennifer, yes I heard." He replied.

"She saw the sign."

"I heard, I was listening beside you."

"Is that not strange?" Braduga asked.

"It is definitely unusual Brad, but I do not know what it means before you ask."

"Me neither, but it is definitely strange." Braduga said quietly as he watched the children settle down for the night at the other end of the cavern.

Socata watched his friend watching the children, aware of the concern in his expression and feeling it himself. No one but a Kavacha could see the sign of the Kavacha; it was something to do with the old lore, so it was indeed unusual that the girl Jennifer could see it.

Socata watched his friend of five years put his weapons on the floor beside his make-shift bed and prepared to go to sleep.

He remembered when Brad had first become part of Sukhoi's Ruedin. Braduga of the Govena had joined them five years earlier to replace his brother Ambar who had been killed protecting Sukhoi from a Gourtak, which had been stalking them. The Gourtak were one of the largest beasts in Sakhalin, they were at least eight-feet tall and bear-like in appearance. They were formidable hunters that had chameleon like armoured scales instead of fur and could camouflage themselves enough to blend into almost any natural terrain. They were intelligent, strong, fierce and fast, and once they caught the scent of their prey, they would hunt it down until the end. They rarely attacked people, but it wasn't unheard of.

Brad had told Socata that he had never wanted to be Ruedin, in fact, he never wanted to be anything, and as an adolescent he was a constant embarrassment to his family. That was until the news came of his brother's death. He had taken it hard; the shock had shaken him to his very core. At sixteen, he was already strong and lithe, built like an athlete and handsome with it; which had all the girls in his village vying for his affections, but he wasn't interested and was prepared to do nothing for the benefit of the tribe. The news of his brother's death changed all that and nearly destroyed him. For some reason he would fight and quarrel with anyone who even looked at him in a funny way. His friends soon steered clear of him and even his family wanted nothing more to do with him especially when he began to take his anger out on a gang of youths in the village, almost killing three of them. It took six of the village's strongest men to restrain him that day, no one could understand why he acted they way he did.

It wasn't until Sukhoi and Socata arrived in the village that Brad began to change. Sukhoi had told him how disappointed he was in the brother of such a brave and noble warrior like Ambar. Sukhoi was so disappointed that Brad had dishonoured his brother that they left the following day, not staying for the funeral service to be completed.

Brad soon regretted his actions and after speaking with his family he decided to go to Enkan Mys to be trained as Ruedin, as his brother had done before him. His family wept with happiness that their wayward son had seen the light and wished him well.

During his relatively short time at Enkan Mys, he soon gained a reputation as a fierce fighter. In just four years, he had become a fully trained warrior and passed with honours as Ruedin. It was an incredible accomplishment, it normally took eight years for a warrior to be trained, and then they had to pass all the required tests to become Ruedin. His instructors were amazed by his abilities, not only was he a master swordsman, but he was equally skilled with a bow, axe and knives. What was even more incredible was that he had adopted such an easy manner with everyone he met, that there was never any jealousy of his abilities or resentment. Not only had he become the perfect warrior, his whole personality had changed, he had become a better man.

Chapter Eight

He was walking down a brightly lit corridor; all white and clinical, an odour of rotten flesh seemed to permeate the atmosphere; the smell strong and nauseating, burning his nostrils with its putrid breath. A dense misty fog crawled along the floor and around his feet, but he wasn't interested in the fog or the smell for that matter; his gaze was focused on the obscure, indeterminate figure before him. He was walking toward that figure now; although he felt as if he was actually floating on the mist rather than walking, the dark figure watching and waiting for his arrival. Before he knew what was happening he was standing before the figure who was dressed in a monk's habit, its face obscured from view by an overlarge hood.

He knew he was shaking with fright, but he could do nothing about that, his body was no longer his own, he had no power over it anymore, the figure before him was in total control. Then he heard the footsteps behind him, faint but there nevertheless, and heading in his direction. His body began to stop shivering and he began to relax, that was until he realised the hooded figure was raising its head toward him. He shouted at the figure before him, "No, you will not have me, leave me alone!"

The figure took an involuntary step backwards in shock but a moment later it lifted its head. He screamed!

David woke dazed and confused, the dream still vivid in his mind. He remembered the dream but still couldn't see the face and that frightened him. He almost felt as if he had won a small victory by making the figure take that step backwards, short-lived as it seemed, he had done it never-the-less.

He rubbed the sleep from his eyes and looked around, almost expecting to find himself in his own bed, but wasn't surprised to find he was still in the cavern.

He slowly got to his feet and got dressed; putting on the clothes he had folded neatly by his make-shift bed the night before. Then he walked quietly past his sleeping brother and sister towards the pool, where he splashed some of the fresh cool water on his face. He turned his head to the left at the faint sound of footsteps; his heart beating rapidly, his imagination expecting the figure from his dreams. Sukhoi's figure came to stand beside him, and he relaxed, exhaling deeply. He hadn't realised he had been holding his breath.

"Did you sleep well my friend?" Sukhoi asked.

"Yes thanks." He lied.

"Are you hungry?"

Now he thought about it, he was a little hungry and said so. They both walked over to the table that had already been laden with flat bread, cheese and fruits and something hot that smelled like porridge. David hated porridge, but it smelled divine.

Sukhoi watched as David began to eat everything but the porridge and wondered what these three strange children were doing here. They were clearly from a faraway land, but he had never seen clothing like theirs before, and had never heard their accents before either.

"David, where are you from?" He asked.

David continued to eat; trying to think of something to say. He had told his brother and sister that he would do all the talking, and now the time had come, he still hadn't decided on what to say. He didn't think they would believe what really happened, but did he really want to lie to these men. He decided to tell Sukhoi as much of the truth as possible, he had no choice really if he wanted their help in getting back home.

So David told him that they were from a faraway land called England, which was surrounded by an enormous ocean. They had entered through a magical door and somehow found themselves at the Guardian's Stone in Sakhalin. He didn't know how it happened or how they got there, but more importantly to them, he didn't know how they were to get back. He just wanted to get all of them back home safe and sound, as soon as possible. He then told him of their mother all alone and probably worried by their disappearance before he finished.

"So you just appeared at Junggar Shan, through this magical doorway?" Sukhoi asked, his face showing no emotion.

"I know it's difficult to believe, but it's the truth, one minute we are walking through the door, the next minute we're in the middle of the desert." David replied. It sounded so inconceivable that even he didn't believe it, but it was the truth, though there were many details he felt he had to leave out. Details such as the strange monk and the foul smelling creature in the corridor and in his dreams. He could tell that Sukhoi was having difficulty in coming to terms with the three children appearing from nowhere, but what else could he say.

Sukhoi smiled to reassure the boy and told him that he believed what he said, though he wasn't sure if he really believed him or not. He didn't think David was lying to him as such, but he did feel that he wasn't telling him the whole truth. He left David at the table to finish his food and walked over to the sleeping forms of his companions to rouse them awake.

David decided he should do the same and with a piece of bread in his mouth he walked over to Christopher and Jennifer and gave them both a gentle shake.

Christopher moaned and groaned as he became awake, whereas Jennifer was instantly on her feet and looking around wildly.

"It wasn't a dream then?" She said dismayed as she looked around the cavern.

"Afraid not sis." David replied.

"Great." She said in return. At least she was speaking to him; he hoped her mood from the night before had changed too, though he didn't voice his opinion on the matter.

"How are our new friends this morning?" Socata asked Sukhoi as he began to pull himself from beneath the furs he had been using for bedding.

"Fine I think, but they are quite strange." He replied wistfully.

"They look lost and scared to me." Socata whispered so they couldn't be overheard.

"I agree they are lost, that much they say themselves," Sukhoi said quietly, "but I do not believe them to be scared."

"Yes, you are right Sukhoi." Brad agreed. "They are not scared, maybe a little apprehensive, but they definitely don't smell frightened."

"We should ask them some questions once they have woken properly." Socata announced.

"I have spoken to David already; there is not a lot to tell." Replied Sukhoi.

He began to relate the details of his conversation with his men, giving his thoughts on what he believed to be half truths, but told them to treat the three as friends for now. Sukhoi didn't believe the children to be Toureng spies, but they had to be careful. If circumstances changed he would let them know, his companions nodded then began to tidy their bedding away

"I'm hungry." Christopher said to no one in particular as he looked around for something to eat.

"Me too." Jennifer said.

"Well I've just eaten but there is plenty of bread, cheese, and fruit on the table if you want some, and oh yes, there's porridge as well." David finished, more as an afterthought.

Christopher rushed to his feet and ran over to the table where he helped himself to everything, including the porridge.

David grabbed hold of Jennifer's arm before she could do the same.

"I've spoken with Sukhoi and told him that we came through a magical door but we don't know how we did it or how to get back."

"Well that's the truth." She said, "But I take it you didn't tell him about the stranger and that thing in the corridor?" She asked quietly in case they were overheard.

"No I didn't but he seemed ok with my explanation."

"Well you had no choice really. What we need to do now is get back to that Guardian's Stone place and find that door home."

"Don't worry Jen, we'll ask them to take us back to the Stone after breakfast, I'm sure the door will be there waiting for us." David said hope written on his face.

"I hope your right Dave." She said as she moved over to the table, picking up a piece of bread before Christopher ate it all.

"Me too Jen, me too." He whispered as he joined them.

The three children were joined a few moments later by the three men and everyone began to eat the remainder of the food on the table. No one spoke, but the silence wasn't awkward. When they had finished everyone in the cavern began to tidy up, putting the cushions back where they found them and then washed the plates and cups they had used in a trough of water beside the pool. When they had finished the three children walked toward Sukhoi who was collecting all his belongings.

"Sukhoi." David said, trying to find the courage to ask the Kavacha if he and his Ruedin would take them back to the Guardian's Stone.

"You wish to go back to the Stone?" He said, not looking at the children, but busily putting his weapons in his belt, boot and up his sleeves.

"Yes please, if that's ok?" David replied astonished that the man knew what he was going to ask.

"You have to leave so soon?" Sukhoi replied

"Yes, we really must be getting home." Jennifer replied. She was going to add that their mother must be frantic by now, but decided it sounded a little pathetic, even to her.

Sukhoi seemed to contemplate this request a long time before answering. "Ok my friends, we will take you back, if that is what you want."

"Thank you, it is." All three children said together.

"Brad, will you bring them their packs please?" Sukhoi shouted over to his companion who was already lifting up three clothe bags from the floor and was now bringing them over to Sukhoi.

"I thought you might be leaving us today, so I have prepared these packs for your journey. There is food, water, clothing fit for the desert and some furs for the cold nights." He said. "There should be enough, but as I do not know how long your journey would take, I had to guess on how much supplies you would require."

"That's really kind of you Sukhoi, but we're hoping we won't need any of that." David said in response.

"Take them anyway, just in case." Sukhoi said with a smile.

David looked towards his brother and sister, who both nodded their assent and he grabbed hold of the pre-offered packs, offering his thanks again.

"Ok, we may as well leave now, everyone got everything they need?" Sukhoi asked.

Everyone nodded and with Braduga leading the group, they made their way up the steps to the desert beyond.

The heat was almost unbearable after the coolness of the Haram; the sun was still only half way in the sky, but scorching never the less.

They had to stand around a few minutes while Sukhoi; who seemed to be praying on his knees, completed some sort of ritual to close the Haram.

"He's chanting something." Jennifer whispered to David, trying to edge closer to see and hear what Sukhoi was doing.

"Yes Jen, I think we all know by now he's chanting." David said raising his eyebrows to Christopher, who smiled back at him. Sukhoi had been doing the same thing for the past few minutes; whatever the thing was. David was happy to wait for him to finish, it was obviously something very sacred and he wasn't about to interfere with any of their rituals.

Braduga and Socata stood silently, waiting for their Kavacha to finish, occasionally looking around, but hardly moving at all, the heat of the day hardly affecting them unlike the children, that couldn't stop sweating.

"Is he going to be much longer do you think?" Jennifer asked impatiently.

David lifted his arms in annoyance. "How the hell am I supposed to know that?" He said trying not to shout. "Don't be so impatient; just wait until he's finished."

"Sorry." She replied and watched as Sukhoi got to his feet and walked the few steps towards them.

"Ok, we can leave now." Sukhoi said as he smiled at them.

"What were you doing Sukhoi?" Jennifer asked.

"Jen, that's none of our business." David reproached.

"It is ok David, I will explain." Sukhoi said as the group began to walk away from the Haram toward the Guardian's Stone. "It takes a little magic to find, open and close a Haram. A little ritual is always required to do this, otherwise anyone and anything that finds a Haram can enter it." He finished.

"So, there are some people that aren't allowed in then?" Jennifer asked, clearly amazed by what Sukhoi had said.

"Yes Jennifer, normally without a Kavacha no one may enter a Haram; providing the magic is still strong." Sukhoi replied.

"And if the magic isn't strong?" Christopher asked intrigued.

"The magic will still keep out all evil creatures, but there are many things that it would not be able to prevent from entering if the magic weakens." He said.

"Like what for instance?" Christopher asked intrigued.

Sukhoi thought for a moment before replying, "Bad dreams for one thing."

David looked toward the Kavacha then, but if he knew anything about David's dreams, he didn't show it on his face; not that he would be able to tell anyway.

"And it's the magic that stops them?" She asked

"Yes."

"Oh, so anyone with a bit of magic could open the Haram?" She asked after a moment's contemplation.

"Possibly, yes, but if that person is deemed to be evil by the Haram, they would not be allowed to enter." He said.

"So the Haram can think? Is it alive?" Christopher asked trying to understand.

David was just about to laugh, until Sukhoi continued, "I would not say it was alive as such, but the magic in the Haram can differentiate between good and evil." He explained.

David pondered this piece of information, but kept his thoughts to himself. Who would have believed that a hole in the ground could have feelings, he thought. But then again, why was he surprised by anything in this place.

The group continued to move silently through the desert, the sun rising in the clear blue sky, its heat beating down upon them. Neither of the companions seemed concerned by the heat or the sun, they just moved through the sand like a fish swims through water, but the children were slipping and sliding along as best they could.

Jennifer was still concentrating on what Sukhoi had said about magic that she didn't see the lizard until she was almost on top of it.

She screamed when she did.

"It is ok Jennifer, it will not hurt you, it is only a skink, a lizard." Sukhoi said trying to calm her down.

The lizard, hearing the shriek, quickly lifted his head and then made a run for it. It was comical to watch the lizard waddle away but Jennifer didn't think so.

From then on, her eyes were glued to where her feet were going and the boys could do nothing but snigger at her obvious discomfort. The men too were trying to keep a bland composure but even they found her discomfort amusing.

It wasn't long before the party arrived back at the Stone and the three companions watched curiously as the children searched it for the supposed hidden doorway. The children were looking for anything really, a lever, a loose brick, anything that would help them find the doorway to take them back home, but the surface to the obelisk was completely smooth, devoid of anything that could possibly help them.

"It's no good, I can't find or see anything that will take us home!" Jennifer exclaimed as she slumped to the plinth floor of the Stone.

"Me neither, Dave, there's nothing here, what do we do now?" Christopher asked deflated, as he too slumped to the floor.

"Not sure, but there must be a way," He replied. "We were in the corridor, then through the door to this Stone, if we can go through one way, surely we can get back the same way, there must be a way back here somewhere, keep looking." He whispered as he continued to scrutinise the Stone.

While the companions looked on, they continued with their search until David stopped and stared at the base of the Stone, where a tiny light was emanating from a small hole.

"There!" he cried as he rushed over to the hole for a closer examination.

Everyone made a rush for the spot David was pointing to and as his arm reached for the hole the wooden door appeared out of nowhere.

The three warriors gasped and then stepped back from the door adopting a fighting stance in their surprise.

David gave a bright, happy smile of success as he surveyed the expressions on the faces of the men and his siblings alike. "I knew we'd find it!" He shouted with joy.

"You were telling the truth!" Sukhoi said in wonder at seeing the door appear out of thin air.

"Yes," he replied brightly, "but we must be going now Sukhoi, thanks for all your help, but we really must be getting home."

"Yes thank you Sukhoi." Jennifer said as she and Christopher stepped up towards the door next to their brother.

"Safe journey then, my friends." Sukhoi replied as he and his Ruedin; who were silently shocked by the appearance of the doorway stepped back.

David smiled and then grabbing hold of the handle, he turned it to open the door.

As the door began to swing open a black robed hand grabbed for David's arm, surprised and frightened he screamed and tried to free himself, but the hand only increased its grip on his arm as he continued to struggle. A body began to push its way through the gap in the door, a body that was wearing a dark robe.

Suddenly, David was pushed to the ground, a shriek of pain erupting from the doorway as Braduga thrust his sword into it. The dark figure took an involuntary step backwards and that gave Braduga sufficient time to push his shoulder against the door to close it. As the door closed it immediately disappeared and with it the strange dark figure that had tried to grab hold of David.

Everyone began shouting and asking questions at once, whilst shaking and trying to recover from the appearance of thing that had tried to grab David a moment earlier. Braduga kept his eyes on the place the doorway had been whilst Socata scanned the horizon in every direction in case of attack from beyond the Stone.

"That was the robed figure we saw yesterday!" Christopher blurted out almost hysterically.

"Calm down Chris, it's gone now." Jennifer said grabbing hold of her brother.

"What do you know of that creature?" Sukhoi asked, concern creasing his face.

Braduga picked David up from the floor; still keeping his eyes on the Stone, and then wiped his sword on a piece of cloth before burying it in the sand to the hilt. "You were extremely lucky David," He said as he replaced the sword on his back. "I thought that thing had you for a minute."

"It would have, if not for you Brad, thanks. I don't know anything about it really Sukhoi," David replied to his question as he brushed the sand from his body. "It was following us yesterday until we entered the door that brought us here and then it was gone." He finished shakily.

"And that is all you know?" Sukhoi asked urgently this time.

"Yes." David replied. He didn't want them to know that the figure had been plaguing his dreams as well.

"Well, from what I have been told, that could have been Nuba Driss, or at least one of his minions." Sukhoi announced.

"That thing was Nuba Driss?" Jennifer asked astonished.

"Possibly, he is very powerful, maybe powerful enough to have conjured that doorway, but we did not get a close enough look at him, so I can not be sure."

"I think I got as close as I wanted to get." David said quietly, although everyone heard him.

"I think you are extremely lucky to still be here, a moment more and that thing would have had you I think." Socata announced sombrely.

"Yes, thank you for saving my brother, Brad." Jennifer said smiling at the warrior.

Braduga smiled, "It was more to luck than anything else that I thought something was wrong and pulled my sword, but it did seem to be waiting for the door to open" He finished solemnly looking over at the three children.

"Well your luck saved David's life, thank you Brad." Jennifer said again and reached up to the big man and kissed him on the cheek.

Braduga blushed and smiled at Jennifer as she went back to her brother and put her arms around his shoulder.

The entire experience had shaken Christopher. "What are we going to do?" We can't go back that way; he could still be waiting for us!" He looked totally dismayed by the prospect of trying to get through the door again. All he could think of was getting home, and now the only way to get home had been blocked by some evil figure, waiting in the corridor for them to try.

The appearance of Nuba Driss or one of his minions had shaken and surprised all of them. Sukhoi couldn't help but think of the coincidence. Meeting the three children at the Guardian's Stone had been a surprise, but now this. Why was Nuba Driss or one of his foul creatures after the children? All his senses and training were trying to tell him this wasn't pure coincidence; the children were important, important enough to warrant the notice of Nuba Driss.

Looking at the children he quickly came to a decision. "I think it would be safer for all of you if you accompanied us back to Enkan Mys," He addressed them. "I do not think you have much choice. It appears Nuba Driss wants something from one or all of you. I do not tell you this to frighten you, but why else would he wait at the door for it to open?"

"I'm not sure." David said looking at his brother and sister and trying to contemplate what to do for the best.

"David, I think you are all safe for now. I think if Nuba Driss could get through that door by himself, he would have done so by now. But, we do not know how long he will remain there. He is a powerful creature of magic, and he may possess the knowledge to return."

"You may be right, but this is the only way we know of to get back home."

"At Enkan Mys, we can ask the Council of Elders to help you return home, but if not, at least you will be safe there. We could always return and try the door again, but next time we will be prepared."

Sukhoi knew the Council of Elders may be able to help the children, but he wasn't sure. He couldn't just leave them there anyway, so he might as well take them with him.

"How far is it to this Enkan Mys?" David asked.

Sukhoi brought his hand up to his chin and began to rub it as he contemplated the length of time it would take the small party to reach their intended destination. He knew he and his Ruedin could probably make the journey in less than ten days, but with the children, he would have to double that. After a few moments he said, "It will probably take us three, maybe four weeks."

All three faces dropped as they realised they wouldn't be able to get home for another month at least, and that was providing there was someone at Enkan Mys who could help them get home. If not it would take another month to return to the stone, to try and find the doorway again.

They looked at each other in despair, but they knew they didn't really have a choice. They wouldn't be able to survive the desert without the three warrior's help and they knew they wouldn't dare enter the doorway again without them being there to protect them. They couldn't expect them to stay with them either, so there really wasn't a choice in the end.

"He's right, Dave, I think we have to go with them to Enkan Mys." Jennifer said dismally.

"Another three or four weeks though Jen." David said to her quietly. "And that's one-way; we may have to come back here, if there's no one there to help us."

"We don't have any choice." She replied shaking her head.

Once Jennifer had made up her mind that they had to go with the warriors a strange thought came into her head. She realised that they wouldn't find their way home through the Guardian's Stone. She didn't know how she knew this, but she knew it to be the truth; though she didn't say so to her brothers.

"Ok, ok, it makes sense; we've run out of options. The truth is we may not be able to find or open the doorway again anyway and we don't want to meet that creature again even if we did." David said glumly as he weighed up the alternatives. He almost laughed to himself as he tried to think of the alternatives, he knew there weren't any.

That settled the matter. Christopher and Jennifer both nodded to David, who in turn; somewhat reluctantly, nodded to Sukhoi.

"We must leave this place now." Braduga interrupted. "It is not safe to remain here too long." He said picking up his belongings.

"Just a quick question before we set off." Christopher said.

Everyone looked at the boy expectantly. "I was just wondering if we had enough food for the journey." He asked.

Sukhoi smiled at the practicality of the boy and nodded that they had indeed, for the packs he had given them earlier had everything they needed for the journey ahead.

David wondered long and hard about that as they began to follow Sukhoi westward towards Enkan Mys. Had Sukhoi known they would meet the creature at the Stone? Had he thought

David was lying and prepared the packs to help them on their obviously long journey, or had he even always planned to take them to Enkan Mys. Maybe he was just being paranoid now but it was thinking about being away from home for another month at least, it frightened him. Jennifer said the three men could be trusted, and he trusted his sister, he just hoped she was right.

He squinted into the distance and could just about make out a ridge of mountains he hadn't seen previously. They were really doing it he thought, they were embarking on an adventure just like Christopher wanted. An adventure into the unknown, they were moving toward the mountains and moving away from the only way he knew to get back home.

Chapter Nine

The little group had been travelling through the baking heat of the day for the last couple of hours, the sun beating down relentlessly on their backs. Sukhoi had told them they wouldn't normally travel during the day, but it was late in the year and the sun wasn't as strong as it usually was.

"I don't know where he got that from," Jennifer said a little while later, "I can't stop sweating and I think my neck is burnt already." She grumbled.

"Yes it is Jen; maybe you should take out the scarf that's in your pack and tie it round your neck, it should give you some protection." Christopher offered.

Jennifer looked at him in amazement, "There's a scarf in there?" She asked.

"Yep, I've got mine on already." He said as he pulled on the piece of material around his neck.

David and Jennifer looked at each other, both of them raising their eyes to the sky at the same time. They hadn't even considered looking in their packs, but obviously Christopher had and taken full advantage of the contents within.

Taking their packs off, they quickly rummaged inside them and retrieved the scarves, quickly tying them round their necks. They then found the water containers inside and took a generous gulp before they packed everything away, and rushed to catch up to the rest of the group.

"We didn't have a choice you know." Jennifer said to David as they caught up with Christopher.

"I know, but four weeks Jen." David replied.

"What about mam?" Christopher asked quietly.

"If you know of another way to get back home, I'm all ears Chris!" He said a little harshly, and regretted it as soon as he said it. He was angry with himself for getting them into this situation; knowing that if he hadn't said anything to them about the fireplace or the stranger they wouldn't be here now, but there was no point crying over spilt milk.

Christopher didn't say anything; he just carried on trying to walk through the sand with his head down.

"Sorry Chris, I know it's not your fault, I miss mam as well." He said.

"It's not your fault Dave, I followed you, I didn't have to, but I did, and so did Jen." He replied as he offered his elder brother a smile.

David smiled back, though he didn't feel like it.

"Do you think we're getting any closer? David asked as he viewed the mountains ahead.

"Probably, but it doesn't seem like it, we just have to try and keep up." Jennifer said slipping and sliding through the sand with each step.

"I wonder where we are." David asked, but didn't really expect an answer.

"Well, it's not Yorkshire!" Christopher exclaimed breathlessly.

Both David and Jennifer looked at Christopher as a big smile came over his face. "Well, it's true, unless we're at the seaside." He said thoughtfully and then for some reason began to laugh.

It was infectious, once Christopher started, so did his brother and sister, it was crazy really, they had travelled through a magical door and arrived in a desert. They were being escorted by a trio of warriors who had offered their protection and were heading for a city that would take them almost four weeks to get to, just to see if someone could help them get home, who wouldn't laugh?

"You're right Chris; I don't think we're in Yorkshire either." David laughed.

"Are you three ok?" Sukhoi asked as he heard the laughter and dropped back to see if there was a problem.

"We're fine Sukhoi, thanks, just having a laugh." Jennifer smiled at him.

Sukhoi's face expanded in a smile as he looked at the children and saw laughter in their eyes. He knew there was something special about these three children and the way they just laughed at the situation only confirmed the fact.

"What will the journey be like to Enkan Mys, Sukhoi?" David asked as he regained control of his laughter.

"It shouldn't be too bad really, we have four maybe five days left in the desert until we reach the Gratishk Mountains. It will take us another five days or so to get through Benglin Pass in the Mountains before we reach the Konare Forest. From the edge of the forest to Enkan Mys will take about two weeks but there are quite a few villages and towns we have to go through, so it may take a bit longer.

"Is there something you're not telling us?" Jennifer asked the Kavacha. She trusted the man but there was something in his words that wasn't quite right; and although she didn't know what it was, she had an idea it must be important.

"You are right Jennifer, the journey will be difficult and there may be many dangers along the way. But we will protect you; with our lives if necessary." Sukhoi replied solemnly.

"I believe you," she told him, "but what dangers do you speak of?" She asked.

"The mountains are quite treacherous in themselves, but at this time of year, we could bump into a Gourtak or even their smaller cousins, a Tek'faskar, which can be just as dangerous."

"A Tek what?" Christopher interrupted.

"Tek'faskar's are the second largest predators in Sakhalin, but thankfully one of the dumbest. If you should unfortunately come across one, just stand absolutely still and they will think you are a tree or something and walk past. If you move though, you could be dead before you know it. Their eyesight is extremely poor, but they are ferocious."

"Oh." Christopher gulped. "What do they look like?" Although a little frightened, he was intrigued never the less.

"Big, black, furry and full of teeth, with two tiny eyes and big strong arms that could crush a man in an instant."

"Oh." Christopher gulped again.

"Do not worry Christopher, it is unusual to see the Tek'faskar, but as long as you stand perfectly still, you will be ok."

"Ok, I will remember that." Christopher beamed at Sukhoi, albeit a little apprehensively.

"And the Gourtak?" David asked.

"Hope that we do not come across one of those creatures," Sukhoi said sombrely, "they are not dumb, in fact, they are extremely intelligent and once they have your scent, they will track you down until you are dead."

Sukhoi went on to describe what they looked like and how they were solitary creatures that lived for nothing but their next meal. All the while David noticed the expression on Braduga's face becoming angrier and darker. He obviously had some issue with these creatures and David wouldn't want to be the Gourtak that met with Braduga when he was angry.

"Great." David replied sarcastically when Sukhoi had finished, "Just what we need."

"I'm thirsty; I don't suppose anyone has any more water available?" Christopher asked, trying to take his mind off of the unpleasant creatures Sukhoi had just been describing.

"My apologies, Chris. Here take a good drink of this." Sukhoi said holding out a leather bag, which sloshed when handed over. Christopher pulled a stopper out of the end and then gulped down the liquid inside. He then returned the stopper with a big smile on his face.

"What you smiling at?" David asked him.

"You should have a drink of that, and then you'll know." Christopher replied still smiling.

"Go ahead." Sukhoi said smiling as well.

Wiping his mouth with the back of his hand Christopher passed the bag to David.

David took a quick sip and then he took a hearty gulp. "It tastes like strawberry milk." He said as he passed the bag onto his sister.

"Really, I thought it tasted like Ribena." Christopher said in surprise.

Sukhoi smiled as he said. "You are both right and both wrong," He laughed when he saw the confused look on both boys' faces. "The liquid content of the bag is from the Khulanha root, it is one of only a few plants that can live in the desert, where its roots burrow deep down into the ground to retrieve water. The liquid taken from the roots possess a magic, which synthesises the taste a person likes, so you think you are drinking whatever you like at the time. It also provides sustenance and vitality for a few hours, which is very much needed in the desert." He added as an afterthought.

"Yes, I think I know what you mean." David beamed. "I do feel quite refreshed, as though I had just been for a nice cool swim.

Jennifer looked suspiciously at the bag and then at her brothers, but could see the delighted expressions on their faces and thought why not. When she drank the cool liquid, she thought she was in heaven. It tasted just like chocolate milkshake; her favourite and it was absolutely delicious. She gulped it down, and she too felt the sensation that David had just described, she laughed.

"This is wonderful," She gulped down another drink. "Just wonderful." She then reluctantly passed the bag back to Sukhoi.

Invigorated, the pace increased as the children chatted excitedly about the drink they had just had.

Sukhoi walked slightly ahead of the children and smiled as he heard them talking about the Khulanha drink as if it were a gift from the gods. He remembered then, the first time he had tasted the drink. As a small boy, his father had taken him to Dakhla; a bustling town two days walk of his little village of Bazan, and situated along the banks of Lake Ghanem. Sukhoi had never before seen anything so wonderful as Dakhla. As a small child, the great stone architecture, which adorned every street, was an incredible sight to behold and a far cry from the earthwork buildings he was used to.

There were statues of various animals; that he didn't know the names of, as well as those that he did. Statues of the gods, of powerful men and women, marvellous and intricate fountains; sprouting water into the air and then disappearing somewhere he couldn't see. There were shops and stalls; which sold anything and everything, all full of colour and life. A truly amazing place that had paled everything he had seen before into insignificance. It was here in this vibrant, exciting place that his father had taken him to test for the Kavacha. Here he had tasted the wonder of the Khulanha drink, and here that his life had changed forever.

Interrupting his memories, Socata sauntered up to him and whispered something in his ear. Although the smile vanished instantly, he remained looking ahead and only nodded to his companion, who then went back to his position on the right flank, protecting the little group.

"Something's wrong." Jennifer whispered to David, who looked at his sister and then at Sukhoi as she nodded in his direction.

"What is it?" He asked.

"Not sure to be honest, but all of a sudden the men feel cautious." She replied, grabbing Christopher by the arm and pulling him between David and herself.

"Oy! What's up?" Christopher asked his sister and when she ignored him he hunched in closer to hear what his brother said.

"How do you know Jen?" He asked his sister suspiciously.

"Your not paying attention Dave, Socata has just spoken to Sukhoi and now they look like they're preparing for unwanted visitors by the way they're checking their weapons." She said pointing to the Ruedin on either side of them.

She was right, David noticed, they were checking their equipment, tying and securing it in place, ensuring everything was where they expected it to be, but David knew there was more to it, he just wouldn't push it for the moment.

"David," Sukhoi whispered as he dropped back a couple of paces. "Please don't be frightened, and do not panic, but we are being followed. By what or whom, we do not know yet for certain, but someone or something is not far behind us." He was still walking and facing forward, but he looked poised and ready to pounce at a moment's notice just as his sister had said.

"What do you want us to do?" He asked just as quietly. "We don't have any weapons to fight with, and to be honest even if we did, we wouldn't be much good."

"You will be fine, just stay close together and if any fighting starts, try and get away if you can."

"What about you?" He asked concerned that he would leave the men behind.

"Do not worry about us, we will be ok, just concentrate on getting your sister and brother to safety, ok?" He said and then smiled reassuringly at him.

Nodding, David said. "Ok."

"Nothing to worry about at the moment; let us just see what we are dealing with." Sukhoi said. "I just wanted you to be aware of the situation."

"Ok thanks, and we'll keep our eyes open." He said to Christopher and Jennifer, but especially Jennifer to emphasize her earlier point that he hadn't been.

She smiled briefly and nodded but there was a nervousness in both his sibling's eyes, David thought, which he guessed was probably mirrored in his.

As they searched the dunes for any sign of movement, David realised the enormity of their situation. Here they were in a strange and frightening place, a place where strange creatures could harm them, if not kill them, protected by three strange warriors. They shouldn't be in this situation. He shouldn't have told them about the corridor and put them in this danger. All he could think of doing now was protecting them himself; as best he could, and get them home as soon as possible.

The minutes passed to hours, but nothing and no one showed themselves to the little group as they continued their march through the desert. They tried to stay alert and vigilant, but it was tiring and even adding extra breaks to take on food and the marvellous Khulanha drink, didn't help the children feel any more at ease or less frightened by the possibility of danger.

Socata and Braduga continued to keep Sukhoi updated on the current situation at each of these frequent stops without seeming to; and then he kept the children abreast of any developments, if any.

He finally told them; after one such stop, that they were being followed by at least eight men, four directly behind, and at least another two men either side. It was apparently unusual for a group of men to just follow another group without making contact. Braduga told them that they were on foot like them. They weren't tinkers or Salt Cake sellers because there was no sign of any carts and they weren't the Caravanners; that roamed this region, for the same reason. They hadn't seen the usual signs of the Toureng, so they could discount them out of hand.

"So who do you think they are then?" Christopher asked as they stopped again for a drink.

"It has to be Koutla Raiders." Braduga deduced, "But it is a little unusual for them to be so brave."

"Yes it is." Sukhoi agreed and explained that the Koutla normally only attacked individuals or twos, it was unheard of for a group to attack a party of six people; even if three of them were children.

David thought he looked worried, but he had realised quite early on that you could never tell with the man, he had one hell of a poker face.

"What do we do then?" Jennifer asked. "Do we stop and wait for them and ask what they want or shall we just carry on as before?"

"Koutla Raiders are thieves and bandits and will rob most travellers given the opportunity, " Socata stated, "but I doubt they would bother us when they realise who we are." He finished.

"Never the less, we have let this carry on too far as it is I think." Sukhoi said, obviously annoyed with the situation. "We shall walk another hour, if they have not shown themselves before then; we shall wait and confront them."

It was just over an hour later when the little group halted and waited for the group of men to make their intentions clear. Braduga and Socata disappeared while Sukhoi stood in front of the children and waited for the people following them to appear over the horizon.

"What do you think they want?" David asked his sister as they stood trying to look in every direction at once.

"I don't know, but I think Sukhoi has everything under control." She replied,

A few minutes later, four heads peered over a sand dune and on seeing Sukhoi and the children they paused before warily continuing in their direction.

Heads swivelled about, obviously looking for the other two companions, but it didn't stop them, as they moved closer to the little group. The four figures were then joined by four more that moved in from the flanks, all heading straight for them.

"Koutla Raiders," Sukhoi spat with contempt, "but I am surprised to see so many together at once. Stay calm and be quiet, I will deal with them."

"Who speaks?" Sukhoi shouted as he stepped towards the Raiders.

"I speak, Soonak is my name," Said one of the men in front.

"You are far from home Soonak, why do you follow us and what do you want?" Sukhoi asked calmly.

"Stand aside Kavacha, we want the children." The Raider Soonak shouted.

All eight men were looking at the children with greed in their eyes, smiling as they thought of the riches they would receive when they handed over their prey to the man who hired them.

"Why do they want us Dave?" Christopher asked in surprise from behind his brother.

"I don't know Chris, but be quiet will you and maybe we'll find out." He replied, shocked by the leader's announcement.

Sukhoi took another step closer to the eight men, directly in front of the children, motioning with a slight movement of his hand for them to take a few steps back.

"So you know who I am Soonak, yet you dare give me orders!" Sukhoi said quietly but with authority at the group of miscreants.

"We know, but you must know that you can't beat eight fully armed men, so stand aside and we'll let you live!" Soonak shouted back undaunted, there was a frenzied look in his eyes as if a strange madness had consumed him.

"That I will not do, nor should you expect me to!" He replied as he faced the men and inhaled a slow deep breath.

"Then you will die Kavacha!" He shouted back as he and his men leapt forward.

All eight Raiders attacked Sukhoi at once, intending to kill him quickly with their superior force of numbers. But Sukhoi was ready; he was Kavacha and trained with the Kavacha knowledge. The children watched in wonder as he appeared to move in slow motion, parrying every blow and thrust, dodging and ducking, kicking and chopping, meeting every attack with a counter attack of his own. One man alone stood against the might of eight heavily armed men and he weaved his magic to avoid being hit by even one single blow.

Every movement appeared to be precise and practised, gliding through the movements as if dancing on a stage. Then he wasn't alone any longer; through the depths of sand appeared his companions, his Ruedin. They shimmered into life and attacked the Raiders with skilful purpose. The Kavacha and his honour guard, three warriors against eight men, but these were not ordinary warriors, these were highly trained, fighting men with sense and purpose, sworn to a task and trained by masters in the arts of death at Enkan Mys. The children watched in awe as their companions disarmed their attackers; breaking bones and smashing heads, until all but one was unconscious at their feet.

Their leader was now crawling along the sand toward Sukhoi, a broken or dislocated arm cradled in his hand, bruised and battered he looked up at his three adversaries.

"You must give me the children!" He screeched as he spat blood from his ruined mouth, his crazed hungry gaze turned to the three children.

"Why? What do you want with the children? Who sent you?" Sukhoi asked the man gently.

"You will die if you do not give the children to me! He will make certain of it!" He shouted, insanely angry and bleeding.

"Who will Soonak?" Sukhoi persisted.

"You will all die!" The Koutla leader promised them.

"We all die eventually Soonak, but if it be my time, I will embrace death as I embrace life."

"Embrace this!" With little warning the Raider leader threw a dagger right at Sukhoi's heart. There was no way he could save himself, the Raider was too close and the dagger's aim was too true. Sukhoi was about to die.

"NO!" David shouted without thinking. Raising his hand as if by doing so he could stop the dagger from killing his new friend, and to his utter amazement; and that of everyone else, the dagger stopped in mid air.

There was complete silence as everyone stared at the now perfectly still knife in the air, inches from Sukhoi's heart. Only Braduga moved after a moment's hesitation to bring down an open handed chop to the back of the Raiders neck, knocking him unconscious with one blow. He had moved with lightning speed, and now he turned to stare at David with the same astounded look as everyone else had in the group.

Suddenly the dagger dropped to the ground by Sukhoi's feet. Everyone stood transfixed looking at the dagger as Sukhoi reached cautiously down and retrieved it from the sand. He raised it to his eyes and gave it a quick inspection before putting it in his belt. Everyone then turned their attention on a very stunned and very frightened David.

"Wow, Dave that was amazing." Christopher cried excitedly. "How long have you been able to do that?" He enquired.

David couldn't breath; all sight and sound vanished except for his own outstretched arm. Had he just done that? Had he just stopped the dagger just by thinking about it? Don't be so ridiculous, he thought, and then it occurred to him. Obviously it was Sukhoi's magic that stopped the dagger, just because he thought about stopping it at the same time, didn't mean that he'd actually done it. Stupid, stupid boy, he thought to himself. With that revelation, he began to come to his senses and he realised that everyone was talking to him at the same time.

"David, are you ok? Sukhoi was asking him, probably for the second or third time with concern in his voice.

"Yes, yes I'm fine; I was just shocked by your magic!" He said feeling a little light-headed and confused.

Sukhoi looked at him as if he had two heads, and then said, "It was not I that stopped the dagger, it was you. I owe you my life!" He finished.

"But, but I didn't do anything, wasn't it your magic that saved you?" David replied unsure of what to believe at the moment. He couldn't have stopped the dagger; he didn't know any magic, not even any magic tricks.

"It was not I David; I did not even see the dagger until it was too late." Sukhoi announced.

"It was you Dave; you reached out your hand and stopped that knife from killing Sukhoi." Jennifer told him, looking a little stunned herself.

"No, I didn't do anything, you've got it wrong." David said flatly, his light-headedness dissipating.

Jennifer gave him one of her creased forehead looks as if she were about to argue with him, then she just stopped and gave him a sympathetic smile.

She had seen the surprised and frightened expression on his face and although she instinctively knew it was the truth; however much David wanted to deny what he had done, she knew, he had performed some real magic. Instead of arguing though, she realised he was in a delicate state and he probably felt as confused and frightened as herself. Ever since they had arrived in Sakhalin, she knew she was different in some way. She felt things, heard half-thoughts and knew instinctively when people were telling the truth. It frightened her, but also amazed and enthralled her. She hadn't told anyone how she was feeling; not even her brothers, but she had hinted that she knew more than she was letting on, she just need time to evaluate what exactly was happening to her before she said anything. Now it looked as if David was able to perform feats of magic, real magic. He must be just as frightened and confused as she was and she sympathised with him.

"I, err." David began and then stopped, as he didn't know what to say.

David looked towards Jennifer who just shrugged her shoulders and smiled at him. She didn't seem surprised at him being able to do magic for some reason. The one thought that kept coming to his mind was that it couldn't have been him. How could he have stopped the dagger in mid-air? No he wouldn't believe it, he couldn't believe it.

"What shall we do with these?" Socata said as he noticed David's discomfort and quickly changed the subject.

"Leave them, they will regain consciousness in a while and we will be long gone by then." Sukhoi said and turned his back on the Raiders.

"Is that wise?" Jennifer asked. She didn't like the idea of eight armed men following them again.

"What would you have me do Jennifer? Kill them and leave their bodies for the buzzards?"

Appalled by the idea, Jennifer shouted back angrily, "No, I just meant, shouldn't we at least tie them up or something, so they wouldn't follow us."

Sukhoi could see how distraught the girl was by his words and wondered why he had said what he had, but immediately apologised to her, "Sorry Jennifer, I did not mean to offend. It is best to just leave them here; I do not think they will be bothering us for a while, do you?"

"No," she said looking at the eight unconscious figures by her feet, "maybe we should get away from here as soon as possible though." She said nervously.

"I agree." Sukhoi said as he ordered everyone to collect their belongings and continue on their journey.

"I wish I could stop daggers in mid air." Christopher said quietly as the little group got underway again. "Somebody throw a knife at me." He said a little louder.

"What? What are you going on about Chris?" David said getting annoyed.

"Well, I might be able to stop daggers as well"

"Don't be silly, Chris."

"You can do it, why cant I?"

"It was an accident, I didn't do anything, just forget it will you." David couldn't believe what happened and just wanted to forget about the entire incident.

"Ok Dave." Christopher said quietly. Christopher knew when his brother was in a mood and didn't want to talk; he had been in plenty of moods since their father had died and knew now, when his brother didn't want to talk about things, especially something as weird as what had just taken place.

David knew he was being unfair, taking his confusion and anger out on his brother; it wasn't his fault. But he couldn't let himself believe the unbelievable. He sidled up to Christopher and tapped him on his arm and gave him a smile, which Christopher returned. The two brothers walked together in silence; each pondering the unbelievable events they had just witnessed. Walking side by side they moved away from the eight unconscious Raiders.

Chapter Ten

As the sun began to set over the horizon Sukhoi pointed out the tops of a few palm trees in the near distance. "Ok, we will rest there for the night."

It was another twenty minutes before they arrived at the small clearing. There were about a dozen palms trees surrounding a small but inviting pond of fresh water. Dried wood and leaves appeared to have been gathered and placed in a segregated area and there were a few utensils hidden in a grass-weaved basket bag that had been conveniently placed beneath one of the trees that Socata had located. Braduga surveyed the surrounding area for signs of life and to ensure they would know if anyone approached the oasis, while the children waited to be told what to do.

When it became obvious that they weren't going to be asked to do anything, Jennifer asked Sukhoi. "Is there anything we can do?" He was kneeling in the centre of the clearing with all the packs, emptying the contents on a flat sand base he had just cleared a moment before.

"Yes Jennifer," Sukhoi said smiling at girl. It had soon become obvious to Sukhoi that the children had never had to travel across a desert before and the weary way in which they looked around the oasis confirmed his thoughts. This revelation posed many questions, but this wasn't the time to ask them, so he gave Jennifer something to keep her busy, at least for a while. "Could you go over to those palms," he said pointing, "and pick some of the fruit and bring it over here."

Jennifer nodded enthusiastically and went to gather the fruit. The two boys waited patiently as Sukhoi continued to empty the packs.

He looked up and noticing their unease, he asked them if they would collect some of the palm leaves that had fallen from the trees, so they could use them later. The boys; given something useful to do, also went about their task with vigour.

Sukhoi watched as the children moved away and couldn't help but smile at their enthusiasm.

"Something funny?" Socata asked seeing the smile.

"These children are strange; I have never seen their like before." He replied nodding in the direction of the children.

"Strange and gifted it seems." Socata agreed. "Did David really stop that dagger, or did you?" He asked suspiciously.

"My friend, I did not get the chance. David stopped the dagger before I knew what was happening, and what is more, I did not even detect the magic he used." Sukhoi replied, his eyebrow raised and a frown creased his face.

He couldn't understand it himself. The Kavacha knowledge granted him the ability to sense magic when it was being used. Today he hadn't detected anything. That was something else he would have to ponder given the time to do so.

Socata looked at him in surprise but remained silent. It wasn't acceptable for a Ruedin to ask his Kavacha about his knowledge.

As the sun set the companions gathered together around a small fire that Socata had started. Roasting on a spit above the fire was a handful of sand larks that Braduga had managed to kill whilst roaming around the camp site. As they waited eagerly for the birds to cook Sukhoi spoke to David about the earlier incident

"I was wondering how you managed to stop that dagger today." He inquired.

David knew it wouldn't be long before Sukhoi asked him about it, but there was nothing for him to say. He hadn't accepted the fact that he had stopped it in the first place, let alone figure out how he did, if he did.

He thought back and tried to visualise everything that happened, and was surprised to realise he could see the events unfold in his mind as if he was watching television.

"I honestly don't think it was me." He said replaying the scene, "All I saw was the dagger heading right for you and I remember thinking that I wanted the dagger to stop, but I thought you must have stopped it."

"No I did not stop it, nor did my Ruedin, so it must have been one of you." He said looking at all the children at once.

"Well it wasn't me, unfortunately." Christopher replied to the look.

"It wasn't me either." Replied Jennifer carefully.

"Did I really do that?" David said, uncertain of anything any more. He had felt as if he had willed the dagger to stop and he had felt dazed and confused afterwards, but to perform magic, it was just unbelievable.

"Have you ever done anything like that before?"

"No, nothing." David replied honestly and thought about the corridor and how it called to him. He tried to block those thoughts now, though he did admit, "I have felt a little different since I arrived here." He finished thoughtfully.

"There is nothing to be scared of David, you seem to have been given a great gift, there are not many people in Sakhalin that could have done what you did, and I for one am thankful that you were here." Sukhoi said as he gave him a genuine smile. "But in what way do you feel different?" He asked.

"I'm not sure, I can't explain it or put it into words." he said shrugging his shoulders, "just different!"

"Do not worry about it for now, clarity will come with time, I am sure." He offered.

Jennifer wanted to tell Sukhoi that she felt different also, but she couldn't explain what that difference was either, so she remained silent.

"I hope so." David replied softly.

"Does it scare you at all?" Sukhoi asked. "This difference?"

"No." Jennifer replied quietly to herself as David gave the same reply.

"It's just unbelievable, it wouldn't have happened at home." As soon as he said "home" he regretted it. Thoughts came flooding in of his mother, his friends and family. He could see by the expressions on their faces that Jennifer and Christopher were thinking the same things.

Sukhoi noticed that the atmosphere had changed, and could see the pain of loss behind the eyes of each child. Feeling as if he was intruding, he didn't say another word but motioned for his Ruedin to follow him to the far end of the clearing, leaving the children to their own thoughts of home.

"What do you think Sukhoi?" Socata asked as they looked out at the desert through the fading light of the day.

"I think they are special children that need our protection and our friendship." He said turning to look at the children.

"Extraordinary to say the least," Braduga agreed. "But if the boy can perform magic like that, surely he should be a Kavacha?"

"Maybe my friend." Sukhoi agreed, "When we get to Enkan Mys he can be tested, then we will know for sure."

"But a more important question at the moment and one I did not want to raise in front of them is who could be after the three children? I believe they were telling the truth when they said they had only just arrived here. So, who else knows about them and why do they want them?" Sukhoi asked although he was mainly speaking out loud and didn't really expect an answer, but Socata offered one anyway.

"Nuba Driss knows they are here." He whispered, as if even his name spoken aloud would make him appear before them, "or at least one of his servants."

"Yes, it could have been him at the door, and he would know where they are, but could he have told his creatures and men that the children were with us in so short a period of time? I am not so sure, but we must make all haste and get to Enkan Mys as soon as possible."

"Then that is what we must do my Kavacha." Braduga stated with hard resolve.

"Will we ever get home?" Christopher asked quietly.

"Yes Chris, don't worry, there'll be someone at Enkan Mys who can help us." David replied. He hoped there was someone there who could help, but he didn't feel confident about it, truth be known.

"I didn't think I would be missing home so soon." Christopher said on reflection.

"I think we all miss home Chris, but Dave is right, we'll be back there soon enough. Let's have some food and then we'll try and get some sleep, ok?" Jennifer said.

"Sounds good to me Jen." Christopher replied as he watched David turn the spit, his mouth watering and thoughts of home momentarily forgotten by the promise of hot succulent meat.

Braduga and Socata returned to the fire a moment later; they had left Sukhoi to stand first watch and the others began to tuck into the food that was on offer. They ate in silence until the children finally rose together and announced they were going to get some sleep.

He was walking down a brightly lit corridor; all white and clinical, an odour of rotten flesh seemed to permeate the atmosphere; the smell strong and nauseating, burning his nostrils with its putrid breath. A dense misty fog crawled along the floor and around his feet, but he wasn't interested in the fog or the smell for that matter; his gaze was focused on the obscure, indeterminate figure before him. He was walking toward that figure now; although he felt as if he was actually floating on the mist rather than walking, the dark figure watching and waiting for his arrival. Before he knew what was happening he was standing before the figure who was dressed in a monk's habit, its face obscured from view by an overlarge hood.

He knew he was shaking with fright, but he could do nothing about that, his body was no longer his own, he had no power over it anymore, the figure before him was in total control. Then he heard the footsteps behind him, faint but there nevertheless, and heading in his direction. His body began to stop shivering and he began to relax, that was until he realised the hooded figure was raising its head toward him. He shouted at the figure before him, "No, you will not have me, leave me alone!"

The figure paused for just a moment as if struck by some invisible barrier, but then pushed forward once more. He watched in horror as the figure began to raise its head. He screamed!

David tossed and turned all night, but after waking for one brief instant he was immediately asleep again and wasn't plagued by the creature in the corridor again that night. Instead he dreamed he was a powerful wizard who journeyed to places far and wide searching for something or someone. He met strange people, speaking languages he seemed to understand, and brought joy and happiness everywhere he went. It was a nice, peaceful dream that ended abruptly when he was woken by a thundering screech.

He bolted awake upright, ripped from his dream by what he believed to be the most fearsome and terrifying scream he had ever heard in his life.

"What in God's name is that?" He shouted fearfully; his eyes wide with shock, until abruptly the scream stopped.

"It's made by blood freeze and the hairs on the back of my neck stand on end." Christopher added his face pale and his blonde hair sticking up in what could only be described as a tangled mess, as he too was shaken from his slumber.

Sukhoi appeared and moved towards the children. "It is ok my friends, do not be worried." Sukhoi addressed them calmly, "it is merely our ride announcing their arrival." He said joyfully, whilst trying to hide the excitement he felt at the prospect of meeting the creature or creatures that had made the distressing sound. It didn't really placate the children as they were all on their feet and looking about in alarm for the creature that had made the sound.

Jennifer's gaze was drawn toward the south; to where the terrible scream had emanated from. She thought she had heard something more than just the scream at one point. It was something fleeting and unusual, but it had gone before she could grasp it, and to be honest, she had better things to think about at the moment without letting her imagination get the better of her.

She had been dreaming they were back home safe and sound; their mother wrapping her arms around them protectively and kissing them all on their heads, telling them how much she missed and loved them. That was until the screams had invaded her dreams and now the comfort she had felt from her mother's embrace was quickly fading.

She thought she might be feeling homesick as her dream thoughts faded but she realised she couldn't help feeling that something spectacular was about to happen, something that was connected to the terrible screams she had been listening to.

Her mind was so engrossed on this thought that she wasn't listening to what her brother Christopher was saying until he pinched her arm quite hard to get her attention.

"Ow, what you do that for?" She asked angrily.

"I've been talking to you for the past five minutes and you were away with the fairies." He replied.

"Well I'm back now, what's up?" She asked, surprised she hadn't heard him say anything, no matter how engrossed she had been.

"I was saying," Christopher began again, "I've never heard anything so terrifying before and wondered if you knew what it could be?" He finished expectantly.

"How am I suppose to know what it is Chris!" she shouted at him. "I'm not exactly an expert on frightening sounds, it could be anything."

Christopher looked a little scared she thought; though he would never admit it and regretted shouting at him and went to put her arms around his shoulders. He shrugged them off and walked over to his brother, who was talking quietly to a very excited Sukhoi.

"Sorry Chris," she said, "It scared me half to death as well." She continued, but he wasn't paying her any attention now, or at least ignoring her. She realised; after thinking about it, that she hadn't been frightened of the screaming at all, though she couldn't tell anyone why, if they asked.

Sukhoi was talking quickly and quietly with his Ruedin while the children waited nervously for them to finish their conversation; clearly frightened by whatever creature had made the terrible sound.

Sukhoi turned toward them, "You are in no danger, that sound heralds the arrival of some friends of mine, who will be here shortly. I would like everyone to remain calm and completely quiet when they get here, ok?" he paused, a smile coming to his lips, "Please do not be alarmed by their appearance, ok?"

The three children nodded, but anything that could make a sound like that one, couldn't be anything nice, of that they were all certain.

"Good, we will wait over by those trees," he said pointing to the trees behind them, "we will not have too long to wait" He said smiling reassuringly as he walked over to the trees and waited for his friends arrival.

Braduga and Socata smiled at each other and then smiled again as the children followed behind Sukhoi cautiously and slowly.

Somehow David found himself standing directly behind Sukhoi, apprehensive wasn't the word he would use to describe himself at this moment in time. It was more like "scared to death" at the impending arrival of Sukhoi's friends, but his new companions didn't seem phased at all, so he stood with them and waited, trying to be brave, trying being the operative word.

A soft breeze heralded their arrival a few moments later, the loose sand swirling up towards the clear blue sky like a whirlwind. They all covered their eyes; but continued to search the ground for Sukhoi's friends when two immense creatures landed softly on the ground from the sky, twenty meters or so from the oasis.

David couldn't believe his eyes, the sight before him consumed all his senses; all thoughts left his mind as he squinted at the creatures. Sukhoi walked over to them as they arrived, while his Ruedin remained with the children, asking them to keep silent and still, as if their lives depended on it, which by the look of the new arrivals, they probably did.

David watched in wonder as Sukhoi stroked first one, then the other creature before turning round and walking back to the waiting group.

It was too much to believe, there standing before him was a pair of Dragons, enormous, majestic, beautiful Dragons. He was gawping, mouth open; much like his brother and sister, when he looked across to see their reaction to the arrival of two amazing creatures of myth and fantasy. He had lost count of the amount of times he had been surprised since they arrived in Sakhalin, but this was definitely the icing on the cake. It was a breath taking sight to witness two enormous Dragons land mere feet away from you and then flex their wings before folding them at their side. His friends back home would be so envious, he thought, if they knew.

They were approximately the same size; which was to say, as tall as a giraffe and probably twice the body weight of an African elephant. The slightly bigger creature had large thick scales of a rich burnt red colour, whilst the smaller one was covered in a mattered silver colour with a blue and greenish tinge. Both had long necks with horned heads and rather large mouths that supported a magnificent array of razor sharp, pointed teeth. Their leathery wings were now folded, but they must have exceeded the wingspan of a small single engine plane. They were truly breathtaking and all three children could do nothing but stare open-mouthed at them in wonder.

"Please do not be afraid, come forward and say hello." Sukhoi said as he motioned with his hands for the children to come closer.

They looked at each other before they cautiously decided to move towards Sukhoi and his friends.

David turned to look behind him, looking for somewhere to run if it all went wrong, but he could see that Braduga and Socata were directly behind him and encouraging him to walk towards the creatures.

The Dragons watched their approach with indifference.

"The male is called Hash'ar'jefar; which means Morning sun-light in the old tongue, and the female is called Sak'ar'jefar; which means Evening moon-light. But I call them Hash and Sak for short." Sukhoi introduced.

"They are truly beautiful," Jennifer whispered as she admired the Dragons before her.

"They are indeed Jennifer," Sukhoi smiled fondly at his friends, "the most beautiful creatures in all of Sakhalin."

The Dragons seemed to look into Jennifer's soul, the tiny hairs on the back of her neck stood on end and goose bumps tingled along her arms. A twinkle in the male dragon's eye seemed to indicate recognition of some sort, but the moment was gone in a flash, and Jennifer thought she was just imagining it.

"Erm, very nice to meet you both." David stuttered to the Dragons, nodding at each of them in turn.

Jennifer pulled her thoughts together and followed suit as she too nodded to each in turn, but Christopher couldn't say anything, he just continued to stare in wonder, whispering to himself the same word over and over, "Dragons."

The two Dragons just looked at the children and then brought their attention back to their friend as he spoke.

"There, you have been formally introduced."

"Can they understand us then?" Jennifer whispered, though for some reason she already knew that question, once asked.

"Not exactly sure to be honest. They do not speak as we do, but they do understand some requests I have made of them in the past."

Jennifer was surprised by that answer, she would have sworn that Sukhoi would have told them they could speak and they could understand each other. Maybe it had been just wishful thinking on her part.

"How did they know we were here, and you said something about a ride?" Jennifer asked.

"Yes sorry, I think I should explain how and when we first met. It must be at least twenty years ago now, when I was a young boy and on my way to Enkan Mys for the first time. I heard a terrible cry of pain, so full of grief and despair that I had to find the source. Little did I know that it would lead me to the two Dragons before us now. Hash had somehow caught his wing in a tree and the more he struggled to get free the more it caught. Sak could do nothing to help except let out a scream of total despair as she watched her companion struggle. I came along and I climbed the tree, eventually freeing him. Ever since then there seems to be a bond between us and when I need their assistance they seem to instinctively know it and come to my aid." He finished.

"So you think they are indebted to you?" Jennifer asked.

"Yes, but more than that now, I believe we have become friends." He said as he stroked the male's flank.

"If you can't speak with them, how do you know their names?" Jennifer asked.

"I think you are asking too many questions Jen?" David said through a tight-lipped smile.

"It is ok David, it is good to ask questions, but to answer your question Jennifer, I named them myself." He finished.

"Well, they are beautiful names." Jennifer said smiling at Sukhoi.

"I think so too." He replied smiling also.

"THIS GIRL ASKS A LOT OF QUESTIONS, DOES SHE NOT?" Hash'ar'jefar said disapprovingly.

Jennifer gasped, had she just imagined the voice in her head or had she really just heard the male dragon speak. She took an involuntary step backwards and stared unbelievingly at the two Dragons, her eyes becoming wide with the shock. She quickly looked around at the three men and her brothers, but they obviously hadn't heard the voice. Was she going mad, she thought?

"IT IS NOT HER FAULT BROTHER, SHE IS STILL YOUNG AND ALL CHILDREN ARE CURIOUS." Sak'ar'jefar replied to her brother's question, a note of sadness and maybe regret in her voice.

Jennifer took another step back, now she heard the female dragon speak, the voice slightly less gruff than the first, but both beautifully musical. She didn't know what to do, should she say something, or was she just imagining it. They would probably laugh at her, she thought if she said anything, and she really hated it when people laughed at her. That was why she fought with her brothers all the time she realised, they knew her for who she was, and she always felt they were laughing at her, even when she knew deep down, that they weren't.

She decided to keep quiet, at least for the moment, just to make sure she wasn't imagining it, she definitely didn't want to look stupid in front of the men if she was wrong.

"I have tried on numerous occasions to communicate with them, but to no avail unfortunately, but never the less, I consider them to be good friends and I hope they see me in the same way and think me worthy of their friendship." Sukhoi finished smiling with affection at the two enormous creatures.

"YES SUKHOI HAS BEEN A GOOD FRIEND, HAS HE NOT BROTHER?" Sak'ar'jefar asked her brother, who merely nodded in agreement. She then lowered her head and Sukhoi laughed as he happily scratched her neck.

Christopher eventually came out of his transient state and began to laugh at the sight. "I think she does understand you Sukhoi." He shouted with joy.

"IF ONLY YOU KNEW AND YOU COULD UNDERSTAND US MY FRIEND." Hash'ar'jefar cried woefully.

"CALM YOURSELF BROTHER, DO NOT UPSET YOURSELF SO, WE MUST ACCEPT OUR FATE." Sak'ar'jefar said gently.

Jennifer couldn't stand the sadness and the pain in their voices; those beautiful voices sounding so full of despair, it was heart-breaking. They were suffering for some reason, maybe from not being able to communicate or some other reason not yet known, but she couldn't stand by and watch as these magnificent creatures suffer so. She had to do something, whether she be ridiculed or not, and she had to do it now.

Closing her eyes to give her strength, she tried to project her thoughts towards the Dragons, she didn't know if it would work, but she had to try.

"C-can you hear mmme?" She said in her head.

Shocked, the two Dragons suddenly roared a deafening cry, unfurling their wings they took a step back away from the group. If they could have expressed their disbelief and amazement on their faces they would have.

Chaos ensued; Sukhoi quickly grabbed hold of the children, and motioned for his Ruedin to take up a protective stance over them as he scanned the surrounding area. Sukhoi had assumed from the Dragons' reactions that there was a potential enemy nearby and they were trying to warn him.

The children were huddled together, shocked and frightened by the erratic movements of the Dragons, who were clearly disturbed.

The Dragons couldn't believe they had actually heard someone speak to them and were frantically looking around for the source of the voice they had just heard. Terrified, all three children moved further away from them and closer to the two warriors who were still looking everywhere for signs of invasion.

Jennifer was almost crying, she didn't know if the Dragons had heard her or not but they were extremely excited about something, but was it her?

She tried to compose herself and closing her eyes again, she took a deep breath and tried once more to speak with them.

"Can you hear me?" She shouted in her mind, willing the voice to be heard.

The Dragons shrieked with excitement, flapping their wings, which brought the sand up from the ground and it swirled about the men and children.

Jennifer began to cough and tried to spit out the sand that had gotten into her mouth, while Sukhoi was trying to calm the Dragons down; his arms flapping, soothing words coming from his mouth.

He was trying to ask them where the danger was and what was it, but the Dragons couldn't be subdued.

Jennifer had to act and quickly, "please don't do that!" She shouted again at the Dragons.

They suddenly stopped what they were doing and looked towards the three children before them with great interest; one of them was speaking to them, now they had to find out which one it was.

With the Dragons calmed, Jennifer felt a composure and control she had never had before. It gave her a confidence that made her walk up to Sukhoi and speak with him, "There is no danger." She told him.

"What? The Dragons?" He began.

She extended her left hand and put it to his lips to stop him from talking, "The Dragons are fine, but I think there could be a surprise for everyone, if I'm right." She said a half smile on her lips in nervous anticipation, even with her new spark of confidence.

"What's going on Jen?" David asked his sister suspiciously.

She smiled at him, "I think I may have just spoken with the Dragons." She said excitedly, "Although, they haven't spoken back to me yet," she announced as an afterthought.

"You've what?" Christopher and David both said together.

Sukhoi and his Ruedin stood motionless, all potential threats forgotten and were just staring at her in open wonder.

"I thought I over heard a conversation between Hash and his sister, I wasn't sure at first, but now I am. I have tried to speak with them, but I'm not sure they can understand me." She said to Sukhoi; who continued to stare in bewilderment. She could see from the corner of her eye the looks of incredulity on the faces of her brothers as they tried to take in what she had just said.

Sukhoi was totally shocked, though the only outward appearance of this was the one raised eyebrow. A calm exterior mask had fallen over his face, although he was finding it very difficult to maintain his composure.

"You are certain of this?" He asked.

Before she could answer the two Dragons moved toward her, Sukhoi and the boys had no choice but to moved out of their way as they slowly and cautiously approached.

Jennifer stood perfectly still, as she watched the magnificent creatures lower their heads together and faced her at her own level.

"PLEASE CHILD; SAY YOU CAN HEAR MY CALL." Hash'ar'jefar whispered.

It may have only been a whisper by the dragon's standards, but to Jennifer the shock of their minds connecting and the full force concentrated on her mind alone, shocked her to her very core. She was a little disorientated at first and took a moment to compose herself before she answered.

"P-please don't shout I can h-hear you." She replied.

Hash'ar'jefar couldn't believe it, he was overwhelmed with joy and couldn't help but unfurl his wings once more, lifting his head, he bellowed a cry of utter jubilation. His sister joined him in his cry of triumph as they both realised they had at last found someone to hear their call.

Sukhoi nervously watched his friends as their excitement consumed them; he had never before seen such a reaction from them and he was a little worried. Could the girl, Jennifer actually be talking with them, he thought. He received his answer a moment later when she smiled over at him and nodded.

"Jennifer," He addressed her, "what is happening?" he asked with an edge of frustration at not knowing what was going on.

"I think they are happy." She said smiling at the Dragons.

"HAPPY, WE ARE EXSTATIC, YOU CAN HEAR OUR CALL." Sak'ar'jefar replied.

"Are you talking with them now?" Sukhoi asked.

"Yes, they're happy that someone can finally speak and understand them." She replied.

Sukhoi didn't know whether to believe the girl or not, he found it difficult to comprehend how a stranger from a faraway land could actually communicate with the Dragons.

He looked at the two boys who were still staring at their sister as if she had gone mad. "What about you two, can you hear them also?" Sukhoi asked them.

David and Christopher looked at each other, then at Sukhoi, then Jennifer and finally at the Dragons, who were in turn, looking directly at them now. Everyone was silent, waiting for the boys to reply. Christopher shrugged his shoulders at his brother, shaking his head slightly, he couldn't hear the Dragons and David did the same, nor could he.

Jennifer exhaled, she hadn't realised she'd been holding her breath waiting for her brothers to answer. So, she thought, she was the only person that could speak with the Dragons, she didn't know how that made her feel yet, but she did know that she felt extremely privileged.

She looked across at Sukhoi as he stared at his friends, the Dragons. "Do you believe me Sukhoi?" She asked him quietly. She didn't know why, but more than anything else she wanted him to believe she was telling the truth.

Sukhoi looked into Jennifer's eyes, she was telling the truth, he knew that and didn't need the Kavacha knowledge to help him see it.

"I believe you." He whispered back.

Jennifer could hear the sadness in that reply; she somehow knew that although he was happy that someone could communicate with his friends, he had privately hoped that, that someone would have been him.

"Is there anything you would like me to ask them?" Jennifer asked him just as quietly. These magnificent creatures were his friends; he had known them since he was a boy and she thought he must have a thousand and one questions for them to answer.

Sukhoi looked towards the Dragons; that were silently and patiently waiting for the exchange to finish, they too must have questions that required answers, he thought, but there was one question he had wanted to ask them since they first met.

"What are their real names is the only question I would ask them right now," he said and paused a moment before he added, "But I would like them to know how honoured and privileged I have been to have them as my friends." He smiled.

Sak'ar'jefar leaned her head closer to Sukhoi and he smiled as he rubbed her neck affectionately. Jennifer translated for her as she said, "Unfortunately men have difficulty in pronouncing our true names, but we would be proud to keep the names you have given us my friend, because friend you are and it is we that are honoured and privileged to call you that." She finished.

A tear appeared in the corner of Sukhoi's eye as the message was delivered and he bowed his head in gratitude before quickly wiping it away and regaining his composure.

"DO YOU REALISE JENNIFER," Hash'ar'jefar said a moment later, "YOU ARE THE ONLY PERSON WE HAVE FOUND THAT CAN SPEAK WITH US IN THIS PLACE." He confided.

"What the only one in all of Sakhalin?" She asked shocked.

"NO, THE ONLY ONE ON THIS WORLD." He replied.

Jennifer was dumbfounded by this discovery, but didn't know how to reply.

"Have you been searching a long time then?" She asked.

Hash'ar'jefar seemed to smile sadly, "A THIRD OF A LIFETIME."

Noting the sadness in his voice but not understanding the reference she asked, "How long is that in our terms?"

Sak'ar'jefar answered the question for her brother," JUST OVER THREE HUNDRED OF YOUR YEARS," she said.

"What!" Jennifer exclaimed out loud in shock.

"What is it Jennifer?" Sukhoi asked frustrated by the situation.

"They have just informed me that they have been searching for someone to talk to for over three hundred years." She replied to his question.

"Three hundred years, that's incredible." Christopher shouted.

"I think that's very sad." David said quietly. He looked toward the Dragons and couldn't help but feel pity towards them. They had been roaming and searching for someone to speak to besides themselves all this time, how lonely must that be for them, even with each other. He realised he could emphasise with them and that knowledge made him feel his own loss; the death of his father, as much as their own.

"As do I my friend." Sukhoi agreed putting his hand on David's shoulder.

Jennifer had a thought, and she wasn't sure how to broach the subject.

"Err, Hash, would you mind telling me how old you are, if it isn't too rude a question that is?" She asked.

Hash'ar'jefar hesitated only a moment before replying, "MY SISTER AND I HATCHED AT THE SAME TIME, WE WERE SEVEN HUNDRED YEARS OLD WHEN WE LEFT OUR HOME AND CAME HERE." He said sadly.

"Oh." Was all she could think to say to them. To everyone else she said, "They are over a thousand years old."

There was complete silence as everyone thought about the implications of that piece of news. From what they could already piece together, the Dragons normally lived for about nine hundred years; as they said they had been searching a third of a lifetime. If they had already been seven hundred years old when they arrived here, they must have already exceeded their normal life span by a hundred years. What that meant, they could only guess, but the majestic creatures before them probably didn't have long to live.

"Well they don't look a thousand years old to me." Christopher said cheerfully.

"I don't know what an old dragon is supposed to look like but Chris is right, they don't look old to me either." David agreed.

"How can you tell when a dragon is getting old anyway?" Christopher asked.

Jennifer asked them and they replied that their scales grew dull and lifeless and would eventually crack and fall off their backs. Their teeth would begin to fall out and their wings would become dry and wrinkly.

Everyone looked at the Dragons before them and all came to the same conclusion immediately. That the Dragons had none of the tell tale signs that they were getting old.

"IS IT POSSIBLE?" Sak'ar'jefar asked her brother.

"IT CAN'T BE, IT HAS NEVER HAPPENED BEFORE." He replied looking his sister over.

"What? What is it?" Jennifer asked. The thought of the Dragons suddenly dying of old age had consumed her thoughts, especially now they had finally found someone to communicate with.

"YOUR BROTHERS HAVE JUST POINTED OUT THAT WE HAVE NONE OF THE SIGNS OF OLD AGE, A FACT WE HAD NOT EVEN TAKEN NOTICE OF OURSELVES. WE NORMALLY START TO DISPLAY SIGNS OF OLD AGE AT EIGHT

HUNDRED YEARS, WE HAVE NO SIGNS, AND THEREFORE WE MUST CONCLUDE THAT SOMEHOW WE ARE NOT AGEING." Sak'ar'jefar said triumphantly.

"WE HAVE NOT NOTICED BEFORE BECAUSE WE ARE CONSTANTLY IN EACH OTHERS COMPANY, BUT I MUST AGREE I DON'T EVEN FEEL THE EFFECTS OF OLD AGE." Hash'ar'jefar interjected.

"ME EITHER BROTHER, I FEEL AS FIT NOW AS I DID WHEN WE ARRIVED HERE." She agreed.

"What does this mean?" Jennifer asked in wonder.

"I AM NOT SURE, BUT MAYBE THE MAGIC IN THIS LAND PREVENTS US FROM GROWING OLDER, OR AT LEAST WE ARE GROWING OLDER SLOWER THAN NORMAL, I DON'T KNOW." Sak'ar'jefar said thoughtfully.

Jennifer explained all this to the group and although they didn't know the reasons they were thankful that the Dragons weren't getting any older.

David was thinking hard, something was familiar about this but he couldn't put his finger on it at the moment, and then it hit him like a thunderbolt.

"Sukhoi," he said, "Didn't you say Nuba Driss wasn't getting old either?" David asked. "Could he be from the same place as the Dragons?"

Sukhoi was shocked; everyone was shocked including the Dragons, who had heard all the stories of the evil wizard, Nuba Driss.

"Maybe if the Dragons told us where they came from and how they came here, maybe we would know something more about this Nuba Driss." David proposed.

"DAVID IS VERY WISE I THINK AND MAYBE WE SHOULD TELL OUR NEW FRIENDS OUR STORY, BROTHER." Sak'ar'jefar said.

"I THINK YOU ARE RIGHT." Hash'ar'jefar agreed.

Jennifer informed the group that the Dragons were going to tell them the story of how they arrived in Sakhalin, although she didn't mention the fact that the Dragons thought her brother was very wise. Well, she thought, she didn't want the compliment going to his head.

Chapter Eleven

Hash and his sister Sak were from a land known to them as Hal Argus. There, Dragons and men lived in a symbiotic state, helping each other to lead a peaceful and plentiful life. The Dragons could speak with the men and vice versa, they lived in harmony and they lived well. That was until a dark day came when a stranger arrived. No one knew where the stranger had come from but he appeared to be a very knowledgeable and amiable young man. Little did they know that he would eventually turn their peaceful and prosperous existence into chaos. What was amazing about the man was that unlike the other men of Hal Argus, the stranger possessed a surprising amount of magic. He wooed captive audiences with his feats of magic and enjoyed the freedom of the realm. The Dragons themselves had a limited capability and were drawn to the stranger and felt he was a kindred spirit. When the stranger asked one day, if he could speak with the council of elders, the Dragons and men agreed without hesitation; an act they were soon to regret. The stranger introduced himself as Merlin; a mage from a faraway land who was seeking a man of great magic, known only as the Guardian. The Guardian; he said, was the only man that could prevent war in his own land. So he began a quest to find him, to try and persuade him to go back to his land and avert an inevitable war. It was a noble and worthwhile cause and both the Dragons and the men were impressed by Merlin's quest.

Unfortunately, neither dragon nor man had heard of this Guardian he sought. But then from the back of the council chamber one of the oldest Dragons entered the council meeting and told everyone the tale his father had told him when he was a small dragon. The tale was of a man; known as the Guardian; who had visited Hal Argus many, many years ago. The dragon couldn't remember much of the tale now, but he did remember that a monument called the Guardian's Stone; which had a Dragon's Eye at its summit, was a memorial to this Guardian. He remembered that his father had told him that the Guardian had arrived when Dragons and men were fighting each other. At that time Dragons and men could not communicate and through fear, they had waged a terrible war. Seeing death and destruction everywhere, the Guardian became overwhelmed with sadness and sorrow and decided to put an end to the war. He erected a tall pillar and at the top, he laid a black orb. The Guardian then performed a miracle of magic, by infusing the orb with a great magical power. It was this orb, the Dragon's Eye, which allowed dragon and men to talk with one another. With men and Dragons finally understanding each other at last, a peace came to Hal Argus. Everyone rejoiced and after days of celebration the Guardian just disappeared.

The old dragon knew of no one else by that name, but it couldn't be the same man as this all happened centuries ago, that Guardian must be long dead by now and therefore not the man Merlin was looking for.

Merlin agreed reluctantly, that it couldn't be the same person, as the man he was searching for was a relatively young man, much like himself, but he would like to see this monument that had brought such peace and friendship to their land. The only problem was that no one but the old dragon could even remember the Guardian, let alone a monument dedicated to him. Both Dragons and men felt they had betrayed the Guardian's memory and his gift of peace, so they searched the entire realm for his legacy.

It was a few days later that Hash himself located the monument and with it the Dragon's Eye. Everyone rejoiced at the discovery and the entire land celebrated for days on end. It was about a week after the festivities had stopped that disaster struck. News circulated that Merlin had betrayed their trust and not only killed a dragon with his magic, but he had also stolen the orb from the Guardian's Stone. Search parties of both Dragons and men scoured the land for the thief. But when they didn't find any trace of him, arguments began to break out amongst the Dragons and men who were blaming each other for the loss of the orb. Finally, war broke out once more in the land.

Hash, Sak and their two cousins were still out searching for Merlin by the Guardian's Stone when they spotted the culprit at the base of the pillar. As they dived to apprehend him a doorway appeared from nowhere and he disappeared through it. Hash felt responsible for finding the orb in the first place and felt compelled to follow the thief. He told his sister and his cousins to guard the doorway; he would retrieve the orb and kill the traitor. Sak could not let her brother go by himself, so she followed immediately after him, telling her cousins to guard the entrance as long as they could.

When they walked through the door they were stunned to find themselves in a vast corridor, but they didn't have time to wonder where they were because the door opposite them was just closing. They assumed the door about to close on them was the one taken by the thief, so they quickly gave pursuit, fearing the thief would escape with their precious orb. Unfortunately, once they entered the doorway the Mage was nowhere to be seen and the doorway disappeared behind them. It was into this land they came and they had been searching for the thief ever since. They constantly returned to the Guardian's Stone in the hope that they would find the doorway and their way home, but it had never shown itself to them again. They realised they had to find Merlin in order to return home, but unfortunately they encountered another problem. No one in Sakhalin could communicate with them. Even worse, everyone they encountered feared them so much that they tried to kill them. They had now been in Sakhalin for three hundred years and had not even had a glimpse of the thief in all that time; they weren't even sure if he was in Sakhalin at all. It had been an endless search of despair, but now finally they had someone to at least listen to their story, someone who could speak with them and hear their call and maybe help them in their search.

The group were stunned and shocked into silent contemplation. Jennifer was almost in tears with the telling of the story, but David's mind was reeling from the events described.

Everything had happened such a long time ago, and this thief was probably dead by now, but the similarities with events of their own story were staggering. They too had found themselves in a corridor; they had also entered through the doorway and found themselves in this strange land. The door had closed on them, and they had no way to get back home; at least for the moment. Could they then be expected to live in this land for hundreds of years with no way of returning home to family and friends, he wondered?

Then thoughts of the thief entered his mind; was it possible that Nuba Driss and this Merlin were one in the same? But Merlin was a mythical wizard from the Arthurian Legends, could that mean that Nuba Driss had been in England as well? Could he have taken that name or was it just all coincidental? And what about the Guardian's Stone; could there really be two of them? Could there be a lot more? Different stones in different lands; but all dedicated to the same person, this mysterious Guardian? If there was more than one Guardian's Stone, could there be more than one corridor, he wondered? Surely there couldn't be two? But if that were true, how many other people were using it and how many other places did the doors lead to? Indeed, did the doors in his corridor each lead to a different world, and a different Guardian's Stone, he wondered? He needed time to think, think about everything that had happened. It was too much information to take in all at once and his head was spinning. He hated puzzles; he had no patience for them, he just preferred to have the answers then and there, and this was becoming one hell of a puzzle to fathom.

David watched as his sister stood and walked over to the two Dragons. He marvelled at her calm exterior as she seemed to take her new gift in her stride. He knew he wouldn't be as cool under the circumstances, the knife incident was still raw in his mind and he still couldn't believe he had anything to do with it, no matter what Sukhoi and the others believed.

Jennifer turned towards him then and said. "I have told our new friends that we will do all we can to help them retrieve the orb and return them to their own homeland."

David was shocked, what the hell was she doing? "Jen," he said trying to keep his voice calm, "you can't go making promises like that, we can't even find our own way back home, never mind helping others." He finished.

"Dave," she whispered to her brother, ignoring the comment made by the Kavacha, "we both know that they must have come through the same corridor we did, which means that one of those doors leads to their home, as one leads to ours. We just have to get back into the corridor and find the right door."

She made it sound all too easy he thought, but it wasn't that easy and she should know that. Even if they did manage to get back into the corridor, how did they know which door would be theirs for a start, she wasn't thinking things through enough for his liking and began to say so.

"Enough Dave, I've said we'll help and we will if we can." She said putting up her hand to allay any further discussion on the subject.

"I didn't say I wouldn't help Jen," He said getting annoyed by her attitude, "I'm just concerned you're promising something we can't deliver."

Sukhoi interjected smoothly, "I believe we will all try and help when and where we can, let us not argue about this."

Everyone nodded their ascent, but David scowled at his sister and she pretended not to notice.

"Could this thief be Nuba Driss?" Christopher asked. It was a question he had obviously been pondering for a while by the look of consternation on his face.

"I was thinking the same thing Chris, but I can't see how he can be." David replied.

"Oh and why not?" Jennifer asked.

David contemplated his words carefully before replying. "Ok, let's look at the facts. A thief steals an orb that allows men to speak with Dragons, ok?"

Jennifer nodded her head slightly in agreement.

"Our friends here have been trying to communicate with the men of Sakhalin for three hundred years. Don't you think if the orb was here, they would be able to use its magic to speak to someone by now?" David asked.

Jennifer looked at her brother and nodded dejectedly; it made sense to her, though she didn't want to believe it.

"Yes, I think you are right David, that was well thought out." Sukhoi praised him. David smiled at the Kavacha but stopped when he saw the sad expression on his sister's face.

"We'll help them get home if we can Jen, but we shouldn't be promising anything, Dad used to say "don't make promises that you can't keep". I agree with him, that's all I was saying." He said quietly.

"I know, but at least we can try." She replied just as quietly.

David nodded in agreement. "That we can do."

"THANKYOU JENNIFER. IT IS WHAT WE HAVE BEEN HOPING FOR, FOR SUCH A LONG TIME." Hash'ar'jefar inclined his head with gratitude.

"We will help you, if it is possible my friends," Sukhoi assured the Dragons.

"I think we must all go to Enkan Mys now; maybe there we can find the knowledge to help you all." He announced.

"We should make haste Sukhoi; we have been here some considerable time," Socata said as he looked up at the baking sun in the clear blue sky, "and time waits for no man."

"Yes Socata is right; we should be on our way." Sukhoi agreed.

"I take it we still have a lot of desert to cover before we get to the mountains." Christopher asked, bringing his hand over his eyes and looking at the vague outline of mountains in the distance.

"You forget my friend, our ride is here and if we ask them politely, I am sure they will take us all as far as they can." Sukhoi said smiling at the boy and then at the Dragons.

"YES, BUT WE CAN ONLY CARRY YOU AS FAR AS THE MOUNTAINS. FROM THERE YOU WILL HAVE TO GO ON ALONE, WE CANNOT CROSS THEM, SO WE MUST FLY AROUND THEM, AND

MEET YOU ON THE OTHERSIDE." Sak'ar'jefar apologised.

"Why is that?" David asked as Jennifer translated.

"WE ARE NOT SURE." Hash'ar'jefar replied. "THERE SEEMS TO BE SOME SORT OF DARK MAGIC IN THE MOUNTAINS THAT WILL NOT LET US
PASS."

"Oh." He said, wishing he hadn't asked.

"There is nothing you can do?" Asked Jennifer.

"NO, I'M AFRAID NOT, WE MUST FLY AROUND THEM." Hash'ar'jefar replied.

"Why can't we go with you then?" Christopher asked.

"WE HAVE TO FLY TOO HIGH; THE TEMPERATURES ARE TOO COLD FOR PEOPLE TO SURVIVE AND BESIDES, THE JOURNEY ITSELF IS TOO DANGEROUS, WE COULD NOT GUARANTEE YOUR SAFETY." Sak'ar'jefar explained.

"But you'll be ok wont you?" Christopher asked a little apprehensive for these new friends.

Jennifer smiled when the Dragons replied that they would be fine but thanked the young boy for his concern, which made Christopher beam.

"We must be on our way then." Sukhoi said, collecting his pack and preparing to mount Hash'ar'jefar as though he had done it a thousand times before.

His Ruedin quickly grabbed their own packs and the children's and also prepared to mount the Dragons. It was obvious to the children that the companions had done this a few times before; they made it look so easy. Unfortunately the children had a bit more trouble climbing on top of the enormous scaled creatures. But eventually; after a few laughs, everyone was settled in a comfortable position and the Dragons soared into the sky, eager with the knowledge that finally they had found a voice and assistance with their quest.

It was an incredible experience; David hadn't witnessed before in his life. He had never been on a plane, but this must surpass the experience a hundred fold. He had been on a couple of rollercoasters at the seaside, but nothing could prepare him for this. They had sprung into the air as if they owned the sky; mind you, he thought; they probably did, it was wonderful. The wind whistled around him as he glided through the air. He didn't know how fast he was going; he didn't really care, caught up as he was in the moment. He looked around at his companions and at Jennifer and Christopher and could see the ecstasy on their faces too. How he wished he were a bird flying in the sky all the time, to experience this everyday would be like being in heaven, he assumed.

Even when looking at the ground he realised he wasn't frightened at all. The sand stretched as far as he could see, dune after dune of nothing but sand, but up there in the sky, with clouds swirling about, it was wonderful. He could just make out the mountains in the distance, it would have taken them a few more days to walk the distance, but the Dragons conquered the distance in hours.

All the while, Jennifer had been talking with the Dragons about their home, their life and the longing to return to their friends and family. This she understood only too well, but had asked them how they could stand to be away from their home for so many years. The answer was simple and honest; they had each other for company and if they couldn't find the orb, everyone and everything they knew before would be destroyed.

Jennifer thought about that for the rest of the flight, but still found the opportunity to enjoy the experience, expressing her joy to the Dragons as they flew.

"YES JENNIFER, IT IS TRULY WONDERFUL." Hash'ar'jefar said as he spiralled through the sky.

Sak'ar'jefar followed suit and everyone was holding on tight and laughing as the Dragons performed a marvellous dancing display in the sky. It wasn't long before the mountains loomed before them and the pace of the flight slowed before finally they descended gracefully to the edge of the desert and the foot of the mountain range.

The group quickly dismounted exhilarated by the flight and collected their packs while Sukhoi spoke with the Dragons through Jennifer.

The Dragons decided the best place to meet the group would be the other side of Konare forest, as their journey would take them many days to get around the mountain range. Sukhoi knew it would probably take the group at least five days to get through the mountains; weather permitting and another two or three days to get to the other side of the forest themselves, so they agreed that if the Dragons weren't there after eight days, they would continue on, and the Dragons would catch up eventually. With that agreed they made their fond farewells, with promises of meeting each other again soon enough.

    Jennifer was almost in tears as the Dragons took to the sky a few minutes later and watched as they became tiny dots in the sky.

Chapter Twelve

The mountains looked quite daunting to the children as they looked upward. They couldn't guess how high they were but they had been told that they had to cross through the mountains in order to carry on with their journey. A journey that no one looked interested in taking; including Sukhoi and his Ruedin.

"Ok my friends, we should really make a start. Stay close together and follow carefully, we do not want any needless accidents." Sukhoi stated as he moved towards the mountain.

There was a narrow path to follow initially that led upward into the mountains beyond; this was obviously the pass Sukhoi had referred to, David thought.

Braduga led the way followed by Sukhoi a few feet behind, then the children and Socata brought up the rear. There was sufficient room for the three children to walk side by side once it broadened further up the trail and they talked excitedly about the Dragons as they walked.

"What was it like?" David asked. He realised he was a little envious of Jennifer, though he'd keep that to himself; "talking with the Dragons?"

"It's just the same as talking to you to be honest, I know I'm talking in my head, but I really don't think it's any different to talking to anyone else." She couldn't believe it herself, but so many things were different here and quite surprisingly she liked this gift she had. She wasn't sure whether David felt the same; he had yet to confirm he could do anything, but she would keep an eye on him, she would keep an eye on both her brothers. Everything was happening so quickly, she thought. First it was David performing magic with the knife and saving someone's life and now here she was talking with Dragons. They were jumping from one surprising situation to another without pausing for breath. She was actually enjoying herself on this adventure, until that was she thought about how much their mother must be worrying over their disappearance. Her mood quickly changed and she became quiet as she walked along the path. Her brothers noticed the sudden change and decided not to bother her with their questions for now and talked quietly to each other instead. She let her thoughts drift to the Dragons and once more her spirit sonred as the Dragons had sonred in the sky. She didn't want to think about home for the moment; not when she knew they had no possibility of getting there for the immediate future. She was going to say something on the subject to her brothers, but she could tell they were caught up in their own conversation and she gave them the same courtesy they had given her, so she said nothing. There would be time to talk about home when they finally reached Enkan Mys, she decided.

"Is everyone alright, I mean, how is everyone coping with this?" David asked as they followed the winding path.

"Yeah, I'm ok." Christopher said. "We've come to a great place, it's just like some of the stories you've told me about at bedtime. Dragons, magic, pirates; well maybe not pirates, unless we say those Raiders were pirate-like. Anyway, we're like those characters now, we're part of a story, but I must admit to keep expecting mum to interrupt the story or wake me up and find myself in my bed.

Jennifer thought Christopher would start getting homesick with that comment but he continued to walk along the path with a smile on his face. Christopher was actually enjoying this adventure as much as she was. She agreed with him, it was just one big exciting story and they were apart of it now; whether she liked the idea of that or not, but personally she couldn't wait for the next chapter to begin. Unfortunately, she wasn't so sure about David. He had seemed awfully quiet since the incident with the knife, more quiet than he'd ever been.

"Good," David said, though he didn't look like he meant it. "Well, we seem to be falling behind a little so let's catch up with Sukhoi." He said noticing the gap that was widening between the children and their companions. With nods of agreement, the three children increased their pace and fell in behind the Kavacha.

"Sukhoi, do you really think the thief the Dragons were referring to could be Nuba Driss?" David asked as they headed up the pass.

"I think it could be David." He replied. He had been giving the subject a lot of thought, and it did make sense. He didn't know how long a mage as powerful as Nuba Driss could live, but if he was from a different land; like his friends the Dragons, then maybe he too wouldn't age. If that was the case, there was no end to how much power he could accumulate over time. The mage would be almost god-like; it made perfect sense and was extremely troubling news, news that he had to pass on to the council of elders at the earliest opportunity.

The group walked up the winding path for hours, stopping briefly for food and drink before continuing again on their journey. The pass was still quite wide and the pace hard but steady, allowing the children the opportunity to admire the scenery around them.

They had travelled quite high already and could see the vast dry desert disappearing into the distance behind them. There weren't any trees or shrubs of any kind on the path. It was just a dirt track between rocks that climbed higher and higher into the expanse of the mountain and beyond. In fact there was hardly any colour at all; everything except the path seemed to merge into one dark, bleak grey colour.

After a few more hours of walking Sukhoi decided to call a halt. It must have been late afternoon by now, and the temperature seemed to be dropping quite dramatically.

"We will stop here and rest for a few minutes." Sukhoi announced. "I will carry on up the trail to locate the Haram, it should not be too far now."

"There is a Haram in the mountains?" David asked Socata in wonder as Sukhoi continued up the trail.

"Yes, there are Haram everywhere David, some in places you least expect to find them. The Kavacha use their knowledge to locate them, though I don't know how they do it. There is even one in the middle of a town called Aquilas Mys, though none of the townsfolk even know it exists." Socata smiled as he remembered his first visit to the town.

"Really?" Christopher asked intrigued.

"Oh yes, they are a great gift from the Guardian." Socata announced reverently.

Some ten minutes later, Sukhoi returned. "All is well and prepared; we must make good use of this Haram, for there isn't another one we can use for a couple of days."

"Isn't that amazing?" David said to Jennifer. "A Haram in the mountains."

"Er, I think there have been more amazing things happen today actually, but yes, I know what you mean." She replied.

Yes, David thought, some pretty amazing things have happened but now he was so tired that he just wanted to get out of the wind and into the lovely warm Haram, where he could have something to eat and rest for a while. He didn't want to think about anything else and especially not about his so-called magic; though he didn't think Sukhoi would let the matter drop so easily.

A little while later Sukhoi called a stop and turned to face an outcrop of rock.

He mumbled a few words and a crack appeared in the rock, which widened to reveal a narrow entranceway. Sukhoi merely walked into the entrance and disappeared from view. The children just looked at each other in wonder until his voice called from the darkness. "Are you coming or are you intending to spend the night outside?" Sukhoi said and then began to laugh.

David moved forward and found himself in a tunnel, similar to the other entrances he had gone through to get to the Haram; moments later he emerged into the cavern. What surprised him was the similarity to the others he had been in, in fact they weren't just similar, they were exactly the same in every detail that he could see.

Jennifer and Christopher followed him in, holding hands as they entered.

As David admired the Haram, he leaned back on the wall, his hands spreading out to the sides and then he quickly stood upright. What was that he thought? He had felt a tingling sensation when he put his hands to the wall. It was similar to the sensation he felt when touching the brick in the fireplace at home; similar but not quite the same. He reached out and touched the spot where his hand had been before; the tingling sensation went through his fingers again, but unlike the brick in the fireplace his hand remained solid. So it wasn't another gateway he could use to get home, he thought, but he felt as if he could feel the magic in the rock. As he continued to feel the rock he realised that it was pulsating rather than anything else. He concentrated on the rhythm and he realised that it was more like a heart beat, a heart beat in the rock. He quickly moved his hand away from the wall in shock; rocks didn't have heart beat's where he came from and the thought of the rock's here having one, made him feel uncomfortable for some reason. He thought for one moment he was just going mad, but why couldn't a rock have a heart beat here, he didn't know what normal was in Sakhalin, maybe every rock had one. He would have to ask Sukhoi when he got the opportunity.

"What's wrong?" Christopher asked him, sensing his unease.

"Nothing really," He replied, it was one thing talking to a stranger about rocks having heart beat but it was something totally different talking to his brother or sister about it. "What with everything that's happened today, I think I'm just a little tired."

"Yeah, I'm pretty tired myself," Christopher replied as he began to yawn.

Sukhoi walked over to the children and could see they had all started to yawn and commented that they would all benefit from a good nights sleep.

"We still have far to go, get some sleep my friends." He said.

"Ok, thanks Sukhoi." David said yawning himself as Sukhoi walked over to his Ruedin and sat down beside them.

The three children all said their goodnights to each other and began to make themselves comfortable on the cushions and furs provided by the Haram.

David quickly arranging his bag and his clothing on one side, folded and ready to put on in the morning, a ritual that hadn't changed even though he was in a strange place. Then he too settled himself to go to sleep.

Unfortunately, sleep didn't come straight away; to any of them. Jennifer couldn't stop thinking about the plight of the Dragons. She was excited by the fact that she was the only person in this land that could speak with them, but she felt such pity for them that she couldn't help but wonder what would happen to them if they had to leave, who would they have to talk to then?

David was kept awake a little while longer as he thought about all the events that had taken place so far, from stopping the dagger, the Dragons and even the pulsating heartbeat of the rock. Surprisingly it was the rock that seemed to ignite his imagination the most. He knew he was tired but he couldn't stop thinking about the feel of it. It felt alive beneath his fingers and he thought it meant something significant, though he couldn't think what that could be at the moment. He would definitely have to remember to speak to Sukhoi about it in the morning.

Even Christopher didn't get to sleep straight away, he was feeling a little left out truth be known. Jennifer could talk with Dragons and David could stop knives in mid-flight, but what could he do, absolutely diddly swat, he thought.

With all the excitement of the day, it took a long while for everyone to put all thoughts behind them and get some well-earned rest. The little bit of magic the Haram possessed pulsated through the night as it tried to protect its inhabitants from the bad dreams that swirled around in the cold night sky. It was successful in only allowing the more peaceful and pleasant dreams to invade its protection, allowing everyone to sleep soundly.

The following morning, the little group woke early; food was eaten quickly and quietly, and then they continued on their journey up the mountain pass. The temperature dropped significantly the higher up they walked, and what made matters worse was a dark threatening cloud had emerged in the sky, promising a foul storm in the not too distant future. It didn't take long for the cloud to conceal them from the warmth of the sun. Sukhoi seemed to be prepared for every eventuality and supplied the children with furs and clothing taken from the Haram.

The children laughed at each other as they adorned the clothing provided; which didn't really fit, but they did provide enough adequate protection from the elements.

Morning came and went as they trudged up the narrow path. The scenery becoming grimmer the higher they travelled. Murkiness settled in the atmosphere and the mood became sombre.

"Is everyone ok?" Sukhoi asked after a spell of silence lingered on the mountain top like the mist that was forming below them. He had notice the children glumly putting one foot in front of the other, without really noticing where they were going. It was a bit of an ordeal and not much of an adventure any more as they climbed higher and higher towards an elusive peak.

"Are we nearly there yet?" Christopher asked sullenly, raising his head to gaze up the trail.

David wanted to laugh at the comment, but didn't really feel in the mood. It normally frustrated him when Christopher made that particular comment, as every time they went on a journey he would repeat it over and over again.

Today though, even Christopher didn't have the inclination to talk.

"We are nearly at the summit of this mountain, but unfortunately we still have a long way to go and a couple more mountains to climb." Sukhoi replied.

On and on they climbed until they reached the summit of the first mountain.

The children were initially dismayed to see a vast array of other mountains before them as they reached the top, until Sukhoi explained it wasn't nearly as far as it appeared.

"We don't have to go over all of those, do we?" Jennifer asked. She was tired, her feet were hurting and she felt as if she had been walking for weeks.

"No, just that one." Sukhoi said as he pointed to the next mountain top nearest the group. "And then the pass veers to the left and into a valley just beyond that mountain." He replied encouragingly.

Darkness came quickly, and even Sukhoi looked surprised by its arrival. "We must find shelter quickly," He said smelling the air. "I think the storm will arrive in a little while."

Oh great, David thought to himself, that's all they needed. It was bad enough climbing through mountains without having a storm to contend with.

An hour passed and the last rays of light had almost faded when Braduga informed them that he had found somewhere suitable to stay the night. It was a small dark cave, which they all cuddled into; luckily for them they found it as the first spots of rain hit the mountain. Squashing inside, they all tried to get comfortable. There wasn't room for a fire but they still had plenty of food available, and there was sufficient room to stretch out and get some sleep.

The storm raged all night, rain thrashing against the mountain, but the cave remained dry throughout.

David woke a couple of times through the night by the thunder clapping outside the cave, but it wasn't long before he soon drifted back to sleep. His dreams were troubled and unpleasant, Nuba Driss was chasing him down the corridor and all the doors were locked, there was no where for him to hide and no one to come to his rescue. He ran and ran, with the footsteps following him, until he couldn't run any more. Exhausted by the chase and near to collapse he turned to face his pursuer, and that's when he woke up. The morning sunlight was trying to break through the dark clouds, but with little success, as he woke.

"You ok Dave?" Jennifer asked as David sat up quickly, a half scream on his lips.

"What? Yes, fine, just a bad dream." He said yawning and stretching to cover his discomfort.

"Oh, sorry to hear that. I had a wonderful dream of flying with the Dragons in a beautiful clear blue sky." She said wistfully, as if she was still experiencing the dream now.

"Lucky you." He said grumpily, the memories of Nuba Driss chasing him still vivid in his mind.

Everyone was awake he noticed, but not doing anything in particular, and he realised the storm was still raging outside. "I take it;

we're going to wait a while to see if the storm subsides a little?"

"That's the general idea." Socata replied. "I don't fancy trying to battle through this lot."

"Too dangerous." Sukhoi agreed. "These winds are strong enough to rip you off the trail and throw you down the mountain. We will wait awhile."

"Thank God for that." Jennifer whispered in David's ear.

Socata passed round what appeared to be dried fruits with bread as they waited for the storm to die down. The fruits were green in colour but tasted like tangerines, and very nutritious they were informed by Socata.

A couple of hours passed before Sukhoi deemed it safe enough to venture out of the now, musty smelling little cave and everyone was thankful for that, especially Jennifer for some reason.

"Ok, we may get a little wet, but we may as well set off."

Onwards they travelled, the children finding the journey particularly difficult now as they trudged through the muddied and dirt ridden path that had been churned by the storm. The hours slowly passed without incident as they climbed the trail, all excitement and exhilaration washed away by the rain. Occasionally they talked, with the children asking the odd question about something or other, but no one was really in the mood for a conversation. Then, just when they thought it couldn't get any worse, the rain turned to sleet and the wind intensified; whipping them remorsefully as they continued to battle the elements.

Sukhoi could tell the storm was going to intensify and wasted little time in asking Braduga to search further along the trail and locate any sort of shelter which could provide protection from the forces of nature. While they waited for Braduga to return they all huddled together to keep warm.

When twenty minutes passed and he still hadn't returned, Sukhoi decided they would head up the trail in case there was a problem. Everyone followed behind the Kavacha cautiously, taking their time as the path they now trod was becoming increasingly slippery as the storm intensified. An hour passed, as they huddled along together in the worsening storm, when finally they met Braduga along the pass.

"I can't find anywhere suitable," He shouted above the howling wind. "I have searched a long way ahead and there is no shelter anywhere, nothing that could offer any protection for all of us." He said worriedly.

Sukhoi was worried also; he looked at the children and realised if they didn't find shelter soon they would perish in this freezing cold storm. "We must keep moving then; if we stop here we will freeze and die!" He shouted and bringing the children closer they set off warily along the trail.

After travelling along the trail for a few more hours David was freezing; the feeling in his toes and fingers had numbed. He was trying to hold onto Christopher, to force him along the trail as he was in a worse condition than himself but it was hard going and he didn't know how long any of them could last in the bitterly cold freezing wind of the storm. If they didn't find shelter soon, they would surely freeze to death as Sukhoi predicted, but still there was nothing ahead of them to offer a reprieve. Slowly, painfully they hugged the mountainside as they moved along the trail and then David stopped in astonishment. Was it his imagination or had he really just felt something familiar beneath his fingers.

His fingers were numb, but as he touched the rock once more, it pulsated warmth into his hand.

Jennifer bumped into him. "What's wrong?" She shouted.

"I think there is a Haram behind this rock!" He shouted back and felt the warmth flooding through him as he placed both hands on the rock. "Feel the rock!" He said.

Jennifer placed her hands on the rock, but frowned and looked back to her brother. "I don't feel anything Dave." She shouted back.

"You can't feel the warmth coming from the rock?" He asked her in surprise.

"No!" She shouted back.

Sukhoi looked behind him to make sure everyone was staying together when he realised David and Jennifer had stopped. He tried to shout to them to keep up but his words were carried away by the howling wind. He grabbed hold of Christopher and walked back.

"What's wrong?" He asked them.

"David thinks there is a Haram behind this rock!" Jennifer shouted at him.

"I am sorry but there is no Haram here, there is not another one now for a few days." He said as he too touched the rock where David had placed his hands.

"I can feel the rock pulsating Sukhoi, just here!" David shouted above the storm.

"I feel nothing David, are you sure?" He asked sceptically.

"Yes, positive." He replied.

"Ok, well I will try the incantation just in case." Sukhoi said as he began to chant at the rock where David indicated.

As he spoke the words, Sukhoi could hardly contain his surprise when a crack appeared and then an entrance to a Haram appeared. Momentarily stunned, he stared at the gap and then at David before motioning everyone to enter the Haram.

Braduga had returned when he realised no one was following him and both he and Socata entered the Haram last.

Everyone gratefully stepped inside and then stared in wonder as they walked into the cavern. This Haram was different from the others; which was unbelievable in itself. For one thing it was enormous, at least double the size of a normal Haram. At the far end of the room was a waterfall, which flowed into a little lake, steam appeared to be rising from the water. Fruit trees surrounded a lawn area, with a round table and six chairs planted in the middle of it.

There were the usual cushions and furs everywhere else as in all Haram, but they appeared new and brighter of colour somehow. It was wonderful and a total surprise not only to the children but to the companions also.

Sukhoi was shocked and surprised, he had made this journey through the pass quite a few times in the past, but never before had he been aware of this particular Haram. His training and knowledge allowed him the ability to find and locate a Haram, no matter where it was. This particular one was incredible, but why hadn't he found it before now he questioned? Was he losing his talent? He doubted it. But what shocked him the most, was the fact that David had found it. This left him with a lot to think about, his senses were trying to tell him something, but he wasn't sure what. How could a young boy from a foreign land find a Haram? He had been born and trained in the knowledge of the Kavacha, but he hadn't even sensed its magic.

"David, how did you know the Haram was behind that rock?" He asked.

David's eyes locked with Sukhoi's and his mind raced. What should he tell him, he thought? A little voice in the back of his mind answered "tell him the truth". "I felt it, when I put my hand out on the rock, I felt a pulse; like a beating heart. I know it sounds silly, but that's what happened." He waited for everyone to start laughing, but no one did, they just stared at him in wonder.

"I meant to speak to you about it before, when we were in the other Haram I felt something similar then and was going to ask you about it, but then, well, I forgot." He finished reluctantly.

"Similar, but not the same?" Sukhoi asked intrigued.

"Yes, this one is slightly different, it feels differently somehow." David said trying to concentrate and describe the difference but failing.

"At least we've got some shelter now." Christopher said happily.

"Yes, and what a shelter it is." Socata smiled as he gazed around the cavern.

"This is getting to be a regular occurrence, isn't it?" Jennifer said.

"What is?" Christopher asked.

"I'm not sure what to call them really, but, these gifts or abilities that keep popping up." She smiled; amazement etched on her face.

David realised she was right. Whenever they came upon one obstacle or another, either Jennifer or himself always found a way to overcome it. Well, that's how it seemed to him, if he could bring himself to believe it was him that stopped that dagger earlier. He should do now, especially as he had located a Haram that Sukhoi couldn't even detect with his magic.

"You are both very special, I knew that from the first day we met," Sukhoi smiled. "But I didn't realise how special, until now. David, I am sure you must be Kavacha, or maybe perhaps something more, "he said on reflection.

"I'm starving." Christopher interrupted them. He looked a little annoyed and David understood immediately that Christopher was probably upset because he hadn't acquired any gifts at all so far. He tried to speak to Christopher about it, but his brother just shrugged his shoulders as if he wasn't bothered and rushed over to the trees full of ripened red fruit and began picking them to eat.

Everyone soon followed, the wind, rain and snow had been gruelling and now everyone just wanted to get out of their wet clothes.

Jennifer walked over to the waterfall and admired its beauty. The water appeared from a hole about twenty feet up the rock-face and cascaded down to a pool below. It didn't look to deep, but the steam and spray as it hit the pool obscured most of the view. She tentatively put her hand in the water and smiled in delight. "This water is lovely and warm!" Jennifer exclaimed. With that she started to take off her wet clothes, wearing only her knickers and bra, she jumped into the pool. Laughing, she splashed around in the water. "This is wonderful" She gasped before plunging her head under the water.

David and Christopher soon followed and all three children were splashing around in the water, enjoying the moment. Christopher's mood changing completely as he jumped into the pool. The three companions looked on, smiling as the children splashed each other.

"How did he find this, Sukhoi?" Socata whispered out of earshot of the children.

"I do not know my friend, I thought only Kavacha could find the Haram." He considered. "It has never been known to have happened before, so one must surmise that David is Kavacha, but it is all very strange."

Braduga had been investigating the Haram with interest and now sat at the table watching the children when Sukhoi and Socata came to sit beside him.

"This place, it looks and feels like a Haram," He began as he looked around the room. "But it is different somehow. It feels new and fresh, more alive than the others." A frown creased his forehead. "Do you know what I mean?" He asked his friends.

Sukhoi knew what Braduga meant, because he felt it too. There was something different, but he could not put his finger on what it was.

David, dripping wet walked over to the table. "Is everything ok?" He asked, watching the three companions with their heads together in conversation.

Smiling, Sukhoi said. "Yes David, we were just surprised you found this Haram."

"Yeah, me too, but I am glad I did. It was freezing outside." He said defensively.

"As are we, my friend." Sukhoi said giving him a big smile.

David felt as if he was about to be interrogated but then Sukhoi smiled at him and then asked him to get his brother and sister so they could all have something to eat before getting some rest.

Relieved, David did so, but he knew the interrogation would come eventually.

As he walked back to the pool he thought back to all the incidents over the past few days and he marvelled at them. He had saved a man's life; Sukhoi's life and now he had found a Haram just when it was needed the most. He didn't think that magic could exist but here, in this place, he shouldn't be surprised to believe anything could exist, especially after meeting the Dragons.

Sukhoi watched David as he walked away and knew the boy was honest and open, and seemed genuinely surprised by what was happening to him, and to his sister, but Sukhoi felt he was missing something. He was probably the most knowledgeable Kavacha there was; after the Keeper, but he had never heard or witnessed magic such as the magic that David wielded. The only problem was that all the children displayed such an air of innocence that it worried him.

They would be so easily manipulated and corrupted he thought, should Nuba Driss and his minions get hold of them. He would have to try and protect that innocence, and protect them all from harm; as his honour guard protected him, something deep within his soul told him he had to, no matter what the cost.

They ate, mostly in silence, the odd cursory word thrown in during the meal, but nobody seemed to have enough strength to talk, the storm had tired them out completely. By mutual consent they decided to get some rest and the children moved to one side of the cavern to prepare for bed. They huddled close together, and spoke quietly of everything that had happened since fleeing from the robed figure in the corridor. It had been an incredible journey so far but they still had a long way to go yet. David and Jennifer spoke quietly for the first time about the strange gifts they had been given, while Christopher listened intently. David expressed his concern about his abilities, he didn't understand how or why he could do certain things, while Jennifer, thought they were amazing and appeared to accept them for what they were, gifts; unexpected and unusual, but gifts never the less.

Christopher lay between his brother and sister and for the first time in his life he felt isolated and alone as they shared their feelings.

"I haven't got any special gifts." He said glumly.

David looked across at Jennifer, and then looked at Christopher. "That's true Chris." He replied. "But who knows what's going to happen tomorrow. We didn't ask for these gifts and quite frankly, if I could give you mine, I would." He said. "They're not as great as you might think, in fact they terrify me. We're in a strange place with strange things happening all the time, maybe your time will come soon enough and then you can be as terrified as I feel right now." He said, but gave his brother a smile to take the sting out of his words.

"It must be quite hard to get use to," he replied, "but I still wouldn't mind having a go though." He whispered.

"It's more than hard to get use to Chris; it's really scary, for me anyway." He said as he looked at his sister. "But you should be careful what you wish for." David said in all seriousness.

Jennifer gave David a stern look then said to Christopher, "Eh, just think Chris, you may be able to do lots of things we can't do in the future." She said smiling.

Christopher thought about that for a moment and then he thought that seemed a reasonable assumption. She could be right; it could be him doing marvellous things in a few days time. If they had special powers, why couldn't he have them too? "I could end up being the greatest wizard ever, shooting fire from my finger tips and maybe fly in the sky like the Dragons, or..."

"Ok, ok, we get the message, mighty wizard." Jennifer laughed.

Christopher laughed with her, but David didn't laugh, he remembered how he felt in the corridor, how he felt with the promise of power. Now he possibly had that power, did he really want it? He felt that Christopher should be careful what he wished for, because he may just get it.

Christopher noticed his brother's sour demeanour, but he decided that if he was given some special gifts, he would use them to his hearts content and not be worried about it. David could be miserable all he liked, but he would have great fun with them.

They awoke early, eager to complete their journey to Enkan Mys, but not too eager to battle the storm which was still raging outside the Haram.

Braduga had risen early to check on the weather and approached Sukhoi with bad news. He was covered in furs which were now crusted in snow, his cheeks and nose were red with the cold and wet, but he had a determined look on his face.

"I don't think we will be able to get through the pass at the moment, the snow has settled, and could be quite treacherous." He looked at the children, who were still getting dressed. "Especially for the children. I would not risk it." He added in a gentler voice so as not to be overheard.

"It is that bad then?" Sukhoi asked, though he knew from the way that Braduga was acting that there was something else his Ruedin wanted to tell him.

Braduga motioned for Sukhoi to follow him to the Haram entrance and left the children with Socata to prepare their morning meal.

As they braved the elements outside, Sukhoi saw a chilling look in Braduga's eyes and something more he couldn't put his finger on.

"What is it Brad?" Sukhoi asked him gently.

"Gourtak." He whispered as he gazed up and down the mountain path.

"Gourtak here? Fresh tracks?" Sukhoi asked though he knew from Braduga's reaction that they must be.

As Braduga continued to look up the trail, Sukhoi was reminded of younger and drunken Braduga at his brother Ambar's funeral, when he promised to rid Sakhalin of every Gourtak he could find. That had been quite a few years ago now, but Sukhoi had never forgotten the look in Brad's eyes as he made that vow, and obviously neither had the warrior. The only difference between then and now was that Brad was probably the greatest warrior Sakhalin had ever seen, and unlike then, if he made that vow now, everyone would not think it an impossible boast.

"That's not all," he paused before finishing what he had to say, "there were two sets of tracks in the snow, it was a definitely a hunting pair."

Sukhoi was shocked, Gourtak were incredibly ferocious creatures and extremely territorial. He knew of no reason why two would be together except in mating season, and this wasn't mating season.

"They were hunting together?" He asked, yet he knew the answer before the warrior could reply.

"Yes, and I think it is our scent they have." He replied. "The tracks pass the entrance of the Haram quite a few times, first in one direction and then the other. If David hadn't have found this Haram..." He left it open.

"Do you know where they are now?" Concern etched on his face. With three young children under his protection and two Gourtak tracking them, the odds weren't in their favour, even with his skills and Braduga's prowess.

"Difficult to say, I couldn't even determine if they were hunting together at first." He sounded disappointed in his ability to decipher that fact.

"Ok," Sukhoi told him. "The pass is impenetrable at the moment anyway; the Haram will give us sufficient protection from the beasts providing we stay inside, so we will stay here today and then re-evaluate our possibilities tomorrow. We can't risk the lives of the children." He emphasised this last remark in case Braduga had some crazy idea about trying to track and kill the Gourtak himself. He was needed, not only to protect his Kavacha, but also to help get the children to Enkan Mys safely.

"Yes, I agree, I will let Socata know." He said as they both walked back into the Haram. Braduga walked over to Socata and offered his assistance in preparing the morning meal as Sukhoi watched him with a slightly bemused expression on his face.

"Well, I did not expect that response." He said quietly to himself as Braduga walked away.

"What's that?" Jennifer asked, standing next to him.

He had sensed her approach him from behind, but he didn't think he had spoken loud enough for her to hear. "It is nothing. Have you eaten yet?" He asked.

She knew that he had been thinking about Braduga, and seemed worried, she could almost hear his thoughts, and they included something that could harm her and her brothers, but she wasn't sure what. "Not yet, you joining us?"

"Yes," He laughed. "I could eat a Tarqasian pie."

"A what?" She laughed with him as they walked over to the others for something to eat.

"You have never heard of a Tarqasian pie? He feigned amazement. "Tarqah is a tiny village near the Konare Forrest. If it was not for the deliciously tasty meaty pie, with a fantastically light crust of fluffy pastry, nobody would have known the village existed. But since the discovery of the pies they bake, people have travelled for miles just to smell the pies, let alone taste them. But the best thing about the pie is, it is as big as Christopher, well not quite, but it is extremely large." He conceded.

"They sound wonderful."

"Yes they are." He said smiling, though Jennifer could tell that he was still worried about something.

Sukhoi didn't mention the Gourtak to the children, providing they stayed within the protection of the Haram, they had nothing to worry about for now. But it did worry him that two of the creatures appeared to be tracking them, one was bad enough, he thought, but two, two could well mean their deaths, unless the beasts found other prey to hunt. He would have to speak with his companions later to devise some sort of strategy, just in case.

In the meantime he told everyone that the weather was to bad to risk continuing with their journey, they would just have to spend a little more time in the Haram. They should get as much rest as possible for once the opportunity arose they would be back on the trail to Enkan Mys.

Throughout the day, Braduga and Socata checked the entrance of the Haram, returning with frowns of frustration. The weather had grown worse, a continuous snowfall had covered all traces of any tracks on the pass and visibility was almost non existent. This combination had made it impossible for the two companions to judge whether they were still being tracked or not.

They couldn't leave the entrance of the Haram either, as that would mean leaving its protection and they could also unwittingly divulge the entrance to the Haram to the Gourtak. It still wasn't clear that the two creatures were hunting their little group, but Sukhoi was not prepared to take the risk. The Gourtak were incredibly intelligent and patient, a combination that could get them killed if they decided to brave the elements too soon to continue on their journey. Fortunately, the Haram protected them for now, which must be frustrating the creatures if nothing else. How hungry the creatures were, would determine how long they would stay on the hunt, unless of course some other prey came their way, which is what they hoped for.

Chapter Thirteen

Sukhoi was sitting on some cushions in the centre of the cavern watching the children with undisguised interest as they talked to each other about Jennifer's incredible ability to talk with the Dragons. He couldn't believe that someone could actually communicate with them. He had spoken at length with the Keeper and the other Kavacha to try and think of a way to communicate with the Dragons but all their attempts had ended in failure. They had checked the Kavacha book of knowledge but again there weren't any references to Dragons or of trying to communicate with any creatures. Disappointed, he had thrust the thought of ever speaking with them firmly from his mind. Now, everything had changed, he had found a girl that could actually speak with them and they could speak with her. He had found a boy with exceptional power for one so young that he could actually find a Haram that he couldn't even detect. What did it all mean? He knew it had to mean something; it couldn't all just be coincidence. But what was he missing? He would just have to wait until he got to Enkan Mys to find out. For now, he would just continue to watch over the children and make sure they arrived safe and sound at their final destination.

"You ok Sukhoi?" David asked as he noticed the man hadn't said anything for the past ten minutes, but merely watched and listened to their chatter.

"Sorry David, I am well, though I am curious about your gifts, I must admit." He replied.

"I take it none of this is normal then?" He asked in return, knowing that he had to talk to Sukhoi at some time about their gifts; he thought it might as well be now.

"Not really, not the gifts you two have displayed."

"Oh." David replied, "What do you want to know?"

Sukhoi smiled at David, realising that the boy was at last ready to talk about his gifts and maybe now he could get some answers to unasked questions.

"You said when you touched the rock you felt a pulse? He asked David.

"Yes, like a heart beat." He replied. "It was a shock at first, and strange, but it was similar to the sensation I felt in the other Haram."

"Hmm, amazing, a heartbeat." He had never felt anything at all when he touched the rock.

Sukhoi asked both David and Jennifer question after question about how they felt about the gifts and if it was usual for people from England to display such abilities. He was shocked when they both replied that they didn't even know they had the gifts and that they knew of no one at home who could do the things they had done. The questions continued, until eventually Christopher decided he'd had enough.

He got to his feet and walked quietly away from the conversation and walked to the entrance of the Haram. Braduga was standing there watching the snow settle on the ground while Socata sat opposite him playing with a knife in his hand.

Braduga turned to face him as he took a couple of careful steps closer.

"Are you ok Christopher?" He asked gently.

"Yes thanks, just a bit bored." He replied quickly, amazed the warrior had heard him; he had been moving so slowly and quietly so as not to disturb them that he was surprised when the warrior spoke.

"The weather is still bad, I don't think we will be leaving here any time soon, I'm afraid." Braduga said as he turned back to look outside.

Socata was flicking his knife in the air and then catching it by its point in his fingertips, without even looking at it.

Christopher was fascinated by it as it spun in the air and the blasé way in which Socata caught it. He sat opposite the older warrior; next to Braduga's feet and continued watch in unbridled envy.

Socata looked at the impressed look on the boys face and then said, "Would you like me to teach you how it is done?"

Christopher couldn't contain the big broad smile that appeared on his face, he nodded vigorously. He rushed to his feet and then went to sit beside the man that was going to teach him his very own trick; it wasn't really magic, but it was close enough in his opinion.

It was mid afternoon when Sukhoi announced to the children that he was going to show them a bit of magic; but it was more in the hope that he could get David to participate than anything else. Socata and Braduga had already left the cavern to check on the weather and to see if there were any more signs of the Gourtak.

The children looked at him with enthusiastic expressions when he stood up and told them to look at a pile of cushions; especially a bright red cushion, to their left. They located the pile and the cushion in question and then clapped in appreciation and surprise when it levitated into the air. The amazement in their faces made Sukhoi smile as yet another cushion followed that one, then a third and fourth. The cushions then began to form a rude circle before they then began to rotate. The children's faces beamed with pleasure as the cushions went round and round. Abruptly the cushions stopped and fell to the floor, all eyes turned to Sukhoi who was standing with his arms outstretched with a faint smile on his lips.

"Even this kind of magic requires some significant amount of concentration to achieve." He said as the cushions now floated into the air but in a straight line, one after the other and then stopped perfectly still. "The difference between what I am doing now and what David did; when he stopped that dagger, is instinct." He noticed David's sombre expression but continued with his narration. "He used his magic instinctively and without really thinking about what he was doing he was able to stop the dagger immediately. All Kavacha have to know what they want to do first and then release the spell. Only a very few could actually do what David did and then only after years of training." He let that remark sink in for a few seconds.

"I didn't know what I was doing though." David said defensively. "I just didn't want you to die."

"And I appreciate that." Sukhoi laughed. "But do you think you could try and use your magic by thinking what you want to achieve first, instead of using your instincts?"

David looked at Sukhoi and his smiling face and then looked at Jennifer and Christopher who were both nodding encouragingly. "I can give it a try." He replied unenthusiastically.

"Ok, good, try and make one of my cushions drop to the floor?" He asked. "In fact, it could be fun for everyone to give it a go." He smiled hopefully at the children and they all nodded their assent, which made David more inclined to take part, he realised.

All three children concentrated on trying to make a cushion move. Grimaces of concentration appeared on their faces as they tried, but nothing happened.

Sukhoi wasn't surprised by their lack of success; it wasn't easy to move something that someone had already moved using magic. As he watched them mentally strain to move the cushion he made another one rise behind David. He needed to know whether David had the ability to do magic instinctively all the time or just in certain situations. The only way he could do that was to test him and although he felt a little guilty for this ruse, he knew it was the only way. Making the cushion move rapidly towards David's head, he shouted a warning to the boy.

Turning quickly, David saw the cushion heading straight for him and his hand shot out instinctively, the cushion stopped in mid-air. David had once again stopped an object in its flight path on pure instinct alone and Sukhoi couldn't help but be impressed. He suddenly felt confused and nauseous but the feeling soon passed.

"Are you ok David?" Sukhoi asked him concerned.

David turned to the Kavacha, "I felt a bit sick, but I'm ok now." He replied.

"Yes that sometimes happens when we are not used to dealing with the magic. The more magic you try the less nauseous you will feel." Sukhoi offered though he didn't explain why he had to feel sick in the first place.

David was just about to ask why he was feeling sick when Sukhoi spoke to him again.

"Can you feel anything David?" Sukhoi asked quickly and with an air of urgency that David didn't understand. "Do you feel differently?" Sukhoi persisted expectantly, hoping the boy could feel the power of the magic around him.

David wasn't happy with Sukhoi at the moment but he was surprised to realise that he did feel something, there was something there, a tingling sensation, weak but definitely there. He nodded to Sukhoi, not wanting to speak in case the sensation vanished.

A big smile appeared on the Kavacha's face at the acknowledgement. "Ok, now concentrate on that feeling and let it empower you, draw it to you." He said.

David did just that, he brought the tingling sensation into him and with it came a feeling of confusion and nauseous-ness. As the unpleasant feelings subsided he felt the power and he realised he was experiencing the same feelings of control he had had in the corridor.

It felt wonderful, he felt as if he could achieve anything.

Sukhoi smiled as he watched David's expression of concentration turn in to one of euphoria. "Now David." He said. "Make the cushion rise into the air."

Jennifer and Christopher looked on in awe as their brother made the cushion rise in to the air as Sukhoi directed.

David could hardly believe his eyes as he watched the cushion do his bidding. He had been frightened when he made the dagger stop before, but now he felt elation as he watched the cushion rise into the air. Here was the proof he had secretly been wishing for, the cushion moved by his thought, there was no denying it. He looked at the cushion and then at the expectant faces, and he realised then that he believed for the first time that he could actually do magic. With that belief came a confidence that he didn't know he had and he wanted to see how far he could go. He made the cushion rise to the ceiling of the Haram and just before it reached the top he brought it back down to sit a couple of inches above Christopher's head.

Christopher clapped and laughed as his brother made the cushion spin on top of his head before he brought it back down to sit in his hands.

Jennifer couldn't believe it, she clapped and laughed along with her brother and even David began to laugh as the realisation of what he had just accomplished finally sank in.

Sukhoi had never experienced anything like it. It had taken him a long time to master what David had done in seconds. He couldn't help but laugh along with the children, what else could he do, he thought, here before him; in the guise of this boy was a Kavacha Master, he had to be, no one else could perform such a feat.

They were all laughing and Sukhoi was patting David on the back with undisguised pride when Braduga and Socata returned.

"What's so funny?" Socata asked bemused.

Christopher rushed over to the two warriors, "Didn't you see? it was amazing!" He shouted and began to tell them all about the flying cushions. The two warriors listened to the boy with surprised looks on their faces as he explained.

Meanwhile, Sukhoi put his arm around David's shoulder and asked him if he would follow him over to the waterfall so they could have a quick chat. David, still smiling agreed.

"I think you must be Kavacha." He said without preamble.

"What?" David asked in surprise.

"You must be, there is no other explanation, I think when we get to Enkan Mys you must be tested." He said smiling.

David didn't know what to say, it must be a great honour; he assumed, but he didn't plan on staying in this place any longer than necessary. He wanted to get them all home, back to Featherstone, and back to their mother, there was no way he was going to go through some test and then train to be Kavacha, not when Sukhoi told him it could take years; even though a part of him wanted to. He didn't know what to say or what to do as Sukhoi waited for him to speak, an expectant look on his face.

"You honour me Sukhoi, but you know we have to get home, I'm not sure I'll have the time to train to be a Kavacha.

Sukhoi smiled, "I agreed to help you get home and that has not changed, but while you remain here would you like me help you master your gift?" Sukhoi said still smiling.

David nodded his agreement, though he wasn't sure he should be using magic at all. It still frightened him; even though he felt a confidence in himself grow when using it. He realised he needed help if he was going to try and control that power but he wasn't sure he should be trying to control it at all. He should just try and not to use it, someone could get hurt if he did something wrong, and that someone could easily be him. His mind raced as he thought of the pros and cons of training to use the magic but in the end he had to agree that it was better to try and control it than not.

"Yes Sukhoi that would be great." He said and smiled in return.

David thought about his gift and the elation he felt when using it, but it scared him. The things he had done with it so far had frightened him, but the potential use of his gift petrified him. He looked toward his new friend and thought about divulging his reservations but somehow couldn't bring himself to tell Sukhoi that he was scared. He felt the man would be very disappointed in him and he didn't want him to feel that way about him. Thinking such thoughts reminded him of his father and if his father would be proud of him now. The emptiness that had been with him since his father left returned in that instant and the jubilation he had felt wielding his magic disappeared.

"Are you ok David?" Sukhoi asked, a little concerned by the boys silence.

"I was just thinking that maybe I shouldn't be using this, this gift of mine," he whispered, "We'll hopefully be going home soon and I'd only be wasting your time." He finished weakly.

Sukhoi focused on the boy's face and using his Kavacha knowledge, he could just about see the conflicting emotions in him. He knew David was scared by his gift and he could also tell there was more to this boy than he first imagined, but he wouldn't push him into anything, not yet.

"It is up to you my friend," he began, "but if you want my help, you need only ask, but there is one thing you must know." He said quietly. "If you decide that you want me to teach you, whatever I do teach you must not be passed on to another, not even your brother and sister, is that understood?" He said soberly, raising an eyebrow as if to emphasise the point.

"Yes, I understand." He said relieved that the Kavacha wasn't going to make him do anything he didn't want to. David didn't think he would ask for Sukhoi's help but at least the opportunity was there if he wanted to take it.

Chapter Fourteen

Braduga was impatient; he was tired of waiting for the weather to improve and was anxious to find any signs of the beast's whereabouts or intentions. He hated the Gourtak with every fibre of his being and wanted nothing more than to go out side and track the monsters down and kill them if possible; even though he had responsibilities, the desire was eating him up inside. He decided to check the entrance again for about the hundredth time that day, he had to do something; the wondering and waiting were almost too great to bear.

Outside the wind had picked up its intensity, the snow was still falling and obscuring his view except for a white bright sheet of whiteness that covered anything and everything. This was useless, he thought, the Gourtak must have surely given up by now, especially as the Haram protected them against such creatures. He was just heading back into the entrance when he heard the blood-curdling cry of the beast, it was a distinctive sound only a Gourtak could make, and it didn't sound too far away. It sounded to Braduga like a battle cry, taunting him to come out of hiding and face his nemesis instead of cowering away in some deep dark hole like a Rabat. He could feel his heart pumping the blood through his veins as his adrenalin intensified. He quickly scanned the immediate area and then decided he had no choice, in order to protect the party from any future attack he needed to know whether the Gourtak were waiting for them or not. He knew it was only an excuse to hunt the creatures down, but the desire for vengeance was still burning deep in his heart. Pulling his furs tightly around him and with both his swords firmly secured on his back; but still easily accessible, he cautiously but deliberately headed down the pass, directly towards the creatures who had plagued his nightmares for far too long.

"How long has Brad been gone?" Sukhoi asked Socata, "I have not seen him for a while." Sukhoi had been talking with the children but he sensed something was wrong. He realised then that he hadn't seen Braduga for at least a couple of hours. He wouldn't have bothered checking but he knew that Braduga still hated the Gourtak for killing his brother and the warrior still ached for vengeance.

"Too long I think." Socata replied grabbing his furs and weapons. "I will go and check."

"Ok, but don't be too long." He shouted back as Socata rushed away to search for his friend.

The snowdrifts were deep in places and Braduga found it difficult to plough through. Visibility was still poor, but at least the snow was beginning to stop.

He couldn't see any tracks; the snow had covered them, but he was determined to find the Gourtak. Forcing his way along the snow-covered pass, he knew he was being reckless tracking the deadly creatures, but he couldn't help it. He hated the Gourtak with a vengeance for killing his brother, and although he had kept his blood lust for the creatures at bay, here and now was his opportunity for revenge. The circumstances weren't ideal, but it was as if his heart had taken over his mind since hearing the foul call, forcing him onward in search of the vile fiends, forward to an inevitable confrontation.

The snow was becoming compact, and he realised the temperature was dropping as the daylight diminished, but he also realised he would soon find it easier to move along the pass. Reckless wasn't the word for it, he knew he was being stupid, one man alone hunting one, possibly two Gourtak and he didn't even have a plan, but it didn't stop him, or even make him pause. On and on he went, eyes darting about and straining to catch one glimpse of movement, his body twisting and jerking at every unusual sound. Time meant nothing to him as he trudged through the snow; his mind focused purely on his search.

He sensed a presence as the last light of day dwindled away to nothingness. The snow had stopped falling, and it glistened in the moon light, sparkling like a sea of diamonds before him. It was cold, even with the furs wrapped around his body and his muscles were beginning to ache from exhaustion inflicted by the unyielding snow and his constant vigilance.

He felt the eyes on his back; he wondered briefly how his foe could have gotten behind him. He was sure the cry of the beast had come from in front of him. Had he made a fatal mistake, had the Gourtak lured him into its trap, he wondered? He stood perfectly still and began to regulate his breathing and relax his muscles before he drew his twin blades from his back and waited.

"He has gone." Socata stated on his return. He was covered head to toe in snow from searching beyond the entrance to the Haram, but even so he had returned empty-handed.

"The Gourtak, any signs?" Sukhoi asked. He knew something was wrong, but had been too slow, or too preoccupied to do anything about it.

"Yes, the young fool has headed down the pass, but a fresh set of tracks follows him" He replied.

"Should we go after him and warn him?" Jennifer asked.

"No," Sukhoi replied quietly. "It is too late for that; Brad will know soon enough that he is no longer the hunter, but the prey. He has wanted this fight for far too long, now he has it and may the Guardian protect him."

"Will he be ok?" Asked Christopher, concerned, "If these Gourtak are as bad as you say they are..." He couldn't finish the sentence.

"He is the greatest warrior Sakhalin has ever seen," Socata announced proudly, "if anyone can survive such an ordeal it will be he. I will wait at the entrance for his return." Socata finished quietly as he walked back towards the entrance with Sukhoi looking on, sadness evident in his expression.

"You don't think he will come back, do you?" David enquired.

"Socata was right when he said Brad is the greatest warrior in all of Sakhalin, but there are two Gourtak out there, they are fearsome, dangerous creatures; the odds are stacked against him, I am afraid to say." He replied.

"Shouldn't we at least try and help him then?" David asked.

"It is too late, he has been gone a long time and I would not risk your lives."

"Is there nothing we can do?" Jennifer asked, tears appearing in the corners of her eyes.

"We must wait and hope." With those words Sukhoi walked back to the table and sat down.

"There must be something we can do?" Jennifer said quietly to David.

"Maybe." David replied, an idea forming in his head.

"What? What is it?" She asked eagerly as her brother seemed to be concentrating on something. David grabbed hold of her sleeve and pulled her gently toward a couple of cushions by the wall furthest away from Sukhoi. They sat down and he whispered to her, "I have an idea, if it works we may be able to help Brad, but if not…" he paused and looked toward Sukhoi who was sitting at the table with his head in his hands, probably wondering if he would ever see his friend again.

"David what is it?" Jennifer said impatiently.

"Ok, sorry. You can speak with the Dragons through your mind right?" He continued.

Jennifer nodded, a thin half smile coming to her lips and a faraway look distracting her gaze as she thought of her new friends.

"Well, do you think it possible that you could speak with those creatures? Maybe tell them not to kill Brad and maybe hunt something else?" He said rapidly, so she wouldn't find this idea ludicrous.

He had been wondering; ever since Jennifer had revealed her gift, if she could speak with other creatures in Sakhalin. It had seemed plausible to him that she would be able to. If she could speak with one creature here; why not others? The only problem being of course was that the Dragons weren't indigenous to Sakhalin, but he thought it worth a try anyway. Now they had been given the opportunity to try out his theory. He hoped it worked, because maybe Braduga's life depended on it, and ultimately theirs.

She stared at him a few moments, and David thought she would laugh at his suggestion at first; then she gave him a weak smile and nodded.

"I'll try," she whispered, and although she didn't sound convinced it was going to work, at least she thought it had the enough potential to give it a go.

Jennifer wasn't sure how to tackle this suggestion of her brother's. It sounded as if it could work, but how was she to make it work. She tried to put an image of the creatures in her mind from the description of them she had been given. Then she tried to push her thoughts out to the image, her face screwed up in concentration, as she shouted in her mind at the image before her. The image kept fading, she realised that without actually seeing the creatures, it would be difficult to communicate with them, but still she tried.

"It's no good Dave, its not working." She said deflated after an intense couple of minutes.

"Try again Jen." He pleaded with her. He knew deep down that this should work, though he couldn't tell anyone why, it just seemed right somehow.

"It's no good, I don't know what I'm doing, and I have tried." She replied dismayed.

David looked at his sister's deflated face and could see tears of frustration appearing. It was wrong of him to push the issue and make her try again but he did anyway, because Braduga's life could depend upon it.

"Jen," he said quietly and deliberately, "you must try again, for Braduga, for us all, please try."

Jennifer lifted her eyes to his and she was surprised to see a confident and focused David looking back at her. David had changed quite a lot recently but she didn't expect to see this doggedness that was now evident in his eyes. She was about to tell him to leave her alone but then whether he meant it or not the look changed to one of encouragement, which suddenly imbued her with a strength she didn't think she had. Behind those eyes was a belief, a belief in what she could accomplish if she only tried.

She nodded, "Ok, I'll try."

"Just feel for the creature Jen," he encouraged her, "there can't be many up here in this weather. Just try and reach out with your thoughts and speak to anything you come across." He finished weakly as he watched intently his sister's expression change from one of improbability to one on dogged determination.

The idea of her projecting her thoughts had just literally popped into his head, but it seemed right, he believed his sister had the ability to communicate with the creatures of this land. He didn't know why he knew this, but he believed it to be true.

Concentration was etched on Jennifer's face as she tried to reach out as

David asked. She wasn't sure if it was going to work, but she was damn well going to give it a good try.

Braduga could sense the Gourtak; he couldn't hear it as it moved closer towards him, but that didn't matter, he knew it was there and he knew it was coming for him. The creature's movements in the snow were slow and calculated, it was built for the hunt and this beast was now in its element. Braduga knew it was just a matter of time before it was close enough to pounce, but still he waited, quiet and unmoving, a statuesque figure waiting for death. He had trained hard to be the best that he could possibly be, and now all his training would be required to defeat this nightmare. The creatures had been tormenting his dreams since the death of his brother, but now he was ready, now he would have his revenge, or he would die.

A fortunate shift in the wind alerted him to the creature's attack and he turned swiftly as the Gourtak leapt at its intended victim.

Time appeared to slow down as their eyes locked for a brief moment. The creature was fierce and immense, its muscles taut as it sprung at its foe. Braduga was surprised to see; what appeared to be a confused look on the beast's face as it pounced. It was a momentary look, but it was sufficient to divert its concentration and Braduga quickly capitalised on this fact. His swords whistled through the air and caught the creature in mid-air, severing its head from its neck, blood splattering his face as he did so. Gourtak were extremely difficult to kill, their bodies were protected by armour-like scales, which couldn't be penetrated by sword or arrow. But they did have one vulnerable spot, an opening between the scales around the neck, and that is where Braduga's blades found their mark; first one blade then the other in one fluid motion. As he struck; with the Gourtak's concentration broken, it fell lifelessly to the ground. Braduga sunk to his knees in the snow beside the dead creature, he couldn't believe what he had done, he had finally killed one of the loathsome beasts. He had expected to feel some small measure of satisfaction, or joy of any kind for that matter, but as he looked over at the corpse, he felt nothing. The creature had died swiftly, two precise strikes had delivered the two blows that killed the creature and Braduga couldn't believe his luck. That was too easy, Braduga thought to himself, the Gourtak were formidable hunters and not easy to kill, but something had broken the creatures concentration, and given Braduga the advantage, an advantage he was grateful to take, but an advantage he shouldn't have had.

He knew he was good; he had been trained by the best instructors Sakhalin had, but he also knew his limitations. When he left the protection of the Haram he hadn't expected to live to see another day, but now, he had been given a chance. It had been foolish to search out the creatures, but now he had been given the opportunity to get back, it was an opportunity he was going to take, because he realised he may not be so lucky the next time. Unfortunately, as soon as he had decided to go back to his friends, a soft but menacing growl erupted from the outcrop of rocks to his left. All thoughts of returning were quickly eliminated from his mind as he turned to face the biggest and fiercest opponent of his life.

"I think I've just made contact with one of the Gourtak?" Jennifer gulped as she whispered to David, "it was terrible, it was just one singular thought, but it made me lose my concentration."

David could tell that whatever the thought was, it had deeply disturbed his sister.

"What was it?" He asked her, though he believed the thought was probably too dreadful to even contemplate.

"Kill." She whispered.

"It said that?" He said, shocked, he didn't even entertain the possibility that the Gourtak could talk, well, not like them.

Jennifer paused briefly before answering. "I don't think it said that to me, I think it was just a thought that was in its mind at the time."

"Brad?" David uttered quietly under his breath.

"I'm not sure Dave, maybe, but I kept shouting, "NO!" At the creature until I lost contact." She said as she wiped back the tears that were falling from her eyes.

David put a comforting arm around her shoulders and then unexpectedly she began to sob into his chest at the thought of what could be happening to their new friend.

The Gourtak had obviously witnessed the attack of his kin on the man before it, because its attention was focused upon the twin blades Braduga held in his hands. It didn't move directly toward Braduga but merely moved around him, forcing the warrior to turn toward his foe as the creature moved. It moved with caution, never taking its reptilian-like eyes off its quarry.

The second Gourtak was huge, and fearsome, and probably half as big again as the corpse by his feet. They were all exceptionally strong and fast for their size but Braduga knew all about the creatures, he had studied their strengths and weaknesses since the death of his brother. He had been surprised by his success from his first encounter with the beasts, and although he was prepared, he wasn't expecting the same success this time.

The wind's direction changed and Braduga was appalled by the stench of rotten flesh which seemed to be emanating from the creature. He didn't allow the smell to impair his vision, even if it was burning his nostrils and making his eyes water. Why hadn't he smelled the other creature he wondered? But now was not the time to focus on whys? Now he had to concentrate on the deadly creature facing him.

Braduga had the feeling that the beast was waiting for something, though he couldn't think what. It was probably just waiting for the best opportunity to attack, so as it circled him, he tried to remain calm and he waited patiently for the inevitable attack to take place.

Braduga knew he probably wouldn't survive this encounter, but he would try and inflict as much harm on to the creature as he could.

The seconds ticked by but still the creature showed no willingness to attack him, it merely circled and watched.

"What are you waiting for you big ugly brute?" Braduga shouted at it.

The Gourtak didn't pause, but continued to walk around the warrior.

Suddenly it did stop. Braduga prepared himself, expecting the creature to attack, and he relaxed his muscles whilst at the same time he increased his grip on his swords.

"Voice!" The Gourtak gave a guttural shout as it banged its head with his massive clawed hands.

Braduga was astounded and gave an involuntary half step backwards. He knew the Gourtak were intelligent but never before had he heard that they could actually speak. It was a fantastic revelation; if he could communicate with it maybe he could reason with it. He was thinking of all the possibilities this presented when the fiend attacked.

The speed in which it moved was amazing, but although Braduga was surprised by the creature's ability to speak he was still prepared for any attack it might offer. He managed to side step, away from the Gourtak's embrace as it sprang forward, barely moving out of the way in time, but still managing to swing his sword in retaliation. Unfortunately the sword hit the scales on the Gourtak's arm which were harder than any armour made by a blacksmith, and the blow clanged off the arm, harmlessly.

Braduga tried to move out of the way quickly to try and acquire a better position in which to prepare for the next attack. The Gourtak anticipated his every move, working to block the warrior's retreat while continuing its own attack. Backing away with every step; slipping slightly on the new snow, which continued to fall all around, Braduga continued to rein blow after blow upon the creature; even though he knew he was doing no harm. The Gourtak merely knocked each blow away with his massive arms as if they were no more than a temporary distraction. Though, Braduga did realise that his foe made sure that its neck was firmly out of reach of the blades he was wielding, which impaired its attack somewhat.

Braduga finally found some firm ground in which he could mount his own attack and waited for the creature to attack once more.

The Gourtak stopped just out of reach and looked at the warrior as he slowly twisted his boots into the ground, preparing to attack.

Again the creature spoke, "Voice!" It shrieked again, once more hitting his head with his hand and shaking it violently.

Braduga didn't know what the creature was trying to tell him, but he wasn't about to be distracted by something as powerful and deadly as the Gourtak.

Like lightning, the Gourtak attacked again, massive clawed arms trying to reach its victim, intending to crush the life from his body. But Braduga was ready this time and had finally realised how best to defeat this foe. He managed to duck and weave around the creature, dancing to avoid the creature's embrace. Strike after strike he landed but the armour-like scales covering the Gourtak's body protected it from harm. He began to make the creature move away from him as he attacked again and again. The force and intensity of the attacks ensured the Gourtak had no choice but to retreat. He wanted the creature to move to the edge of the path; he had noticed that there was a large hole that dropped a thousand feet, but it appeared from the reluctance of the Gourtak to do just that, that it too knew of the hole. It increased its own ferocity and mounted its own attack, forcing Braduga back. He couldn't believe how fast it could move, and couldn't help but think how lucky he was to have killed the first one. He could do with that luck again he thought as the Gourtak mounted yet another attack. Braduga knew he was getting tired, but he was relentless in his attacks, matching the beast blow for blow. This made it angry especially as he always managed to evade each of the blows the creature made.

The seconds laboured into minutes as the contest continued each searching for a way behind the other's defences. Braduga couldn't understand why the creature just didn't rush him, the armour would protect him against any attack he could mount, but a small smile appeared on the mouth of the Gourtak. He hadn't seen it before, but he realised that all along the creature had been playing with him.

The Gourtak were a formidable killing machine, whatever they hunted they killed. Braduga had been lucky enough to kill one of he beasts, but it was pure luck, nothing more. This beast had weighed up all factors and realised that the man before it, probably didn't have any magic and could be defeated like all the rest of its prey. It had been playing a game of cat and mouse with him, probably to sap his strength until he had nothing left, then and only then would it attack without mercy. The realisation hit Braduga hard. He had heard all the stories about him being the greatest warrior Sakhalin had ever had, and maybe he had even come to believe them a little. But here he was, on top of a snow capped mountain trying to destroy a creature that knew nothing but killing and it was playing with him.

Anger flared in his heart, his head pounded and he felt the rush of adrenalin enter his limbs. Renewed with a strength found from deep within himself, he faced his foe and smiled.

Christopher didn't want to disturb Sukhoi and it looked like David and Jennifer didn't want to be disturbed either so he walked over to the entrance to the Haram and found Socata staring at the falling snow.

"Are you ok?" He asked the warrior, though he knew it was a stupid question to ask, he really didn't know what else to say.

Socata turned to face the boy and said in reply, "He will return." Then he turned back to the falling snow to wait for his friend.

"I hope so." Christopher whispered and stood opposite the concerned warrior and kept him company through his silent vigil.

"Jen?" David whispered into her ear. She had been crying silently on his chest for a few minutes now but he had to get her attention. There were two Gourtak on the mountain and he wanted to know if she could reach them.

"What?" She said lifting her head and looking into his eyes.

"I'm sorry to ask you this sis, but could you try and communicate with the Gourtak again, we need to know what they're doing." He replied.

"We know what they're doing," she whispered, "Kill." She said in disgust, "Killing is all they know." She finished.

David could hear the fear and repulsion in her voice but he needed answers. He didn't want to think about what was happening out there to Braduga, and didn't really know how he was going to explain it to his sister but he wanted to know if the Gourtak would still be interested in the rest of them if they had killed the brave warrior. His heart sank as the thought hit him, especially at his own reaction to the possible demise of someone he had begun to know and like. Thoughts of his father immediately came to his mind, but he had no choice but to put them to one side. He didn't have time to think about that for now, he needed to know if they were still in danger and the only person who had a possible answer was his sister.

As gently as he could he explained his thoughts to her and when he finished she sat there staring at him as if he were a stranger.

"What?" He asked. He knew he was being callous for thinking of them and not of Braduga, but it was his responsibility to take care of his brother and sister and he had to make sure they all got home safe and sound. He had to think of them now and if that made him sound callous, so be it. Deep down he knew he was right to think about it this way, but as he looked into Jennifer's eyes he could tell that she found his words heartless so he looked away, unable to face her. If he could do anything to help he would have, but Jennifer was the only one that could possibly help now.

Jennifer instinctively knew that her brother was only thinking of her and her brother, but the way he explained himself sounded so cold and detached. As he looked away from her, she realised he must have seen something in her look that hurt him, so she softened her look and tried to give him a slight smile of acknowledgement.

"Ok," she whispered, "I'll give it a go."

She sat up straight and folding her hands together in her lap she closed her eyes and tried to concentrate of the Gourtak once more. The seconds ticked by as beads of sweat ran down her face as she focused her attention on communicating with the creatures. She tried to imagine the Gourtak in her mind and then imagined herself shouting at it. Again and again she called out to the image in her mind, trying to re-establish the tiniest link she had experienced earlier.

The creature attacked again but Braduga was ready now. With determination fuelled by the thought of the creature laughing at him he attacked with vigour. Thrust after thrust he aimed at the creature's neck, only to be pushed aside, but with satisfaction he could see that the smile had left the Gourtak's face; presuming it was a smile at all, he thought. He tried to bring his sword up under its chin, but it merely shrugged its shoulder in the way of the sword and crawled at his shoulder in a counter attack. He wasn't fast enough as the claws ripped across his shoulder and he could feel the blood running down his right arm followed by an intense pain from gashes. He knew he had to finish this soon or he would be dead. He moved backward and staggered, going down on one knee. He still managed to lift the sword up in his left hand in case the creature attacked, but the right arm wouldn't move now. The Gourtak snarled at him in what seemed to be amusement, sensing its victory, it finally moved in for the kill. Working its way over to the wounded warrior it gave a cry of triumph. It reached forward to its injured quarry; the half smile had returned to its lips. The Gourtak had underestimated the strength of its victim and as it moved closer Braduga was ready.

He knew the creature was going to attack at that moment and had in fact planned for it. As he crouched on the ground he had taken a firm hold of the sword in his right hand. The gashes inflicted by the beast's claws were deep but Braduga knew he had sufficient strength left for one more blow. As the Gourtak reached forward Braduga tried to attack him with the sword in his left hand which the creature knocked away with ease. It was at that moment that Braduga lifted his sword in his right hand and thrust the blade into the Gourtak's throat. It hadn't perceived any threat from the wounded arm and had not expected the attack.

It cried out in pain and then shouted in agony as it shook its head. "Voice!" The blade which was lodged in its throat moved upward with every turn of its head and forced its way up into its brain. It staggered back, but immediately Braduga was on his feet and grabbing hold of his sword with his good arm he slashed at the creature's neck with the last of his strength.

The Gourtak fell to the ground and thrashed about as its lifeblood drained from a gaping hole in its neck and throat. It tried in vain to grab its foe but Braduga dived and rolled to safety. Retrieving his other sword he attacked the creature mercilessly again and again, trying to penetrate the beast's armour. With its strength ebbing away, the Gourtak rasped one final cry of defeat and then it died.

Exhausted, Braduga looked at the two dead creatures before him. He knew he had been lucky, stupid, but lucky all the same. He didn't know why the Gourtak had kept saying what it did, but the voice it was hearing had probably saved his life. He shook his head in disbelief, and then raised it to the sky above. It had finally stopped snowing, with the last snowflakes floating down from above to land on his eyes. He gave a deep sigh as he looked at the two corpses again and as he turned away a tear fell to his cheek.

"For you Ambar, for you my brother, rest in peace." He whispered, then pulling his furs around his shoulders, he set off back down the pass, and back to the warmth and protection of the Haram.

Chapter Fifteen

"Damn." Jennifer cursed.

"You ok Jen?" David asked concerned as he watched her eyes flicker open and an annoyed look appear on her face

"Yes," She replied, "I thought I had made contact a few times there, but I've lost it again". She finished.

"You tried your best Jen." David said giving her a thin lipped smile. "It was a long shot, but at least you tried." He said trying to comfort her.

"I'm sure I can do it," Jennifer said as she scowled in frustration, "but I must be doing something wrong." She whispered to herself.

"I'm sorry I can't help you sis." David said in response, though Jennifer seemed not to notice or hear him as she continued to scowl in thought.

"I could have sworn it tried to talk to me." She said. "Then there was nothing."

David felt defeated, he thought if anyone could have helped their friend it would have been Jennifer, but obviously he had hoped for too much. He told her to rest and then went to fetch her something to drink. When he returned, she leaned against him and went to sleep, totally exhausted. He combed her long blonde hair with his fingers and regretted trying to make her do what she had; just on a flash thought that came into his head. He just thought it would work, and now his sister was paying for his stupid idea.

David eventually managed to put his sister's sleeping head on a cushion and then he got to his feet and walked over to the table where Sukhoi was still sitting. He sat down next to him, but didn't say anything, even when Sukhoi smiled weakly at him.

They both sat there silently as they waited for any news. All sense of time disappeared in the silence and then they were joined by a sleepy looking Jennifer, who sat down next to her brother.

Socata and Christopher approached the table covered in snow a little while later and by the look on both their faces, there was still no news.

"The temperature has dropped considerably over the last couple of hours." Socata said to Sukhoi, who nodded in response.

"You can't see anything outside now." Christopher added gloomily.

"What you been up to Chris?" David asked trying to change the subject.

"Socata has been telling me all about Brad, from when he first arrived at Enkan Mys and the trouble he caused, to him finishing his training with full honours." Christopher said with a sad smile on his face.

Socata smiled fondly at the boy before turning to his Kavacha, "At least it's stopped snowing."

Sukhoi nodded, but still didn't say anything.

"Socata, tell David about the time Brad defeated four of the best swordsmen at Enkan Mys with just a staff." Christopher said with a glint of excitement in his eyes.

"That story is grossly exaggerated." Braduga said as he entered the cavern.

Everyone was on their feet immediately as they all rushed over to help the warrior as he staggered into their midst.

"He's wounded!" Jennifer shouted as Socata grabbed him before he fell exhausted with blood dripping from his arm.

"Bring him over to the table Socata." Sukhoi shouted as the children parted to make way.

"Is it bad?" Socata asked in concern.

"I will survive." Braduga said and smiled weakly at his friend, "It's not as bad as it looks." He said quietly and then dropped into unconsciousness.

Socata checked his friend over for wounds but only found the one, which he tended to quickly. "He has lost quite a lot of blood, but I think the cold prevented more loss. I think he will recover with rest."

"Do you think he killed the Gourtak?" Christopher asked.

"We will let him sleep now, questions can wait until tomorrow." Sukhoi replied.

Socata applied a foul smelling poultice on the wound, saying it would draw out any poison that maybe infecting the area and he would change it himself during the night. He tended to Braduga all night, worried about infection and fever, but Braduga was strong and he surmised the only thing the warrior needed was plenty of rest.

The weather improved through the night, but Sukhoi knew they couldn't leave the protection of the Haram until Braduga was feeling better. The journey through the pass would be too difficult in his present state. Braduga slept all night and most of the following morning, but when he did wake, he was ravenous.

"I know, you don't have to tell me," Jennifer smiled at him as he woke rubbing his belly. "You could eat a Tarqasian Pie."

Astonished, he laughed. "That's right I could."

"Well, we haven't got any, but I'll find you something."

"Thank you Jennifer." He said gratefully.

"You seem to be recovering well?" Sukhoi said with a smile as he walked over and sat beside his friend.

"Yes, feeling ok I think, what's the weather like?" He enquired.

"It is clearing, but we shall rest here another day, our path is still full of snow and ice, it takes time for the snow to melt." He replied still smiling.

Braduga knew Sukhoi well enough to know that behind the smile he wasn't happy with him putting his life in danger and that of the party. He also knew that the only reason they were staying in the comfort and protection of the Haram was to allow him some rest and respite. So instead of replying he merely nodded to say he understood the situation and that he also knew this incident wouldn't be forgotten until the two of them had spoken about it.

"Brad!" Christopher shouted as he ran over to the wounded warrior, excitement dancing in his eyes. He had been waiting rather impatiently for the warrior to regain consciousness. He quickly plumped up a cushion and then settled down on it. "You have to tell me all about the battle with the Gourtak." He said to his new hero.

Braduga smiled somewhat sadly at the boy with the big expectant grin on his face. He didn't really want to speak about the incident but then Jennifer appeared with some food, followed by David and Socata. They were all there now and waiting for him to tell his tale.

Braduga didn't like to talk about himself or his exploits; which were normally grossly over exaggerated, but he felt he owed everyone an explanation about his actions. Besides, he thought, there were a few questions he wanted answers to and maybe someone would be able to provide those answers, if he told his story.

"Ok, but I will keep it brief." He began.

Everyone waited patiently as he slowly raised himself into a sitting position.

"First of all I know it was stupid to leave the protection of the Haram, and I know by doing so, I put all your lives in danger, so I apologise for that!" He said meekly.

"I for one am just glad you are alive." Jennifer said blushing.

"So are we all." Socata echoed, "But please, tell us what happened."

"Ok," He laughed in appreciation, "I heard and then found the first Gourtak down the trail." And then he told them what had happened and emphasised how lucky he had been, and how stupid he felt for doing it in the first place as everyone listened intently.

When he had finished his tale, everyone just stared at him but for different reasons. Sukhoi and Socata could hardly believe that their friend had killed two of the creatures never mind one.

It was an amazing feat that had never before been accomplished.

Although the children couldn't really comprehend the full impact of what Braduga had told them, they did understand that the Gourtak were ferocious creatures that couldn't be killed easily, yet their new friend had killed two of them.

"Did you say that the first Gourtak seemed distracted somehow?" Jennifer asked, her forehead creasing in thought.

"Yes, it was really strange, but when our eyes met, it was as if its attention was else where."

"I think that was you Jennifer," David whispered to his sister.

"If not for that distraction, I don't think I would be here now." Braduga said quietly as he remembered the confused look on the face of the first Gourtak.

"Maybe." Jennifer whispered back, but David noticed a slight smile of triumph on his sister's face as she thought about it.

"It's funny, but the second Gourtak kept shouting about some voice in it's head and if it hadn't shook its head the way it did, it would have probably killed me. As it was, it probably killed itself by lodging my sword into its brain."

"That must have been the second time you tried to make contact with the creatures." David whispered again excitedly.

Jennifer just nodded, but her mind was racing by the thought of what she may have accomplished. Not only had she possibly managed to communicate with some fearsome indigenous creatures, but through her actions she may have contributed in saving the life of a member of their small group. Her head was spinning and she was finding it difficult to focus as she deliberated on what all this meant to her; to them.

Sukhoi had heard the conversation between the brother and sister; though no one else appeared to have heard. If he had heard them correctly it was the girl that had been instrumental in saving the life of Braduga through her talents. He was aware that she didn't really know what she was doing, and he could understand her reluctance to tell anyone, but it opened up many more questions on who these children were and where they came from. They had saved two lives since joining the group; one of which was his, so he was extremely grateful that they had found them.

Both David and Jennifer had a magic that he could only dream of, which made them both amazing and dangerous at the same time. If anyone else found out about these abilities and tried to exploit them, he wouldn't want to think about the results.

Braduga went over every little detail of his experience; prompted mainly by Christopher, who was insatiable, until finally David told his brother that Braduga needed some rest.

The morning of the following day, Braduga was adamant he was fit enough to continue the journey. Socata checked his wound but reluctantly agreed he had sufficiently healed enough to carry on. So with that, the group packed their belongings and with plenty of food they left the Haram behind them.

The weather had cleared beyond their expectations, as they travelled along the pass.

It wasn't long before they came across the bodies of the dead Gourtak. The children were amazed by their appearance, liking them to a cross between a bear, a lion and an armadillo, but the size of them had obviously been the biggest surprise. Christopher's face turned ashen as he looked them over, especially their teeth and sharpened claws.

Their respect for Braduga seemed to increase ten fold after seeing the dead bodies especially that of Christopher, who constantly chatted to the warrior as they walked along.

With the weather clearing and the snow melting, the journey along the pass grew increasingly easier. Sukhoi pointed to strange plants and animals they came across, trying to give them as much information as he could, and the children breathed it all in. The rest of the journey through the mountains passed without incident and when they finally came to the last ridge and looked to where the path lead they couldn't believe the sight before them.

At the base of the mountain was a vast forest, in the distance they could see a river running through it and at the far end they could just make out an enormous lake, or maybe the sea, they couldn't tell from this distance.

Everything looked so small, yet so full of life.

"There." Sukhoi pointed. "There is Enkan Mys." He said.

There was nothing to see, it was too far in the distance, but Sukhoi assured them, it was there, and there also, was their way home.

Their journey the other side of the mountain was both quicker and easier as the land on the other side of the mountain was higher above sea level. Their pace quickened so by nightfall they finally came to the end of the pass arriving at the edge of the forest. It looked frightening and uninviting, and Sukhoi could see that the children didn't relish the idea of entering it in darkness.

"Right," Sukhoi said as he stopped by the nearest tree. "It is late; we will camp here tonight, and have a good start on the morning."

The children were clearly relieved and nodded their agreement with Sukhoi's plans.

They laid their furs on the ground in a circle and ate a quick meal before settling down to sleep. Socata kept first watch but it was a long time before the children felt comfortable enough to go to sleep. Their dreams were full of strange creatures, the Raiders and Dragons, but David's dreams were consumed by one thing, and that was Nuba Driss.

They all woke often in the night, but when they did so; there to comfort them was one of the companions, speaking softly to them until they found sleep again.

He was walking down a brightly lit corridor; all white and clinical, an odour of rotten flesh seemed to permeate the atmosphere; the smell strong and nauseating, burning his nostrils with its putrid breath. A dense misty fog crawled along the floor and around his feet, but he wasn't interested in the fog or the smell for that matter; his gaze was focused on the obscure, indeterminate figure before him. He was walking toward that figure now; although he felt as if he was actually floating on the mist rather than walking, the dark figure watching and waiting for his arrival. Before he knew what was happening he was standing before the figure who was dressed in a monk's habit, its face obscured from view by an overlarge hood.

He knew he was shaking with fright, but he could do nothing about that, his body was no longer his own, he had no power over it anymore, the figure before him was in total control. Then he heard the footsteps behind him, faint but there nevertheless, and heading in his direction. His body began to stop shivering and he began to relax, that was until he realised the hooded figure was raising its head toward him. He tried to shout again and again, "No, you will not have me, leave me alone!" But the figure's head continued to rise.

The footsteps were getting closer, their pace more frequent but he could not take his eyes away from the figure before him. He couldn't do anything and the figure lifted its head. He screamed!

David woke the next morning feeling restless and irritable. His sleep had been plagued by bad dreams yet again. He had been protected from them whilst he was in the Haram but now he was away from that sanctuary they had returned worse than ever. One dream that really disturbed him was his inability to help his brother and sister with his gift when they were being attacked by some warriors. He was lying on the floor and watched in rigid terror as both Jennifer and Christopher were killed before him. He had tried to change the dream; as he had done so often at home, but this dream always ended the same way. It unnerved him that at the most crucial time in his life, in the protection of his family; his abilities had let him down. It was one of many dreams, but the worse dream was always the one that featured Nuba Driss.

Shaking his head; trying to erase the images in his mind, he rose to his feet. He nudged his brother and sister awake and as he stretched the weariness from his body he smelled something delicious emanating from a large warm fire tended by Socata. All dreams were firmly put aside as they all walked over and watched strips of meaty flesh being roasted on the fire.

"What is it?" David asked.

"Meat." Socata replied, taking some of the cooked meat away from the fire and replacing it with more raw strips.

"Yes, but what type of meat?" David inquired.

"Rabat." He replied. Their blank expressions induced him to provide a description of the creature. The Rabat was a large rodent that could be found in almost every part of Sakhalin and it was something resembling a rabbit; they deduced, but without the big ears and fluffy tail.

"It smells lovely." Christopher said, mouth watering, obviously not bothered which animal the meat came from, provided he had his fill. Though the look of Jennifer's face implied she wasn't half as excited as her brother about trying the food.

"Tastes even better and it's almost ready now." Socata added. "Go and freshen up over there and by the time you get back it will be done." He said pointing to the side of the mountain where a light cascade of water was dripping down into a shallow pool.

True to his word, Socata had the food read when they returned and it wasn't long until everyone was tucking in wholeheartedly. The meat was a little spicy to the taste but wonderful never the less and was quickly devoured. The spirits of everyone were definitely rising when they had finally finished their fill of Rabat, washed down with the re-energising Khulanha drink.

Refreshed and full of the delicious meat, they continued on their journey. The route through the forest was difficult to follow, changing from quite a wide path to following what appeared to be an animal trail at times, but no one seemed particularly bothered at first.

After a while of cutting through one trail onto another, David was getting a little confused by the general direction and disarray the tracks were taking them. "Is there no direct path through this forest?" David asked Sukhoi as they changed direction again for the third time in twenty minutes.

"Not this way David; not anymore, long ago there was a direct path from the mountains through the forest to Enkan Mys. When the four tribes lived together in harmony, all the roads were well kempt, but now we must rely on the animal trails through the forests."

"So there's another way then." He asked.

"Yes, there is another easier trail through the mountains and through this forest but to take that one would have added an extra month at least onto our journey." Sukhoi replied.

"Another month." David said quietly. "I should be thankful then."

Sukhoi smiled as he watched the boy trudging along behind his brother and sister; head down and looking bleak.

"Our path does improve, especially the closer we get to the towns and villages." Sukhoi announced. "There are a few roads which have been maintained to some degree; for visiting tinkers and merchants, but I must admit, even those are in need of repair."

"Will we actually visit these villages and towns?" He asked intrigued but a little frightened as well. He wanted to meet more people from this land but was a little apprehensive; especially if they were like the Raiders he had met, but he didn't voice his trepidation.

"Yes, "he replied, "Although I must admit we will try and steer clear of some."

"Why's that?" Christopher asked. He had been listening intently and was eager to see other people.

"Let me just say that some places have bad men, like the Raiders we bumped into earlier." He replied shrugging his shoulders.

Christopher gulped as he remembered the Raiders and the half smile he had on his lips vanished.

They continued to walk through the forest until finally Braduga; who had been scouting further up the trails, returned.

"Baveystock is about a half mile ahead, but I'm surprised the Archers haven't approached us yet!" He said, a concerned look creasing his brow.

"Archers?" David asked.

Sukhoi turned to the three children. "Sorry, I should have explained, Baveystock is a small garrison; commanded by an old rascal friend of mine, Maroc. It is the furthest most outpost from Enkan Mys. There are a detachment of soldiers posted there that are to act as lookout against any attack. The soldiers assigned there were personally trained by Maroc who used to be the Master at Arms in Enkan Mys many years ago. Those soldiers were trained to the highest standard; more as Ruedin than mere soldiers and are exceptional warriors with most weapons but predominately the bow. Hence, everyone now refers to them as the Archers. They have been following us for the last five or six miles."

The children's heads moved around nervously, looking in one direction and then another to see if they could locate the Archers.

Sukhoi laughed. "Do not worry my friends; if they thought we were a danger to them, they would have tried to kill us by now."

David couldn't help but continue to look around the forest but didn't miss the remark Sukhoi had made about trying to kill them. They would try, but Sukhoi was obviously confident that they wouldn't succeed.

"Do not try and look for them either, they are masters of camouflage and concealment." He said as he continued to walk along the trail.

David edged up to his sister and asked, "I don't suppose you can sense anything?"

She looked over at her brother before shaking her head. "No." She knew roughly were the Archers were, but they moved about so quickly that she couldn't tell where they were now or how many of them were out there.

As the daylight began to fade they finally saw signs of recent use along the trail and a few strips of land that had been fenced off and used for farming. They smelled the village long before they actually came across it. The village was surrounded by a large timber perimeter construction and the ground before it had been cleared at least a hundred feet to the forest. The clearing probably ran around the entire village so anyone approaching would be spotted immediately as they left the protection of the trees. The mild westerly wind brought a whiff of wood smoke from the drab wooden houses which were hunched together in a circle to form the little village, which could be seen through the one open gate of the main entrance.

As they drew closer they could smell the human and animal stench that seemed to permeate the atmosphere. The ground was still wet from an earlier storm, which only enhanced the smell the closer they got. It was the smell of the cooking fires, which gradually began to overwhelm all other smells, and saved their nostrils. Seasoned meats were being roasted on the open fires that could be seen through the open windows, pleasant odours that tantalised the taste buds as they walked through the open gate and peered into the nearest houses.

Most villages were known to be markets and gathering places for people who lived in the area; this village was far from that. It still looked like a village, but there was an atmosphere of readiness about the place. This was emphasised by the way the guards watched them as they passed through the gate. It appeared that the guards were just looking them over, but a feeling of intense scrutiny followed them as they walked past. Once through the gates, everything seemed organised and controlled. There was a neatness and tidiness that wasn't normally associated with a normal country village. The one path leading into the village was swept and smooth and everything seemed to have a dedicated place. The Guards made no effort to stop them but there was a soldier waiting for them as they walked up to the guard house. He was quite a big man with a stern look on his face and with his hands on hips, he didn't look happy to see them. Remarkably, there were no other people to be seen anywhere else. There were no children playing in the mud, causing a raucous and getting into mischief, no village women chasing or chastising them for it. No women gossiping over the fence with a neighbour about village life or how lazy their good for nothing husbands were. The village was almost deserted, and they could tell that the soldier before them was more agitated than angry; though the cause was unknown.

"Is everything well?" Sukhoi asked as the soldier approached the group. Sukhoi didn't recognise the soldier and that worried him, he knew all the Archers by name and this soldier wasn't one of them.

The soldier looked Sukhoi up and down and regarded the others in the group quickly before coming to attention and addressing him.

"All is well Kavacha, for the moment, "He added, "but we have been receiving reports of too many Koutla in the forest." He said nervously.

"Yes, we bumped into a few ourselves." Sukhoi replied.

"Where is everybody corporal?" Braduga asked the soldier.

The soldier turned toward the warrior who had just spoken and was just about to report when recognition suddenly lighted his face. He had noticed the crossed swords on his back, but the penny didn't drop to who the warrior was until now. The swords were better than any picture or painting and only one warrior could carry those swords that way. Every soldier knew it and some even tried to emulate their hero, but didn't have the skill and expertise to draw their weapons with the same grace as Braduga. Something incomprehensible came out of the corporal's mouth, the meaning merely lost in his surprise and awe in being confronted by his hero. The corporal tried again to relate what information he knew and he was at least partially coherent.

"Is he ok?" Christopher asked Socata quietly, surprised by the reaction of the soldier.

Socata smiled at the boy." He's fine, he's just realised who he's speaking to, and Braduga always gets this reception from any soldier posted away from Enkan Mys for a long time."

"Why?" Christopher asked.

"Braduga has a fierce reputation, he is a master swordsman first and foremost but he is also a master with most other weapons that we use. He is revered by almost every soldier, loved by the ladies and envied by the Lords. He has everything they wish to one day obtain;

prowess, adoration, respect and so on, he is their hero in many respects.

Christopher blushed at that last remark, for he felt the same way about the warrior, though he didn't believe he looked as googly-eyed as the corporal before him did.

The corporal eventually divulged that almost every member of the village was in attendance at the village's only public house. He pointed to the largest building in the centre of the village but Sukhoi and his Ruedin had been to the village many times before and did not need directions.

The buildings surrounding the Inn appeared dull and lifeless in comparison as it was obvious that it had just been painted. The walls had a bright white look, but the painter had obviously been in a rush as there were splashes of paint everywhere. The building still looked decidedly weathered and in need of some repair but the paint helped. "Guardian's Rest" proclaimed the new wooden sign hanging over the wide thick wooden double doorway. The doors themselves, their thick brass handles glinting in the last light of the evening, were folded back against the wide timbers of the front wall and a bright warm and inviting light shone out from every window.

Socata addressed Sukhoi, but everyone heard his words. "Looks like Maroc has been busy."

"Yes my friend, but it is about time. The place was looking a bit run down the last time we passed through here.

Socata nodded in agreement but didn't say anything.

"I wonder why all the villagers are in the Inn?" He said, one of his eyebrows lifting to emphasise his point.

A deafening cacophony escaped the Inn at that moment; cries of laughter pervaded the silent village like a cockerel screeching his call into the breaking dawn of a new day.

"Ok, wait here, I need to find out what is happening." Sukhoi announced and then marched towards the front doors of the Inn without further hesitation.

Dogs barked as he approached the doors and a few children came running out of the doorway to see why the dogs were barking. They stopped suddenly and stared at the strangers in the street. A small boy, with a shock of flame red hair ran back into the Inn, shouting as loud as he could, leaving the other children staring, watching and waiting.

A large; rather plump, round faced woman appeared a moment later with the wailing child held in her arms and watched as Sukhoi motioned for everyone to come forward and then approached her.

"Sukhoi!" The woman shouted heartily as she smiled in recognition. She straightened her clean, bright white apron and quickly tried unsuccessfully to tidy her hair behind her ears as she waddled down to the group.

"I see you have lost some weight, Sheila." Sukhoi laughed as he rushed over to the big women and greeted her with a big kiss on the cheek; which made her blush, and a long heart felt hug.

"Oh, Sukhoi, it is so good to see you again, fit and well." She crowed, hugging him to her chest with vigour.

"And you too, but please release me so I can breathe." Sukhoi said as he feigned being crushed.

Sheila laughed and held the Kavacha at arms length while she looked him up and down. "You look too thin my friend, have your Ruedin not been looking after you like I told them to?" She turned her gaze on to Socata and Braduga, who merely smiled at her fondly.

"He has been well looked after; as promised Sheila." Socata replied.

A slim, wide eyed young girl about ten years old rushed out of the Inn and to Sheila's side.

"Ah, good, Liselle, go bring Maroc. Quickly now child, and don't dawdle!" She admonished the girl as she kept looking back over her shoulder while going back inside to find Maroc.

"You have come at a good time, my friends, a most fortuitous time." She announced with a slight knowing smile.

"Has something happened since we were here last?" Sukhoi asked a little apprehensively.

They had taken a different route to the Amal Desert that had by-passed the village and hadn't been back for just over four years. The signal network between the village and Enkan Mys was well established since Maroc had assumed command of the outpost, but even so, Sukhoi was concerned something bad may have happened to his friends.

"No, nothing like that be calm Sukhoi. There have been too many Raiders in the forest and in the towns and villages; which is why we have additional soldiers here, but they haven't bothered us yet. I think the Archers are enough deterrent anyway, but I will wait for Maroc to tell you everything." She replied quickly to alleviate any fears he may have.

"Good." Sukhoi said in relief. "But where are my manners, I would like to introduce some friends of mine, David, Jennifer and Christopher." Sukhoi indicated to each in turn, "say hello to an old and beautiful friend of mine, Sheila."

The children smiled and said hello and Sheila smiled back, but blushed at Sukhoi's remarks and said, "You flatterer!"

"Sukhoi!" The name boomed from the biggest man the children had ever seen. He was a mountain of a man, as wide as he was tall, with long dark hair tied back in a ponytail with just a hint of grey. He was wearing tough-looking leather breeches and a white open necked shirt embroided with lace.

His muscles were straining to be contained within the shirt and a big smile occupied most of his bearded face. His eyes twinkled as he said the name again, just in case somebody up the mountain hadn't heard him the first time.

"Sukhoi, my friend, how are you?" He boomed again.

"Maroc! my old friend." Sukhoi replied rubbing his ears. "Could you speak up, I think I am going deaf."

Maroc laughed, the sound reverberating around the village. And as the two men hugged each other, a wave of people began to pour out of the Inn, enveloping the small group.

As the big man hugged Socata and Braduga, others came over to greet them and their friends.

As the forming crowd greeted old friends and the children, Sukhoi grabbed hold of Maroc and took him to one side.

"Is there much news my friend?" He whispered.

Maroc's brow knitted together before answering. "A couple of strange things have happened recently. Someone appears to be organising the Raiders; controlling their movements. We have seen lots of them in the forest lately. I sent news to the city to ask for re-enforcements for all the villages, which they sent promptly. They even sent some here; even though I told them that my Archers could handle any trouble they could cause. They did cause a bit of a ruckus with the locals in Aquilas Mys. Sukhoi raised an eyebrow, but didn't say anything as Maroc continued with his narration.

"There were about twenty of the devils in the town itching for a fight and that's exactly what they got. It was only a brawl; no weapons were used, but still, it seemed too organised, too controlled by the reports I've had.

"There have been too many such stories of late, as if something is brewing." Sukhoi replied, looking a little worried.

"Yes too many, but that is nothing to what I heard a few weeks back." He continued, his voice dropping to a whisper, which was difficult for the big man.

Sukhoi nodded for Maroc to continue.

"Tamrin the tinker came by and told me of something he had seen whilst travelling through the mountains. You know Tamrin don't you?" Maroc enquired expectantly.

"Yes, quite well." Sukhoi replied. He had met the tinker on numerous occasions as he travelled from village to village selling his wares. He had even seen him in the Aral Desert one year, trying to establish trading links with the Toureng, but he hadn't been successful in locating them. But then, no one had.

"Well you know then that the man can be trusted?" He said. Maroc was a good judge of character but needed to Sukhoi to acknowledge this fact before he continued.

Yes, thought Sukhoi, Tamrin could be trusted; he had used him to pass his own information onto others when the need arose. He nodded.

"Tamrin saw a pair of Griffins, just by Eagle's Peak." He said blankly.

Sukhoi stared at Maroc, who merely nodded back. Eagle's Peak was close to the other path through the mountains that he had told David about. It was a long way off to the north but no one had seen a Griffin in Sakhalin since Nuba Driss brought his army of creatures across five hundred years earlier.

"A pair of Griffins?" Sukhoi asked amazed.

"Yes." Maroc replied thoughtfully.

"Strange events indeed my friend, have you informed the council about the creatures?" Sukhoi asked.

Marco looked troubled, "Yes, but I'm not sure they believed me."

"They will believe it when I get back." Sukhoi promised his friend. Sukhoi didn't have to see the creatures himself. If Tamrin said he saw the creatures he would believe the tinker; by Maroc adding his own belief to the tale, it only added weight to the story.

But there was more to know as Sukhoi looked past the big man; which was difficult to do with a man Maroc's size. "But what of this gathering, what is happening here?" Sukhoi asked eagerly, he would leave talk of the Griffins to a more opportune time, now he wanted to know why the village had congregated together.

"Ah," the big man smiled at his friend, "Now that is good news!" He said as he began to laugh in pure pleasure.

"What is it my friend?" Sukhoi asked again, smiling at the change in his friend's demeanour.

"A wedding." Maroc replied when he finally contained his mirth.

Sukhoi laughed along with the big man and said. "A wedding?"

"Yes, my friend. Kane and Hannah are to be married this day." He said.

"What, little Han, is ready for marriage?" He asked, shocked, he hadn't seen the girl on his last visit, she had been sent to Aquilas Mys to train as a seamstress, but he was sure she wasn't old enough to be married, was she?

Maroc smiled at his friend. "She is no longer the little girl you knew; she is a woman now, a beautiful woman." He said with pride in his voice. Hannah was his only daughter, the youngest of four children, and the apple of his eye.

It was then that a vision of beauty distracted Sukhoi from his thoughts of the little girl that use to sit on his lap as he told her stories of his adventures. The blonde haired goddess, covered in a silky white dress ran straight at him and jumped into his arms, laughing.

"Sukhoi." She said in an angelic voice. "Is it really you?" She smiled as she kissed his cheeks and then finally landed a big kiss on his lips.

Sukhoi; a big smile covering his face, could not believe what he was looking at

Hannah, she had only been a little girl a few years ago. Well, actually he thought, it was quite a few years ago, and now before him was a beautiful woman. Where had the time gone he wondered?

"Hannah, is it really you? You are beautiful!" He exclaimed. He didn't think she could look more lovely, until her eyes sparkled with his compliment and her smile widened with joy.

"Thank you." She laughed demurely as she dropped from his arms.

"I am Kane, Sukhoi of the Kavacha." A tall, blonde haired, muscle bound man with bright blue eyes and a cheeky smile introduced himself.

Sukhoi could see the attraction for both of the intended. Both were beautiful, and both had a mischievous look in their eyes. The babies they would inevitably create would be envied for their beauty throughout Sakhalin, he thought.

Kane was flanked by three giants; who were the spitting image of their father. They were huge, strong and powerful, but still retained the easy demeanour of their father, and his disarming smile.

"Hello boys." He said to them as they approached.

They just grabbed him one at a time and gave him a bear hug as a greeting, smiling and laughing as he was passed from one to the other. Their father looked on in amusement as his sons greeted his oldest friend.

Introductions were made, as more and more men joined them, and then preparations for the wedding began again in earnest, for now the bride and groom had the fortune of a Kavacha at their wedding, which was known to bring good luck to the happy couple. The entire party of companions was seen as honoured guests and they would be seated next to the bride and groom at the feast tables.

As preparations continued, Jennifer asked Sukhoi. "Have you known Maroc long?"

"Yes, a very long time." He replied fondly. "I met Maroc at Enkan Mys when I was being test as a Kavacha many years ago. He was the Master at Arms then and training the warriors of the honour guard and I interrupted one of his lessons asking for directions.

He just looked at me, and then boomed; with his great voice, "get out of his training yard." He laughed as he remembered the incident as if it was yesterday. "I was very obnoxious back then, and I decided to teach this mountain of a man a lesson in manners, so I levitated a nearby bucket of water above his head, intending to turn it upside down. He realised what I was about to do though and grabbed the bucket, throwing its contents over me. Only, the bucket wasn't full of water, as I assumed, it was full of horse manure. The disgusting smell hung around me for a week." He laughed as he finished his tale.

"You deserved that." Maroc laughed walking over. "And I had never laughed so much in all my life as when that muck fell all over you."

"Fell over me! Don't you mean thrown over me?" Sukhoi laughed.

"Well, yes, now you come to mention it." Maroc agreed still laughing.

"We have been friends ever since, even when Maroc left Enkan Mys to find fame and fortune." Sukhoi finished.

"Not fame and fortune." Maroc smiled back at his friend, a look of sadness entering his eyes.

"I am sorry my friend, I did not mean..." Sukhoi didn't finish what he was about to say.

"It's ok my friend, it was a long time ago now." He smiled. "And now my daughter is to be married." He laughed jovially once more.

Maroc walked back to shout at people as they prepared for the forthcoming wedding. Jennifer had to ask. "What happened?"

Sukhoi stared at his friend for a long time as he walked away and then looked into Jennifer's eyes, seeing nothing but concern; he decided to tell her, though he didn't really know why.

"Maroc; as I said, was the Master at Arms at Enkan Mys, he was respected, well known, and liked by everyone. He fell in love with Asmara, a beautiful woman of the Govena, who arrived at the training camp one day. As soon as their eyes met, Maroc knew he was in love and it was not long after that the couple got married. As they years passed by happily, Asmara gave birth to three strong boys and one beautiful girl. Then without a word to anyone, she just disappeared, leaving her husband and children by themselves, never to return. Obviously, Maroc was devastated; he believed something must have happened to her. He couldn't believe that she would just leave the city and leave her family without reason. He began to see conspiracies where there was none, and accused everyone of killing his beloved and hiding her body. Eventually he was convinced that there had not been any foul play, but by then he had entered into a deep depression. Distraught, he decided to leave his children with his sister and search for his wife beyond the boundaries of Enkan Mys. The search lasted three years, the length and breadth of Sakhalin he wondered, but he finally returned empty handed. On his return; he decided he could not stay at Enkan Mys any longer. He didn't want to raise his children in the city that had taken his wife from him, so he decided to leave. He took his three sons, Thane, Faran and Bamako and his daughter Hannah; who was still a baby then and left the city. He found this village eventually and informed the elders that he would stay here and watch the border; as protection against any threat. They sent him a squad of soldiers; which he trained to become the Archers. And that is where he has been ever since."

Tears welled up in Jennifer's eyes as he finished the tale, she felt his sadness, and as she focused her thoughts on the big man walking away, she was amazed to discover she could actually feel the loss he kept well hidden within the depths of his soul. Such a sad, sad story, she thought.

"Do not tell anyone this, especially today." Sukhoi requested. "The big man hides it well, but he still mourns the loss of his wife."

"Yes, he does." She whispered. "And of course, I won't tell anyone." She didn't know how she knew it, but she did know that Maroc had never gotten over the disappearance of his wife.

The preparations were almost complete, the children had refreshed themselves and there was an expectant buzz in the atmosphere. As the last of the sunlight faded, torches were lit and a great fire became the centrepiece for the ceremony with clean, white, clothe covered tables, circling it.

The bride and groom, resplendent in their finery gave their vows to each other before the entire village and honoured guests. Then Sukhoi said a few words to wish the couple a joyful and happy life. He joked about Hannah sitting on his knee as a child listening to his stories, and finished with the joy he felt being present at this wonderful time and how proud her father must be. Before he finished his speech, most; if not all of the guests had a tear in their eyes. Once all the speeches had been completed it didn't take long for the rest of the ritual side of the ceremony to end and the feast and festivities to start.

There was dancing and singing, laughter and tears, as the happy couple enjoyed the moment. There was food and wine aplenty as everyone over indulged. It was a wonderful end to the day, and one the children would find hard to forget. Stories were told later by the fire, the village children sitting wide eyed in their parents' laps. Sukhoi related one or two himself. Socata related the battle between Braduga and the Gourtak, which had the children hiding their faces in their hands. He made the creatures come to life, with his story telling that had even David, Jennifer and Christopher on the edge of their seats. When he finished the story with the death of both of the creatures, the children laughed and clapped, as Braduga just sat there with a half smile, looking embarrassed. It hadn't quite happened like that he thought, but he wouldn't spoil his friend's account of events with something as trivial as the truth.

As the stories were being told, Hannah came to sit beside Sukhoi and looked into his eyes. "I was in love with you." She began. "When I was a young girl and you came to visit, I was in love with you." She waited for his response with a smile on her lips.

He thought for a moment before saying. "I know." He smiled at her. "You will always be in my thoughts and in my heart. But I think you have found a good man to love you back."

"Yes, I think so too." She said looking towards her new husband smiling.

"Be happy and live a long, wonderful life Hannah." He said as she started to get up.

"I will." She replied. "And I hope you will find what you're looking for one day." Then she walked back to her husband.

"I hope so too." He whispered back, but she had already left.

The morning brought a crisp new day, a light sheet of dew covered the ground and without the smells of cooking, the stench of urine permeated into the room the children had been put into after the festivities had finished.

"That smell is disgusting." Christopher complained as he stretched and yawned.

"Yes, but when we leave here today, I will be sad to go. I had a great time last night." David replied as he too began to yawn.

"Everyone was so friendly." Jennifer stated. "And Hannah looked absolutely amazing in her wedding gown." She said wistfully.

Christopher tutted. "I enjoyed the food, and Socata even gave me a little taste of wine."

"Yes, it was nice, but I think we really must be on our way, Sukhoi is probably waiting for us already." David said.

So, the children got dressed and tidied their room before they went looking for Sukhoi and the companions. They found everyone in the main common room, seated together and deep in conversation. They all smiled as the children joined them.

"Did you sleep well?" Maroc boomed at the children.

"Yes, thank you." David lied; he hadn't at all, but he still wasn't prepared to tell anyone about his dreams.

"We should be leaving soon." Sukhoi announced.

"Not before you have something to eat." Sheila said walking into the room carrying two trays of hot food; she was followed closely behind by Liselle; who was always at her side, carrying another tray.

"Yes, a good meal to start the day, before you continue on your journey." Maroc smiled.

"Dig in, come on, there's plenty to go round." Sheila ordered as she put the trays on the table.

They chatted constantly as they ate a banquet of hot porridge, meats, cheeses and bread. They were soon joined by other guests at the Inn who had travelled from the neighbouring villages to attend the wedding, and it wasn't long before the Inn was full of people.

Eventually they were joined by the radiant, newly married couple, who were clapped into the dinning hall by their friends and family. Everyone was surprised to see them up so early and commented on the fact jovially, with a few nods and winks as the happy couple blushed.

"We wanted to say goodbye to our friends and the children, we thought they would be leaving early." Kane explained with a yawn.

"I hope my sister didn't keep you up all night with her constant chattering?" Faran remarked to Kane with a wink and a smile as he seated himself at one of the tables.

Thane and Bamako couldn't help but laugh as Kane's face began to glow bright red and Hannah's became one of indignation.

"I do not chatter, constant or otherwise." Hannah said sternly, but couldn't maintain the false look of outrageous indignation when everyone began to laugh.

"Do you have to leave so soon Sukhoi?" Hannah asked him as she sat down next to her new husband, squeezing his hand gently.

Sukhoi smiled. "I do and quickly, these are troubled times and I have reports to make, but I am so glad to have been here on your wonderful day." He said.

"It is always a pleasure having you here my friend." Maroc boomed across the table.

"Yes, it truly was." Hannah agreed.

"I wish your mother could have seen you yesterday though." Maroc said quietly, with a real pang of sadness in his quavering voice.

Hannah grabbed his hand in hers and smiled at her father warmly.

"Me too, but at least I had you by my side, and that gave me enough joy." She whispered into his ear.

Jennifer watched and listened to the exchange, that everyone else seemed to have missed, or chose to ignore. Maroc still missed his wife, the pain still evident in his voice; even after all the years that had gone by. She felt his sadness and a tear came into her eye, before she looked away.

It was some time later when they finally finished their meal. Sheila brought a large sack full of "something for the journey," which she handed to Socata.

So it was on a full stomach that they made their farewells. As they said their goodbyes, most, if not all of the village turned out to bid them a good and safe journey. Sukhoi hugged Maroc and Sheila warmly, and then Hannah ran into his arms, kissing him lightly on the cheek.

"Don't leave it too long the next time." She whispered as they hugged each other.

"I wont, take care." He replied.

As the others began to walk away down the trail, Jennifer turned to look toward Maroc who was standing slightly in front of the crowd and once again she saw such sadness when she looked at him that she was compelled to stop.

She turned round and began to walk back to the big man as he stood there waving them off. The others in the group stopped in surprise and watched as she walked up to Maroc.

When she reached him she stopped and her heart felt as if it was going to burst. Jennifer felt that Maroc was still consumed by his pain and she wanted to take that pain away from him.

"Is something the matter my dear?" He asked in concern as he watched Jennifer's face contort in concentration.

With his warm smile, Jennifer asked him to bend down to her as if she had something she wanted to tell him.

So the big man knelt on the floor with everyone looking on, intrigued.

The words came out of Jennifer's mouth, as if by a mystic ritual. She felt in control of the situation but she didn't really know what she was doing. All she really knew was that she wanted Maroc to be happy and she whispered in his ear. "Forget the past Maroc, be happy and live for the future." She said and then instinctively she reached out her hand and touched his heart beneath his tunic, "be at peace". She finished.

A small white light appeared from her hand as Jennifer touched him.

Maroc's eyes opened wide in shock at her touch, he felt a warmth flowing into him, a warmth that opened his heart. It consumed him totally and in that instant he could see what he had in his life. He could see the love from his sons and daughter, the friendships he had forged throughout his life and the love his wife had felt for him. The love he felt for his wife had left a large hole in his heart but everything he had and held dear in life now, helped to fill that gap. It was as if in that instant he had finally found peace and contentment. He could feel the tears flowing down his cheeks uncontrollably and as the girl removed her small hand from his chest she smiled at him; a bright sun-filled smile that filled him with joy.

No one else could see the light, but they could see that Maroc's face began to brighten and he began to smile, until eventually he began to laugh. He called over his sons and daughter and hugged them all together. Although they didn't know what had happened to their father, they did notice a change in his expression and his laugh became infectious.

Once Jennifer took her hand away from Maroc; she felt a little dizzy, she had shared in Maroc's thoughts and feelings and those feelings overwhelmed her. She had felt his sorrow down to his very soul as she touched his heart, but then she had felt that sorrow consumed by the love he had for his family and friends. Maroc had finally found peace and she had helped him to find it. Although she didn't understand how she had done it, she was happy that she had and she began to smile.

Jennifer walked back to the waiting group but turned her gaze to the big man who was standing in the centre of his family, laughing and crying at the same time; embracing them one at a time and telling them how proud he was and how much he loved them.

"What did you say to him?" Sukhoi asked with undisguised interest as she rejoined them.

"Nothing really." She replied smiling at Maroc as he looked toward the departing group of travellers and waved farewell.

He mouthed a thank you to her and she smiled back in return.

"I just told him to be happy."

This was one special gift she wanted to keep to herself, she thought as she turned towards the trail before her and followed her brothers and companions.

Chapter Sixteen

Braduga ran through the trees in silence. His shoulder had healed extremely quickly under the circumstances, Socata always managed to put him back together on the odd occasion he got injured, and he was thankful for his friend's ability in that department. He had decided to scout a bit further than what was really necessary, but he liked to be prepared. He didn't like surprises; especially the dangerous kind that could get someone killed, so he moved silently through the trees, searching for danger. He found a potential problem a few minutes later. He came across another Koutla Raider party, which again consisted of eight men and they were camped in the direct route his little party were headed in. This couldn't be coincidence, he thought, they must be waiting for them, but he had to find out their intentions. He stealthily positioned himself as close to the group as possible, and listened in on their conversation.

"Why us?" One Raider was moaning to what appeared to be the leader of the band.

"What do you mean why us, Krutak? Have you got something better to do?"

The rest of the men laughed as they listened to the exchange.

"I'm not saying that, Gismarl." He replied sullenly. "But I thought Soonak and his men were dealing with the situation, and they've probably got the bounty now!"

"Well, he obviously failed and now we get the opportunity to get rich." Gismarl snarled back. From the obvious frustration in Gismarl's voice, the conversation had been going on for quite some time. Gismarl looked formidable dressed all in black with twin swords strapped to his back and various knives deposited everywhere else, but Braduga could tell that the man was no weapon's master from the way he moved about the camp.

Braduga weighed up every man there and knew instinctively that they were not use to the forest environment. From the way they looked and acted they were probably more use to towns than the outdoors. There were signs everywhere that they were inadequately prepared, from their clothes to the fire they had lit, everything was wrong. They wouldn't be a serious threat, but Braduga never took anything for granted, incredible and surprising things happened all the time and so he took note of everything. Every detail was consumed as he peered around the makeshift camp; information gleaned now could potentially help him in the future he knew.

Braduga brought his attention back to the conversation between Gismarl and Krutak and realised he had heard the name Soonak before. Yes, it was the name of the leader of the last Raider party they had come across, the one that nearly killed Sukhoi, and would have, if not for the intervention of David. So, he thought! More Raiders looking for the children. But who wanted them? It was obvious that the Raiders were just being paid for a service, but who was this service for? And why were the children wanted so badly?

"Who are these children anyway Gismarl?" Krutak asked.

Now he would get his answers Braduga thought as he listened intently.

"You ask too many questions for your own good Krutak." He replied. "Be quiet or I will cut out your tongue! Just do as your told and when we get the children, we will be rich!" He growled as Krutak closed his mouth, another question on the tip of his tongue as the rest of the Raiders began to laugh once more.

Braduga waited a few more minutes, to see if he could glean anything else before he reluctantly decided to return back to his friends and report his news.

"So." Sukhoi said. "Another party of Koutla Raiders, eight you say?" Surprise evident in his voice.

"Yes, but not equipped to fight in the forest." Braduga added.

"Why are they after us?" Christopher asked worriedly. "What have we done to them?"

"That I can not answer, Chris." Braduga replied. "But do not worry, you will be safe."

"Oh, I'm not worried. He smiled back. "I am protected by the greatest warrior in Sakhalin, my brother can stop daggers in mid flight and my sister can speak to Dragons. I've got nothing to worry about at all." He said utterly convinced that he was well protected.

Sukhoi chuckled. "He has got a point."

"Sukhoi, are there a lot of Koutla Raiders?" David asked smiling at his brother but still worried by this unwanted turn of events.

"There seems to be more and more each year. They normally band together in small groups, just enough to menace unfortunate travellers, but it is not unheard of for groups larger than these to band together. Maroc thinks that there is someone controlling and co-ordinating the Raider attacks, but I need to speak to the council about this."

"Do you think someone is co-ordinating the attack on us?" He asked dismayed.

"Possibly," He conceded. "The Raiders are only interested in money; but to hire this amount of Raiders would require an enormous amount to pay for their services."

"Yes it would, wouldn't it?" David said as he realised the truth of that statement and a look of relief cleared his brow.

"Don't worry Dave, we can handle them." Christopher said to his brother.

David laughed. He had nothing to worry about he realised, Chris was right. He had a little magic, as did Sukhoi, and they did have Socata and the formidable Braduga. He had seen all three companions in action; nobody in their right minds would intentionally mess with them.

The three companions discussed their options as the children listened attentively. After careful deliberation they decided they had no choice but to follow their current path. To deviate from it would probably get them lost in the forest, and there were worse things in there than the Raiders to contend with. On hearing this, the children automatically looked anew at the forest, thinking that some creature would pounce at them any moment. But Sukhoi told them not to worry; he doubted anything would attack them if they remained on their current path. So it was decided they would keep walking until they came upon the raiding party, then they would assess the situation and decide on the best course of action to take.

Braduga would scout ahead as usual, Socata would take the rear and the children would follow behind Sukhoi. This decided, their journey continued.

It was twenty minutes later that they heard the Raider party. The children were told to stay where they were as the men assessed the situation.

They waited for a couple of minutes nervously awaiting the return of the companions. Socata appeared ahead of them and motioned for them to follow. Slowly and quietly they did as he asked.

"We will take you in front of the group and find a safe place for you to wait,

Sukhoi wants to ask these men some questions, then we will come and get you, ok?" He asked, but not waiting for an answer he crept away.

The children followed him through the trees. They could hear the voices from the raiding party as they passed close by, but within moments they were beyond the group and Socata found a place for them to wait

"Ok," He said. "We will be back shortly, keep quiet and wait here, we won't be long."

"Ok," David whispered, and they settled down to wait

Socata was back with his companions a few minutes later. They discussed their plan of action and would wait a few minutes for everyone to get into position before putting it into action.

A few minutes passed and Sukhoi presented himself from behind a tree along the path the group had been taking. "Hello in the camp." He said as the raiding party nervously jumped to their feet brandishing their weapons.

"Who's there?" One of the Raiders asked.

Sukhoi looked at the man, he was obvious the leader, as described by Braduga. "You must be Gismarl?" He asked.

Gismarl was shocked, who was this man who knew his name, he wondered.

"Yes, who are you?"

"I am Sukhoi; I believe you are trying to find three children?" Sukhoi realised his name meant nothing to the Raider but the mention of the three children did.

"Yes, yes, what do you know of them? Do you know where they are?" He enquired excitedly.

Sukhoi noticed all the Raiders were now paying attention to the conversation with interest, news of the children obviously meant something to them all.

"Why do you want them?" He asked.

"That is no concern of yours, but if you have information to their whereabouts, I may be able to offer you something in return." He suggested elusively.

"Really? What?" He asked intrigued.

"Your life for one thing." Gismarl laughed.

"I may offer you the same deal, if you tell me why you want them and who paid you to find them." Sukhoi countered.

Gismarl laughed again, but his men began to look around nervously.

Why would a lone man walk up to a band of eight fully armed men and offer them their lives for information if he didn't have something to back it up with.

"You make me laugh, Sukhoi is it?" Gismarl chuckled. "What do you know of the children?"

"You first?" Sukhoi replied.

Gismarl stopped laughing and walked towards Sukhoi. "Enough of this, tell me what you know or I will rip your tongue out." He said, it was his favourite phrase and used it often. He reached out to try and grab Sukhoi, but Sukhoi read the leader's intentions and deftly sidestepped the move, grabbing the outstretched arm and twisting it up the leader's back. His other arm he placed round the Gismarl's throat. The movement was finished in seconds as the other Raiders looked on in amazement.

"Now Gismarl, are you going to tell me what I want to know, or shall I break your arm first?" Sukhoi asked in a pleasant voice.

"Kill him!" Gismarl shouted as he tried to twist out of Sukhoi's grasp.

As the Raiders moved towards Sukhoi, weapons in hand, two figures emerged from the trees and arrows reigned down on the unsuspecting foe. It was over, really before it started. In seconds the Raiders were writhing on the ground with arrows protruding from various parts of their bodies as Socata and Braduga released one after the other into the unsuspecting group of Raiders.

Gismarl stopped trying to break free of Sukhoi's grip and looked at his men on the ground. Then, he watched the two men move toward him with their bows in their hands and an arrow notched and ready to use. He could barely see them, but with that snippet of information came realisation, these men were the honour guard of the Kavacha, which meant, the man holding him in a vice like grip must be the Kavacha himself.

Sukhoi could almost see the thought process going through Gismarl's mind and the ultimate conclusion. "Now will you answer my question?" He asked.

"I know nothing Kavacha," He said. "I was merely told to take the three children into my custody; no matter the cost, and I would be well paid." He spat.

"And to whom and where were you to take these captives on the completion of your mission?" Sukhoi asked.

"To Enkan Mys." He said. "But I don't know who wants them."

Sukhoi and his companions stood there in shock. Gismarl was to take the children to Enkan Mys. "I do not believe you do not know who to deliver them to!" He said. "How are you to be paid then?" He asked. He couldn't believe what the leader was telling him, who in Enkan Mys would know of the children, he wondered?

"I do not know, only that I was to deliver them to the South Gate before the second bell of the day." He replied. "There I would receive my payment." He finished.

The second bell was wrung at eight O'clock in the morning. It was a good time to go to the gate as there wouldn't be many people about at that time.

Sukhoi released the leader and pushed him towards the moaning men on the ground. "See to your men, and then leave this place." He said and motioned Socata and Braduga to follow him as they walked away. "Would you like me to tie them up before we leave?" Braduga asked.

"No my friend, I think they have enough problems attending to their wounds, let us be on our way without further delay." He replied somewhat dourly.

"You believed him then?" Socata asked quietly.

"Yes my friend, I do unfortunately." He replied just as quietly. "Which presents us with another problem? Someone at Enkan Mys knows of the children, and it appears, they will pay any price to have them delivered to them, even if it means killing a Kavacha and his honour guard."

"I would definitely call that a problem." Braduga said.

"I wonder what's keeping them." Christopher asked impatiently.

"Probably the eight Raiders waiting to kill them and capture us." David replied.

"Maybe we should go and help them then?" Christopher said hopefully.

"Don't think that'd be a good idea, Chris." Said David, contemplating the same idea. "We'd just get in the way."

"Yeah I know, but I don't like this waiting." Christopher replied looking in the direction of where their friends and the Raiders would be.

"Why do you think they want us Dave?" Jennifer asked worriedly.

David looked at his sister and then at his brother. He didn't have any answers, he didn't know why anyone would want any of them, but he had to say something, he had to keep strong for them. He didn't like the responsibility but there was no one else.

"I don't know Jen, but we have found some friends who are willing to help us and protect us from these Raiders, so we're not alone. We'll be just fine." He finished.

"Yeah, Dave's right Jen." Christopher said smiling at his brother and then moving close to his sister and putting his hand on her shoulder. "We'll be ok."

"Everyone ok?" Sukhoi asked as he appeared from nowhere, followed by his companions.

The children jumped as one, caught by surprise, but each smiling as their friends came into view, uninjured.

"Yes fine, but what happened? Are you ok? What did they say? You're not injured are you?" David bombarded them with questions.

"Slow down my friend, one question at a time." Sukhoi laughed.

"We were worried." Jennifer said. "We didn't know if you were in danger, or what to do, or anything."

"It is ok, we are ok." He replied softly. "We just had a little chat with our friends in the trees, and now we can be on our way."

"What did you find out, anything?" David asked.

"Only that they did not really know who hired them." He replied.

"Did they say why they want us?"

"No, only that someone is paying a lot of money to apprehend you. I do not think they were interested in the reason provided they got their money."

"Oh." David sounded disappointed. "I suppose there's no point speculating."

"I think you are right." Sukhoi said, looking slightly troubled.

Everyone collected their belongings and with Braduga scouting ahead and

Socata bringing up the rear, the little group continued on their journey once more.

Sukhoi was pondering what the Raider leader had said to him. It just didn't make sense he thought. How could anyone at Enkan Mys know about the three children? It just seemed inconceivable that anyone would know of the children. Even if that could be believed, what reason would they have for trying to capture the children?

Jennifer didn't need any special ability to see that Sukhoi was worried about something. From his silence; as they continued on their journey, she knew that he was thinking hard about something in particular and she had caught him on a few occasions staring at one or all of them.

"You ok Jen?" David asked noticing her frown. He had been thinking about the comment his brother had made about magic and about Jennifer's ability to speak with the Dragons. He was feeling a little confused and overwhelmed by everything, and if he was, maybe his sister was too. He desperately needed to talk to someone about it but Jennifer seemed to be constantly consumed by her own thoughts. He couldn't believe how easily he came to accept her abilities, and wondered if she thought the same of him. She was looking decidedly tired, and a constant frown seemed to furrow her face now, but she seemed to be taking everything in her stride.

"Yes, just thinking." She replied quietly.

"What about?" He asked.

"Something seems to be worrying Sukhoi and I believe it's something to do with us." She replied.

David thought she was actually going to open up to him and express her feelings, doubts and concerns about her gifts or his, but even with everything going on, she was still thinking about someone else.

"What do you think it is?" He asked quietly.

"Not sure, but whatever it is, it must be serious."

"Try not to worry about it Jen, if it is important, I'm sure Sukhoi will say something eventually." He advised.

"Yes, you're probably right." She replied smiling. "Was there something else?" She asked, as she turned to look at her brother then and could see he too had something on his mind.

"No, nothing." He replied, the moment had passed, he thought to himself, he would just have to deal with the situation himself. He decided he needed time to think things through and try to work it all out in his own mind first.

"Ok, but if you want to talk about anything, I'm here." She replied, not wanting to push the issue, but making a point of telling him she was prepared to listen to what he had to say.

"It's ok, just try not to worry about things; once we get to Enkan Mys, I'm sure everything will be fine." He said.

"I hope so Dave." She replied.

She then began to smile.

"But I must admit, even with everything that's happening I am actually enjoying myself."

"Yes," He laughed. "Me too, but I would still like to get home in one piece." He finished solemnly.

Christopher hung back as they walked along the path; the track narrowing to allow one person at a time to go between two large trees.

Socata caught up to him, looking down at the little boy who seemed lost in thought.

"You ok Chris?" He asked.

"Yes, thanks, just thinking." He replied.

"What are you thinking about? Anything I can help with?"

"I don't think so." Christopher said as he looked up at the warrior walking beside him.

"Well, if you change your mind, let me know."

"Well, actually..." Christopher started. "I was just wondering when I was going to do some magic."

Socata contemplated this for a while before asking. "Do you want to do some magic?"

"I think so. Well, to be honest, I'm not really sure, but both Dave and Jen can do magic, so why can't I?"

Again Socata thought a moment before replying. "If you only want to perform magic because other people do, do you think that is a good enough reason to do it?"

Christopher thought for a few moments. "Maybe." He said unconvincingly.

"I can not do magic Chris, I never have, and I have never wanted to, but I am still happy." He said. "Would you be happy if you never performed any magic?"

"Well, I haven't done any so far," He replied. "And I'm happy enough. So I suppose if I didn't do any it wouldn't really make any difference."

"That's right; you don't miss what you don't have." Socata said as he smiled at the boy. "You don't need magic, Chris, and if you can live your life without it, you will be stronger for it."

"I suppose so." Christopher said a little sulkily. "But Dave and Jen can do really great things. I can't do anything."

Socata regarded the boy for a moment before coming to a decision. "How about it if I teach you how to use the bow?"

Instantly Christopher's face brightened; a hungry look on his face as he smiled up at Socata. "Really? You'd teach me how to use the bow?" He asked enthusiastically.

"Yes, and I will even ask Braduga if he will show you how to use the sword."

Christopher looked into Socata's eyes; he could feel his own about to fill with tears.

How wonderful would it be to learn to be a great warrior, he thought. "Thank you Socata that would be great." He said quietly as he walked a little quicker to catch up with everyone.

Socata smiled as Christopher caught up to his brother and sister, but was surprised that he didn't say anything to them about their conversation, he just walked along as if nothing had happened; albeit with a big grin on his face.

Later that day he asked Braduga if he would be willing to teach the boy, when the opportunity arose. As he thought, Braduga was willing and even looked like he would enjoy the experience, so he gave Christopher the good news.

"That will be just marvellous." He said excitedly and then looked at Socata with a serious look on his face. "Can I ask a favour?" he said quietly.

"What is it?" Socata asked suspiciously.

"Could we, I mean, would it be ok if we, you know, that we keep this a secret from Dave and Jen." He said, looking round to make sure they weren't listening.

"Why?"

"Well," he thought for a moment before continuing, "I want to do this for me, it will be all mine, and. ..." He trailed off.

"And you think they may say no if you told them?" Socata guessed.

"Yes." He replied looking at the ground.

"Ok, for you Chris, we will keep this between the three of us."

Christopher gave him his biggest grin and hugged the warrior, "Thank you Socata."

"Ok, ok, don't squeeze so hard." He laughed.

Visibility began to deteriorate rapidly as they trudged through the forest. The tall elegant trees were already blotting out quite a bit of the sunlight, but as time raced on, it began to grow darker and darker. The party continued to follow the ever-winding track as it narrowed and widened inconsistently, until Sukhoi finally called a halt.

He chatted quickly with Braduga; who had been navigating the party through the forest; by what seemed like instinct alone as the fading light disappeared, until they decided to stop.

With everyone tired and visibility poor, Sukhoi made the decision to stop there for the night.

A small fire was lit but it provided little warmth as the group huddled around it. They ate the food from the sack they had been provided by Sheila. Pies and cakes were a welcome surprise to everyone.

The conversation steered clear of their meeting with the band of Raiders and centred more on meeting up with the Dragons and the rest of the journey to Enkan Mys.

"I have been wondering Jennifer if your ability to speak to our friends is limited in any way?" Sukhoi asked her but continued to express his thoughts when she returned a blank look. "Do you think you have to be standing next to them to talk with them or could you hear their thoughts from a long way off, for instance?"

Everyone in the little group turned their attention on Jennifer and she blushed under their scrutiny, awaiting her reply.

"I don't know," she replied honestly, "I haven't given it much thought."

She had in fact given it quite considerable thought; especially since her experience with the Gourtak. They could have killed Braduga, but something or someone had distracted them; she wasn't a hundred percent certain, but she believed she was that someone. She had also thought about trying to contact her new friends, but had decided against it in the end. They were probably too far away to hear her any way and she had dismissed the idea as soon as it had formed. She was surprised by Sukhoi's suggestion never the less. What did the Kavacha know? Or guess? She wondered if Sukhoi had actually overheard her conversation with David when expressing her views on making contact with the Gourtak. She decided not to mention it and just shrugged her shoulders instead.

"They are probably too far away, but I was wondering if there was a limit to your gift." He said finally. One eyebrow rose expectantly but she chose to ignore the look he gave her.

"It could be worth a try Jen!" David said encouragingly.

Christopher nodded and smiled and Jennifer found that she had no choice but to at least give it a go. It probably wouldn't work, but she wouldn't know if she didn't try.

"Ok, I'll try." She replied.

Sukhoi nodded to her and smiled, while her brothers held their breaths.

Taking a deep breath; though she didn't know why, she didn't think holding her breath would actually make any difference after all. She tried to picture the two Dragons in her mind and once she could see them clearly she attempted to push her thoughts out to them. She waited a moment expectantly, but there were no sounds in her head. She opened her eyes to see numerous eager gazes watching her, so she tried again, this time concentrating on just Sak with a single thought, hello. The result was still the same; there was no acknowledgement of any kind.

David watched his sister intently as she tried to speak with the Dragons. He wasn't sure if she would be successful or not, but the fact that she was willing to try, never the less made him think about his own abilities. He was scared to use them; he had felt in control in the Haram for the first time, but could he control his magic all the time? He wasn't so sure and it was that fact that made him loathe to even try. But more than that, it was the possibility of failure that scared him the most. Since his father's death, he had felt there was a part of himself missing, a part that was lost and wouldn't return. When he had entered the corridor that first time, he had felt in control, and now these gifts were providing the means to harness that control and finally fill that gap. He had been nervous about using the magic in case that feeling didn't return. He couldn't stand the thought of losing everything and the emptiness returning. He smiled at Jennifer and thought how much braver she was than himself. He knew he shouldn't let his fear control him this way, but he couldn't help it. He watched his sister trying to use her gifts and realised that he must try and do the same. He couldn't let his fear rule his life this way.

A few seconds later, her face full of disappointment, Jennifer shook her head. She had tried but she couldn't reach the Dragons.

"Do not be too disappointed Jennifer, they are probably still too far away and it may also be that your gift will only work when you are physically with them." Sukhoi offered.

She smiled weakly at him in reply, but his words didn't alleviate her disappointment. Even though she thought it wouldn't actually work, a small part of her hoped that it would.

"What about you David?" Sukhoi said as he swept up some dried meat from the bowl in front of him with his fingers and put it in his mouth.

David looked sheepishly at his sister and then turned his attention on the Kavacha. He knew that Jennifer had tried her best to contact the Dragons and although she had failed, she didn't look too disappointed. With everyone's attention now focused on him, he wasn't sure if he could do as well and his old fears came flooding back. He needed courage and the strength to at least try, but where could he get those from, he wondered?

Jennifer squeezed his hand then and to his surprise, he realised he had nothing and no one to fear but his own lack of confidence. He had to at least give it a go, so he nodded.

"Ok, "Sukhoi said smiling. "Just imagine this stick floating in the air." Sukhoi told him as he picked a twig from the ground and placed it in front of David.

David concentrated on the twig, willing it to float. He saw the stick in his mind, floating before his eyes. The twig didn't move.

Sukhoi watched the boy as he concentrated, but somehow knew he wouldn't be successful. "Try and picture the stick David." He suggested.

"I am." David replied through clenched teeth, but still the twig didn't move.

"It's not working." David said hollowly.

"Try again Dave." Jennifer encouraged, squeezing his hand again.

David looked at his sister's hand on his and then at her encouraging look, and he thought he would give it one more go.

He concentrated on the twig, putting his mind to the task with all his might and then to his surprise and jubilation he felt a tingling sensation. He felt the confidence return and he felt empowered once more and thankfully the feeling of nausea was much less. But he was shocked when the twig rose into the air and kept rising.

Everyone looked expectantly as David stood up and followed the stick with his gaze.

"Now make it come back." Sukhoi suggested, trying to see the stick as it rose out of sight.

"I can't even see it." David said in a half laugh.

"What goes up must come down." Christopher laughed.

Everyone was on their feet looking for the stick when suddenly it dropped and landed by David's feet.

"Did you make it do that?" Sukhoi asked him.

David was a little stunned, he couldn't see the stick but wanted it back where it was before and then with that thought the stick dropped from the sky to land by his feet.

"I think so" He laughed, shrugging his shoulders.

Sukhoi could hardly contain his excitement, "try and make it raise again David."

David smiled as he looked at the stick and this time the stick did exactly as he wanted. He made it twirl in the air and then made it stick in the ground when he'd finished. He couldn't stop himself from smiling, he had performed more magic and he loved the feeling that infused him.

"Well done David." Sukhoi praised him.

David watched the twig and then he felt the power leave him, allowing the emptiness to return.

Jennifer and Christopher were clapping and smiling at him and he joined in with their revelry, proud that he had overcome his fears and managed to perform his magic.

Sukhoi decided then that it would be in everyone's best interest to get some rest as they still had a long journey ahead of them.

The next day, everyone was up and ready to move at the break of dawn.

They could see the first whispers of light coming through the trees as they set off down the track.

David was still on a high, the previous night's success still vivid in his mind, even though his dreams were still plagued by the hooded menace, it didn't dull his spirits.

Jennifer on the other hand was still thinking about the lack of her own success in trying to communicate with the Dragons.

"Hash, Sak, can you hear me?" Jennifer tried to project her thoughts. She had been trying to speak to the Dragons since she woke up.

She decided she would continue to try and contact their friends every so often, just in case. She was still learning to control her abilities and determine their limits, but for some reason she knew that if she concentrated, she would be able to make contact. She didn't know why or how she knew this, but it felt right, she was certain of it. So, she continued to try and communicate as she followed everyone else.

Christopher had been enjoying a pleasant dream, where he was fighting side by side with Braduga and Socata; saving the people of Sakhalin from the forces of Nuba Driss, when he was woken. It was still dark, though the sky had patches of red and orange breaking with the new day, when Socata roused him and asked him to follow quietly.

"What's up?" He asked when they had walked out of sight of the camp.

"I wanted to start your lessons; we have about an hour or so before the sun rises." He replied.

Although still a little tired, Christopher gave Socata a big smile as he was given his first lesson with the bow.

He was initially disappointed, he couldn't even draw the bow without assistance, but when aiming his shot, he demonstrated a keen eye, which Socata had complemented him on. Socata instructed him on the use of the bow; how to hold it correctly, how to aim and how to fire. He practised for at least an hour, and although his arms and shoulders had begun to ache after the first few attempts, he kept trying and he loved every moment of it. Socata taught him numerous exercises to conserve his energy. He explained how to relax his muscles and how to increase his flexibility and strength. At the end of the lesson, Socata had given Christopher a salve to put on his shoulder, his arm and his fingers to help relieve the discomfort he was feeling, that worked immediately. As Braduga prepared a breakfast, Socata continued to chat to Christopher about his next lesson and what he should be doing in preparation for it. Christopher listened intently, nodding every so often and both Socata and Braduga were pleased by his enthusiasm. After twenty minutes; with a deliciously smelling breakfast ready, they woke the rest of the party up, just as the sun began to break through the trees and illuminate the camp site.

Chapter Seventeen

"I've got to keep trying!" Jennifer whispered to herself underneath her breath. "I just know I can do it."

Jennifer had continued to focus her thoughts on the Dragons and project those thoughts, trying to establish a communication link, but to no avail.

She had tried standing still, she tried moving, holding her breath and breathing normally, closing her eyes, everything, but nothing seemed to work. In fact the more she tried, the more frustrated she got and her head had begun to hurt her through the effort.

She refused to give up though. She was still adamant that if she tried hard enough, she would finally succeed. David had tried to engage her in conversation at one point as they travelled through the forest, but one stern look with her eyebrows knitted together had soon discouraged him from trying again.

They had been travelling for approximately three hours and Jennifer decided she wouldn't try again until after they had stopped for lunch. With a little food inside her, she believed she would have enough energy to try again.

"Ok, one more go then." She said to herself, she knew she was pushing it, but something in the back of her mind told her to keep trying, so she did.

"Hash, Sak, can you hear me!" She shouted for the fourth time that morning.

"Jennifer?" Sak'ar'jefar whispered, stunned by the thought that had just entered her mind.

She and her brother were soaring through the clear blue sky over the southern end of the Gratishk Mountains. There wasn't a cloud anywhere to be seen and they were enjoying the flight until they would meet with their friends.

"What was that?" Hash'ar'jefar asked his sister as he gracefully brought his muscular body to an immediate stop, hovering in the air with an ease born from centuries of experience.

"I thought I heard Jennifer calling us." She replied as she caught up to him and the pair of them hovered above the vast array of mountains below them.

"I very much doubt that, we are still two days away from our meeting place." he said, indicating with his great head the direction they were flying, "not even the men from Hal Argus could communicate with us that far." He said wistfully, thinking back to his home, family and friends.

"Yes, my brother you are probably right." She sighed as she flapped her wings in the cool currents of air. She was almost certain she had heard something, but now there was nothing. It must have been wishful thinking, she assumed and she followed her brother's flight path over the snow capped mountains.

Jennifer's eyes widened for an instant and she suddenly stopped.

"You ok Jen?" David asked in concern as he almost bumped into his sister.

Had she just heard something in her mind? No, she must have imagined it, she thought on reflection. Her head ache was getting worse, and she needed some food to replenish her energy levels.

"I thought I heard Sak for a moment, calling my name, but..." she trailed off.

David could tell she was disappointed, and she looked tired as well.

"Never mind, we're probably too far away from them still, you look tired Jen." David said.

"Maybe, but I'm sure I heard my name being called," she said, she was trying to think of how to describe it, when the idea came into her head, her tiredness disappearing in her enthusiasm. "It sounded like an echo. You know that sound you get when you call someone in a cave for instance." She said excitedly.

David nodded, surprised at her enthusiasm.

"Well it's just like that, I heard someone calling my name as if calling to me from within a cave."

"And you think it could be one of the Dragons?" David asked sceptically, though he tried to not to show his disbelief.

"Exactly." She replied.

David smiled at his sister; she needed a bit of encouragement he thought, even if she had imagined it. It was up to him to offer her as much support as possible. If he was in her place, he would want that same encouragement.

"Well, you have to keep trying then Jen and maybe you'll get through to them eventually." He said trying to emulate her enthusiasm.

She gave him a big smile of thanks, "Yes, I will, but you are probably right, they are too far away."

"Forget what I said, if you think you heard them just now, try again, maybe you'll get through this time." He said encouragingly.

"Yes, you're right, thanks Dave." She said smiling again and then concentrated on the images of the two Dragons once more. Closing her eyes, she could see them before her and then she squeezed her eyes even more, scrunching her nose and focused all her thought on her words.

"Sak, can you hear me?" Jennifer shouted in her mind as loud as she could. She put in that shout, all the strength and determination she could muster and then listened intently for any reply. She wasn't sure what to expect; maybe another echo perhaps; probably nothing, but she waited patiently for the faintest sound.

She was shocked, surprised and elated when a reply came back to her a few seconds later.

"JENNIFER, IT IS YOU?" Came the reply from an evidently shocked Sak'ar'jefar.

"Yes, yes it is!" She replied excitedly. "It is wonderful to speak to you again, how are you?" She asked.

"WE ARE FINE, BUT HOW CAN THIS BE, WE ARE SURELY TO FAR AWAY TO BE TALKING TO EACH OTHER?" The dragon replied in wonder.

"I don't know my friend? I thought you might be able shed some light on that." Jennifer replied, amazed that it had actually worked.

"I WILL SPEAK WITH MY BROTHER AND DISCUSS THIS WHEN WE NEXT MEET." Sak'ar'jefar replied after a slight pause.

"When will that be?" She asked excitedly.

"IN PROBABLY TWO DAYS TIME IF ALL GOES WELL." The dragon replied.

"Ok see you then Sak." She replied elated by the conversation.

There was no reply from the dragon, but the arrangement had been confirmed and Jennifer was thrilled that she had managed to talk with one of the Dragons; especially over such a great distance.

David had been quietly watching and waiting for some outward sign that his sister was conversing with the creatures but she just stood there perfectly still that was until she began to smile. He instinctively knew that she had made contact and was now chatting away merrily. He envied her ability, it seemed amazing to him that she could actually speak with these creatures from a different place and reminded him of the film he had seen a few years back, Doctor Dolittle, a film about a man that could speak with all the animals. He remembered laughing at the time; but that had been when his father was alive, he had laughed a lot back then, not so much anymore he realised.

"David!" Jennifer shouted in excitement as she opened her eyes.

"You did it then?" He smiled at her.

"Yes, it was wonderful." She said beaming at him.

Everyone had looked around at once on hearing Jennifer call her brother's name excitedly, thinking there was some danger they hadn't seen, but noticing the big grin on Jennifer's face, they soon relaxed.

Sukhoi walked over to the two children, "what was wonderful may I ask?" He enquired.

"I have just spoken with Sak." She said proudly. "They are well and only two days from where we are to meet with them." She finished laughing at the surprised look on his face.

Everyone stopped and gathered round as Jennifer explained that she had been trying to communicate with the Dragons since her failure earlier. She had tried and tried until just recently, when she had finally made contact with Sak. Sukhoi listened with obvious surprise, which made her laugh. Sukhoi couldn't help but smile at her excitement and eventually joined in with her when she began to laugh. The tiredness around her eyes seemed to just vanish as she thought of her accomplishment.

"This is just wonderful." He said happily.

"You really spoke with them Jen?" Christopher asked in awe.

"Yep!" She replied with a proud grin on her face.

"Wow."

"Two days, Sak said, two days?" Sukhoi asked, trying to recover from his shock.

"Yes, two days." Jennifer replied.

"Good." He said after a moment's hesitation. "That means we should probably arrive there at approximately the same time then." Sukhoi announced smiling.

There was a buzz of excitement as the group pushed through the forest with renewed vigour. They knew that once through they were through the forest they would be reunited with the Dragons, and it wouldn't be long before their journey would come to an end at Enkan Mys.

The next day and a half seemed to fly past as the group; full of excitement and anticipation pressed on, along the track. Luckily, it had evolved into an overgrown road through the trees, which made it easier to travel. In the afternoon, they came upon another village, which they approached with caution. A caution, which seemed well placed when Braduga and Socata reported back to Sukhoi what they had found.

"The village has been plundered," Braduga stated. "Burned and decimated, and no signs of anyone still living there."

"Can you tell what happened?" Sukhoi asked as the children looked at each other in shock.

"I would say the villagers abandoned their homes before the attack and escaped into the forest." Socata said. "They must have been forewarned, and I also think, it was the work of that Koutla Raider party we came across earlier." He finished.

"Yes, I think so too." Braduga confirmed. "The attack was sloppy and very disorganised, but effective never the less. There are many tracks leading in to the village which were made by the same sort of boots made by the Raiders. So it's either them or there is another group in the forest at the moment."

"What do you think?" Sukhoi asked him.

He thought for a moment and then replied. "Probably the Raiding party we bumped into."

"Ok, makes sense, but we must stay alert just in case." Sukhoi said. "Was there anyone injured?" He added.

"No, I don't think so, but the Raiders destroyed everything they did not take with them, such vandalism was not called for." Socata replied, disgusted by the waste.

"Well, I am sure the villagers will return eventually and I do not suppose our friends will be bothering them again any time soon with their injuries." Sukhoi stated before telling everyone they should carry on with their journey.

They moved cautiously through the village when they came upon it, looking incredulously at the burnt out shells of the villagers' homes as they passed by. There was an eerie silence as they walked by each building in turn, amazed at the unnecessary desecration of people's property.

"Why did the Raiders do this?" Jennifer asked in disgust.

"I don't know, they are vile people at the best of times but they normally just take what they need then they leave. I have never seen or heard of this sort of vandalism before." Socata replied, clearly worried by what had taken place.

"But what did these people ever do to them?" She continued, trying to understand the meaning behind the actions.

"Oh, probably nothing, except exist." He said vehemently.

Jennifer noticed what appeared to be the charred remains of a small animal.

She ran over and knelt down beside the creature and began to weep when she discovered it had been a puppy. Sukhoi walked over and saw that the poor little thing still had its lifeless eyes open.

He gently pulled Jennifer away from the sight and held her in his arms.

"There, there, be still." He said as he rubbed her back and whispered comforting little comments to her.

"They even burnt that little dog." She sobbed. "How can those men be so cruel?"

"Yes, I know." He replied. "Come." He said gently. "Let us leave this place."

They walked away from the village dismayed and outraged at the pointlessness of the destruction there and continued along the path. They walked without rest for the next few hours, to get as far away from the village as possible, as if the distance would erase the memory.

When the light began to fade, Sukhoi called a halt and the weary travellers settled themselves in a little clearing beside the road. They chatted briefly as they ate a couple of Rabat Socata had caught, but after sensing the mood Sukhoi announced they should all try and get some sleep.

A fine rain dropped from a grey sky through the trees as the little group woke the next morning. The mood was still sombre; made worse by the weather.

No one felt like eating, so it wasn't long before they were back on the road, headed for their meeting with the Dragons.

It wasn't until late morning that the rain finally stopped and as it did, with the sun shining through the trees, the group finally saw the end of the forest. As they moved along the road they could see people moving around further up.

"Aren't we going to wait nearby while you scout ahead?" David asked nervously, as they got closer and closer to what now appeared to be a village locked between the forest and a large lake.

"No need David," Sukhoi replied. "This is Kahin, the roughest fishing village this side of

Lake Ghanem, there will not be any unusual trouble here." He said matter-of-factly.

David had no idea what that was supposed to mean, but he tried to reach out for his magic as he approached the village. He felt the tingling sensation immediately and he smiled in relief. He wasn't sure he could control the magic properly yet; he probably needed some instruction and some practice, but just knowing it was there made him relax somewhat.

They walked through the last of the trees and into the clearing that formed the outskirts of the village. The stench was incredible, the odour of beer and rotting fish permeated the atmosphere as they moved into the village; not that Sukhoi and his Ruedin seemed to notice as they scanned the area for Raiders. The village consisted of about twenty rough buildings on either side of a road that ran straight up to the lake ahead.

There was a ramp attached to a wooden structure; like a pier, with a couple of small boats moored on either side. A wooden platform reached out either side of the pier and out of view, there were a few people walking along the structure heading for the pier. The village itself seemed particularly busy, there were a few shops, selling various wares; from cloth to meat, from copper pans to game birds. There were two Inns; one located half way down the left-hand side of the village between a bakers and a cobblers and another on the right hand side almost directly opposite, situated between a Blacksmiths and what seemed to be an ordinary house. Painted signs, swinging on wooden posts identified the two buildings as "The Travellers Rest" and "The Boot and Shoe."

The villagers were all dressed in various garments, some with turbans, and some without, drab colours and bright, the differences were startling. They appeared to be people from different places who had just congregated in this village, though most were obviously passing through by the startled looks on their faces. As with the children, they gawped around at the various buildings and the odd person that was dressed differently to themselves in wonder.

As the group walked through the village they were given a few cursory looks, they even received a few nods of acknowledgement, but with the companions in the lead the children were herded up the road.

They stopped at the house next door to "The Travellers Rest" and Sukhoi knocked twice on the door, and then waited.

A few seconds later the door opened and a large, fearsome, bear of a man, wearing clothing similar to what the companions were wearing answered.

"Who is it?" He growled. But he took one look at Sukhoi and smiled, and then he saw Braduga and Socata and he began to laugh. "Well, well, well, so the travellers return, eh?" He said as he opened the door wider to allow everyone inside.

"Well met, Quince." Sukhoi replied with a big smile.

"Come, come, you know the way." Said the big man as he moved his bulk out of the way so everyone could get through the door; with a bit of a squash, it was barely achievable.

Sukhoi led everyone down a narrow, dimly lit corridor to a wall at the far end.

He touched the wall and the entrance to a Haram appeared. He beckoned everyone to follow him as he walked through.

As they entered the cavern they were met by two men, one young; about twenty years old, who greeted Sukhoi as a brother, the other, in his late thirties, clasped hands with both Socata and Braduga. Everyone smiled and laughed and greeted each other as the children stood by watching.

A few minutes passed until the twenty year old nodded askance at the children behind the men.

"Yes, sorry, please forgive me." Sukhoi said to the children. "May I present, Ruddale Safir of the Kavacha." The young man nodded to the three children.

"Please call me Ruddy." He offered to the children.

"Adan Ismail of the Ossora." A tall, well-built man nodded solemnly at the children in acknowledgement. "And I think you have already met Quince Ibrahim of the Palana." The bear-man smiled warmly.

"May I present David, His sister Jennifer and his brother Christopher from England." Sukhoi finished as an afterthought.

By the look they gave to Sukhoi, the three men obviously didn't know if the Kavacha was making that name up or not, but never the less, they managed to smile again in acknowledgement.

Once the introductions were finished, Sukhoi asked the children to make themselves comfortable while he had a word with his friends. He pointed out a table with plenty of food on it and told them to help themselves to what they wanted. The children tucked into the food as they watched the friends move to one side of the Haram for a private conversation.

From the looks they kept receiving from the other Kavacha and his honour guard, they realised that Sukhoi must be telling them of their journey so far.

"I wonder how much he's telling them." David asked, a little nervously. He wasn't sure he wanted everyone knowing their business.

"Not nearly as much as he probably could." She replied.

"What makes you say that? Can you sense something?" David asked her quietly.

"Nothing like that," she replied, "I have been watching them closely and they haven't been too surprised by what Sukhoi has told them yet. If he was telling them everything that had happened to us, surely they would find some of that quite interesting, especially if he told them about speaking with the Dragons." She finished.

That was true enough, David thought, as he covertly watched the conversation, Jennifer was right, none of the three men looked at least surprised by what the Kavacha was telling them.

After about an hour, the men rejoined the children and everyone chatted about what they had been doing. It appeared that Ruddy and his men had been on their way to the Guardian's Stone, and were hoping their paths would cross with Sukhoi on the other side of the mountains.

It emerged that the Kavacha were constantly crossing the mountains not only to search for the Nadym Varsk but also for any signs of the Toureng. It was now Ruddy's turn to cross the mountain pass; though he admitted that he didn't like this particular journey.

"At least you shouldn't run into any Gourtak." Christopher said. "Braduga killed them." He said proudly.

"What is this?" Quince shouted intrigued.

It was obvious that Braduga's little excursion into the mountain by himself to find and kill the Gourtak hadn't been mentioned by anyone.

"It was nothing really." Braduga said with a wince.

But it was too late; the other Ruedin wouldn't let it go and so Socata had to re-tell the story of Braduga's triumphant battle over the Gourtak, which he only embellished ever so slightly.

"You were very lucky, my friend." Adan said as Socata finished the tale, though he was clearly impressed.

"Yes I know." Braduga replied.

"But I wish I could have been there." He said laughing. "Only you Braduga could have faced two Gourtak and lived to tell the tale."

All the companions nodded in agreement and laughed as Braduga just blushed and finally joined in with the laughter.

They continued to talk and to eat as the day wore on, discussing events taking place throughout Sakhalin and other journeys the friends had been on since they last met. During a lapse in conversation Sukhoi took Ruddy to one side for a private chat.

Both David and Jennifer could tell from the expression on Ruddy's face that Sukhoi was finally telling his brother Kavacha the rest of the tale. They couldn't tell if he was told everything but from the surprised gasps that came from their direction it was fairly obvious he was telling him most things. This became more evident when later on they noticed that Ruddy kept staring in their direction, though he tried not to make it too obvious.

Ruddy was still quite young and newly trained as a Kavacha. His abilities had not had a lot of time to mature and he was constantly learning new things about the knowledge and about himself. Sukhoi had related most things to the young Kavacha, and what had surprised him the most was Jennifer's ability to communicate with the Dragons. He had never actually met the Dragons before himself but he knew a few Kavacha that had and everyone knew of the bond of friendship between Sukhoi and those magnificent creatures. He believed everything his Kavacha brother told him without question, but he found it difficult to believe that this strange girl could actually speak with the creatures. He couldn't help but to stare at her, even knowing that he had been seen by her and her brother. He decided eventually that he should probably go over and apologise if he was making them feel uneasy. Besides; he thought to himself, it was a good excuse to speak with her himself and see if he could find anything else out about the three strangers.

"Jennifer, David, I would like to apologise for staring, but after what my brother has just told me about you two, I must admit, I am finding it difficult to take it all in." Ruddy said as he approached the children.

Jennifer smiled and replied, "I know what you mean, we don't believe it ourselves and we were there."

Ruddy's ear twitched ever so slightly and then he suddenly began to laugh.

David and Jennifer just looked at each other and then as they looked at the young Kavacha, they too began to laugh.

"It must be a little bit frightening for you? These gifts?" He asked a moment later trying to put them at ease.

"It is a bit." David replied quietly. He liked this young Kavacha he realised. He seemed only to be a few years older than Jennifer and he could tell that he had a warm and inviting personality. Jennifer appeared captivated by him; smiling at his every word, but then, Ruddy didn't know Jennifer like he did, and it wouldn't be long before it was Jennifer doing the captivating. He had seen it too many times with his friends and he had no reason to believe that the people in Sakhalin would be any different.

"I'm going to speak to Chris." He said leaving the young Kavacha to speak with his sister and then walked over to his brother who was chatting away merrily to the bear, Quince.

Ruddy watched as the boy walked away but then immediately focused his attention on the girl. "May I talk with you a while?" He asked with a big smile; showing his dimples on his cheeks.

She smiled at him knowingly and then replied. "Yes, what would you like to talk about?" She asked, though she had an idea what the topic was going to be.

"Sukhoi said you could speak with the Dragons?" He said quietly as if he still wasn't convinced by the idea.

"Yes, as amazing as that sounds." She replied, raising her eyebrows emphasising the point.

"Sorry, it is not that I disbelieve anything that was said, I would trust Sukhoi with my life, it is, just so, incredible." He said apologetically.

"It's ok," She laughed. "I know what you mean. I'm finding it difficult to believe it myself."

"You can not speak with any creatures in your own land then?" He inquired.

"No." She laughed again. "Though I must admit, I haven't even thought to try." She finished after a moments consideration. It crossed her mind then that maybe she could talk to the animals at home, but quickly dismissed the idea as ludicrous.

They talked for a long time, Ruddy asking lots of questions, Jennifer answering the ones she could as truthfully as she could. She then began asking him lots of questions about his training as a Kavacha, his family and friends, which he answered enthusiastically. Before they realised it, it was getting really late; nearly everyone else had retired to get some sleep, so reluctantly, they did the same.

Sleep did not come easy for Ruddy, he thought long and hard about what Jennifer had said to him and he realised that he too; like Sukhoi, believed the children were special. He didn't know why, but he found himself wanting to watch and protect them; especially Jennifer. Sukhoi had tried to explain to him a similar feeling he had experienced when he had first met them and now Ruddy was experiencing that same feeling. He did not think there was evil magic at work, but it was worrying that he felt such compulsion to assist these strange children. He also realised that something wonderful was happening here and now, he felt that history was in the making, and these children were an integral component of it. He realised he wanted to be a part of it and he promised himself that on the morning he would speak with Sukhoi on the matter and ask his Kavacha brother if they could accompany them on their trip back to Enkan Mys. With that decision made, he fell into a blissful sleep.

David woke in the night, rubbing his eyes; he got out of his bed and walked toward the entrance to the Haram. He didn't know what had woken him or why he felt drawn to the entrance, but he knew he should follow his instincts and find out. A moment later he was standing at the door to the house and staring out of a window at the deserted street. There was no one to be seen; although there were still a few lights on in various buildings up and down the street. He noticed a light from a candle in the window opposite their building; he could tell it was an Inn from the sign swinging in the light breeze, though he couldn't make out the name of it in the poor light. Still half asleep he was mesmerised by the way it flickered in the darkness, until a shadow moved and a cowled, white face peered through the window and looked out in his direction.

He gasped and stepped back quickly from the window, it was a familiar face that looked back at him. When he regained his courage and stepped up to the window again to look out, the face had disappeared. The candle was still flickering gently, but there was no one there anymore. Had he imagined the monk's face? He was tired, he knew that, and he was beginning to get a headache; which didn't help, but he was certain he had seen the stranger's face in the window. He waited, staring at the window across the street for a few minutes, but still nothing appeared. Finally, he decided he couldn't stay there all night and turned back down the corridor to enter the Haram. A few moments later he was tucked up in bed and sound asleep; the monk's face forgotten as he dreamed of soaring through the sky on the back of a dragon.

The stranger had seen the young boy; David, peering at him through the window from the house across the road. He had sensed him too late to hide from that look and that annoyed him. His magic allowed him the ability to sense anyone looking at him and stop them if need be, but the boy had caught him before he could do anything about it. He was surprised by this; but he shouldn't have been. He had been told to expect the unexpected with the boy and now he knew why he was given the warning. David had great potential, he had been informed and he knew he had to be more careful in future. If he underestimated him in any way, he would probably regret it.

He watched from the shadows, as finally, David left the window and disappeared from view. He dissolved the spell that cloaked him in darkness and stared at the window for a long while. David had arrived in Sakhalin safe and sound as expected, and as predicted he brought his brother and sister with him. He was told that the three children were needed for their abilities, although he hadn't been informed what those abilities could be. They were each special in their own way, but it was David and Jennifer that had a role to play; they just didn't realise what that role would be until it was too late.

His plan to send the Kavacha and his Ruedin to the Guardian's Stone this time had been the right thing to do. They would protect the children from harm and he knew that Sukhoi would gain the children's confidence and help to nurture their gifts when they emerged. Yes, he was happy, everything was going to plan; well most of it, he thought on reflection. Not every plan survived first contact; he knew, but it was still on the right track and time was still on his side.

"It won't be long now." The monk whispered to himself with a half smile. "Not long at all." Then he collected his belongings and left the Inn, disappearing silently into the darkness like a thief in the night.

Chapter Eighteen

Morning came too soon, David thought, as he was woken by the noises of everyone eating and talking, while he was still trying to sleep. He decided reluctantly to get out of bed, there was no point trying to sleep when everyone was chattering away. He didn't know why everyone had to get up so early, but as he stepped out of bed he realised that the sun was up and he was the last one to wake. He quickly got dressed; all his clothes had been laid out where he left them in a nice neat row, and he went over to the table. He looked around the table for something to eat as everyone else began to clear away their dishes.

"You took your time getting up this morning, didn't you sleep ok?" Christopher asked him.

"Fine Chris," He replied and then asked, "Is there anything left?"

"There's some smoked fish; they taste like kippers, and there's some fruit." Christopher offered. David hated kippers, but thought he should try them just in case. He took one small piece and put into his mouth and was relieved that it was in fact quite tasty. He ate a bit more and had some of the fruit, before he helped clear away the table. When he had finished he looked about to try and find out what was happening.

Christopher was talking avidly with Braduga and Socata. He had noticed of late that his brother had formed some sort of bond with the two warriors. They all seemed to get along very well and they didn't appear to mind him tagging along. He was quite happy about that, because the last thing he needed at the moment was to answer all the incessant questions his brother was bound to ask about his gifts.

Jennifer was chatting with Adan and Quince, about something or other; he couldn't quite hear, but he wasn't really interested anyway and Sukhoi and Ruddy were deep in quiet conversation. From the way they were acting, their conversation looked a little conspirational. He decided to walk over and find out if they were talking about him or his siblings. Their conversation stopped with his arrival.

"Sorry, didn't mean to interrupt." He said feeling a bit awkward now.

"No, it is fine David." Sukhoi said. "Ruddy was just asking if we minded them joining us on our journey to Enkan Mys, what do you think?" He asked.

"Me? You're asking me?" David asked amazed.

"Yes, my friend, you are part of our group and you speak for Jennifer and Christopher."

I suppose I do, David thought, but then he realised one problem with this proposal, the Dragons. "It would be great to have you and your honour guard accompany us to Enkan Mys, Ruddy but, I don't think Hash and Sak would be able to carry everyone." He replied regretfully.

"What?" Ruddy asked in surprise.

Sukhoi gave a little smile as David addressed Ruddy. He hadn't mentioned his friends to his brother Kavacha, but he was thrilled that David had realised the logistical implications of the two groups travelling together. It demonstrated a quick mind that he knew the boy had.

"My friends are meeting us this morning and have agreed to carry us to Enkan Mys." Sukhoi added.

"Would it be ok if we joined you as far as your rendezvous point?" Ruddy asked hopefully. He still hadn't met the Dragons, although he had heard all about them from both Sukhoi and a few of the other Kavacha that had the privilege of meeting them.

"Yes, of course." Sukhoi agreed happily.

"Good, that is settled then!" Ruddy replied smiling. "We will follow on behind and meet you at Enkan Mys later."

"Agreed." Sukhoi said. "Time to be on our way then."

Outside the house, the village was busy with daily chores. The fishing boats had just arrived back and the smell of stale fish had been replaced by another unsavoury smell of fresh fish. Seagulls swarmed around the boats as crates of fish were loaded onto carts and whisked away to various shops and stalls.

Other shopkeepers were laying their wares outside their shops, a couple of girls were sweeping the floors of the Inn across the road and the smithy was hammering on his anvil. Everyone seemed busy as the six men and three children made their way towards the pier where a queue was forming to get a boat to cross the lake.

As they reached the pier a group of at least twenty Raiders appeared from behind a boathouse and catching sight of the group, headed right for them.

The leader, flanked by two large men broke from the main group and approached Sukhoi.

"Kavacha, I am Abdi Salut." He introduced himself, as if his name should mean something to Sukhoi. When it didn't, he continued. "My guard are Timak and Cory."

"I am Sukhoi, what can we do for you Koutla?" Sukhoi asked calmly.

"I think you know what we want." Abdi said, directing his gaze to the children.

"Yes." Sukhoi replied. "And you know what my answer will be."

Braduga and Socata had positioned themselves either side of their Kavacha as the Raiders approached and now they were poised for action as they waited for the Raiders to make a move.

Adan and Quince did the same to Ruddy, and the children were now protected by both groups of companions.

Abdi Salut was a large man; almost as big as Maroc himself and he was adorned with numerous weapons that looked immaculate as the morning sun shone on them, but they also displayed tiny nicks that could only be obtained through frequent use. His brown eyes were intense, and determination blazed hot in the look he now directed towards Sukhoi.

Sukhoi recognised something in that look, but couldn't quite put his finger on what it was. He knew instinctively that this man was dangerous; the way he moved and talked displayed an authority that brooked no nonsense. The two giants either side of Abdi were at least a couple of inches taller than the leader, and although they didn't look as dangerous, they were a good twenty years younger. They were identically in every way, from the way they were dressed; with the same armour and weapons, to the same vicious expressions on their face. They were twins from head to foot. It was also obvious, that these three men were different to the other Koutla Raiders too, especially the ones Sukhoi had come across. They were more confident, alert and probably more able than any others he had seen. These men were dangerous, he had no doubt about that. But he had to protect the children at any cost, even if he had to face the twenty Raiders alone, he would to keep them safe.

"If you want to live." Sukhoi began. "I suggest you walk away now Abdi." He finished quietly.

Abdi stared at the Kavacha; deeper and deeper he looked into his eyes as if he was trying to see into his soul. He then looked at the other companions, until his gaze found that of the children, protected by the men.

He was weighing up his options, Sukhoi thought, he and his men were obviously proficient with their weapons, but surely even twenty men against two Kavacha and their honour guard were still not evenly matched. Either the man was very stupid, or extremely confident in his and his men's abilities.

Some of the villagers were witnessing the exchange and men began to appear from every doorway within the village, each carrying a weapon of some description, and headed towards the confrontation.

The Kavacha were known and respected everywhere they went; no matter what village or town they were in. Any violence toward them was not tolerated; even though they knew that the Kavacha; and especially their Ruedin, could look after themselves, the people believed they shouldn't have to. So when they witnessed the Koutla confronting two Kavacha and their Ruedin, they knew something would have to be done to stop any violence which may ensue.

The Koutla leader looked from the companions to the large procession of villagers. He seemed to come to the obvious conclusion with a controlled fury. "There will be another time, Sukhoi." He spat and then he and his men walked back the way they came, rounding the boathouse at the end of the street without looking back.

The villagers waited until the Koutla were out of sight before a large thickset man with a long black beard told them to return to their own chores and go about their business as usual. After a few minutes, the street was almost deserted apart from the group of companions.

Sukhoi nodded to the man in appreciation; who returned his nod with a smile, and made his way back to the blacksmiths from where he came.

Returning his attention to the retreating Raiders, Sukhoi spoke to Ruddy.

"Have you seen this band or this leader before?" He asked.

"No." He replied. "I have never seen so many Raiders together at once either. They are obviously not the same ones that attacked you before?" He asked.

"No, and it is worrying that so many of them are congealing together." Sukhoi frowned as he watched the men walk away.

"Well, I have not seen any of them before now."

"What about the leader, you did not recognise him?" Sukhoi asked. "He seemed familiar to me somehow."

"No, I do not think so." Ruddy thought.

"Ok." He said. "But there is one thing for sure; those men are dangerous, more so than any other Raider parties I have come across." Sukhoi said as he watched the Raiders leave.

"They were after the children then, like the others?" Ruddy asked.

"Yes," He replied. "But this group were not concerned that two Kavacha and their honour guard were protecting them. If the villagers had not come over I think they would have tried to take them."

Ruddy laughed. "They must be mad then! Not even a band double their size would try to fight two Kavacha and their honour guard."

"No, my friend. I do not think they were mad, but I know those men were on the verge of attacking us then. A fact, that makes me extremely nervous."

Ruddy stared at his friend and then at the departing images of the band of Raiders. He couldn't believe that anyone in their right minds would willingly force a confrontation with one Kavacha and his honour guard, let alone two.

Sukhoi nodded to the few villagers who were now busily displaying goods from their stalls, but still watching for trouble, ensuring that everything was still ok. All the Kavacha had a good relationship with every village and town in Sakhalin. They were respected by almost everyone and often seen as a talisman of luck. There was always one or two Kavacha in Kahin, and the villagers knew most that passed through. Sukhoi himself had passed through the village on numerous occasions and had never experienced any problems. But even if they didn't know the Kavacha, Kahin was a tough fishing village that didn't tolerate trouble of any kind; especially caused by anyone as despised as a band of Koutla Raiders. Many unfortunate people had found that out, to their detriment. So, the group headed for the end of the pier and were soon aboard two small boats being rowed to the other side of the lake.

Abdi Salut watched the Kavacha; their honour guard and the children leave the village and head across the lake. Abdi Salut was not like the other Raiders; he had been trained at Enkan Mys as a boy; to become one of the honour guards of the Kavacha. Unfortunately, he had been banished from what had become his home for killing a young woman. He had managed to convince the Council of Elders it had been a terrible accident but they had banished him in any case. The whole incident had been hushed up and very few people alive still remembered what had happened that fateful day. So he had been given no choice but to leave the city and the most talented warrior; at that time, had left in disgrace. After seeking work and finding nothing, he eventually joined the only people who didn't care what you had done in a past life. The Raiders were loathsome to him at first, but over the years he had come to accept their way of life, as if born to it. He had only been with them a couple of months before his skill as a warrior and his intelligent and ambitious nature was noticed by one of the Koutla leaders. It wasn't long before the training he had started at Enkan Mys was put to good use. He would never forgive the council for making him leave, and the pain of his disgrace would be with him forever, but as he watched the two boats cross the lake into the distance, he vowed; as he had each day since, to make them all pay.

Timak and Cory approached Abdi and stood patiently waiting for their leader to notice their presence.

"Yes." He said quietly, still looking at the two boats fading from view.

"The boats are ready." Timak replied.

"As are the men." Cory finished.

He turned to look at the towering twin pillars before him. They were his best warriors, loyal and trustworthy, a rare commodity to be found in the Koutla.

As teenagers they had once tried to rob him, but they soon learned the errors of their ways. Abdi had disarmed them with little effort and gave them a beating for good measure, but from that day, they had followed him everywhere. They did his bidding and in return he taught them everything he knew. They could have left him at anytime, but they decided to stay and acted like his own personal guard of honour. In fact, he reflected as he watched them patiently waiting for his orders, they were like the sons he should have had. He smiled at the thought and putting an arm around each of them, he guided them towards the waiting boats and the rest of his men.

"Ok, let's get to those boats." He said quietly.

Yes, he thought, let's get to those boats and make them all pay.

The two boats reached the other side of the lake a few hours later. As they drew near, the children were disappointed to see nothing but a small jetty where their boats would join quite a few others already moored. There was but one small building, where an old man was sitting on a bench, mending a fishing net and that was it. No village, no people, nothing.

Their disappointment must have been evident, for when they stepped out of the boats, Sukhoi asked. "Were you expecting something different?"

"I thought there may have been another village this side." David said.

"Yes, me too." Answered Christopher.

"Dakhla Mys is a small town, about a mile away," He said, remembering fondly the first time he had been to that town. It hadn't been described as a small town when he was a boy, he reminisced. "But there are normally quite a few Raiders there, so I asked the boatmen to row us here instead."

"A good idea," Ruddy said stepping out of his boat. "We don't want to draw unnecessary attention to ourselves."

The children nodded in agreement, they didn't want any attention at all and they definitely could do without any more trouble. So the small party of travellers walked through the sand and shingle towards the lone building and the old man.

Chad Macchi was seventy seven years old, he had lived by the lake all his life, it had been a hard life, but one he had enjoyed never the less. He didn't see many people these days, he thought, but he recognised the men by the way they dressed as they walked up to his home. He couldn't tell who they were until they got closer; his eyesight had been failing recently and everything further than in front of his nose was nothing more than a blur. But then he did recognise a few of the men so he stopped repairing his fishing net and waited for them to approach. "Are you well Kavacha?" Chad croaked eyeing them all up in one blurry glance.

"We are well Chad, and you?" Sukhoi asked.

"I am well thank you." He replied graciously, though he seemed a little subdued to Sukhoi.

"Has there been much news?" He asked pointedly.

"Nothing much, well nothing that makes much sense." He said soberly. "I have heard many tales of Raiders causing bother against the tribes, but I suppose that is nothing new." He finished smiling, knowing that it wasn't usual for the Raiders to attack so often.

"Oh." He said in surprise.

"Yes, a couple of travellers passed by here a few days ago now and said they had seen numerous groups of Raiders of maybe twenty or more together. They managed to stay out of their way, but it wasn't easy as more and more Raiders seemed to be joining them."

Everyone looked surprised by this revelation, but remained quiet as it was obvious the old man still had more to tell.

"Then there have been reports of villages being burned, homes and livelihoods taken away from honest hardworking folks. I don't know what it all means but I can put two and two together. When you see a wolf pack or two roaming about, the intelligent thing to do is put your chickens in the coup." He finished with a slight nod of his head and touched his nose with a wrinkled old finger.

"And have you seen any Raiders hereby?" Ruddy enquired.

"A few small groups, but they leave me alone; I haven't got anything they could use or want."

"Have you seen them recently?" Sukhoi asked.

Chad's eyes indicated a spot behind him, but replied. "No, not for a while."

Sukhoi had already sensed there was someone lurking in the bushes to his left, and now Chad had confirmed it. He quickly looked at his companions, who from their body posture and cautious looks had also noted the same, but were waiting for Sukhoi to give some word or command.

"Well thank you for your help old friend," Sukhoi announced a bit more louder than was really necessary. "But we must be on our way to Dakhla now. Braduga, have we got some spare food to give to our friend Chad?"

Chad smiled as Braduga handed over a small bag of provisions.

Sukhoi heard a faint noise from the bushes and maybe even footsteps running away when Braduga whispered in his ear.

"There was a small boy in the bushes, but he has now gone. I believe he was alone but do you want me to check to be certain."

"No, let him go tell his tales." He whispered back, but then said louder, "It is safe now Chad, what is going on here?" He asked.

Quickly the old man told them that a young boy had been seen running up and down this part of the lake for the past two days. He had been told that the same boy had been talking to Raiders in Dakhla only yesterday. He thought it best to say nothing for fear the boy would pass the information on.

"So, Chad, what else do you know?" Sukhoi asked.

"There are about fifty Raiders currently in the town; split into groups of about eight or ten; so as not to draw attention to themselves. They are staying away from each other but they cover the entire town," He said. "They are asking questions about three children; two boys and a girl." He said looking at the children knowingly. "They were behaving themselves until recently, now with more than fifty in the town they have started to cause trouble, and as more and more of them come into the town, the more trouble they cause."

"And you believe it is these that have been destroying the villages?" Socata asked concern in his voice.

"I'm not certain, but if the rumours are to be believed, yes I think so."

He was silent for a while but then added quietly, "but there is worse." He whispered.

"What?" Sukhoi asked just as quietly.

"There are stories of hideous creatures hunting in the forests and drinking the water from the lake, strange dark shapes have been flying in the night sky and even more outlandish stories of the Toureng returning and attacking the tribes once more." He whispered.

"I believe some of those tales could be true my old friend." Sukhoi said. "We have just come from Junggar Shan, over the Gratiskh Mountains, where we bumped into a pair of Gourtak ourselves, but as for the Toureng." He trailed off and shrugged his shoulders.

"I am only telling you, what I have been told." He replied, thinking they were just trying to humour an old man.

"And we are thankful for your news my friend." Sukhoi replied.

"Good." Chad answered with a smile.

"If the situation gets worse, I think you would be wise to make your way to the city." Sukhoi offered.

Chad thought for a while before answering, "You are probably right Kavacha, but my home is here, things would have to be very bad, to make me go all the way to the city, especially with my eyesight failing as it is. But you must be careful if you are going into Dakhla, the Koutla are looking meaner than usual." He advised.

"We will be ok Chad." Sukhoi replied and thanked the old man.

After a short discussion, it was decided that Ruddy and his men would recce Dakhla Mys first and report back on the current situation.

If there were too many Koutla present they would just have to go around the town instead of through it. With the decision made, Ruddy and his Ruedin followed the track behind Chad's home and headed for the town.

"Do you think there'll be trouble?" David asked Sukhoi.

"We will try and avoid any trouble, David." Sukhoi replied. "But with that many Raiders in town we must be cautious."

"Where are we meeting the Dragons?" He asked.

"The other side of town, there is a big clearing about three miles beyond the outskirts, I have met my friends there before; they know it well."

"Is there no other place we could meet them, away from the town?" David asked hopefully. He wanted to avoid a confrontation with the Koutla Raiders if possible and the obvious decision would be to meet the Dragons somewhere else.

"I do not think so, we need to get to Enkan Mys as soon as possible and this is the only option I can think of." He said regrettably.

"Couldn't Jen send them a message to meet us here instead then?" He inquired.

"Good idea but they do not like to land near water. We should be leaving now; I think Ruddy has a sufficient lead on us by now."

Slowly, they made their way toward the town, but it wasn't long before Adan met them. "Ruddy thinks there are too many Raiders in the town." He greeted them. "I will take you on a path around it; Ruddy and Quince will keep watch and give warning."

Zigzagging through the trees and over rocks, the companions and the three children followed the warrior to within throwing distance of the town.

As they moved cautiously from one building to another, Sukhoi noticed Ruddy and Quince surrounded by eight Raiders. They appeared to be having a heated conversation and things didn't look too good.

"The young hot-head." Sukhoi remarked quietly. "Adan, I think we will be ok from here, and besides, your Kavacha could use your skills more than we, at this time."

Adan looked over and smiled, "he's still young and enthusiastic. I will look after him." He said quietly and then nodded to Braduga and Socata before he left to be with his Kavacha.

"Will they be ok?" Jennifer asked in a whisper, mindful of where they were.

"Yes Jennifer, Ruddy may be young but he is still a Kavacha, he will be able to handle a few Raiders." Sukhoi reminded her.

"Ok, keep close and keep quiet, it is time to move again." He whispered to everyone. With Braduga leading the way now they continued on the path chosen by Adan. They only saw a few people as they moved swiftly around the town, moving stealthily from building to building. But those that saw them didn't really pay much attention anyway. They still had to be careful never the less and it took a little longer than expected to get to the meeting place.

They stopped by the last building and Sukhoi pointed out a wood just ahead. The clearing was in the centre of the wood but first they had to cross a road in front of them. Braduga went to check to see if all was clear but he came back shaking his head. "There are Raiders everywhere." He told them. "They are guarding the road, but we should be able to cross it, if we move one at a time." He suggested.

"Ok, we cross one at a time, everyone ok?" Sukhoi asked. Everyone nodded and with Braduga co-ordinating the crossing, everyone moved into place.

The Raiders weren't very diligent in their duties and the small group managed to get across the road eventually without any problems and more importantly, without being seen. When they reach the other side and entered the wood, Sukhoi put his finger to his lips, enforcing the need for silence as they made their way to the clearing.

The wood was quite dense and there were bushes and brambles everywhere, which hindered their progress. When the clearing was finally in sight the children knew that something was wrong. Both Braduga and Socata were constantly scanning the trees all around them and they had drawn their weapons.

The clearing was just ahead of them, it was a wide open space surrounded by trees but Sukhoi was reluctant to give the order to enter the open ground.

"We are surrounded Sukhoi." Braduga stated as the group stopped and stared at the clearing in anticipation.

"Yes my friend, it appears we have underestimated the Koutla and now they begin to close in." Sukhoi answered him.

"Do we stay in the woods?" Socata asked his Kavacha.

Sukhoi thought for a moment and then replied. "No, let us see our enemies face to face."

He turned to David and said. "You must stay out of this, do not use your magic. Only use it as a last resort to protect yourselves, ok?"

When David nodded he continued, "We will form a triangle, stay in the centre of that triangle." Then as one they entered the clearing.

The children moved closer together as Sukhoi and his Ruedin moved into formation. They looked toward the trees expectantly and with dread and they weren't disappointed as armoured clad figures began to emerge from them. They were indeed surrounded; there must have been at least fifty Raiders if not more. Each one was brandishing a sword or an axe and they closed in on the little group. They were all smiling and jeering as they brandished their weapons and pointed them at the three men protecting the three very frightened children.

As terrified as he was, David couldn't help but think that if the Raiders had brought bows with them, they would have had no choice but to surrender there and then. But amazingly they didn't and he knew then that they still had a chance. Sukhoi and his Ruedin were formidable warriors, if Ruddy and his Ruedin could get there in time, he was almost certain that they would be ok, even against fifty Raiders.

One man stepped forward from the crowd surrounding them and smiled at Sukhoi; it was not a friendly smile. "So Sukhoi, we meet again." Said Abdi Khouna.

Sukhoi was amazed to see the Koutla Raider they had met on the other side of the lake so soon, though he kept his expression blank. The Koutla leader had crossed the lake and wasted little time in banding together the Raiders, but how had they known where to find them, he wondered? He was just about to speak to the Raider leader when Jennifer whispered in his ear.

He paused for a moment and then said to the Leader. "You seem well organised Abdi, how did you know we would be here?"

"I don't have to answer your questions." He spat back, "just hand over the children and I'll let you live." He said menacingly.

"I can not do that, but tell me why you want them so badly?" He asked.

"We are being well paid for the service Sukhoi, well paid indeed, now hand them over."

"You know I can not do that?" Sukhoi replied.

"I know." Abdi acknowledged and a big grin appeared on his face. That grin said everything, he knew they had no choice but to fight and with the odds in their favour he knew that the Raiders would be triumphant.

"Get ready." Sukhoi whispered.

Abdi gave the order to attack and the Raiders charged the Kavacha and his Ruedin with careless abandonment as if their force of numbers would be enough to overpower the three men in that first instant, they were wrong.

Sukhoi unleashed his magic into the first few unfortunate Raiders that crossed his path. Waving his arms with purpose, he directed tiny balls of fire into their midst, knocking them to their feet and scorching their armour. He moved like lightning, trying to disperse his magic evenly around the small group. Surprisingly the Raiders were neither shocked nor frightened by the Kavacha's magic, but it did slow their attack on the small group.

Socata's axe and Braduga's swords were a blur as they tried to counter the attack, striking, thrusting, and stabbing with precision and skill. But there were too many and the attack was too fast and furious. It should have been all over, the Raiders should have killed them all but then Jennifer shouted as loud as she could.

"They're here!"

Hash'ar'jefar and Sak'ar'jefar shrieked as they plummeted from the skies above into the clearing. Raiders scattered with frightened yells as they trampled each other to get out of the way of the Dragon's descent. Only the Koutla leader and his bodyguard didn't move, although they weren't really in the Dragons' path.

Running for their lives the Raiders scrambled out of the way and retreated into the dense woods, where they cowered behind the trees and watched the creatures from the safety of the trees.

Hash'ar'jefar gave one more piercing screech and then folded his wings and walked over to the smiling, yet exhausted faces of his friends, while Sak'ar'jefar stood guard.

Jennifer had been trying to contact the Dragons ever since Braduga had said that they were surrounded and having spoken with them, she asked them to come to their aid as soon as possible. It was Hash'ar'jefar's response; that they would be there in a few minutes that she had whispered to Sukhoi.

Sukhoi thanked the Dragons for coming to their aid so swiftly and then he turned to look at the Koutla Raider leader, who was watching the exchange.

Abdi Khouna realised yet again that the children would be beyond his grasp as he watched the Dragons land in front of him. He stood staring at the Kavacha for a few seconds with hate burning in his eyes. He noticed that Sukhoi had seen him looking at him and after a moment's hesitation he told the twins to gather his men. Slowly, he turned away and with the twins following behind, they left the clearing and disappeared amongst the trees.

Sukhoi watched him leave, this Koutla leader impressed him, but there was also something else that he couldn't quite put his finger on. Then it struck him like a thunderbolt, he realised for the first time in his life that he was also scared. He couldn't remember the last time he had been scared of anyone or anything. But he knew this man was dangerous and somehow, he knew that given the opportunity, this man would kill him. It shocked him to his very soul, his Kavacha knowledge told him that if this man Abdi Khouna tried to kill him, he could very well succeed. He also realised that he had seen the man before, but the when and where, still eluded him for some reason.

There were so many questions that needed answers, but he didn't have the luxury of time. He had to get the children to Enkan Mys, safe and sound. With the arrival of their friends, it would make his mission considerably easier.

The arrival of the Dragons was cause for celebration, not just they had arrived at a most crucial moment, but because it was a joy to be with them once again, especially now they could communicate through Jennifer.

As the group waited impatiently, Jennifer chatted with the Dragons, thanking them for their speedy arrival. They would have continued to talk for hours if Sukhoi had not eventually interrupted the discussion. The Kavacha and his Ruedin were still nervous about being in the open and with justification, as they told the children they were being watched from the trees.

"What about Ruddy and his Ruedin?" Jennifer asked, "Will they be ok?"

"I think they will be fine." Sukhoi replied, "It is not easy to get rid of a Kavacha and his Ruedin, but I will leave him a message before we depart." He finished as an afterthought.

"How are you going to do that?" David asked intrigued.

"A little magic." He replied evasively.

The children watched as he performed his incantation, David tried to listen to what the Kavacha said, but he couldn't really make any of it out clearly enough to understand it. It only took a couple of seconds and then he was finished.

"Ruddy will know what happened here when he arrives and I have left him with instructions to follow us to the city, so we should be on our way, from these prying eyes."

The three companions and the three children mounted the Dragons' backs as they had done so once before and within moments they were soaring in the clear blue sky above the clearing.

Abdi and his twin protégés watched from the trees in wonder, at the unbelievable exchange between the Dragons and the group. Abdi had seen the Dragons before, a long time ago now, but he had never witnessed them ever actually communicating with anyone. Abdi noticed things other men missed and he had noticed a difference in the way the Dragons behaved, from when he had last seen them. He was certain beyond any doubt that the Dragons were actually talking with the group, more importantly, to one member of that group.

"The girl seems to be doing all the talking." He said out loud, though he hadn't realised he had said anything until Cory agreed with his observation.

"Yes, from the way she addresses the Dragons and then the Kavacha, it appears she acts as an interpreter." He replied.

"This is a very interesting piece of information and could be potentially very important." Timak agreed.

"Very important indeed." Abdi smiled at his protégés. He couldn't help but smile; he had wasted the opportunity to capture the children, twice in one day, but his training of the twins had been proved once more. They too had noticed the unexpected and marked it for use in the future, not everyone could do that.

He turned to the twins. "You must always try and obtain as much information about your enemies as possible." He said. "Either our friend wasn't aware of this or he kept it from us for some reason. But that is not important for the moment. We must now re-evaluate our position, then adapt and prepare for our next meeting, ensuring we take all we have learnt into the situation." He said watching his foe mount the Dragons' backs and rise into the sky.

Twice now they had eluded him, he thought. The next time, he would be better prepared. He would not only deliver the boy; as he had been directed to do, but he would also deliver the girl, the girl who could speak with Dragons.

Chapter Nineteen

"How long will it take us to get to Enkan Mys?" David shouted across to Sukhoi as they soured through the cloudless blue sky. It was exhilarating being on the back of a dragon; although you wouldn't believe it to look at David as he hung on, as if his life depended on it. It did actually; they were at least five hundred feet up and travelling faster than anything else he had ever been on.

"Probably a couple of hours by our current speed." He replied, the thrill of travelling this way evident on his face.

"Are we going to land right in the City?" Jennifer asked.

"No, I do not think we should do that, a lot of the people have not seen a Dragon before." He replied. "They can be quite intimidating." He laughed thinking of the expressions of the Raiders as the dragons arrived in the clearing earlier.

"Where shall I tell them to take us then?" Jennifer asked.

Sukhoi described the place, which was a small copse of trees, about four miles from the City gates. It was an ideal location to land, there were no people nearby and the trees and a rocky mound would afford them sufficient privacy for them to land there and provide some protection from the elements.

"What can we expect when we get there?" David inquired.

"A request will have to be submitted to the council of elders, then I will tell them of our journey and of your goal to return home. They will make a decision on what to do after that." He said, though he smiled encouragingly at him.

"Oh." David said, looking at Sukhoi worriedly.

"Do not fret so David," He said. "I have promised to help you all I can. You will get home safely." He promised.

David brightened at this and smiled back, relief evident on his face. He then leaned forward on Hash's back and tried to enjoy the thrill of flying through the sky on the back of a real live Dragon, even if his knuckles were turning white from the effort of holding on as tight as possible.

They arrived at the copse of trees at midday; dark clouds had appeared from nowhere and now obscured the sun. A thin drizzle of rain had begun to fall as they landed and the mood of the party had turned sombre. The rocky outcrop wasn't big but with the trees surrounding it, it was large enough to offer some protection against the rain. So the companions huddled under the rock as the Dragons sat under the trees, but they didn't seem to mind.

"Are we not heading straight for the City?" Asked David as he watched Braduga began to make a fire and Socata prepare some food.

"Not yet David." Sukhoi replied. "There is something we must do first."

"Is there some ritual you must perform before you enter the city?" Christopher asked, thinking he had the answer.

Sukhoi laughed. "No, my friend. I just thought we should talk about the elders, the council and what you can expect when you enter the city."

"Oh." Christopher replied, shrugging his shoulders. "Worth a guess." He said.

As they ate their meal around the fire, Sukhoi told them that the council consisted of seven elders. Two elders were nominated from each tribe to perform the duty for three years. The council leader was nominated and voted in for five years to provide continuity, by all the tribal leaders. It was a duty that all the tribal elders would eventually perform on more than one occasion if they lived that long. Anyone could request an audience with the council, but it had been known to take weeks for that audience to be given. The only way to ensure your case is heard immediately is if a Kavacha spoke on your behalf. They should receive an audience virtually straight away because he was requesting it himself. Once all information pertaining to a case had been heard the council would debate and present their findings in due course. It could in theory be a slow process, but Sukhoi was optimistic the council would be able to decide on the best of course of action immediately.

"Do you think they could help us get home?" David asked, unconvinced and worried about the length of time the council might take to make a decision to help. David was well aware how long it had taken them to get this far, if they had to wait weeks and weeks for an audience, he would be pulling his hair out.

"And help the Dragons?" Jennifer added, "They have to get home as well, don't forget.

"I have not forgotten our friends, "Sukhoi acknowledged, "Once the council agrees, we can ask the Keeper to check in the Kavacha book of knowledge to see if there is a means to get you all back home." He replied. He hoped so, anyway, though he didn't voice this out loud.

"But what if there isn't anything in this book of knowledge?" David asked.

Sukhoi looked at all the children then and replied. "Then we will find a way to get you home together and we will not rest until this is accomplished."

David nodded, but he now realised that getting home wouldn't be as easy as he first anticipated. In fact, he wasn't sure if they would get home at all this way, and they may have to go back to the Guardian's Stone after all.

The hours ticked by slowly as they discussed how they would present themselves to the council. Sukhoi would lead the children into the main hall followed by Braduga and Socata.

Jennifer would summon the Dragons when the time was right, they would stay out of sight until that moment. This would allow the children sufficient time to tell their story without everyone being distracted by the Dragons presence.

The rain continued to fall as they chatted about the council, the city and the people of Enkan Mys. Plans were discussed and formulated and then revised as they tried to think of every contingency. The rain continued to fall about them as they chatted, with the only protection coming from the outcrop of rock. They didn't really mind, they were almost at Enkan Mys, which meant they were almost home. The buzz of excitement was electrifying, as the children spoke of returning home and through Jennifer; the Dragons talked of seeing their family and friends once more. There were tears of happiness as well as sadness that night. All their journeys were coming to an end and they couldn't wait for the morning to begin. Darkness came swiftly and everyone retired early, the following day was going to be busy, and Sukhoi wanted everyone refreshed and ready to leave at first light.

He was walking down a brightly lit corridor; all white and clinical, an odour of rotten flesh seemed to permeate the atmosphere; the smell strong and nauseating, burning his nostrils with its putrid breath. A dense misty fog crawled along the floor and around his feet, but he wasn't interested in the fog or the smell for that matter; his gaze was focused on the obscure, indeterminate figure before him. He was walking toward that figure now; although he felt as if he was actually floating on the mist rather than walking, the dark figure watching and waiting for his arrival. Before he knew what was happening he was standing before the figure who was dressed in a monk's habit, the figure's face obscured from view by an overlarge hood.

He knew he was shaking with fright, but he could do nothing about that, his body was no longer his own, he had no power over it anymore, the figure before him was in total control. Then he heard the footsteps behind him, faint but there nevertheless, and heading in his direction. His body began to stop shivering and he began to relax, that was until he realised the hooded figure was raising its head toward him. He tried to shout again and again, "No, you will not have me, leave me alone!" But the figure's head continued to rise.

The footsteps were getting closer, their pace more frequent but he could not take his eyes away from the figure before him. He couldn't do anything and the figure lifted its head. He screamed!

It was cold, dark and wet when the group set off for the city the next day. The dark menacing clouds ensured a dismal morning with extremely poor visibility but they could still see the high walled city in the distance. All the trees and shrubs had been cut away from around the City as an obvious defensive measure. No one would be able to approach the city walls without being seen straight away. From this distance the city itself looked like a fortress. The huge wall completely surrounded it and must have been at least twenty feet high; with guard towers situated along its length at intervals. They could see a pair of large wooden gates along on length of wall as they drew closer. It didn't take them long to walk the four miles distance to the South Gate and they had to be there before the second bell rang. Even though the clouds were becoming dark and menacing, and the rain had turned torrential, the muddy ground hardly hindered them at all. The companions were hunched over with cloaks covering their heads when they finally arrived at the gate.

Sukhoi knew he was taking a risk by bringing the children to the South Gate at this time, but it was a risk worth taking if he could find out who was paying the Koutla Raiders to capture them.

Braduga and Socata were ahead of him, poised and prepared to act if required, while Sukhoi listened and watched, and walked in front of the children acting as a shield. He had not told them what the Raider leader had said to him, but from his countenance they knew something was wrong.

The South Gate was just being opened as they drew near, alert for anything unusual the group walked to the entrance. A guard approached them; visibility was pretty poor with the torrential rain, so he had to walk a few yards from the gate to get a look at the group of people heading his way before allowing them to enter.

As they sloshed closer, recognition lighted his face. "Welcome back Sukhoi of the Kavacha!" He shouted through the wind and rain.

"Sush." Sukhoi said putting his finger to his lips, but it was too late, a dark shadow passed behind the gate, running away from it in obvious flight.

"After him!" Sukhoi shouted.

Braduga and Socata charged after the shadow as the guard looked around startled and surprise by this turn of events. "What's happening Kavacha?" He asked worriedly.

Sukhoi recognised the guard but did not know his name; he stared into his eyes as he asked. "Who was waiting by the gate as we approached?"

"No one that I know of, Kavacha." He replied clearly agitated by this unexpected turn of events.

"Are you sure?" He used all his training to determine whether or not the guard was telling the truth.

"Yes, positive, there was no one here a moment ago."

"It will go bad for you, if I find out you are lying to me." Sukhoi said menacingly.

The guard paled and looked extremely worried. "I swear Kavacha, there was no one there a moment ago, that I saw." He said nervously looking around for someone to confirm he was telling the truth, but finding no one.

Braduga and Socata returned a moment later shaking their heads. "We lost him." Braduga said.

"He was too fast." Socata confirmed.

"What's going on?" David asked, totally confused by what was happening. "Who was too fast?"

"Ok my friend, I am sorry, you have done nothing wrong," Sukhoi apologised to the guard though inwardly he was annoyed that he had lost the opportunity to find out who had been paying the Koutla to capture the children.

"What is your name?" Sukhoi asked the now extremely nervous guard.

The guard straightened, head held high, with his shoulders back. "Benjika, Ben." He replied.

Sukhoi nodded in recognition, he remembered where he had seen the guard before and he berated himself for not remembering his name. After all, it was this same guard that had accompanied him on a journey to Dakhla Mys once before.

"Right Ben," He said. "I would ask a favour of you."

Ben relaxed a little, though he didn't feel like it. "Yes Kavacha, anything?" He said, though he wished he hadn't been on duty this morning now; especially as he was only standing in for one of his friends; who had gotten a little drunk the night before.

"If anyone acting suspiciously comes to this gate, will you let me know?"

Sukhoi asked.

"Certainly," He replied. "But to be honest, this gate is rarely used." He said helpfully; which was why he had agreed to do the duty in the first place.

"Yes, I know." Sukhoi replied and gathering the children and his companions he started forward and into the City of Enkan Mys.

Ben stood there drenched and watched as the group entered the city.

"I'm going to bloody kill Wayan Droon when he sobers up!" He said under his breath.

Sukhoi told the children what the Koutla leader had said about delivering the children to Enkan Mys via this particular gate and at this time.

"Why didn't you say anything?" Jennifer asked suspiciously.

"I didn't want to worry or frighten you. I said you would be safe here. I thought we would be able to identify the man responsible for trying to capture you and end it here and now." He replied sincerely.

"I wish you would have just told us, maybe we could have helped." Jennifer said reproachfully.

"Yes, you are right." Sukhoi admitted. "It will not happen again."

"Good." She said, and walked through the gate to Enkan Mys, with everyone else on her heels.

"Oh my!" Jennifer exclaimed in amazement, stopping just inside the entrance to the city and gaping at the sight before her. The rain stopped just at that moment and the clouds broke to reveal a startling and glistening city beyond.

Sukhoi and his companions smiled as they saw the expression of wonder on the faces of the children. With the sunlight bursting through the clouds Enkan Mys dazzled the children with its beauty. They had entered through a side gate, so the view wasn't as spectacular as the main entrance, but it was still breath taking all the same.

There were straight streets with stone roads, and buildings running along the side, leading towards an extremely large round stone structure in the centre of the city. The roads had pavements and every ten metres or so there was a tree or shrub; well trimmed and nurtured. There were signs on almost every building they could see. Shops of every description could be seen. There were fountains and statues, shops and stalls everywhere.

David stared, he had seen this place before, he thought. The sight of the city overwhelmed him and he felt a warmth grip his heart. It was amazing, just like some pictures he had seen in a book on the Romans, with the centre building being the spitting image of the Colosseum. He wondered if that was why he thought he recognised this city, but that didn't make sense, the Roman Empire had perished hundreds of years ago. Whether it was in a book or not; he couldn't quite recall, but the city was magnificent, and as he gazed upon it in wonder, he felt at home.

"Welcome to Enkan Mys." Sukhoi announced as he opened his arms and introduced them to the city.

A bell rang twice.

"Why is it so quiet?" Christopher asked, his eyes darting from one building to another, drinking in the sights before him.

"Everyone will be gathered in the Corinth by now. " Sukhoi told them pointing to the structure. "The elder will speak to the people of the city and praise their efforts in keeping the three tribes strong. Afterward, everyone can watch the Ruedin as they train. It has been a tradition since the tribes split.

"And everyone goes along?" David asked incredulously.

"Yes, it is the one tradition we hold dear to our hearts."

"The entire city attends?" David asked again, unconvinced.

"Mostly, except of course the soldiers that guard the city gates." He added.

"Incredible." He replied in wonder. He noticed as he looked at all the various streets and buildings that they all converged in the centre of the city and the Corinth. He couldn't believe how much the city resembled the Roman city of ancient times and the Corinth resembled the Colosseum.

As they walked toward the centre of the city, Sukhoi pointed out various structures, statues and buildings, providing them with a guided tour of the city as they drew ever closer to the impressive structure; where all the people of Enkan Mys were congregated.

The closer they got to the stone structure, the more David was convinced of the similarity. He had recently written a story about a gladiator who had to fight for his life in the Colosseum in a history project. This stone structure; in the middle of the city, was almost identical, he thought. If he remembered rightly the Roman emperor's used their Colosseum for their own amusement with murderous intent; David hoped the people of Sakhalin didn't do the same.

"It looks like the Colosseum, doesn't it?" Jennifer whispered in his ear as they walked along the streets.

David had to smile to himself, "Yes it does a bit Jen." He replied. Jennifer was supposedly quite good at history, and she had just confirmed that he had been right to make the analogy.

David was surprised at how long it seemed to get to the Corinth, but he shouldn't have been, it was a massive city. He had only seen small villages and relatively small towns so far, but this was something entirely different. There must have been thousands and thousands of people living in this city, and he couldn't believe that they were all tightly packed in the inside of the building he had finally reached. He craned his neck as he tried to take in the full view of the stone structure before him. To say it was impressive was an understatement and he felt overwhelmed by its ornate beauty. As the children stared in open amazement they were escorted along a corridor of tall stone pillars, until they reached a large wooden door. Sukhoi pushed it open to present a gap wide enough for everyone to squeeze into one after the other. Following closely behind the Kavacha they walked up a series of steps and were then confronted by a scene from Roman antiquity.

The Corinth was immense; they had walked up to a terraced area that was full of people, all watching the scene in the arena below. But even with the Corinth totally packed from pillar to post there wasn't a sound being muttered. They appeared to be in the middle of the lowest level of a five-tier seating area, with the arena about fifteen to twenty feet below them. The arena was full of soldiers standing in square formations of approximately forty men, some with their backs towards them. Different coloured clothing and weapons distinguished the squads; their weapons held on their left-hand side. The soldiers were deathly still; anticipation fizzled in the air. All was silent, even the crowd of spectators seemed to hold their breath as a figure emerged opposite the group on the third level; they had arrived just in time. The man looked old and frail dressed in flowing robes of brown as he stepped forward to address the crowd and the soldiers alike.

"That is a surprise. " Sukhoi whispered to the children. "The old man is the leader of the council, Elder Hanish."

"People of Enkan Mys." The old man's voice resonated throughout the Corinth to reach everyone in the audience. "We bless this day, and bless our lives; we shall conquer our fears and be strong in the face of adversity."

He boomed to the ensemble with enthusiastic temperance.

He carried on talking for quite a long time about the roles and responsibilities of each individual to ensure the city maintained a peaceful society. The city would remain prosperous and would benefit all the tribes if everyone worked together. He then addressed the soldiers in the arena and told them, with their skills and dedication they would find the Nadym Varsk and fulfil the prophesy. He then told everyone how proud he was of their achievements and then ordered the ceremony of the newly appointed Ruedin to take place.

"That explains it." Sukhoi added. "You are lucky to see the passing out parade of some newly appointed Ruedin, which is why Elder Hanish is overseeing the proceedings today." He enlightened the children.

The children watched with undisguised intrigue as column after column of warriors performed an elaborate dance with their chosen weapons. Swordsman were swinging their weapons in majestic arcs in unison; to the wholehearted cheers of the crowd. Archers were using their bows as staffs and twirling them around, only to pull arrows from their quivers and shoot at various targets across the arena; finding the red circles with ease. Each column of warriors performed something different for the enjoyment of the crowd, and for the benefit of the other soldiers present. The spectacle continued for approximately thirty minutes, until eventually the ceremony was concluded and the old man raised his hand for silence.

He stood there waiting for the noise from the crowd to subside and then after a significant pause the old man addressed the crowd once more, "People of Enkan Mys, let us rejoice in our salvation and praise these new warriors." He finished.

A deafening cheer emanated from the crowd and the soldiers as the old man took a step backwards and reached out to take his seat on the chair provided behind him.

Smiling, laughing and chatting to one another the crowd began to disperse to carry out their duties for the day. Sukhoi, the companions and the children now seated, watched and waited as the Corinth emptied. Sukhoi had told them it was pointless trying to get to the other side of the Corinth until most of the crowd had left. The soldiers were ordered to attention and under control of the numerous squad leaders, began to march out of the arena. Some of the crowd were still seated and watched as the soldiers marched away, leaving three squads behind. Eventually; after some considerable time, the Corinth was empty except the three squads, the companions and the old man sat on the opposite side.

The squads broke formation and under orders began to prepare the arena for training; people appeared from behind closed doors to provide additional weapons and training aides; the arena becoming a hive of activity once more.

Sukhoi stood, and watched the old man a while until eventually he motioned for the children to follow him.

They walked along the terrace to reach the old man; it took a while as they were still a few stragglers leaving the corridors.

As they walked around the Corinth, David asked. "Does this happen every week?" Amazed by the spectacle and by the attendance of probably the whole of the city.

"The ritual, yes, but the ceremony of selecting the Ruedin only happens a few times a year." Sukhoi replied. "The displays are similar but the newly chosen Ruedin try to improve on the previous event if possible." He said with excitement.

"Well, this was one was brilliant." Christopher said thrilled to have witnessed such an event.

"Yes, there is much competition between the Ruedin and their ceremonies." Sukhoi smiled at Socata and Braduga before turning his smile on Christopher.

"So we're going to meet the leader of the council now?" Jennifer asked.

"Yes, I had thought to find him in his quarters, but I am glad I came here now, I am sure he will speak with us." He replied.

"Does he come here often?" Christopher asked.

"No, just a few times a year to coincide with the appointments really, but I think he misses the training and likes to watch the soldiers."

"He misses the training, what do you mean?" Christopher asked.

"The training, Nakfa Hanish was once of the Ruedin himself; it was a long time ago now, but he has never forgotten the training he was given here."

"I would have thought," David said after thinking about the situation, "that one of the Kavacha would be the leader of the council of elders."

Sukhoi smiled. "No, we are merely seekers for the truth seer, that is our sole purpose and why we are trained with the Kavacha knowledge. There are not that many of us either, so every one of us is needed to find the Nadym Varsk."

"What will you do when you find the Nadym Varsk and the search is over?" Jennifer asked.

Sukhoi looked into the girl's eyes. "Rejoice," he replied after several moments, "for then, we will have found a way to destroy Nuba Driss and I will be able to do what I please."

They walked on in silence, until eventually they came upon the old man. He turned and smiled in recognition as Sukhoi inclined his head slightly towards him in acknowledgement.

"Sukhoi Mikoyan." The old man rasped. "How are you?"

Elder Nial Hanish had led the council of elders for almost five years now, and it would soon be time to choose a new leader. He felt as if he had made a contribution to the tribes, but he had done his time, and now all he wanted to do was to spend a bit of time with his grandchildren.

Sukhoi smiled back at the old man. "Elder Hanish, I am well, thank you. But it is good to see you. How are you?" He replied fondly and a little concerned by the frailty of the old man, which was more evident than it had been since the last time they met.

"Good my friend, tired, but good." Elder Hanish sat down again. "Who are your young friends?" He asked intrigued that the Kavacha would be escorting three children.

Sukhoi introduced the children, who greeted the old man with great respect, a fact that made him chuckle to himself quietly.

"And what stories have you to tell?" Elder Hanish inquired.

"That." Sukhoi began. "We shall save for the council." He said to the old man.

"Ah, I see. You wish for an audience then?" He asked, a thin smile on his lips.

"Yes, Elder, as soon as possible. It is a story worth listening to and could change Sakhalin forever."

Elder Hanish was not Kavacha, but he knew people, he looked from Sukhoi to the children and back again. Yes, he thought, there was something about these children. He didn't know what, but he thought Sukhoi was right, but would it change Sakhalin for the better or for worse? Now that was a question to ponder, he thought.

He gave everyone a big smile. "Well then," he said, "we should go and summon the other elders; an audience is required by a Kavacha."

With the old man leading, the companions and the children left the Corinth.

The three squads were training hard in the arena below oblivious to the conversation above them. They had been training for a gruelling four years and they now had only one more task to complete, before they could enjoy some time off with their families and friends as fully trained honour guards of the Kavacha.

Chapter Twenty

The leader of the council of elders found a soldier on duty as he left the Corinth and commanded him to summon the other elders for an audience with one of the Kavacha. They meeting would take place in the Audience Chamber in two hours time, which gave Elder Hanish enough time to speak with Sukhoi and the children. They decided to take the scenic route so Elder Hanish could perform his own guided tour of the city, divulging his extensive knowledge on the buildings and the people who created the city in the first place. The children found it incredibly informative, enjoying the old man's enthusiasm for his wonderful city.

When they finally arrived at the Audience Chamber they were surprised the time had gone by so quickly, but thanked the Elder for sharing his love of the city with them.

They walked through a long corridor and stopped in front of a pair of large wooden doors. The Elder asked them to wait and sit on the two stone benches provided, which were positioned either side of the door. He then went inside, closing the doors firmly behind him. Before he left he told them they would be called forward shortly when everyone was seated and ready to receive them.

As they waited, citizens and soldiers alike began to walk through the corridor, now and again Sukhoi and his companions received a friendly nod or smile, but no one stopped for a chat.

"You seem to know a lot of people Sukhoi, but no one stops and talks to you, is it something to do with the Audience Chamber?" Jennifer asked after a few more people passed that obviously recognised the Kavacha.

"Yes, Jennifer." Socata replied amazed at her insight. "Waiting here for an audience with the council is deemed as a significant event. Therefore, something so important should not be disturbed by idle talk or distractions." He explained.

"Sounds sensible, but it still seems a little strange." She admitted.

"I suppose it is a bit." He agreed.

They sat there waiting patiently for another twenty minutes until the big doors began to open and a guard asked them to enter. Sukhoi flanked by his two companions and the children following behind, entered the Audience Chamber a little apprehensively.

Sukhoi knew he had to help these children, by helping them he was also helping his friends, the Dragons. He had a lot of information to tell the council and on reflection, maybe he should have talked to them alone first. But having made his decision to address the council with the children, he would now stand bit it.

As they entered the room they could see the council members at the far end. They had at least a hundred metres to walk to reach them, and it was a little frightening and intimidating to the children. They were flanked by enormous marble pillars running up either side, which were intricately sculptured and decorated. A faint light shone through stain glassed windows on the right hand side, depicting fight scenes of one description or another. Torches adorned each pillar; but instead of fire in the torches, there was a crystal, which shone with a faint blue glow. The pillars stopped at the far end of the room where seven figures were seated upon a dais. As they finally reached the dais, two benches with cushions were brought into the room for them to sit on.

"Please be seated." Elder Hanish said, pointing to the seats with a friendly smile for the obviously nervous children.

Braduga and Socata positioned themselves at either end of the two benches as Sukhoi and the children sat facing the council.

"I think introductions are in order first of all." Elder Hanish announced as everyone made themselves comfortable.

Pointing to each individual from left to right, the old man introduced the council.

"Haber Bashir of the Palana, Jallo Turabi of the Ossora, Issa Garang of the Govena, Sanag Awdaal of the Palana, Erita Burao of the Ossora and finally Harg Srabat of the Govena." He finished, with an expectant look on his face.

Sukhoi stood and addressed the council. "You all know me Elders, and my honour guard." He said as the elders nodded. "But let me introduce you to three new friends of mine, David, his sister Jennifer and his brother Christopher."

Each child stood as they were named following David's lead and bowed to the Elders before them. "We are honoured to meet you." He said respectfully, although a little croakily.

The Elders nodded their heads and Sukhoi and the children sat back down.

"Why do you request this audience, Sukhoi of the Kavacha?" Elder Erita Burao asked. Erita was from Sukhoi's tribe and although he didn't really know her well, she was respected by all the tribe and was a formidable woman.

She was renowned for her direct, no nonsense approach to situations. She was extremely blunt and forthright on occasion, but likeable never the less, and obviously this was one such occasion where she felt the direct approach was needed.

"I have a story to tell, troubling news to relay and requests to make." He replied as his gaze took in all the elders before him.

"Is there any news you bring that needs our immediate attention?" Another Elder asked. Harg Srabat was old now but had been a fierce warrior in his day. He still retained a keen mind and always maintained a suspicious nature that had been bred in him since he was a child. Sukhoi knew and liked the man, and the feeling was reciprocated. They also had a very good friend in common, Maroc. Maroc had once courted the elder's daughter and had hoped they would marry, but although Maroc had found love else where, there remained a firm bond of friendship between the two.

"That you must decide for yourself, Elder Srabat." He replied respectfully.

"Let him tell his story and give his news." Elder Bashir interrupted. "Then we can hear his requests." Haber Bashir was the voice of reason, and was always eager for information. He had people reporting to him all the time with one titbit of information or another. The only problem was, he always insisted on corroborated information before making any decisions or taking any action. It was wise sometimes, but foolish at others; a bit like the man himself.

"Yes, let him speak, I would like to hear what our young Kavacha has to say." Said Elder Awdaal. Elder Sanag Awdaal had joined the council late the previous year, a tall, thin, ambitious man who had approached the council with his application to join it from his tribe, the Palana.

Elder Hanish raised his hands for quiet. "Speak Sukhoi of the Kavacha, before we start a riot." He said smiling and then settled down to hear what he had to say.

Sukhoi stood and described his journey to Junggar Shan and the surprise encounter with the children there. He told them about the magical doorway; though he never mentioned where that doorway came from or how they managed to walk through it. He didn't mention that they may have been attacked by Nuba Driss himself either, but everything else was described in detail, almost every conversation and every incident without omission. The journey through the Gratiskh Mountains, the Koutla in Konare Forest and Dakhla Mys, were all described. He told them what Chad Macchi had said about the sightings of dark creatures and of the Raider and the Toureng. He described everything, even how David had saved his life with his magic. He also added at this point that the boy showed great potential and should be tested.

As the story unfolded, his audience was mesmerised by what the group had to go through to get to the city and what obstacles they had to overcome.

The biggest surprise came when he told them about Jennifer and her ability to communicate with his friends, the Dragons. This brought raised eyebrows from every member as well as a few uttered remarks from beneath their breath. He would have been interrupted on more than one occasion; especially after his remarks about the Dragons and their quest, if Elder Hanish hadn't used his authority to keep everyone quiet. Sukhoi decided not to mention that the Dragons were waiting to be called at a moment's notice; there would be time for that later. He continued to tell them about the stolen orb and the fact that they couldn't and wouldn't return to their own land until they had it back in their possession once more. He added at this point that the Dragons didn't know how to get back to their own land; although they too had entered Sakhalin through a magical doorway, and like the children, were hoping that the council would be able to help them. Sukhoi kept the narration to the point; clear and concise without any interjector or supposition on his part. There were quite a few details he didn't mention that David; for one, picked up on, but he remained silent. Sukhoi had his reasons for not mentioning the conversation with the Koutla leader that had divulged the fact there was a traitor in Enkan Mys and he could appreciate the Kavacha's caution.

When he had finished he sat back down and waited for their response. He had made his request to help the children return home and to help the Dragons search for their missing orb, now all he could do was to wait and see what their response would be.

David looked searchingly at the faces before him. The tale sounded so unbelievable; even to him, would the council believe what Sukhoi had just told them? He felt he should say something to them himself, not that he really wanted to, but Jennifer and Christopher were looking to him to get them back home, he had to do something. He began to form the words in his mind, trying to decide what he should say that would make the council help them. Images of his mother, his friends and his home came flooding into his mind and then one image of his father; who was smiling down at him, gave him the strength to stand up.

Everyone stopped talking and all eyes went to David as he cleared his throat and addressed the council.

Jennifer squeezed his arm in support and he acknowledged it with a brief half smile as he spoke to the council.

"Hmm," He cleared his throat again. "We are strangers to your land and the events described by our friend Sukhoi of the Kavacha are true. We have travelled a long way to reach you here in the hope that you know of a way to get us home, another way to take us back through the doorway." He paused then as he tried to grab the words he had formed in his mind, but he couldn't think what to say. He looked down at his sister for support and she responded by squeezing his arm once more. "We need your help to get home and so do the dragons, please help us."

Jennifer smiled as David sat down, he had read her mind, she thought. More than anything else she wanted the Dragons to get some help.

She hoped when David stood up to speak that he would say something to encourage the elders to help and he had. She desperately wanted to know what they were thinking about. She felt a responsibility for the Dragons ever since she knew that she was the only one that could communicate with them. Their story was a sad one and every time she thought of their futile search and their absence from home she wanted to cry.

Her feelings and thoughts must have been projected in someway, because it was then that she heard Hash calling to her softly in her head.

"IS EVERYTHING OK JENNIFER?" He asked her gently.

"Yes, I think so," she replied trying to get a grip of her feelings, "they are just thinking things over at the moment. It's a lot to take in I suppose, but don't worry, I will let you know of any developments." She finished trying to put the dragon at ease.

"OK, WE WILL BE READY." He replied as his voice left her mind.

"I will let you know Hash." She replied but wasn't sure if he heard.

"Is that everything Kavacha?" Elder Hanish asked, looking a little bewildered.

"Yes." He replied.

"Magical doorways to new lands, it sounds incredible!" Elder Bashir expressed.

"Nevertheless, Elder Bashir," Sukhoi interrupted, "A magical doorway was there for us to see at the Guardian's Stone."

"Incredible." He whispered this time, finding it difficult to comprehend.

"David." Issa Garang said, looking at the boy intently.

"Yes, err." He began, trying to remember the elder's name.

"Elder Issa Garang." She helped him.

"Yes Elder Garang, sorry?" He continued nervously.

"Would you do something for me?" She asked him.

Issa Garang was a beautiful woman; she was in her forties and maintained a fitness regime that any athlete would be envious of. She was the youngest elder the Govena had sent to the council, but age did not matter when wisdom was needed. Her hair was blonde but already had hints of grey at the temples, though when the sun struck it, it glistened like gold as it flowed unhampered down her back.

"Yes, Elder Garang, what would you like me to do?" David asked wondering what the elder would want from him.

He was staring at her beautiful, bright blue eyes when he glimpsed a knife heading straight for him. Without thought or reason he instinctively put up his hand in defence and the knife stopped in mid-air.

Suddenly, Braduga crashed into him and they both went sprawling over the floor. Braduga had seen the dagger too and had desperately flung himself towards the boy to try and protect him. There was commotion everywhere; Socata had dived in front of Sukhoi to protect him, thinking him the intended target and now both the Kavacha and David were lying on the floor with the Ruedin on top of them. Jennifer was screaming in fright and shock and Christopher stood up wide-eyed and pointed at Elder Garang. "She just tried to kill my brother!" He shouted angrily.

The elders were all on their feet and speaking at the same time, trying to make sense out of what had just happened.

"Silence!" Elder Hanish shouted.

Everyone stopped shouting and screaming and stood in silence all eyes on the old man. Sukhoi, David and the Ruedin were quickly on their feet and everyone was looking at the old man expectantly.

"I am sorry David." Elder Garang said. "But I had to know the truth." She smiled meekly at the boy in what was supposed to be, an apology.

"And are you satisfied now, Issa?" Sukhoi shouted his face red with rage, forgetting the honorific in his anger. "He is but a boy and under my protection, how dare you attack him in this way." He shouted.

"I did what I had to, to find out the truth, but I am sorry Sukhoi of the Kavacha." She said and then faced David, "and I am extremely sorry to you, young man. I hoped that you would be able to avert my dagger's flight."

"You doubted my word?" Sukhoi asked quietly but through clenched teeth. "I am first of the Kavacha, how dare you insult me this way!" His expression of surprise and indignation and turned into one of anger that would have made a band of Raiders tremble in fear.

Issa stared at Sukhoi of the Kavacha as he controlled his obvious anger. She had not only insulted one of the Seekers, she had insulted the most powerful Seeker; after the Keeper, but she wanted to explain her reasons for doing so. "I did not doubt you Sukhoi, but some of what you have spoken of today is almost too much to be believed. I just wanted proof, now I have it." She said carefully.

"Whether you believed me or not is irrelevant, it does not give you the right to attack anyone." Sukhoi turned on her.

"Yes, I know and again, I apologise." She said trying to placate the Kavacha.

"Everyone sit down!" Elder Hanish ordered, "Issa, we will speak of this later."

Issa Garang nodded to the old man that she understood. This incident was not over and she knew the Council Elder would find some fitting punishment for her when this meeting was concluded for insulting the Kavacha so.

Eventually, everyone sat down and contained their anger at what had just happened. Everyone except Sukhoi and David. Both man and boy were finding it hard to contain their anger. Sukhoi was shaking with rage and had to call upon all his strength and training to stop himself from approaching the elder and slapping her senseless. David, on the other hand, was motionless, his arm was stretched out in front of him and his hand was facing the elders. He was staring at the dagger in front of him with his wide blue eyes as if seeing it for the first time.

"Sukhoi, Sukhoi." Jallo Turabi shouted. "Please sit down." Jallo was Sukhoi's uncle, they were very similar in appearance, but Jallo had a good twenty years on his nephew. Sukhoi sat down, still staring at Issa, who had the grace to look abashed.

David hadn't been listening to the exchange; he was staring at the knife. Once he got to his feet he couldn't take his eyes off the dagger that was still directly in front of him about five feet away. It didn't move or waiver, it just hung there as if suspended.

He was angry, but that was only one of a host of feelings that were now raging through his mind. He knew he could control his magic to a certain degree but he had resigned himself to not trying to perform any more magic if he could help it. But now he couldn't help it, it was either stop the dagger or die and he wasn't happy about having to do that. Seeing the dagger heading straight for him had instinctively awoken the power deep within himself and he had called it forth. But as he held onto it this time, he realised that it was significantly more intense. This time the power promised him anything he wanted, providing he had the strength and courage to use it. He suddenly realised that he could sense an immense reservoir of power in the city; though he didn't know where it was coming from. He also realised that if he could just find a way to tap into that power he would be invincible. The only problem was, the power was so intense that it frightened him, he felt that if he unleashed it, it would burst through him and escape to the outside world and wreak havoc and chaos. It was then that he heard his father's words, "You must be strong, it is better to have order not chaos!" With those words reverberating in his ears he began to regain control.

His mind rushed back to the present and he realised he could hear shouting, and someone was pulling on his sleeve.

He looked down and saw his brother, concern clearly displayed on his face, and he could now hear Jennifer calling his name. Everyone else was watching him in silence, but he couldn't help but to look back at the knife before him, his anger was still there and wanting to vent itself.

The power was ready to be used if he wanted, but he didn't know what he should do to show how upset and angry he was at the elder. He needed to show them that they couldn't treat people this way, and especially not children who were strangers to their land. They had travelled on this perilous journey through many hardships to find a way home and just when they thought they were safe and they had found the people who could help them, one of them tries to kill him. He was angry and frightened and the power he held in his hands was desperate to be released and if he didn't vent his anger somehow he would surely explode.

"What shall I do with this?" He growled angrily; he summoned the power but as it flooded into him, he almost drowned with its intensity, and he struggled briefly with it until he once again controlled it.

No-one spoke, no one knew what to say, truth be known. They all stared and then everyone gasped in surprise as the dagger slowly turned in mid air and faced the other direction and toward the council.

David grabbed hold of the magic inside him and pictured the knife turning, it did just that. He felt in control as he pictured it in his mind; just as he had told Jennifer to picture the Dragons in hers. He thought about the knife rising up to the ceiling and the knife did exactly as he thought. Everyone was transfixed as the knife moved around the room, turning their attention from the boy to the knife and back again.

Everyone was watching the knife, but Sukhoi was watching the boy with one eyebrow raised in concern. Sukhoi knew the boy had power and talent, and this surpassed even his wildest hopes, but he saw something in David's eyes that concerned him. The boy seemed to be struggling with the power, and it appeared to be a fierce battle. When Sukhoi used the power, he felt nothing but peace and harmony, why wasn't it the same for David? He must speak to the boy as soon as possible, there must be a reason.

David made the knife turn again and head for the double doors at the end of the hall, making it stop just before it struck. Everyone was still silent as he turned the knife to face the council once more and then he brought it back to head straight for Issa Garang's heart. She gasped in shock and surprise as the knife headed directly towards her. She was paralysed, and could only stare as the knife suddenly reached her; bringing yet another gasp from her lips, but it stopped inches from her chest. Elder Issa Garang held her breath for fear that the knife would pierce her heart, beads of sweat began to cascade down her forehead as she slowly turned her head to look at the other elders sat with her.

Their expressions were ones of surprise, and a little fear, but no one could do anything to help her. She turned her attention back to the boy; the boy she could have killed with this same dagger a few moments ago. Oh, she didn't want to hurt the lad but she wasn't sure a strange boy from a strange land could actually do what she had been told, even if the person telling her was a Kavacha.

She swallowed and tried to put moisture in her mouth before she spoke to him, "I am truly sorry David." She said with sincerity. "I meant you no harm."

Jennifer couldn't believe what her brother was doing with the knife, but enough was enough. The elder had been wrong to throw the knife at her brother and was appalled that she even thought to try, but she couldn't let her brother stab the Elder with her own knife.

"David," she whispered.

He turned his head slowly to look at his sister.

"I think you have their attention, please stop it now." She pleaded.

She could see that he was still angry, she could see it in his eyes, but his outward appearance was one of perfect calm and control. It was a little bit frightening to see her brother this way, but she had to try and stop him from doing anything stupid.

"Please." She whispered again.

What happened next surprised even David, but there was an audible sigh of relief and then other gasps of surprise from everyone present when the knife suddenly disappeared. He didn't even know how he did it only that he had done it. One minute the knife was inches from Elder Garang's heart, and then it had disappeared to be replaced by a bright red rose.

Although he had been angry, clarity of thought finally came to him through his sister's words. If they were ever going to receive help from these people, the last thing he wanted to do right now was stab one of them with a knife, even if he did think it justified. Once he had made that decision, he suddenly thought of a red rose, the ones his mother liked on her birthday, and then the knife had changed. It was as much as a surprise to him as everyone else, but it was David that had thought of the rose and it had been David that had changed the knife into one.

He stared at the rose that had a moment before been a knife and realised that the power inside him almost made him use that knife. He had fought to control the power this time, but would he be able to control the power in the future; if he were to use it again, he wondered.

Everyone stared at the rose, and then at David in disbelief.

He knew he had to say or do something, even if it was just to apologise, but he couldn't bring himself to say anything. He had been so angry, but now that anger had finally subsided and he was just a small boy standing in front of lots of adults supposedly asking for their help to get home.

He reached out with his right hand and the rose slowly moved towards him until it landed in his outstretched hand. Then passing the rose to his sister; who accepted it with a hesitant smile, he sat down and closed his eyes, so he couldn't see the shocked and possibly disappointed expressions on everyone's faces.

Everyone was silent; they couldn't believe what they had just witnessed. The Elders had seen magic performed often by the Kavacha, but they had never seen a boy so young have such control as the boy did. Everyone was still mesmerised by what they had seen and couldn't speak.

Elder Hanish finally broke the silence and said to the rest of the elders. "We see now, the truth of Sukhoi's words, I think we all owe Sukhoi and his friends our sincerest apologies and maybe we should have a break for a short time so everyone can calm down."

Before anyone else could say a word the big wooden doors flung open and in stepped Hash'ar'jefar and Sak'ar'jefar, looking magnificent in the sunlight from the stained glass windows as it reflected off their scales.

Everyone stood up and stared in awe as the two Dragons, majestically walked up the chamber towards them. The incident with the dagger was instantly forgotten by everyone with the arrival of the magnificent creatures as they gracefully moved along the chamber to stop before the council. Even David had to smile at the looks on the elders' faces as they approached.

"INTRODUCE US, JENNIFER." Hash asked the girl with a bright open smile on her face.

"Sorry," She said out loud. "Elders, I have the privilege and honour to introduce Hash'ar'jefar, and his sister Sak'ar'jefar, Dragons from the faraway land of Hal Argus, and our friends."

She smiled at the wonder on their faces. "But you can call them Hash and Sak."

Elder Hanish was the first to recover and through Jennifer, he introduced himself, and the rest of the council to the Dragons. He was just finishing the introductions when a squad of six armed guards rushed into the chamber.

Everybody turned to watch them as they cautiously approached the Dragons with swords and spears drawn; though not actually pointing towards the Dragons themselves; which was fortunate, as the Dragons didn't like anyone pointing weapons at them.

They looked at the Dragons in wonder but also in terror, but they finally made their way to stand in front of the council. They all looked towards the Elders, wondering what to do, until the corporal of the guard appeared to take control of his fear and stepped forward.

"Is there anything I can do, Elders?" He asked a little nervously. He secretly hoped they wouldn't ask him to do anything, but it was his responsibility to protect the council; even if he knew he would be dead in an instant if the Dragons attacked.

"You may leave us in peace corporal, everything is under control." Elder Hanish told them, and laughed out loud at their expressions as they departed. "Did we have the same look on our faces as those guards?" He said as they closed the doors behind them. "When Hash and Sak first came into the chamber?"

"I think we did." Elder Srabat said smiling, but with less mirth.

"Well, I know I did," Elder Turabi confirmed laughing.

"I think we had better have that break now, so my fellow council members and I may discuss a few matters in private." Elder Hanish said, looking directly at Issa Garang purposely.

A bell sounded and immediately a group of servants came rushing into the hall and almost dropped the platters of meat, fruit and bread they were carrying. The servants carrying the pitchers of drink careened into them but amazingly didn't even spill a drop; though how they didn't was a feat of magic in itself. They were so shocked at seeing the two magnificent creatures that it took them a few seconds to realise where they were and what they were suppose to be doing. Until finally, Elder Hanish coughed and the servants carried their trays and drinks to the table provided, before they hastily left the chamber. Then the council members made their way through a single door on the right hand side, behind the Dias. There were many such doors but this was the only one that had a sign above it which said "Private". They were gone for approximately ten minutes before they promptly returned with hungry looks on their faces. It wasn't hunger for the food though, but news of the Dragons. Only Elder Garang returned without that look as she walked back into the chamber. She was harbouring a sour and chagrined look on her face as she followed the rest of the council back into the hall.

The atmosphere had suddenly changed with the arrival of the Dragons. Jennifer spoke for them as numerous questions were asked. The audience was supposedly pausing for a break but there was little relief from the incessant amount of questions that were directed their way. Dragons and the children tried to answer as many questions as they could before Elder Hanish finally called a halt, "Lets all eat, we can ask more questions after we are nourished."

Everyone nodded their agreement and began to attack the plates of food. It wasn't long though before the questions began again in earnest though.

After a few more hours, Elder Hanish finally called a halt; to the children's relief and the dismay of the council members.

"I think everyone is tired, and in need of rest, we will reconvene in a few hours time. It will give us time to digest all this information and see if we can help both the Dragons and the children."

"Yes, that is a good idea." Elder Awdaal agreed.

Servants were called and asked to find suitable accommodation for their guests, including somewhere for their esteemed dragon friends to reside.

The Dragons thanked the Elder but declined his offer as they felt more comfortable out in the elements, but if they were needed, Jennifer would be able to get in touch with them at a moments notice. They departed as quickly as they arrived and then everyone else left the chamber to carry out their other duties.

Chapter Twenty One

An hour later, the three children were sat alone in a large room resting on three luxurious beds piled with brightly coloured cushions. The room had a balcony; which had a fabulous view of the city and a small pool in one corner, which was used to bathe in. They had been given plenty of food and drink, and now they sat chatting about the events in the Audience Chamber.

"Well," Christopher said, "I thought it was amazing, changing that knife into a rose, truly amazing." he finished, smiling at his brother.

"Well, I don't know how I did it; it was as much of a surprise to me as the rest of you. But I'm still upset that Elder Garang threw it at me in the first place."

David replied still angry with the elder.

"You are very lucky she didn't kill you." Jennifer agreed. "But at least you had your magic to protect you, if she'd have thrown it at Chris or me, we'd be dead now."

"And so would she, if that'd happened." David replied darkly.

"David, don't say that!" Jennifer exclaimed in shock.

"Well, what do you expect me to say Jen, she could have killed me and would probably have killed you if you were her target. I would have made her pay for that." He replied angrily.

"You can't go round killing people Dave." Jennifer insisted.

"If she harmed either one of you I would." David said, but sounding less convincing.

Jennifer smiled at him then, she realised it was all bravado, well, she hoped it was.

"What do we do now then?" Jennifer asked, looking round the room.

"I suppose we just rest and wait for this evening, we will be speaking with the Elders again later." David replied.

"Suppose so."

"What are Hash and Sak doing?" David asked his sister.

"They decided to go back to the copse of trees outside the city for now. They didn't feel comfortable with all these people about." She informed him.

"Can't blame them," he said, "All those people and no one to talk to, it must be quite frustrating."

"Do you think the council will help them Dave?" Jennifer asked.

"I'm sure they will if they can." He replied.

"How did you do it Dave?" She asked changing the subject.

"The rose?" He said watching his sister twist the rose in her hand. "I don't know really, the picture of a rose just came into my head and there it was."

"Why a rose?" She asked, admiring its perfection.

"I don't know. It was the first thing that came into my head. I was angry and wanted to show them, but then you said something to me. I realised that I couldn't let my anger take control and then I thought of mam and her roses for some reason, and there it was." He finished with a shrug of his shoulders.

"Better a rose than something that could kill you." She said thoughtfully.

"Yes, that's true." He agreed.

"We could be home tomorrow." Christopher said to them. "We could be away from here and back home with mam."

David and Jennifer both looked at their brother, he seemed unhappy about that possibility, which worried them.

"What's wrong Chris?" Jennifer asked concerned.

"Nothing really, I just think it's a shame with have to leave without seeing everything." He replied gloomily.

"Well don't start worrying yet, we can't leave for a while," Jennifer said. "We're not sure the council will help us and we still have to help the Dragons get their orb back. They need to get home as well."

"Jen, if we get the opportunity to get home, don't you think we should take it?"

David asked gently.

"Not until we help the Dragons. We promised them we would help, and If I don't help them, who will?" She said raising her voice.

"But there may not be another chance, don't you think we should get back home, I'm sure mam will be frantic by now."

"Dave, I know mam will be frantic, but we have to help our friends. We're not leaving until we help them, mam would understand." She said with the attitude that she was right and she wouldn't change her mind on the matter.

David had seen the signs, she would be in a right strop unless he relented, but surely if they had the opportunity to go home, they should take it. Then he realised how selfish he was being. She was right, Jen was the only person that could speak with the Dragons, without her they were lost, and they would never get the orb or see their home again, how would he feel in their situation?

"Sorry, Jen, you're right, we help the Dragons first, and then we go home."

"Good." She said and reached over to hug her brother.

Christopher then jumped on the pair of them, and they all began to play fight, hitting each other with the cushions, and laughing.

"Am I interrupting?" Elder Awdaal said as he walked into the room.

The children stopped what they were doing, embarrassed.

"No Elder Awdaal, please come in." David said politely.

"Good, I was just wondering how you were all getting on." He said.

"Fine, yes fine, thank you." David replied, wondering why the elder was really there.

"Good." He said as he looked around the room. "And the room has everything you need?" He asked.

"Yes wonderful, thank you." Jennifer replied, tidying the cushions up.

"And there is nothing else you require?"

"No, thank you, we have everything." David said looking worried now. What was the man after, he thought. The Elder wanted to ask them something he was sure, but was reticent about asking for some reason.

"Ok, well, I will leave you to it then, see you tonight." He said as he turned around and walked out of the room.

"He seemed a nice man." Christopher said helping Jennifer tidy up.

"Hmm," David said. He walked to the door which was still partially open and looked first one way, then the other but the Elder was nowhere to be seen. "He's a fast walker, I can't see him anywhere!" David said from the doorway and then closing the door he walked back to his bed.

"Anyone find that a little weird?" David asked.

"No, I don't think so, he was just asking if we had everything we needed, nothing weird in that is there?" Jennifer asked.

"It seemed a little strange to me, but I suppose your right." David replied, though something told him there was something not quite right about Elder Awdaal. He didn't know if it was instinct or some early manifestation of another ability but he had a bad feeling about the man that made the hairs on the back of his neck stand on end.

Sukhoi came to see them a while later; he had been to see some friends, but wanted to know how they were. He didn't stay long, but told them he would return well before they were needed, so they shouldn't worry. David told him they were happy to relax in the room for now, but Christopher added they would like some more food if there were any available. Sukhoi had laughed, and said they could have as much food as they liked, he would have some sent to them immediately and anything else they wanted besides.

So, it was a short time later, that there was a knock at the door.

"Come in." David said. He was dressed in just his underpants and had been just about to get in the pool where Jennifer and Christopher were already, but quickly grabbed a towel from the bed as he ran to the door when no one entered. Opening the door he was confronted by two extremely large men. They were dressed in the servant's garb of white linen trousers and shirts and they were both carrying a heaped tray full of hot delicious smelling food.

Wrapping the towel around his waist David opened the door a little wider for the men to enter and then asked them to put the tray over on the table in the corner of the room. Both men nodded in understanding and walked over, placing their trays on the table. David followed them in and was stood right next to one of the men as he put his tray down, so he didn't see where the backhand came from to throw him across the room.

Jennifer screamed as David's body hit the wall and landed next to the pool, blood oozing from a cut where he had hit his head on the wall. One of the men produced a couple of thin pieces of rope from his shirt and walked over to the unconscious David and began to tie his hands and feet together.

"Leave my brother alone!" Christopher shouted.

Jennifer was almost hysterical, as she watched the other man move towards her and Christopher with an evil grin on his face.

Christopher was instantly by her side, as if to protect her, but Jennifer pushed him behind her; trying to protect him, and he slipped. He fell back into the pool with a yell, splashing water everywhere and spluttering it out of his mouth as he tried to regain his feet.

Recognition came when she looked into the man's eyes; she realised that the two men were the Raider twins they had encountered in Kahin and again outside Dakhla Mys, Timak and Cory, she believed they were called.

The Raider's smile grew wider when he realised that she'd recognised him.

"I'm Timak." He informed her. "My brother over there is Cory." He indicated as Cory looked over at her and waved, and laughed at her stricken face.

David groaned as Cory pulled tightly on the rope to fasten his hands together, although he looked to be still unconscious.

"What do you want? What are you going to do with us?" She asked on the verge of hysterics.

"You and your brother over there are going to bring us quite a bit of money, and a little more prestige." Timak replied happily.

"But why?" Jennifer asked, as she began to cry in fear and frustration of not being able to do anything to protect her brothers.

"You both have special gifts..." He began.

"Enough Timak, information is power." Cory reminded his brother.

"Yes, enough talk, you're coming with us." He said as he grabbed for her.

She pulled away just as his hand shot out. "You don't need to do this." She cried at them, "We haven't done anything wrong."

She was shaking with fear but she knew she had to keep talking, she must find some way out of this predicament, with David hurt and unconscious and Christopher by her side, it was up to her to save them all. She scanned the room, looking for anything that could offer any assistance to her plight, but she realised she wouldn't have time to do anything even if she could find something to use. The realisation frightened her to her very core, they were all going to get captured or worse; killed and she couldn't do a thing about it.

It was then that the door flew open and the twins turned to face a lone figure standing in the doorway.

Recognising the twins immediately Braduga shouted at them, "Picking on small children again I see."

The twins turned to face him; all thoughts of the boy and girl forgotten as they faced this new foe. They watched with mild amusement as Braduga Sikorsky of the Govena and honour guard of the Kavacha, entered the room. They didn't look frightened of the warrior, even though he had a reputation of being the greatest warrior in Sakhalin.

Braduga himself was a little surprised to see the twins in Enkan Mys and warily looked around for their leader just in case he was also in the room, and was a little relieved to see that he wasn't. It was bad enough trying to fight two foes, but three would have been too much in such a confined space. Besides, Sukhoi had said that all three Koutla had seemed dangerous men to him, and if Sukhoi thought that, then there was no way Braduga was about to ignore what the Kavacha said. He would not underestimate the warriors before him, if he did, he could find himself dead.

Adopting a stance designed for close quarter fighting, Braduga waited as the twins approached him.

"So this is the great Braduga Sikorsky, is it?" The twin called Cory sneered.

He was surprised they had heard of him, but not enough to be distracted from any attack that could be forthcoming.

"He doesn't look like much to me, what do you say brother?" Cory mocked.

"I agree, but it will be a pleasure to gut the great Braduga." Timak laughed with malice.

"Let me guess, you are Daisy and your sister here is Daffodil." Braduga mocked.

"You think you're funny. He actually thinks he's funny. " Cory said to his brother in mock surprise.

"Will he still be laughing when we put his guts in his mouth to stop him from crying though brother?" Timak replied viciously.

"Let us dance then, and we will see who laughs and who cries." Braduga challenged.

Jennifer and the boys forgotten, the twins moved to engage Braduga in combat. They were strong, fierce and highly trained; Braduga realised as soon as they began their attack. Their combat techniques were equal to his own; all movements were conducted with confidence and precision. Additionally, it became apparent that they had obviously trained to fight an opponent together, with each movement made by one, opening an opportunity for the other. It was going to be extremely difficult to fight the twins by himself if they maintained their control and coordination. Braduga never underestimated any opponent; even now he could appreciate the skill and grace of the twins as they attacked him together. He realised immediately that if he was to come away from this fight with his life, he had to use all his knowledge and experience; use it wisely and use it quickly.

Moving with vigorous intent, they quickly launched into their attack and the battle of skill began in earnest. Blow after blow reigned down on Braduga, from every direction at once it seemed, as he parried, dodged, jumped and ducked out of the way. They were efficient, effective and potentially deadly, but he still managed to evade each blow, even if by a hairs breadth. The skill displayed by all three warriors was tremendous, though Braduga looked the most impressive as he danced between the two brothers. It was a dance of death, the twins moved just as fluidly as Braduga, it was as if they had been taught by the same master of arms, as they followed his every move with a counter move of their own. All Jennifer and Christopher could do was to watch in dread fascination as they attacked each other relentlessly.

Timak and Cory slashed and thrust, attacking with calculated precision that only years of training could achieve. They moved with confidence and incredible speed; each thrust seemed to only just miss its mark. Timak smiled at Braduga as he managed to avoid a killing blow from his brother Cory, only to take a slash on his arm from him. Braduga bled from the wound, but he knew it wasn't deep and he ignored the pain that was creeping up his arm.

He had to concentrate on his foe; he knew if he lost that concentration, he would be dead.

Again and again they attacked, while Braduga weaved his magic, he avoided every blow as if he had cast a spell against their swords. The onslaught continued relentlessly as the twins vied for a weakness they could finally exploit.

Finally, it was Timak that made a fatal mistake; a clumsy thrust which made him stretch a little too far, Braduga twisted and ducked out of harms way and then slashed the unfortunate soul under his arm pit. Uselessly, the sword fell from Timak's hand as he lost all feeling in his arm. Surprise and anger twisted his face as he scrambled for the blade. Unfortunately for his brother the movement obstructed Cory's killing thrust to Braduga's throat, his sword whistling harmlessly by his head.

Braduga moved like lightening; sensing an advantage, he swivelled and turned to bring his blade down on Cory's exposed back. He cried out in pain as Braduga's blade slashed him, blood spurting everywhere and soaking his white shirt.

Both brothers were down, but not out, they recovered faster than he would have thought possible, but they did realise that they had underestimated their foe. They were both bleeding and losing blood quickly. Timak had lost the use of one arm, and his brother was still losing blood from the nasty gash on his back, the pain of which must have been intolerable. Even so, they still attacked him relentlessly, and with fire in their eyes. But the attacks were becoming more frenzied and erratic now; the realised they needed to put an end to this dance. Timak and Cory suddenly changed tactic; fighting Braduga individually, each trying to find their own way passed his defences. It was this change that lost them their main advantage. They were still attacking the warrior in turn, but they had lost the ability to read each others movements as they searched for an opening. They almost had the warrior a couple of times, but a lack of understanding gave Braduga the opportunity to evade the killing blow. Braduga recognised every calculated movement; every thrust and every turn and again waited for that one mistake that would bring him victory.

It was Cory who made the first fatal mistake, he had lost a lot of blood and his movements became sluggish and imprecise, which resulted in a miss-timed blow that left his right side open and vulnerable.

Taking advantage of the mistake, Braduga's blade bit into Cory's ribs, and towards his heart. He died instantly, the pain and surprise hardly registering on his face as his life ebbed away from him and he fell to the floor.

Timak was incensed as he watched his brother die. He turned on Braduga with his sword in his other hand and attacked with a fury. Slashing to the left and to the right, heavy blows barely missing the now exhausted warrior. Time after time, the remaining twin thought he had the better of him, but Braduga continued to thwart his efforts. Braduga slashed but Timak grabbed hold of his sword and pushed him back against the wall, with the blade of his sword against his neck. Hatred, pain and anger filled his eyes as he pushed, trying to sever Braduga's neck from his body. Braduga recognised his opponent's last effort to defeat his foe before all his strength diminished. Timak had a crazed look in his eyes, a look that had seen his brother fall and a look that said he too would fall unless he could end it now. With the last of his strength Timak pushed and pushed, but the best warriors in Enkan Mys had taught Braduga. Not only that, he had eventually beaten those warriors, and had taken with him all the skill and knowledge they could offer. He now used everything he had been taught, every movement and every tactic to defeat the man before him.

Turning and twisting, re-positioning his body, Braduga danced away from Timak, releasing a torrid succession of blows in his wake. Timak could not stop the onslaught, as he crumbled under the attack. Finally, Braduga caught him with a killing blow to his stomach. Timak, holding his stomach, folded to the ground, a look of utter surprise on his face and a fierce hatred in his eyes as his last breath left him.

Exhausted, Braduga would have collapsed if not for his sword, which he used to support his weight as he looked at the two dead bodies before him. They were the best warriors he had every fought, as good as his teachers had been, if not better he realised.

That troubled him; the twins had adopted most of the fighting stances and manoeuvres as if they had trained at Enkan Mys themselves, impossible as that sounded. Every warrior that was still living and had trained there was known to him, yet he didn't recognise the brothers, and he was certain he would have remembered them. He would have to speak with Sukhoi about this as soon as possible, maybe he would be able to shed some light on the matter.

Braduga gathered his strength and focused his attention on the children.

Jennifer was still holding Christopher protectively, both their eyes were brimming with tears, both of them looking relieved that he had survived, even though still a little frightened and shocked. David's body was beginning to stir by the wall and there were re-assuring grunts coming from his direction; the boy was injured, but thankfully still alive.

Braduga motioned for Jennifer and Christopher to get out of the pool as he made his way over to David. Bending down he searched his body for injuries and any bleeding or broken bones. He was amazed that the boy seemed relatively uninjured except for a large cut on the side of his face and a bump on his head. He untied his bonds and then carried him over to the bed and gently laid him on it.

"Is, is he ok?" Jennifer stammered, tears still running down her distraught face.

"Yes," He said re-assuringly. "Just a couple of cuts and bruises, but I think he will be ok."

Braduga walked then toward the door, exhaustion evident by his slothful movements.

"Don't leave us Brad!" Jennifer shouted in dismay.

"Calm down, Jennifer, I am just going to call for a guard, I will not leave you." He promised.

Jennifer and Christopher rushed over to their brother while Braduga called for a guard. It was a few moments before a guard finally heard his call and came to investigate. Braduga quickly explained what had happened, though not that he knew who the assassins were, and then asked him to find either Sukhoi or Socata, but both if possible. The guard peered through the door and could see the dead bodies, but nodded and ran to do Braduga's bidding.

Jennifer was gently mopping David's brow with a wet clothe she found by the pool when a few moments later Sukhoi and Socata entered the room.

Sukhoi saw the dead bodies as he entered. "What happened?" He asked trying to take in the scene before him. "Is everyone ok?" He asked and then he saw David lying on the bed with Jennifer and Christopher by his bedside.

"We had a couple of unexpected visitors," Braduga began. As Socata rushed over and tended to David, Braduga explained how he had heard the commotion coming from the children's room and the presence of the twins. Sukhoi listened intently and quietly as Braduga told him of his battle with the two warriors that were almost his equal. When Braduga had finished, Sukhoi asked the children if they had anything to add, but they just shook their heads, it had all happened so quickly and they had been taken by surprise.

"He will be ok in a while." Socata announced. "Nothing too serious, I have stopped the bleeding and he has a couple of bumps and bruises, but nothing serious." He announced as David began to rouse awake.

David opened his eyes slowly and eventually focused on his sister's face. He smiled weakly but didn't have the strength to do anything else.

Sukhoi approached the bed. "How are you feeling David?" He asked in concern.

"I'm ok I think, just a little headache." He managed to reply. "What happened?" He asked confused as he noticed all the concerned faces around his bed.

"I was so worried Dave." Jennifer said, tears beginning to fall once more down her face. "I thought he had killed you."

"I'm ok Jen, honest." He added as he saw the worried look on her face.

"I was worried too." Christopher said meekly. "I tried to help but I fell over and couldn't get back on my feet." He said giving Jennifer a pointed look that she chose to ignore.

"There was nothing you could have done anyway Chris." Braduga smiled at the young boy. "They were extremely skilled and dangerous warriors and I think I was lucky to survive their attack."

Christopher hero-worshipped the warrior and didn't believe for a second that the twins could have beaten him, but he nodded at his friend anyway. He knew that even with the little training he had received, it would have been no good against warriors of their obvious prowess.

"What happened?" David asked. "Everything is a little hazy. The servants entered the room and the next thing I know I'm waking up with a splitting headache..." He trailed off.

A knock at the door brought everyone's attention towards the man entering the room. Elder Sanag Awdaal pushed open the door and walked into the room.

"Is everyone ok?" He asked. "I have just spoken with a guard who informed me of a..." he paused momentarily as he saw David on the bed with a bandage wrapped around it, "situation." He finished.

"Elder Awdaal." Sukhoi said. "Everything is fine now, thank you."

Sukhoi asked Braduga to explain to the Elder and to David what had transpired. Elder Awdaal was visibly shocked to hear that two Koutla Raiders had violated Enkan Mys and vowed to hold an inquiry into how the men had just walked in; as he put it, without a care in the world.

"It is a good job Braduga was near by to offer his assistance." Elder Awdaal stated.

"More than that Elder," Jennifer said. "If Brad hadn't come when he did, we would probably be taken prisoner, captured or even dead, by now."

"Well, we owe you our thanks then Braduga." The Elder smiled towards Braduga.

"I am only glad I arrived in time to stop them." He replied.

"So are we." David said quietly. "Thanks Brad, for saving our lives."

Braduga smiled back at David. "Any time my friend."

"I will inform the rest of the council members of this incident at once." Elder Awdaal announced and then left the room.

"I think everyone should get some rest." Sukhoi announced. "I will ensure there are guards on the door with instructions to let no one enter until I come back."

"I will rest here a while Sukhoi, at least until the guards get here." Braduga stated as he looked over at the three children, "I promised I wouldn't leave them alone."

"Ok," Sukhoi agreed reluctantly, "but I will ensure the guards make haste."

Jennifer smiled her thanks at Braduga, who returned the smile. He could see she was still shaken by the incident and he wasn't going to leave them alone to think about what could have happened, had he not turned up when he did.

"I will make my own inquiries. See you in a couple of hours then." Sukhoi said as he too walked out of the door followed closely by Socata.

As they left the room, Braduga told the children to try and relax, Sukhoi would find out exactly what was going on and put a stop to it. In the meantime, he decided to tell them stories of his youth, to help them try and forget the ordeal they had barely survived. They were brave children Braduga thought, as brave as his own brother Ambar had been when they were children growing up together. Ambar had protected him then, from everything and everyone. He had continued to protect people as he grew older; becoming one of the Ruedin, until that fateful day when he had died trying to protect Sukhoi from the Gourtak. Now, he thought, as he looked at the children, now he would do the protecting. He wouldn't let any of them come to any harm, he would make Ambar proud.

Chapter Twenty Two

Sukhoi returned a couple of hours later as promised and roused everyone from their slumber. Braduga had been relieved by Socata and had returned with the Kavacha.

"I have some news." He said as everyone gathered round. "You remember Ben?"

They nodded that they did and he continued. "He came to find me with news of our surprise visitors."

"The Koutla entered via the South Gate then?" Socata asked.

"No, but three men did enter via the North Gate." He said. "Ben had sent a priority order to each gate; requiring news of anyone the guards didn't recognise or anyone acting suspiciously. They were to report to him and him alone with any information they obtained. It paid off; if a little late, but three large men were reported entering via the north gate a short while after we arrived."

"How did he get away with that?" Socata asked intrigued. "I've never heard of a guard giving orders."

"If the story I heard from one of the other guards is true, he walked up to his Lieutenant and told him to write the order on my aufnority." Sukhoi said and then smiled as he tried to imagine the look on the Lieutenant's face when one of his own guards ordered him to write the letter.

"He's a brave and clever lad, that Ben." Socata praised the guard.

"He is indeed." Sukhoi agreed. "What is more, he even had the three men followed."

"Even better." Braduga added with a smile.

"It could have been. Two guards followed the three men, which was fortunate when the men split up. Unfortunately though, the guard that followed two of the men lost them in the crowd around the Colosseum and the guard who followed our third man is still missing."

"I think we can guess what happened to him then?" Braduga deduced, and could see the same look on Sukhoi's face.

"As soon as the guard lost the two men he reported it to Ben."

"Well, at least we know where they are now." Socata stated with a smile towards his friend.

"Yes, but where is our third man?" Braduga asked.

"We have no idea yet, but our friend Ben has now sent another order to the gates stopping anyone from leaving, until I give the word." Sukhoi added.

"So, the third man is still in the city." Braduga stated with an angry look on his face.

"Yes and the guard provided us with one more piece of information."

"Oh and what's that?" Asked Socata intrigued.

"The guard confirmed that the third man; by his description, is the Koutla leader, Abdi Salut."

"I don't think he'll be too happy to hear about his protégés." Said Braduga; with a slight smile returning to his face at the thought of the leader hearing the news about his bodyguards.

"I think you may be right." Agreed Sukhoi.

"I think our friend Ben deserves a promotion after this." Socata stated.

Sukhoi nodded in agreement I will have to speak to his superiors about all the help he has provided the Kavacha.

"What do we do now?" Asked David.

Sukhoi regarded David and then Jennifer and Christopher. He had brought them here to try and help them get back to their homes. All they had experienced so far was people trying to capture or kill them, for reasons yet unknown. He believed that both David and Jennifer had special gifts and maybe someone knew of those gifts; though he didn't know how, and they were going to try and exploit them. He was certain that the council was going to help them; how could they not under the circumstances, but whatever the outcome, they needed him. He would protect them as well as he could, but who wanted the children and why? It was frustrating not knowing the answers, but all things came to those who waited, and that was what he was going to have to do.

"It is pointless to speculate." Sukhoi said. "There are guards on the door and either Socata or Brad will stay here with you." He paused, thinking. "The council will be calling us forward soon, we shall have to wait and hear what they say on the matter."

"So we're just expected to sit around here and wait for some more assassins to kill us then?" David said annoyed and angry.

"This is the safest place for you to be at the moment David." Sukhoi said gently.

David looked at his friend and could see the concern on his face, but he didn't like to be confined in this place, especially after what had just happened. He knew Sukhoi was right though, he just didn't like it.

"I will stay here with you David." Braduga said. "No harm will come to any of you."

"I know Brad, and thank you, but I hate all this waiting." He replied.

"You are right; I will go and speak to the council." Sukhoi said to them and he left the room.

Sukhoi returned with news that the council was ready to speak with the group again.

"We must go back to the Audience Chamber, my friends. He informed them and they quickly left the room.

The children were escorted from their building to the Audience Chamber by a squad of armed guards. They found out later that Elder Awdaal had arranged the escort to ensure no more incidents happened.

They were shown directly into the chamber on arrival. The elders were already seated and awaiting their presence when they were shown to their seats.

"There has been some trouble?" Elder Hanish asked, although he probably knew every detail of the incident already.

"Three Raiders entered the city; two of which tried to kidnap the children, Elder." Sukhoi replied; his face was without expression but one of his eyebrows was raised as he spoke. "Those two have been dealt with, but we are still looking for the third Raider." He finished.

"No one was seriously injured I hope?" Elder Issa Garang asked, though by now she had noticed the bandage on David's head and she half rose in concern.

"The children are fine, except for David who has a few bruises." Sukhoi said motioning for the elder to remain seated.

"Where are these fiends that would attack children within our city?" Elder Jallo Turabi bellowed with anger. He had obviously not been informed of the incident until just recently and was only now getting the true facts of what had happened.

"The two Raiders are dead." Sukhoi announced without emotion.

"I am conducting an inquiry into the incident." Elder Awdaal interjected. "We will find out how these rascals managed to infiltrate the city."

"Very good, Sanag." Elder Hanish said.

"I have personally ensured that the children have protection wherever they go from now on." Elder Awdaal added.

"Very good," Elder Hanish nodded in appreciation that the elder from the Govena had everything under control.

"You think that is a necessary precaution considering the Raiders are dead?" Elder Srabat enquired.

"There is still one Raider roaming the city, Elder." Braduga said, "But we will find him!" He finished, as if making a promise.

"And you are ok?" Elder Hanish asked the children, concern evident in his voice.

"We're fine Elder Hanish." David replied for them all.

David quickly looked at his brother and sister as he answered the Elder's question and they nodded that they were fine. David was still a little light-headed and feeling rather weak, but he wanted to know if the council were going to help them or not, so he insisted on attending this audience. He would have said they were fine even if he had had one of his arms chopped off, he thought to himself.

"Well, if that's settled?" The elder looked around to see if anyone would contradict him, but no-one did, so he continued, "let's now concern ourselves with the reason we have called you here. I wouldn't want to keep you in suspense and time runs on."

Elder Hanish looked around at each of the other elders in turn before continuing. "I'm afraid the news I bear isn't good." He began. "We presented your problem to the Keeper, who checked the Book of Kavacha Lore and he informed us that he knows of no way to help you get home." Elder Hanish said with sadness in his voice.

The children were shocked, their faces dropped in amazement as the Elder explained that they knew of no way of returning them back to their own land. They had searched all the old texts on the subject and referred to the Kavacha lore but there wasn't anything that could be of assistance. There was some reference to a doorway, but nothing tangible that could be used to create one or where one could be found.

Their hopes and dreams for the future were shattered in that instant; they had travelled all this way and now the council told them it had basically been a waste of time. The children looked at each other as the reality of their situation began to sink in.

David looked at the distraught faces of his brother and sister as they looked at the council members. He knew he should be angry that they had travelled one end of Sakhalin to the other, especially with what had happened to them since arriving there, but he was feeling relatively calm under the circumstances. Somehow he already knew that the council couldn't help them, though he didn't know how he knew. It was just a feeling he had, but the feeling had been right. A part of him was still disappointed with the news but now his mind began to think of a way to get home; if they couldn't help them, then they had to help themselves, he concluded. There had to be a way home, he would just have to find it.

He realised then that he knew the answer already. The only doorway that existed; that they knew of, was the one at the Guardian's Stone. David realised that the only way to get back home now was through the doorway at the Stone. Even if there was someone, or something waiting for them, they really didn't have any other choice.

He realised they had travelled all the way to Enkan Mys for nothing, or had they? Numerous images appeared in his mind, images of the places he had seen. He saw the faces of people he had met and made friends with, he saw the dragons; everything, all the images rushed through his mind. The strange and wonderful land of Sakhalin, it hadn't been a waste of time after all, they could have stayed at the Stone, but then he would have missed everything else. The Barnes children had been lucky enough to find themselves in a strange new world, a world totally different from their own, a world full of magic and of incredible sights. He had performed magic; his sister could speak with Dragons. Yes, they had almost been killed on more than one occasion, but they had survived. Who else did he know, that could boast such experiences? No, it hadn't been for nothing, they had had their adventure, but now it was time to go back to the stone, and find their way home.

Taking a deep breath, he coughed to get everyone's attention and then waited until everyone stopped talking. With everyone's attention totally focused on him, he felt nervous, but then he remembered his mother; probably distraught for the whereabouts of her children. He could almost see her in his mind and he knew he had to say something, for her sake, if not for his own.

"You wish to say something David?" Elder Hanish asked gently. He was a perceptive man and from the look on David's face, he knew that he had something important to say.

He didn't like speaking to crowds of people, especially adults; he had enough problems speaking to his friends, who weren't half as intimidating as the people before him now. But everyone had stopped talking when the elder spoke and now with all eyes on him, David cleared his throat again.

He was surprised that he felt quite calm under the circumstances, but maybe that was because he knew exactly what he was going to say; hoped he did anyway. There was only one thing they could do; although he knew his sister wouldn't be happy, they really had no choice now.

"There is one way we know for sure that will take us back home," he said directing his gaze to Jennifer and Christopher.

"What is this way?" Elder Hanish asked, looking around at the rest of the council members as they leaned forward to hear what the boy had to say.

"The way we came here," David replied, pausing momentarily before continuing, "we must return to the Guardian's Stone," he finished.

He looked at Sukhoi then to gauge his reaction. The Kavacha stared back, before a small smile appeared around the edges of his mouth and he nodded in agreement.

"That is along way from here David, and are you sure the magic doorway will appear to you again?" Elder Turabi asked sceptically. He assumed that the reason the children had travelled all this way to the city was because the doorway hadn't re-materialised.

Elder Srabat had obviously been thinking the same thing and added. "It's a long way to go; only to find when you get there, that there isn't a doorway to walk through." He pointed out.

"We have no other choice," David reminded them, "you can't help us, and we know of no other way except the Stone."

"Why did you not wait there in the first place, maybe after a short period of time the doorway would have re-emerged?" Elder Garang asked.

David looked at the group of elders before him and then turned to Sukhoi for help. He didn't want to mention Nuba Driss, mainly because the Kavacha had left it out of his story, but they had no choice but to bring the evil magician's name into the equation.

"The doorway did return." Sukhoi said to the elders.

One or two were about to ask more questions but he interrupted them.

"The doorway opened but they did not get the opportunity to go through it." Sukhoi told them.

"Why not Sukhoi?" Elder Hanish asked the Kavacha suspiciously.

"Nuba Driss obstructed their path." He announced. "Or maybe one of his minions, we are not certain."

"What, what is this?" Elder Srabat shouted, as the rest of the council were on their feet and shouting questions at the Kavacha.

"Be silent!" Elder Hanish ordered, and as the elders regained their seats he asked Sukhoi to explain why he hadn't mentioned this crucial fact in the telling of his story.

Sukhoi's face became calm, with little, if any emotion present as he explained to the elders that he wasn't sure who the creature was behind the door. But that creature had tried to grab hold of David. Luckily Braduga had saved the boy, but they knew they had to leave the stone and find another way for the children to return home. Nuba Driss or one of his creatures could still be there waiting for them, but now they had no choice. They knew of no other way for the children and the Dragons to get home except through that doorway.

The elders were quiet when Sukhoi finished, but Elder Hanish was frowning at the Kavacha in what looked like disappointment.

"You should have told us of this sooner Kavacha." Elder Srabat berated Sukhoi.

Sukhoi's back tensed for a split moment and his mouth opened a fraction as if he was about to give some retort, but he knew he should have said something and therefore remained silent.

"Whether Nuba Driss was there or not," Elder Hanish said after a few moments of consideration, "it appears that the Guardian's Stone is the only way to get the children and the Dragons back to their homes. We must help them return. If we send them a big enough escort, maybe they could get home safely."

The elders began to talk at once on whether that was a good solution to the problem.

"Surely, the children would be better off staying in the city, where they would be safe from harm." Suggested Elder Garang, who seemed to feel responsible for the children ever since the knife throwing incident.

"We have no choice, the children are not from this land, and must return. If Nuba Driss is still waiting for them, then they must have sufficient forces to try and protect them from the danger he represents." Elder Hanish insisted.

"But it's such a long way Elder Hanish; anything could happen on the way!" Elder Garang argued.

"You're right elder we would need some help." David replied staring straight ahead and trying not to look at Sukhoi. He wanted to ask for Sukhoi's help but couldn't bring himself to ask for help in front of everyone else. He would try and get the Kavacha alone and then plead with him. It was the only way; he had to make sure he got his brother and sister home, safe and sound, and if he had to beg for help, that's what he'd do.

As it happened he didn't have to, because just then Sukhoi spoke. "It is my fault the children are here. I thought the council would know of a way to get them home. I made them travel the long journey here; through many dangers. Therefore I am responsible for their safety. I and my Ruedin will return them to Junggar Shan, if that is what they decide to do."

David did look at the man then and smiled in thanks, and received a sad smile in return. Sukhoi was adamant the council would be able to help and it was as if that smile apologised for the time the children had been apart from their home.

David realised instantly and whispered, "It's ok my friend, it isn't your fault, you were only trying to help."

"What about the Dragons?" Jennifer said before anyone could say anything else. "What can be done to help them?"

"We would like to help the Dragons Jennifer but we do not know how to," Elder Hanish replied, "we do not know if Nuba Driss has their orb; but even if he has, to regain possession of it would be almost impossible. And if they arrived the same way as yourselves, the only way home for them, is to follow you back to the Guardian's Stone." He finished with a shrug of his shoulders.

She knew the elder was right, but they had to do something, they surely didn't go through everything to get here, for nothing to be done.

A dark figure emerged from an open doorway; nobody had heard anything from the shocked faces as it approached. Whether it had heard everything discussed was anyone's guess but it moved quietly and with purpose toward Elder Hanish. The figure was dressed in a dark robe, but the body beneath was indistinguishable, even the face was shrouded in darkness as it approached.

There was an uneasy tension in the atmosphere from the group of elders, but they all remained quiet as the figure spoke with the head of the council.

Everyone waited patiently for the conversation to cease, but it was Jennifer who spoke first.

"There must be something you can do?" She pleaded.

"Jennifer." Elder Bashir said giving a side-long glance in the robed figure's direction before continuing. "We have never heard of this orb you speak of, we do not know where Nuba Driss is hiding and we still have no idea how to help the Dragons get home, except by maybe following you. How do you think we can help them?" He finished.

Jennifer knew he was speaking the truth but she was not happy with his answer. She was not happy with any of the answers. They had come to this place with high expectations, and now, well, they had nothing, only the realisation that the only way to get back home was the way they got there in the first place.

An uneasy silence settled on the chamber as everyone contemplated what had been said, but then the figure that was still standing statuesque next to Elder Hanish spoke quietly, but with enough volume to be heard by everyone, without seemingly to try. "Nuba Driss can always be found where there is death and destruction." The dark figure spoke venomously, and as it did it reached its hands up to its cowl and removed it from its head to reveal a young face with long white hair. It was the monk that the three children had seen by their window in the living room and they all stared at him now and at each other in recognition. The monk continued to speak as if reciting some ancient scripture. He talked about Nuba Driss as if he was talking about a vile creature that was bent on the destruction of the world, each phrase spoke with just a bit more distaste than the last.

The room went deathly quiet as everyone stared and listened intently to the monk; telling them of the death, destruction and chaos this evil had plagued upon Sakhalin.

"He can be found in the land of the Toureng, who bow down to him as if he is a God. He has the Dragon's Eye and access to a portal to many worlds." He concluded.

In that one last statement he had given the answers to all the questions asked. He had told everyone that there was a way home for the children, Nuba Driss had stolen the orb and there was also a way home for the Dragons. How he came by all this information was anyone's guess, but none of the elders asked him, they just took it for granted that the monk was speaking the truth.

"That's the monk we saw at home, isn't it Dave?" Christopher asked his brother, though he already knew the answer as David nodded.

"How does he know all this though?" Jennifer asked in wonder.

"I don't know," David whispered to his sister, "but I for one believe him."

Jennifer nodded that she too believed what the monk had just said.

"Please forgive me for my lack of manners." The monk said after a moment in which he seemed to physically compose himself, "I am Belmokhtar, and I am Keeper of the Kavacha Lore and teacher to the Kavacha."

"Belmokhtar is THE teacher of Lore and has been doing so for many, many years." Sukhoi whispered to David.

"He doesn't look old enough." David whispered back, confused by what Sukhoi had just told him.

"Looks can be very deceptive David." He replied and listened silently to the conversation between Belmokhtar and the Elders.

"Surely you are mistaken Belmokhtar, the Toureng are believed to be a nomadic people now, scattered and desolate." Elder Srabat said sceptically.

"They are not as scattered and desolate as you may believe." Belmokhtar interrupted. "Their land is far beyond the Amal Desert where they flourish and expand their empire. It is here where Nuba Driss rules the descendants of the Toureng; and are known as the Imazaghan; the free people."

"How does he know all this Sukhoi?" Jennifer whispered as she stared at the monk in wonder.

"He is the teacher of Kavacha Lore." Sukhoi replied as if that answered everything.

"If we're to help our friends, then we must go back to the desert and get the orb back from Nuba Driss." Jennifer said quietly to her brother. But obviously not quiet enough, because Belmokhtar had heard her and stared at her as he spoke. "There is no need to go searching for Nuba Driss, he has amassed a great army which is already on its way here as we speak." Belmokhtar said just as quietly but everyone heard his words and there were gasps of disbelief.

"What nonsense is this Belmokhtar?" Elder Burao exclaimed. "Toureng coming to Enkan Mys, with Nuba Driss, no impossible."

Belmokhtar raised his hand and interrupted the Elder. "The Toureng are not the same people as those written in the ancient texts Elder Burao, the Imazaghan are fierce and highly trained warriors."

"Toureng, Imazaghan, they are still our enemies." The elder insisted.

"True." Belmokhtar conceded.

"Is that why we haven't seen you for these last few weeks Belmokhtar? You have been gaining this information?" Elder Hanish asked the monk with a frown on his face.

Belmokhtar merely smiled at the Elder, but didn't reply.

Everybody spoke at once, talking and shouting over each other. David couldn't keep his eyes off the monk and noticed that a slight smile came to his lips as he saw David looking in his direction, as if in recognition.

David, stunned at first that the monk recognised him, gave him a weak smile in return, and was surprised when Belmokhtar winked at him.

Everyone was still shouting and asking for answers when Belmokhtar raised his arms for silence and asked everyone to calm down.

"I am the teacher of Kavacha Lore, what I say is the truth." He announced, and then right on cue, as if the entire incident had been arranged somehow, there was a loud bang on the door, which reverberated around the room. All the talking stopped instantly as a guard entered and approached the Council nervously.

"I am sorry to disturb you sir," The guard addressed Elder Hanish with sweat dropping from his brow; though it couldn't be determined if it was from the exertion of running to the chamber or through his nervousness, "The guard commander gave me this report to bring to you immediately and he says I must remain to hear your orders, sir." The guard said quickly and a little nervously, which was quite understandable in the circumstances, with all the dignitaries in attendance.

"You had better give me the report then soldier." Elder Hanish said quietly and a little annoyed by this unprecedented interruption.

The guard handed over a folded piece of paper then stepped back and folded his arms behind his back and waited trying to look anywhere but at the elders or the children.

The old man read the words on the piece of paper and then appeared to read them again, just in case he had read them incorrectly.

"Are you aware of what is written here soldier?" He asked the guard.

"Yes sir." He replied immediately in a firmer voice.

"Were you told to tell me anything else?"

"Sir!" He replied nervously, clearly thinking about the question but then deciding he wasn't told anything else he replied, "No sir!"

Everyone was quietly waiting to see what would happen next as the old man read the note for a third time. Then he gave a deep sigh and spoke so everyone could hear him clearly.

"Grave news I'm afraid," he began, "Belmokhtar is correct, as we speak there is a vast army approaching the city from the east, initial reports can't estimate the number or disposition at the moment, but it must be the Toureng, the Imazaghan." He corrected as he looked at the Keeper.

"What, impossible!" Harg Srabat shouted as he came to his feet.

"I have not finished." The leader of the council said quietly as he forced the other man back into his chair with a no-nonsense look alone.

Once Elder Srabat had taken his seat he continued. "The report continues to say that there are a vast number of people heading for the city, indeed some people have already arrived who tell tales of the army. These are the villagers and town's folk which have deserted their homes and livelihoods to escape the approaching army." He finished in dismay.

"This can't be true, the Kavacha would have known if an army had crossed the desert or at least the Gratishk Mountains. We would have had indications and warnings well before now, surely?" Elder Erita Burao said looking at Belmokhtar and then at Sukhoi.

The monk remained silent, his hood back up and his head down, as if in contemplation.

"I can't believe it, I won't believe it, it's just impossible." She continued, though she couldn't bring herself to look at the monk again.

"I agree there must be some mistake." Elder Awdaal agreed, though he didn't sound very convincing.

"There is no mistake," Belmokhtar announced quietly, "Nuba Driss is on his way, of that I am certain. War and death will soon be knocking on our door." Belmokhtar added as if announcing the end of days.

"Elder Hanish, I think we should speak to these people, confirm these reports and find out exactly what's happening before we start getting as scared as a Rabat being chased by a fox-hound." Haber Bashir added calmly, not one for flapping about in a crisis.

"I agree, but I also agree with Belmokhtar that we should at least make adequate preparations should the reports be true." Elder Turabi suggested.

"Yes, and I think it would be prudent to call a war council and make the necessary preparations, just in case." The old man stated and then turned to the guard, "inform the guard commander that he is to gather as many officers and dignitaries as possible, they will be de-briefed on the current situation in one hour."

He said. "And bring me some of these people." He ordered, slapping the piece of paper in his hand.

The guard nodded and rushed out of the chamber without another word, speed was of the essence now, and he knew his duty as the discussion continued about the report the elder had been given.

The monk Belmokhtar, disappeared as quickly as he had arrived; no one actually saw him depart, which was unfortunate because the council realised they needed some answers to some very worrying questions.

The three children were requested to leave the chamber; although it wasn't really a request, especially when Braduga and Socata were asked to make sure they returned to their rooms immediately. Sukhoi; as the First of the Kavacha, would have to remain behind to discuss this, unprecedented news.

The children were almost knocked down on one or more occasion by high ranking officers, rushing to get to the chamber and receive their orders. From the amount of soldiers that appeared and were also rushing around carrying orders with them, you would think that the army had already arrived.

The children received the occasional odd look from some of the soldiers as they passed by; especially as they were being escorted by Sukhoi's Ruedin and more importantly in their eyes, by Braduga himself. Socata informed them that word of the attack on the children had been circulated, together with a description of the Koutla Leader, Abdi Salut. Orders had been given to ensure the children were protected at all times; though the soldiers didn't really understand why three children were so important, they would obey the orders given.

Two soldiers were even waiting outside their room when the children escorted by Braduga and Socata arrived.

"You know your orders?" Braduga asked harshly as he looked at the men critically.

They both nodded and flushed uneasily under his scrutiny until he told them to remain alert and having told the children he would return shortly, he and Socata left them alone.

Chapter Twenty Three

"So, he's called Belmokhtar and he's the Keeper of Kavacha Lore." David said excitedly as he rushed into the room and closed the door firmly behind him once his brother and sister had entered. "I have been wondering if we would actually see him here, but when we didn't, I thought he probably went through one of the other doors in the corridor." He concluded.

"Well, it's definitely him, but why didn't he say anything to us?" Jennifer asked, "Or at least to you Dave." She said.

"Maybe he is waiting for the right time." Christopher proposed.

"Maybe, but from what Dave has said about our mysterious monk he wanted our help. Why would the Keeper of the Kavacha Lore need our help? We're just three kids from Featherstone, how can we help such an obviously powerful man like him?" Jennifer asked her brothers.

"It does seem a bit strange," David agreed, "especially as everyone seemed to hold him in such high esteem."

"Maybe he didn't recognise you Dave." Christopher offered.

"No Chris, he definitely recognised me, he smiled and winked at me, he knew who I was, who we all were." He said smiling.

"I don't like it Dave, there's something not quite right here." Jennifer said wrinkling her nose as if smelling something foul.

A soft knock at the door made all three children jump, before they knew what they were doing; they had all drawn their daggers and faced the door nervously.

The door slowly creaked open and a white haired head appeared round the door frame.

"May I come in?" Belmokhtar asked smiling at the weapons in the children's hands as he pushed the door open a little further.

They hastily put the daggers away, each blushing in embarrassment as the monk entered the room and closed the door behind him.

"I haven't got much time but I had to see you before I left." Belmokhtar whispered with a slight anxious smile, as he walked over to the children.

They each looked at one another, uncertain what to do or what to say as the monk moved closer.

"Your going somewhere?" David asked nervously. He was actually speaking to the apparition that he had seen in his home and at his school. It brought back memories of his mother and his friends and the thought of the monk leaving them now before they got the opportunity to ask him what they were doing in this strange land made him want to cry.

"Yes, urgent matters to attend to, but I need to speak to you three first." He replied quietly.

"You, you are the same man who visited me aren't you?" He asked hesitantly, uncertainty clouding his thoughts now the monk was standing before him.

The monk stopped and stood in front of David and smiled, "Yes I am, well, in a manner of speaking," he continued on reflection. "I managed to get my spirit into your world but not my physical body."

"Where are you going?" Jennifer asked before the monk could continue.

I'm sorry, but I haven't got time to explain now," he said, looking around the room apprehensively, "but I had to come here and warn you about Nuba Driss."

Both David and Jennifer let out an involuntary gasp, but Belmokhtar continued, "He knows you are here at Enkan Mys and wants you both."

"What does he want us for?" David asked shakily, "we haven't done anything to him, we haven't even met him." Though David had the feeling that wasn't exactly true, the nightmare dreams he had been having came to mind unexpectedly.

"He wants news of the Guardian and he believes you hold that knowledge." He said quietly, waiting for some response expectantly. "Do you have knowledge of the Guardian?" He enquired.

David looked at Jennifer; who shook her head, and then at Christopher who returned his look blankly, before turning back to the monk.

"We hadn't even heard of the Guardian until we came here, so how Nuba Driss thinks we have news of him, beggar's belief."

Belmokhtar looked at David for a long time, obviously thinking about what he had just been told, "You're absolutely certain you know nothing of the Guardian?" He asked again, urgently this time.

"Nothing." David replied quickly and then added, "Why did you want us to come here?"

"What?" he replied absentmindedly, "Oh, I thought you might be able to tell me where the Guardian was before Nuba Driss found him?"

"For what purpose?" Jennifer asked suspiciously.

Belmokhtar turned to look at the girl before answering with a slight smile, "To ask him to help us against Nuba Driss, what else?" he replied.

"You brought us here for that. You thought we might know something of this Guardian and you brought us here to find out?" Jennifer asked in a fury barely contained.

"Calm down Jen," David said trying to placate his sister, sensing the eruption that was about to explode.

"Calm down, you want me to calm down. Why didn't he just ask you when he was at our home or at school even? Then you could have said no and we wouldn't have had to come all this way, gone through everything we have and not be stuck here with little chance of getting home without being killed by some monster of a magician called Nuba bloody Driss!" She shouted back at her brother.

"You managed to get through the portal yourselves Jennifer," Belmokhtar replied, "I had nothing to do with it, except to show you the doorway. As to the Guardian, he was last seen entering the doorway to your world. The doorway that leads into your house." He explained.

"The Guardian came into our world?" David asked excitedly, trying to comprehend the significance of that piece of knowledge.

"Yes David, and to my knowledge he hasn't been seen since." Belmokhtar continued.

"So you think he could still be there?" David asked, surprised by this revelation.

"It seems to be a reasonable assumption. When I entered the doorway myself to look for him, I found only you, the Guardian was nowhere to be seen." He said.

"I don't get this!" Jennifer said trying to keep up with the conversation, "It sounds to me that you were trying to find the Guardian just before we got here, but he left here centuries ago; according to Sukhoi, so how do you explain that?"

"Time runs differently in Sakhalin to your world, with both being connected by the corridor as a sort of gateway. I haven't time to explain everything now, but when I return I will get you home and you need not concern yourselves with what is happening here any more." Belmokhtar promised them and before any of the children could say anything he was out of the door.

"Time runs differently, what does that mean?" David asked out loud.

"Never mind that Dave, did he just say, what I thought he said?" Christopher asked with a huge smile on his face.

David thought about what Belmokhtar had just told them and when Christopher raised his eyebrows and extended his smile, he realised what his brother meant. "Yes, I think he did." David replied smiling too and then began to laugh with excitement. They had at last found someone who could help them get back home.

"We're already concerned with what's happening in Sakhalin," Jennifer said with a slight frown on her forehead, "but more importantly, he was lying about something." She said to herself as her brothers began to pat each other on their backs and laugh at the prospect of finally returning home.

Jennifer strutted around the room as David and Christopher sat talking about what they were going to tell their mother when they finally got home. She kept looking over at them as she paced wanting them to notice that she wasn't happy, but they were so excited and probably relieved that they would be finally going home, that they chose not to notice. Belmokhtar concerned her; she didn't like the man, but was that sufficient cause not to trust him? She didn't know if it was her gift or her intuition, but it was more than an obvious dislike. She knew without doubt that he had been lying; holding something back, something that was important, but unfortunately she didn't know what that something was. She had to tell her brothers; warn them that the man couldn't be trusted, but what proof did she have? She only had a feeling that he wasn't telling them the truth, and she didn't think her brothers would accept that as a good enough reason when the monk had promised to take them back home. Since he had left their room, they had talked about everything he had told them, and the spirits of her brothers had raised a hundred fold. She tried to get excited about the promise herself but she just couldn't escape a feeling of dread. Now, her brothers were getting on her nerves by their consistent chatter and she had to say something.

"I wish you'd shut up about him." She said to their chagrined looks.

"What's wrong Jen?" Christopher asked, a little worried by his sister's attitude.

"There's something wrong here, I don't know what, but I don't trust Belmokhtar."

David looked at his sister and the expression of concentration on her face as if she was trying to figure out a complicated puzzle that was just beyond her grasp. She appeared frustrated, and he found himself annoyed by that frustration. They had just been informed that they would soon be on their way home and she was acting all weird for some reason, what was wrong with her?

"Jen, Belmokhtar said he would take us home, that's good news, don't you think?" He asked her calmly; aware of the mood she was in, but not wanting the moment spoilt by whatever was on her mind.

"Do you really think he can help us get home when the council couldn't do anything?" She replied.

"Of course, why not? He is the Keeper and he's got the book of Kavacha knowledge. He was the one that brought us here really and now he wants to help us get back. He's done it himself, so why wouldn't he be able to take us back home?" David asked her, a little annoyed by her reluctance to believe what Belmokhtar had told them.

"I don't trust him." She replied. "He's not telling us everything, I'm sure of it!"

"He did say he would help us get home though Jen." Christopher interjected.

"He opened the gateway for us, and now he knows we don't know anything about the Guardian, he will take us back home, we should be thankful. If he's not telling us something, maybe it just doesn't concern us, don't you think?" David argued.

"We can go home and back to mam." Christopher added with a big smile.

"I'm not convinced; I've got a really bad feeling about this." She said stubbornly.

"Ok you've got a bad feeling, there's nothing I can do about that, but think things through Jen. Belmokhtar said he will take us home, if he can take us home, he can surely take our friends Hash and Sak home also. That's what you want isn't it? We've found someway to help them and help us at the same time; I think that's great news, don't you?"

Jennifer thought for a few moments before replying, "Yes, it is wonderful news." She said relenting and tried to smile but failed miserably as she tried in vain to shake the bad feeling that was gnawing away in her head.

Aware of the changing mood Christopher added, "I expected more from the council, they weren't very helpful."

"Not really helpful at all." David agreed allowing the subject to change slightly. He didn't want to start arguing with his sister, not now, not when he was so happy and somewhat relieved that they would be returning home as soon as Belmokhtar returned.

"I must admit I was a bit angry at first. Especially when they said they couldn't help Hash and Sak. But if they could, I'm sure they would." Jennifer stated.

"Maybe." David whispered back unconvinced, especially after hearing that Belmokhtar could and would help them on his return. He was sure that if the monk knew of a way to get them home, the council must know of the same way; though he kept that to himself.

Not hearing what her brother said, Jennifer continued. "I'm worried about this army. I can't believe Nuba Driss would send an army against Enkan Mys. I can't see the point in going to war!" She added.

"Stupid." Christopher agreed.

"You don't think there's going to be a war because of us do you?" Jennifer suggested.

"I doubt that Jen. I can't see Nuba Driss going to war because of us and besides we haven't been in Sakhalin all that long, have we?" David said.

"No, you're right, "She said smiling, "I just didn't want to be responsible for anyone getting hurt." She admitted.

"I think this has been brewing for quite some time," David reasoned, "It can't be easy to organise an army and march all the way here from beyond the desert. It must take weeks and weeks of preparation, if not months to organise all the supplies and weapons, etc. More likely, I think Nuba Driss has been planning this attack for years and we're just in the wrong place at the wrong time." He concluded.

"That makes sense." Christopher said. "Brad told me that the three tribes have been on the constant lookout for any indications of the Toureng returning to Sakhalin. I think they have been expecting them to come back for a long time."

"It's the Imazaghan now Chris." David reminded him.

"Yeah sorry."

"Well, hopefully we will be out of here before the army arrives and they can tell Nuba Driss; if he asks, that we didn't know anything about this Guardian." David said.

"You think it will be as easy as that Dave?" Jennifer asked her brother, incredulous of his naivety.

"No, but it's nothing to do with us, it's not our fight." David said.

"Aren't you even a little concerned about our friends?" Jennifer asked in amazement.

"What can we do Jen, what can we really do against an army and Nuba Driss?" David replied getting angry.

"We can try and help them!" Jennifer shouted in response.

"No we can't!" David shouted back, "As soon as Belmokhtar gets back, we're going home and away from all this." He replied.

Jennifer stared at her brother; she couldn't believe what her ears were telling her. Her own brother was prepared to leave Sakhalin and its troubles without even trying to help, what was wrong with him. Was he such a coward that he wouldn't even try and help? She realised there wasn't a lot they could do, but to just leave and not think anything more about it was a horrendous thought.

"What about Hash and Sak, what about them when we go back home, what will they do?" Jennifer asked, tear drops falling from her eyelashes on to her cheeks. She wiped them away gently, without taking her eyes of her brother.

"They will come with us, they can enter the corridor and find their own doorway back home when Belmokhtar shows us the way, can't they?" He offered.

"They won't leave without the orb, that's why they came here in the first place!" She replied matter-of-factly.

"Look Jen, I haven't got all the answers, all I know is that Belmokhtar has promised to help us get back home, and I'm sure he will help the Dragons. I don't know anything more than that. But once that opportunity comes knocking at our door, we're going to take it, whether the Dragons come with us or not." He said with as much authority as he could muster.

Jennifer scrutinised her brother and realised he was right. The Dragons may not like it but the only way they could get back home was if they went with them, whether they had the orb or not. She knew, deep in her heart that they wouldn't leave Sakhalin until they had their precious orb, even if it meant they couldn't return home, but what other choice was there?

"Yes, I know you're right, but we can't leave them here if they choose not to go with us, we must try and help them retrieve their orb. What about the rest of our friends? You could leave them as well, in their time of need?" She said making a deep, slow sigh, which was tugging on the edge of despair as she wrestled with her conscience.

"We haven't really got much choice Jen." David said soothingly aware of what could happen to all their new friends should the army attack the city. He didn't ask Nuba Driss to send an army against his friends, it wasn't even their battle, it was nothing to do with them, couldn't she see that?

"I know but it's just not right. We all made a promise, a promise to help our friends if we could, do you remember that promise Dave?" She said quietly through tight lips.

David nodded and realised he was getting angry because he knew his sister was right. He didn't want to leave his friends either, but they were three children, strangers to this land, what could they do really? Nothing!

Jennifer watched the emotions unfold in her brother and felt guilty for making him confront the feelings she was desperately trying to hide herself, but she couldn't just abandon their friends. Someone had to stay and help them, she wasn't prepared to leave them to the mercy of the army and to Nuba Driss, "I'm sorry Dave, I know your right, but I for one, am going to keep my promise." She said quietly, and stood defiantly waiting for the impending explosion.

David was surprised by the calmness in his voice, when he replied, "If we stay and help the Dragons and the rest of our friends, and something happens to Belmokhtar; for instance, if he gets killed by the approaching army, how will we get home? If the opposing army wins, we wont be able to get back to the Stone either. No one else knows of a way to get us there, do you really want to risk that on a promise to someone you have only just met?" He asked angry with himself for having to ask that question, and being put in this position in the first place. He didn't want to abandon his friends, but he wanted to make sure they both understood what they would be letting themselves in for, what they would be sacrificing if they stayed. He was becoming angry more by the futility of the situation than with his sister but someone had to think about them, about getting them all home, and he felt responsible for that. They shouldn't even be in this situation, and they wouldn't be, if not for him. But was he really prepared to sacrifice going home for people and creatures he had only just met? Did his friendship extend that far, he thought? Yes it did, he knew it did and now all he wanted was for Jennifer and Christopher to agree.

"Yes." Jennifer replied quietly, without hesitation.

Christopher had been listening intently and had remained silent until now and he added his own thoughts to the conversation. "I think we should stay and keep our promise as well Dave." He said sheepishly. It was probably the first time ever that his brother had sided with his sister over him. But the decision was made.

He knew they had to help and that was the problem, they had promised, but what could they do against an army and against the dreaded Nuba Driss, even with the little magic they had. He had expected Jennifer to argue the point of communicating with the Dragons, but she either thought it was too obvious or didn't even realise its significance. They couldn't really leave until the Dragons left, otherwise, who else would be able to speak with them; she would have won the argument straight away with that one. It was the right thing to do; their father and mother would have wanted nothing less of them. David would not abandon his brother and sister. He knew it and they probably knew it as well. Oh, he wasn't happy about the situation, but he really didn't have a choice, they would face whatever was thrown at them together. So no matter how much they talked, discussed or argued, they all knew that they would act as one.

"Ok I think we've all decided. What we do now, we do together and we will stay and help our friends, agreed?" He said.

Jennifer ran to him and hugged him as she laughed with joy, repeating over and over again her thanks.

"Ok, ok, you can let me go now. Let's sit down, we need to think this through, but I honestly can't see what we can do to help."

They sat huddled on the bed as they discussed all that had happened to them since arriving in Sakhalin. They tried to remember every conversation about Nuba Driss and what everyone had told them to see if there was anything they could do.

"So let's think about this. There seems to be three doorways to take us home. The Guardian's Stone, Nuba Driss and his portal and Belmokhtar." Jennifer said excitedly.

"Possibly, but Nuba Driss could be using the Guardian's Stone; we know he knows of it and it makes sense, which just leaves Belmokhtar's way." David said thoughtfully.

"And there's still the matter of the orb." Christopher remarked. "Nuba Driss won't just hand it over to us if we ask politely and I bet he's got some of his minions guarding the Stone by now." He added.

"You're probably right." Jennifer conceded. "But with his army heading here, would he need to protect the doorway if we're all here? And if he is here with his army I doubt he will leave the orb behind. So there's a chance that we can get hold of it and get back to the Stone, especially if Belmokhtar doesn't return." She said.

"Why wouldn't he return Jen?" Christopher asked confused.

She thought a moment before replying, "Well something may happen to him, as David said, and we need to look at every contingency."

David realised that his sister was holding something back. He didn't know if it was anything to do with Belmokhtar, but she had already expressed her feelings about the monk. She didn't like or trust the Keeper of the Kavacha Lore, and that was her choice. He wasn't about to start another argument about that and decided to hold his tongue. If she thought it was something important, he was certain that she would mention it in due course.

They chatted at length while they waited for any news to filter down to them.

David moved over to the window again and when he was sure he wasn't being watched he practised moving objects around the room. He wanted to be prepared to use his gift if he needed to and a little practice wouldn't hurt. He was amazed how quickly he picked it up, but was confounded when he couldn't change an object into something else, no matter how much he tried.

Jennifer communicated the events of the audience to the Dragons. They said they would investigate these rumours themselves and report back when they had some information.

Christopher just sat on his bed and waited quietly, he was practicing something himself but you wouldn't think it to look at him. Socata had taught him how to concentrate his thoughts to tense and relax his muscles at will. He continued to do that for twenty minutes or so but soon lost his concentration and decided to go and find Braduga. While his brother and sister seemed to be lost in their own thoughts he left the room quietly, they didn't notice him leave.

"Jen, where's Chris?" David asked searching the room for his brother.

"He's, well, he's here somewhere." She stuttered, as she scanned the room.

They searched the room from top to bottom, shouting Chris's name as they looked, shouting that they would be annoyed with him, if he didn't stop messing about and show himself. There was no reply, and no movement, so they rushed over to the door, which was still being guarded by two soldiers.

"Has Chris come through this door?" David asked one of the guards.

"Yes." The guard on his left stated. "He went down that way, about thirty minutes ago." He finished pointing down the empty corridor.

"Well, why didn't you stop him?" Jennifer asked reproachfully.

The guard on the right shrugged and glancing at his comrade for obvious confirmation, said. "Sorry, but our orders were to let no one in. They didn't say anything about letting anyone out." He said in their defence.

"We have to find him." Jennifer cried. "Where could he have gone?"

"Hmm." The guard on the left cleared his throat. "The boy was looking for Braduga." He said helpfully. "We told him to try the third room on the left down the corridor and around the corner."

Leaving the guards to shrug their shoulders at each other in apparent confusion of what their orders meant, David and Jennifer ran down the corridor to the room the guard had described and knocked on the door. There was no reply, so they began to bang on the door loudly. After a few seconds there still wasn't any reply, so David tried to open the door; it was locked. The two guards had followed them; they decided they might as well since there was no one in the room to guard and on instructions from Jennifer they managed to kick the door open. There was no one in the room after a cursory search so they began to bang on every door in the corridor searching for their brother.

In the shadow of a blind exit, Christopher listened to a sinister conversation between two men. He couldn't hear everything that was being said, but he had heard enough to know that he needed to tell someone immediately. He had sneaked out of the room to find Braduga but the warrior wasn't in the room the guards had indicated, so he decided to have a look around by himself. David and Jennifer were both engrossed in whatever they were doing and he was bored. He had tried the relaxing techniques he had been shown by Socata, but after a while he wanted to see if Braduga had the time to give him some more lessons. Truth be known, the two Koutla had really frightened him when they came into their room. Well, to be honest it wasn't so much them; though they were scary enough, it was more his inability to do anything about it. He really wanted to discuss this with the warrior, he knew from his chat with Braduga when he had faced the Gourtak that he would understand Christopher's feelings. He realised that he couldn't do anything really to help against two seasoned warriors that were almost a match for the greatest warrior ever seen in Sakhalin, but it didn't really matter, he didn't like that feeling of helplessness and he wanted to talk about it. He would normally speak to David about such things, but he felt his brother had enough on his plate at the moment and he really couldn't speak to Jennifer about it. As his new mentors, he felt he could speak to either Braduga or Socata about his fears, and he was almost certain that they wouldn't tell his brother and sister about them.

The guard on the door had given him directions to Braduga's room but when he turned the corner he had spotted Elder Awdaal talking to a tall stranger that was concealed within a long dark cloak. Christopher didn't know why but he thought there was something familiar about the way the stranger moved. He couldn't place the figure, but it did raise his interest in the pair as they walked along the corridor. They were walking away from him, he didn't know why but he began to follow them, just beyond their sight. The corridor had lots of twists and turns so it was easy to stay out of sight, and that's what he did. He edged closer to try and find out what they were talking about and now he was listening intently.

"They were like sons to me, Sanag." The tall stranger said. "I've known them since they were boys."

"You will get your revenge, Abdi, I promise you that." Elder Sanag Awdaal replied, trying to console the man who appeared genuinely upset.

The name registered in Christopher's mind straight away and he could do nothing but stare at the two men as they continued to walk away from him.

"Yes, I will get my revenge, no fear of that." He agreed with a steely determination.

Christopher was shocked, as the two men continued to walk away he realised that Elder Awdaal was having a conversation with non other than the Koutla leader, Abdi Salut. He was not only talking with the Koutla leader but he was familiar enough with him to call him by his first name. He must get back and warn everyone about the elder, who was obviously a traitor.

He turned round intending to run back to his room, but realised instantly that he didn't have a clue where he was. He had been trying to be careful not to be spotted by the two men that he hadn't been paying attention to where he had been going. Now he stood in a corridor not knowing which way to turn.

He walked along the corridor anyway, trying to find his way back, but it was like a maze, sometimes he turned a corner only to hit a blank wall and he had to turn back the way he came, it was frustrating.

"He must be here somewhere?" Jennifer shouted, distraught.

"We'll find him, Jen." David said trying to console his sister, but he was just as worried something had happened to his brother that he could feel his anger rising in the pit of his stomach, and with it the power he knew was lying dormant; waiting to be released.

The guards assisted the two children as they searched for their brother, speaking to everyone that passed them in the corridor and in the rooms they were looking in. No one had seen the boy however, and word of the missing child spread quickly. It was about an hour later that Socata found them, anger turning to relief when he caught up to them.

"I thought you had been kidnapped." He said as he came running down the corridor.

"Chris has gone missing and we can't find him anywhere." Jennifer said distracted.

Socata had been told by one of the soldiers they had spoken to about a boy going missing, though there weren't any details given. He had run as fast as he could to try and locate them, but he hadn't seen Christopher or Braduga. "You have no idea where he is?" Socata asked.

"Do you think I would still be looking if I did?" Jennifer shouted back at him, tears running unashamedly down her face.

"Sorry." He said quietly.

David couldn't believe this was happening, not after everything they had gone through. Why had Christopher left the room, what was wrong with him? Why'd he have to go off like this? He was just thinking about how stupid his brother was when an idea popped into his head. Ideas seemed to be forming in his head a lot recently for some reason, but he knew instinctively that this idea would work, if he could get his sister to try it.

"Jen." He said cautiously, aware of his sister's raw emotions at the moment. She had been gradually getting angrier and angrier since discovering Christopher's disappearance and he knew he had to be careful how he handled her.

"What!" She shouted back at her brother.

"Try speaking to him." He said calmly.

"I've been shouting his name for the last hour, what do you think I've been doing all this time!" She yelled, tears filling her eyes.

"I mean," David said patiently, "try speaking to him with your mind."

"Don't be stupid David I can't do that." She replied bitterly.

"Are you sure? Have you tried?" David insisted, trying to remain calm.

"No, but I..." She stopped and considered the possibility. She had been so distraught that it hadn't even occurred to her to try and use her gift to find her brother. She wasn't sure it would actually work, but she had to try, she wouldn't be able to live with herself if anything happened to Christopher and she hadn't tried everything.

With David's open and encouraging smile, Jennifer nodded, "Ok, I'll give it a go."

She concentrated on her brother, forming an image of him in her mind, she concentrated on his face, his voice, the way he moved, anything that would bring his image to her mind. Then once she had him in her mind she forced her thoughts out to that image and she called to him as if her life depended on it.

"Chris." She said. "Where are you?"

Christopher had just taken another wrong turn; he knew that because the turn ended in a dead end. He heard Jennifer's voice as a whispered echo coming from the corridor behind him.

"Is that you, Jen?" He asked out loud, turning round expecting to see his sister standing next to him in the corridor, but seeing nothing.

"Chris!" His sister's voice became excited.

Christopher looked up and down the corridor but he couldn't see anything or anyone, he scratched his head in wonder.

"Jen, stop messing about, where are you?" He said out loud.

"I'm here." She replied in his head, sounding amazed and excited all in one. "Where are you?"

"Where are you?" Christopher said in surprise.

"I'm in your head; I'm speaking to you in the same way I can speak with the Dragons, I suppose it's telepathy." She replied.

"Wow, that's great." He said excitedly, "How'd you manage that?" he asked amazed by this revelation.

"Never mind that, where are you?" She asked crossly.

"Don't know really, I'm lost." He admitted reluctantly.

"Right, you stay exactly where you are, don't move a muscle, and we'll come to you, ok?"

"Yes, don't move a muscle, stay where I am, I understand." Came his reply.

Jennifer shouted for the guards and with David and Socata in tow, she walked around the corridor trying to concentrate on her brother as she talked to him about anything that came to mind, to keep a sort of link established with her brother. She feared that if she didn't maintain that link, she wouldn't be able to find him, so she encouraged him to talk whilst she concentrated on his voice.

The walk gradually turned into a run with Jennifer leading the way, she would pause occasionally when she came upon a junction with a choice to be made, but she would then make a decision and start running again. They passed a few people in the corridor at first, who gave them questioning looks, but as they travelled down less used corridors, they didn't see anyone. Socata briefly stated that no-one had used these particular corridors for years but Jennifer wasn't interested about if people used the corridors or not, she was totally focused on only one thing, her little brother's voice.

It was about twenty minutes later when they turned yet another corner to find Christopher sat against a door; knees bent with his chin resting on them.

He turned his head at their approach and an enormous relieved grin broke over his face.

"You took your time." He said as he got to his feet and began walking over to them.

Jennifer and David ran over to their brother, hugging him, and then berating him for leaving the room, and then hugging him again in relief that he was safe.

The guards and Socata smiled as Christopher was smothered by his brother and sister.

"What were you thinking?" Jennifer berated him again.

"I was looking for Brad and..." He began to explain.

"You should have told us." David broke in.

"I need to tell you something..." He began again.

"Well, it doesn't matter now, you're safe and that's all that matters." Jennifer interrupted.

"Stop it, stop talking and listen to me!" Christopher shouted trying to get a word in edge ways.

Everyone looked questioningly at Christopher, as he appeared to gather his thoughts and cleared his throat.

"I followed Elder Awdaal." Christopher began.

"You should not be following anyone." Jennifer interrupted. "What were you doing following the elder?" She asked him with a frown on her brow.

Christopher stared her into silence before continuing. "I followed Elder Awdaal who was speaking with another man. They seemed to know each other very well." He paused, looking at everyone waiting for him to finish. "The man was covered from head to foot in a cloak but there was something about him that I thought I recognised. I followed them and listened to a bit of their conversation and then I realised who this mysterious stranger was. It was Abdi, the Koutla leader." He finished.

"What?" David said. "Are you sure Chris?" He asked in amazement.

"Of course I'm sure, I'm not stupid." He replied sulkily.

"What happened? What was said?" Socata asked hurriedly.

Quickly he described how he had come across the two men when he was searching for Braduga. He had recognised the Elder and then to his astonishment had recognised the man talking with him. He knew this meeting could be important so he decided to follow them and try and hear what they were talking about. He just didn't expect to get lost, and he had almost given up finding his way back when he had heard Jennifer's thoughts in his head.

"We must tell Sukhoi at once." Socata announced. "Quickly, follow me." He said as he turned and began walking briskly back the way they had come.

They walked back to the room where they found Sukhoi and Braduga waiting for them, with worried looks on their faces.

"Where have you been?" Sukhoi asked, relieved to see them as they entered the room. "When we got here and there were no guards on the door and the room was empty, we thought something had happened to you all."

"I think you should listen to what Chris has to say Sukhoi." Socata interrupted the Kavacha before he could continue.

Christopher quickly described what had happened while Sukhoi listened intently, raising his eyebrow in surprise.

"So the threads begin to knit together." He said, as his thoughts organised and came together like a jigsaw puzzle. "Elder Awdaal was obviously the contact within the city. Abdi Salut and his protégés were to bring you to him. The why, we still have to determine, but I am sure all will become clear eventually."

"I have been thinking about the twins a lot recently, Sukhoi." Braduga said. "The way they fought was reminiscent of the time I spent here. A few of their moves were different, but you find that when you have fought in a few battles and you have to adapt quickly to compensate for an unexpected thrust or stab. But in essence, their movements, skills and techniques were the same. If they were trained at the city or by someone who trained at the city, it would definitely explain a lot."

"That does make sense." Sukhoi thought. "But how can that be? I am sure we would all know about a set of twin warriors, especially with their abilities." He said after some consideration.

"That is true." Braduga conceded though he was sure he was right about the twins being trained as warriors here in the city, maybe even as Ruedin.

"What about Abdi Salut then?" Socata asked. "You said he seemed familiar to you."

"Yes, maybe he had been trained here, and then he taught the twins." Braduga smiled triumphantly, that made sense.

"It could be possible," Sukhoi agreed. "He did speak his name as if I should know it. I think you may be right."

"That would also make sense." Socata suggested. "If he was trained here when he was younger, he could have met Elder Awdaal then."

"Yes, it all fits together." Sukhoi smiled. "We should ask the council and tell them about Elder Awdaal and his associate. We must start a search to find them both before they have the opportunity to escape."

The guards had been patiently waiting for their orders and now Sukhoi tasked them to find and detain the elder and the Koutla leader if possible. They were to approach each with caution, but get assistance in their search from every guard they met.

"Oh, and there is some other news that is of great interest." Sukhoi said. "More villagers have arrived in the city. They say they were forced to leave their villages by Koutla Raiders and not the Imazaghan.

"What does that mean?" David asked.

"It probably means that the Raiders and the Imazaghan are in league together. Maybe the Raiders are the vanguard of the Imazaghan army."

"So there's going to be a war?" Jennifer asked nervously, not wanting the answer to be real.

"If the reports are true, yes, I am afraid there is." Sukhoi replied.

Chapter Twenty Four

Hash'ar'jefar and his sister Sak'ar'jefar soared into the sky to search for any indications of an army marching on the city of Enkan Mys. They flew together; they went west initially; the most likely route an invading force would take, but found nothing. They then headed east towards the Gratiskh Mountains, and were greeted by a large army obviously heading towards the city. The army was still quite a long way from the city, but they did appear to be advancing quickly, and were probably only slowed down by their supply wagons, which were trailing behind.

They realised from their uniforms that the soldiers were Koutla Raiders, but they knew from overheard conversations that such numbers had never been seen before now.

They continued to fly in an easterly direction until they reached Dakhla Mys and were shocked to see another greater army of soldiers crossing the Lake. They realised that these soldiers were different, better equipped and more organised from the way they moved. This force was immense compared to the Raider army; at least four times larger if not more. They calculated that there must be at least thirty thousand soldiers, descendants of the banished tribe and now called the Imazaghan. They decided to return to the city as soon as possible and inform their friends of their plight before either force got too close.

"JENNIFER." Hash'ar'jefar said as they headed back towards the city.

"Yes Hash, any news?" She replied promptly.

Hash'ar'jefar thought it strange that he could once again speak with the humans, but enjoyed the feeling immensely. It had been too long since he had found the opportunity, but it thrilled him to do so.

"THERE ARE TWO ARMIES HEADED TOWARD THE CITY. A SMALL FORCE OF KOUTLA RAIDERS ARE MOVING QUICKLY TOWARD THE CITY. BUT A MUCH LARGER FORCE OF APPROXIMATELY THIRTY THOUSAND SOLDIERS, I THINK THE IMAZAGHAN, ARE ALREADY CROSSING THE GHANEM." He finished.

"You're sure?" She asked, but she already knew the answer.

"YES." He replied.

"Ok, thank you my friend, I will pass this information on."

Jennifer had been sitting in her room and listening to Sukhoi re-tell what he had heard from the villagers that had entered the city, when she heard Hash'ar'jefar's call. Everyone else was listening intently as he told of Raiders sweeping through the villages and taking everything that wasn't tied down, then burning the villages when they'd finished. They didn't notice her lack of attention but when she had finished her conversation it was Socata that noticed her pale complexion.

"What's wrong Jennifer?" He asked.

"I'm afraid I've got some bad news!" She told them.

"What is it?" Sukhoi prompted.

"The situation is worse than predicted." She said. "I have just been speaking with Hash."

"About the army?" Sukhoi inquired.

"Armies! There is an army of Koutla Raiders coming this way quickly; but more importantly, there is another army of at least thirty thousand crossing Lake Ghanem as we speak and Hash thinks they are Imazaghan."

Shocked into silence, Sukhoi could only stare at Jennifer. It was incredible to believe there were thirty thousand Imazaghan soldiers heading toward the city; incredible and unbelievable.

"We must speak with the elders at once." He said quickly, standing up.

They arrived at the Audience Chamber amidst an atmosphere of panic throughout the city. The streets were full of families who had fled the villages and towns and were now seeking refuge within the city walls. With so many people, it had taken them a while to get to the Audience Chamber. When they finally got inside the building the corridors were full of people trying to gain an audience with the elders. They pushed forward regardless of the outcries from the homeless people gathered there queuing. Even with Braduga and Socata clearing a path through them, it was a slow process to get to the door. Luckily one of the guards recognised them and commanded that the crowd let them through, which they did, albeit reluctantly.

"It's been like this all day." The guard informed them when they were within hearing.

"Are they all waiting?" Jennifer asked, feeling sorry for the plight of the villagers and townsfolk.

"I'm afraid so. But you don't have to wait. My orders are to let you in as soon as you got here, Kavacha." The guard informed them.

"Good, thank you." He said as he and his companions entered the room.

If there was chaos outside the chamber there was anarchy inside with everybody shouting to be heard at once over the noise. Sukhoi, his Ruedin and the three children pushed their way forward; between a various assortment of soldiers, elders and advisors until they reached the front.

"Elder Hanish!" Sukhoi shouted over the din. "Elder Hanish!" He shouted again, not heard the first time.

Elder Hanish was on his feet. "Silence!" He commanded, raising his arms and lowering them in a movement to decrease the noise level. He might have looked a frail old man but he still had the steely strength in his voice that demanded notice, when raised.

The room gradually went quiet as the elder glanced around the room, daring anyone else to speak. Silence ensued, no one was stupid enough or brave enough to speak against the leader of the council once he had shouted everyone to silence.

"Sukhoi of the Kavacha. You have news?" He asked as he motioned the small group forward. The group moved forward again with all manner of officers and officials making way for them as they approached the council.

"I do Elder Hanish." He replied as he reached the old man.

"Then speak, so all might hear."

"The news is not good Elder," he began almost reluctantly, "not good at all." Everyone was silent as Sukhoi of the Kavach turned to face the throng of dignitaries and advisors.

"There are two armies heading this way as we speak." He began.

The crowd erupted with this announcement and once again Elder Hanish had to shout for the noise to stop. "I will have silence!" He commanded as he berated the ensemble.

Sukhoi waited for the noise to abate again before continuing. "An army of Raiders are moving quickly toward the city, though I do not have any more details for the moment." He paused, looking round the room, trying to gauge the audience. "But a more serious problem is that of a larger army of about thirty thousand strong, which is crossing Lake Ghanem now; they are Imazaghan soldiers, descendants of the Toureng." He finished.

Uproar met this announcement. This was impossible came the general cry, everyone wanted their say about the situation.

Elder Hanish just looked directly towards Sukhoi who nodded to confirm his statement and the old man seemed to gain a few years in age as he closed his eyes and let out a steady sigh.

"Where does this information come from?" Shouted one officer of the guard.

"The Raiders haven't got an army, and who are these Imazaghan lot?" Asked another voice from the crowd.

Question after question came his way, but he didn't get the opportunity to answer one before another one was asked.

One of the other elders tried to ask for everyone to calm down, trying to tell them that the Kavacha couldn't answer their questions over the commotion but to no avail. Elder Hanish continued to sit quietly, control was lost for the moment and he had no choice but to wait for the noise to recede. He didn't have to wait long though, because after a few minutes the arrival of the two Dragons in the chamber had everyone's tongues stuck to the top of their mouths in shock. Indeed a couple of dignitaries actually fainted in shock at seeing the creatures.

Hash'ar'jefar and Sak'ar'jefar had been summoned by Jennifer when reports of the two approaching armies had been questioned. She concluded that the only way to convince the crowd was for the Dragons to appear and for her to translate exactly what they had seen on their travels. The Dragons had agreed to come even though they hated crowds; especially crowds of people that couldn't hear their call, but they had agreed to come never the less.

Hash'ar'jefar roared as he entered the room and everyone stared in surprise at his arrival, and that of his sister Sak'ar'jefar.

The Dragons made their way towards the front of the crowd, which parted to let them through with great haste for some reason. Probably the fact that two enormous creatures were heading in their direction and had no intention of slowing down, gave them little choice but to move out of the way.

"THEY DO NOT BELIEVE WHAT I HAVE REPORTED?" Hash'ar'jefar asked as he turned to face the crowd, who were still staring at him with awe and wonder.

"I think they will now." She replied.

Elder Hanish stood and addressed the crowd. "May I introduce our friends?

Hash'ar'jefar and his sister Sak'ar'jefar." He said smiling as each Dragon nodded their heads in acknowledgement of their names. Silence greeted this introduction as everyone continued to stare.

"Jennifer." Elder Hanish said, motioning for the girl to come to him.

The silent crowd parted once more to allow the girl to walk up to the old man and stand beside him. She whispered in the Elder's ear as he nodded with everything she told him and then he faced the crowd once more.

"This is Jennifer." He said. "She is a very important person."

Murmurs arose from the crowd as they looked from the girl to the Dragons in wonder. Questions were already forming on some of the faces. Who was the girl? What significance did she have with the current situation? Did she have anything to do with the Dragons?

Elder Hanish could almost hear the thoughts himself as he slowly raised his arms for silence again. This time it came quickly and he said. "I realise there must be lots of questions, but first I give you proof of the armies." He looked at Jennifer and smiled. "Jennifer can communicate with the Dragons." He continued as the murmurs rose, "It was the Dragons that brought us news of the armies and if you have any questions she will translate them for you."

The crowd couldn't contain themselves even with the arrival of the Dragons and question after question was shouted at the council and indeed at Jennifer.

"How do we know she can communicate with these creatures?" Asked one man.

"That's right, she could be saying anything." Agreed a middle aged woman dressed all in black.

"She's only a girl." Came another shout.

Then Hash'ar'jefar roared and swayed his head from left to right in order to get everyone's attention. The silence was deafening as he spoke to Jennifer, while the crowd waited hungrily.

"THEY JABBER LIKE CHILDREN." Hash'ar'jefar stated. "NO OFFENCE INTENDED JENNIFER." He added quickly recovering from his blunder.

"None taken my friend." She laughed.

'What is he saying?" Asked a tall Kavacha named Fassut.

"Hash," She said to the crowd. "Was commenting on the fact that you jabber like children."

The crowd looked at the Dragon standing before them and then at the girl, who was still smiling and couldn't contain their disbelief.

"It can't be true, she's lying!" A man shouted from the back of the crowd.

Jennifer heard what the man had said and she could feel her anger rising. How dare they think she was lying, she thought.

"Maybe she could ask them to do something?" The woman in black suggested.

"I am not lying!" Jennifer shouted, "But I am not going to ask my friends to perform some sort of tricks just to prove the point. You either believe me or not!" She said a little louder at the now silent crowd.

"Elder Hanish." Sukhoi said, moving to the front of the crowd to be seen clearly. "May I address the council and this audience?" He asked.

"Speak Sukhoi." Elder Hanish said.

"My friends listen to me now." He began. "Jennifer speaks the truth, she can speak with the Dragons, on my word as Kavacha it is true. But listen to me now; there are more urgent matters to discuss. Our friends the Dragons have brought news of two armies heading this way. There is little time to prepare already, let us not shout and argue here, we must make plans and make them now." He paused. "We need your help and co-operation. We need to organise, to plan and be ready to fight. All other considerations can be discussed at a later date. Can we count on everyone to do their duty?" He asked, his arms open to emphasise his request.

Duty was one word the inhabitants of Enkan Mys knew. Since before the last battle with Nuba Driss they had known that word and what it represented. The Toureng had spat on that word and crushed it into dust, but the remaining three tribes held it dear to their hearts, they knew their responsibilities and they would not shirk from them now. Yes, they would do their duty and they would do it willingly.

"Will the Dragons help?" Fassut asked. Aran Fassut was tall and thin, with a sharp face and a keen eye. He had known the relationship between Sukhoi and the Dragons existed, but he had never seen them before now. The stories he had heard about them did not do them justice, they were magnificent creatures, and he couldn't help, but stare at them.

"WE WILL HELP, WHERE WE CAN." Sak'ar'jefar nodded and replied taking a step forward to face the surprised but smiling Kavacha, when Jennifer repeated her words.

"We will all do what we can." Elder Bashir agreed as he witnessed the exchange with the rest of the audience and then the council stood and addressed the crowd.

With everybody in agreement and the decision made, the elders began to segregate officers and advisors into groups and plans began to formulate for the defence of the city.

Five men grouped together with Aran Fassut approached Jennifer, who now had Sukhoi standing beside her to give her strength and support, if she required it.

"Sukhoi, my friend." Aran said. "Is it really true?" He asked looking at Jennifer in something bordering on awe.

"Yes Aran and there is little time to prepare." He said.

"I am sorry my friend, I knew this day would come, but I just find it hard to believe that after all this time the Toureng have returned." He said shaking his head.

"Not the Toureng anymore my brother, but their descendants, the Imazaghan." Sukhoi reminded him.

The two Kavacha discussed the Imazaghan in detail, passing on their own thoughts and conclusions as to why the army was attacking now. The rest of the congregating group listened intently to the conversation, which provided

Jennifer with a means to slip away and search for her brothers who had disappeared from view when the groups were being sorted out.

She found them with Elder Hanish as they were discussing the traitor Elder Awdaal and his Koutla accomplice.

"So you have no idea where Elder Awdaal has gone?" David asked the elder.

"No David." He replied. "I have guards searching everywhere for him, but I can not believe he would betray us."

"He has, I heard him." Christopher said, slightly annoyed that the Elder didn't believe him.

"I did not say I did not believe you Christopher," He said to the boy, sensing his unease, "I just find it difficult to believe that an Elder would betray his own people in this way." He remarked.

"There doesn't seem to be another explanation." Jennifer said, "Unless you can think of one Elder?" She inquired.

The leader of the council of elders looked Jennifer in the eye, anyone else would have looked away from that gaze, but Jennifer thought there was something not quite right with Elder Awdaal and she was genuinely interested in any thoughts the old man might have. So, she returned his look with one of innocent expectancy.

"No," he replied after a moment, "I can think of no reason why he would be talking to the Koutla, especially with such familiarity." The old man replied reluctantly.

"Me either." She said with a hardness she hadn't expected in her voice.

David had been watching the exchange, and thought it more a battle of will than a mere discussion. He knew his sister could be quite formidable, he had often lost the arguments they had; even with Christopher's backing, but he had never seen his sister seem so confident. He had never seen her so hard or cold either for that matter.

"If you will excuse me, there are some matters I must attend to." The elder said as he left the three children.

They watched him depart and when he was out of hearing, David rounded on his sister, "what was all that about?" he asked her.

"What do you mean?" She replied innocently.

"Don't play dumb with me, what's got into you?" He said forcing the issue.

"I told you I didn't like Elder Awdaal, there was something not quite right with the man, and then there was Elder Hanish trying to find some reason for his actions. I didn't like it, if he knew of some reason why the elder would do that to his own people I for one was interested in what that reason could be." She finished adamantly.

"Do you think it was your gift telling you something then?" David asked realising it could be another addition to his sister's abilities. The thought had crossed his mind before, but both their gifts were changing and improving he didn't know what to think anymore.

Jennifer hesitated before replying, she hadn't even thought of that, but now he mentioned it, maybe it was her new gifts that were helping her to see the truth in what people said. It had happened a few times now, where she instinctively knew whether someone was telling a lie or not. In fact, now she thought about it, it had actually happened quite a lot recently.

"Maybe," she conceded as she continued to think it through, "but I'm not convinced it works all the time; if at all, at best it's happening intermittently."

"Well, if you can tell if someone's lying that could be very useful in the future." David said as he thought about the implications of having someone who could tell the truth from a lie.

Christopher listened to the exchange and a crazy thought came into his head. Well, he thought it was crazy, and couldn't help but laugh as he said out loud.

"Sounds like you could be the Nadym Varsk the Kavacha are looking for."

"What?" David and Jennifer said in unison.

"You know, the Nadym Varsk, doesn't that mean "truth seer?" he asked with mirth, though from the looks on their faces, it was soon swallowed.

"I was only saying, I didn't mean anything by it." He said defensively as they stared at him.

David looked toward Jennifer, who stared at Christopher and then looked back at David, unable to say anything for a few seconds.

"No," she said, shaking her head, "impossible." She protested.

"Is it Jen, is it really?" David asked, not convinced it was impossible at all.

The more he thought about it, the more it made sense. They had arrived in a strange land and had started to display certain talents, but

Jennifer more than himself. She had given him warning on a few occasions when she thought someone was lying, and had also given him council when she thought someone could be trusted. She thought there was something odd about one of the elders and now he had been found to be a traitor. All those things added together sounded something a Truth Seer would see, so why not? Why couldn't she be the Nadym Varsk, she was displaying all the characteristics attributed to the one the Kavacha were searching for.

"No David, I can't be the Nadym Varsk." She said defensively, but once the words left her lips, once she said that she couldn't be the Nadym Varsk, she knew then that she was. It was like a light being turned on in her head and David had flicked the switch. She remembered the times when she had seen the truth and tried to deny it to herself, that she hadn't seen it after all. But now, the switch had been turned on and she could see that her brother was right, that both of her brothers were right.

David could tell there was some sort of internal wrangling happening to his sister, he could see it in her eyes. He wasn't exactly sure what was taking place and could do nothing to help her, but he knew she was thinking very hard about what had just been innocently suggested. She seemed to silently weigh up the options, trying to determine if she was who he now believed her to be. He was sure that Christopher had hit the nail on the head about Jennifer, without even realising it. He wasn't extremely happy about it, this would undoubtedly complicate everything, but it felt right, she really could be the Truth Seer.

He laughed inwardly at that thought. Why was he so sure she was the one? Wasn't he himself, displaying some of those same characteristics he thought his sister had? Could he now see the truth as well? No, if there was one thing he was sure of more than anything else; he knew he wasn't the Nadym Varsk.

"Jen, you ok?" He asked after a nudge and a nod from his brother when she hadn't responded to his same question.

"What? Yes, just been thinking about things." She replied in a somewhat disorientated state.

"Forget what I said Jen." He began, the last thing they needed right now was for Jennifer to be thinking she was the chosen one, but it was too late, she interrupted him before he could finish.

"Actually Dave, I think you could be right." She said, "I have felt for a while that there was something different about me, about us, and it sounds right, do you know what I mean?" She said in explanation.

David breathed a deep sigh, knowing that she was right, "Yes Jen, I do." He replied. Whether he liked it or not, it had to be right, because everything fit perfectly. Unfortunately, he could now see all the potential problems the announcement of this fact would bring to his sister and to them on a whole.

"So, she is the Nadym Varsk?" Christopher asked sceptically

"Yes, I believe she is Chris!" He replied, "Isn't that right Jen?" He asked her.

"Yes." She replied without hesitation and a heavy silence descended upon them as they thought of where this would lead them.

"Everyone ok?" Sukhoi said joining the children with his Kavacha brother Aran Fassut. But the three children continued to look at each other in silence as if they hadn't heard the question. They were still struggling to come to terms with this new revelation.

"Are they ok?" Aran asked his friend when the children didn't reply or even take their eyes off each other.

David tore his eyes away from Jennifer and apologised for being rude.

"Everything ok?" Sukhoi asked again.

"Yes, fine. We were just wondering if there was anything we could do to help?" he said as he smiled at the Kavacha. Now wasn't the time to be telling their new friends that one of them was the one person in the whole of Sakhalin that they had been searching for. Not when they had been searching all their lives and not when he remembered that the Nadym Varsk was suppose to be instrumental in the fight against Nuba Driss. Had his sister even realised that small point when she admitted she could be the Truth Seer, because he very much doubted it.

"Ok, well, it has begun at last." Sukhoi announced. "Plans are being made for the defence of the city and responsibilities are being assigned. I do not think you can help at the moment but we will let you know." He said as he smiled at the three of them."

"It is a shame there are not more of us here." Aran expressed quietly, "that would certainly improve our chances."

"How so?" David asked intrigued.

"Well for one thing, there would be more warriors." He laughed. "Each Kavacha has his Ruedin, each warrior worth twenty of the local soldiers. But more than that, we would have our brothers with us, and that would bring us great power. Using the Kavacha knowledge together would make us a formidable opponent."

"You can join together and use the power? Sukhoi has mentioned it before but hasn't really said how it can be used!" David asked.

"I am sorry my friend, only the Kavacha themselves can know of that." Sukhoi reminded him of the discussion they had on their journey to Enkan Mys.

"Sorry, just thought I might be able to help."

"We will talk of this later David, if that is ok?" Sukhoi said to the boy with a sly smile and a discreet wink.

David nodded his ascent and smiled back, though he wasn't sure what the Kavacha had planned.

"Wouldn't most of them know about the army and be returning here anyway?" Jennifer asked.

"Yes, to the east." Sukhoi replied. "But there are still many towns and villages in every other direction that are probably not aware of the armies."

"I know of a way, maybe." Christopher stated with a big grin on his face.

Everyone looked toward him as his smile grew with all the attention he was receiving and Jennifer thought he was going to say something about her being the Nadym Varsk and gave him a challenging look, just in case.

"Well?" Jennifer asked impatiently.

"Well." He wanted to mimic but decided against it and instead broadened the smile on his face, if that was possible.

"Why don't we just ask the Dragons to go and find them? They could scour the countryside quicker than anyone else for a start and if there was some way of knowing where the Kavacha were?" He asked, looking pointedly at Sukhoi, "We could give them a note or something. The note could say something like, "get back to Enkan Mys as quickly as you can, there is an army on its way to destroy the city". I think that would work." He said quickly before anyone could interrupt him. He was always prepared to put his thoughts forward, he was a lot braver than David in that respect, thought his brother. David wouldn't normally suggest anything, he normally kept his thoughts and suggestions to himself; well, until recently that was. But Christopher was fearless, if he thought of something that could be of any use to anyone, he would just come out and say it.

As he looked at everyone's astonished faces, he realised yet again that his idea had merit, if nothing else.

"There may be a way to find the Kavacha." Sukhoi suggested cautiously, impressed by Christopher's suggestion.

"What do you think then, is it possible?" He asked, eager for their thoughts.

"Hash and Sak would definitely be able to cover a lot more ground than anybody else." Jennifer agreed.

Everyone realised immediately that his plan could work. If they could somehow find out where the rest of the Kavacha were and then get the Dragons to deliver a note, once located, yes it could work.

The boy was a genius David thought, and not for the first time. He just had this ability to come up with the simplest, but most obvious idea that everyone else seemed to have missed.

"How do you do it?" David asked with a smile.

"What? The ideas? Just talented I suppose." He replied with an even bigger grin, which really did extend the full length of his face.

"You are truly wise beyond your years, Christopher is it?" Aran said with a smile.

"Yes, that's right, but everyone calls me Chris." Christopher beamed at the praise, nodding at his sister as she gave a big sigh at his response.

Reluctantly, Jennifer smiled at her brother, "that is a great idea Chris," she said to him as he gave her a deep bow of appreciation.

Smiling, she turned to David, "we're not going to hear the last of this, are we?"

"Doubt it." David conceded, but couldn't help but laugh at Christopher as he shrugged his shoulders and raised his hands in a gesture that said, "What?"

Sukhoi said to Jennifer, "Each Kavacha has a little magic; I believe our friends would be able to sense that magic. I believe that is how they have been able to find me when I needed them. If that is true, then the same method could be used to locate the other Kavacha."

"That sounds plausible." Jennifer replied.

"It makes sense; if Hash and Sak could find the rest of my brothers it would mean a great difference to the defence of the city." Sukhoi added.

"I will go and speak with Hash and Sak and see what they think." She said and then walked up to her brother. "Will you be here when I get back?" She asked David.

"Not sure, Sukhoi wanted to have a word with me about the Kavacha knowledge." He said looking over at the man who was gesturing him to follow him.

"Ok, I won't be long, but I'll come and find you when I've finished." She said as she walked toward her friends.

Although Jennifer could have spoken with the Dragons anywhere in the room, she walked over to them and could see the relief in their expressions. They were surrounded by people asking them questions, but the people still hadn't realised that the Dragons couldn't answer those questions without Jennifer.

She motioned them to follow her as she led them to the far corner of the room.

"We have just been having a chat about the other Kavacha who are still outside the city," She began as she leaned against a marble pillar; one of twenty that were in a line holding up the ceiling. "It has been suggested, "She had no intention of saying it was her brother Christopher's idea, "that if we could get those Kavacha to return to the city, we would have considerably better odds for when the army arrived."

Hash appeared to ponder this for a moment before speaking. "I HAVE NOTICED THAT THE

KAVACHA HAVE A LITTLE MAGIC, THIS INDEED WOULD BE USEFUL FOR WHEN THE ARMY ATTACKS THE CITY." He replied carefully.

Jennifer thought for a moment as she absorbed what Hash had told her. "Yes, Sukhoi said the same thing; do you think you could find the Kavacha by their ability to do magic?" She asked expectantly.

"YES, I BELIEVE SO." He replied.

"Would you be able to give them a message from us?" She asked.

"YES." Sak'ar'jefar said quickly, looking around at all the people in the audience chamber. Anything to get away from the crowd of people who couldn't communicate with them, Jennifer could almost read that thought in the Dragon's face.

"Hash," Jennifer said quietly. They both brought their gazes back to the girl as she pushed herself away from the pillar to come between the pair of Dragons.

"YES JENNIFER?" He asked expectantly.

"You said that the Kavacha have magic. Can you detect any magic in my brothers and me?" Jennifer asked almost reluctantly.

He scrutinised her for a few moments and looked toward his sister who shook her head before answering. "NO, I CAN DETECT NOTHING." the dragon replied with a slight frown. Well it looked like a frown to Jennifer. But she was surprised by the reply, because David had already demonstrated his ability to perform magic on more than one occasion, and if she really was the Nadym Varsk; which she believed she was, then surely they would be able to detect the magic in her too.

"IT IS A LITTLE STRANGE, BUT YOU THREE ARE DIFFERENT FROM THE REST OF THE PEOPLE WE HAVE MET IN SAKHALIN." Sak'ar'jefar agreed.

That must be the reason, Jennifer thought. They weren't indigenous to Sakhalin, so maybe their gifts wouldn't be seen in the same way. It made sense, she thought.

"Ok never mind." She replied and changing the subject said. "I will get Sukhoi to write a note that explains everything and bring it back here."

"WE WILL LEAVE WHEN WE HAVE THE NOTE THEN. BUT PLEASE HURRY." Hash'ar'jefar said looking at the crowd of people amassed in the room.

"HE IS NOT COMFORTABLE WITH ALL THESE PEOPLE ABOUT AND NEITHER AM I." Sak'ar'jefar said by way of an explanation as her brother fidgeted from one massive foot to the other.

"IT IS MORE THAN THAT." He expanded. "IT IS FRUSTRATING NOT BEING ABLE TO SPEAK TO THEM."

"YES, IT IS NICE TO SPEAK TO SOMEONE AGAIN AFTER SUCH A LONG TIME." Agreed his sister, who gave Jennifer what was suppose to be a big smile, she thought.

"It must have been terrible for you." Jennifer said.

"IT WAS, BUT EVERYTHING WILL BE OK NOW, BECAUSE WE HAVE YOU." Sak'ar'jefar replied.

A tear appeared in Jennifer's eye, though she couldn't understand why she was getting emotional. "We will try and get your orb back,

Sak. I promise you that." She said wiping her eyes.

"WE KNOW JENNIFER, AND WE APPRECIATE YOUR HELP." She replied gratefully.

"Ok, I will go and find Sukhoi and get that note for you." She said and left the Dragons to find Sukhoi and her brothers.

Chapter Twenty Five

"This is the book of Kavacha Lore." Sukhoi said to David with a reverence that he hadn't heard in his friend's voice before.

"And it holds all the knowledge of the Kavacha?" David asked as he gazed upon the magical book. Although it wasn't anything to look at, he noticed. It was quite non-descript really, the brown leather exterior of the book was faded and torn and some of the pages beneath were brown and upturned with obvious constant use. But there was something about the book that attracted him to it, as if a force was pulling at him to read its contents. A familiar sensation overcame him all of a sudden and the unexpected shock of it must have shown on his face because Sukhoi asked him if he was alright.

"I just felt as if I was back," He hesitated, trying to decide if it was the same feeling, "Somewhere else." He finished.

"The book has great power David." Sukhoi told the boy, "All the Kavacha that have read the book have felt that power and gained some of its knowledge."

"Have all the Kavacha read the book then?" David asked.

"Yes, though some Kavacha are given more knowledge than others. We do not know why this is, but we know it to be true." He replied.

"It sounds as if the book decides how much knowledge a person should have!" David said thoughtfully.

"I think you may be right." Sukhoi agreed.

"And the Keeper protects the book?" David asked.

"Yes, in a way. The book is protected by an incantation made by the Guardian himself. The Keeper believes that the book can not be taken from this room."

"Have you tried to move it?" David asked intrigued.

"No, not that I know of, and why would we want to move it?" He asked.

"Well, if nothing else, to see if the spell on the book works." David replied.

"It would not be allowed and there are Kavacha incantations on this room to ensure it is not considered." He added.

"May I touch it? I wont damage it!" He asked then, an overwhelming desire to touch the book ripped through his mind.

Sukhoi hesitated for a minute, trying to sense anything from the book or the boy, but he sensed nothing. So he nodded and opened the glass cabinet in which the book was held and put it down on a nearby table.

David looked at the book and was amazed by his reaction. He wanted nothing more than to touch the book, open it and read it, but he wasn't really one for reading books and couldn't understand why he wanted to read this particular book.

Placing both hands over the book he slowly lowered them. When his hands finally touched the leather binding of the book he almost cried out in shock.

Sukhoi watched in amazement as a green light suddenly sprang from the book where David had his hands placed on it and the boy went rigid with his head back and his eyes wide open.

David couldn't believe what was happening at first. But when the light moved through his body he realised that it contained the knowledge held within the book. The book was imparting its knowledge and power into his very being. He could see in his mind all the words and pictures the book held and what's more he understood what they meant.

Sukhoi wanted to grab the book; fearful for David's safety, but he couldn't do anything, it was as if he was paralysed. He hadn't seen the book react this way before and he felt frustrated that he could do nothing to help his young friend. The seconds ticked by as Sukhoi watched David being consumed by the light. He tried to grab the book, but it was as if a barrier had been placed between him and them. Helplessly he watched as David seemed to fight the light until eventually David scrunched his eyes and lowered his head. The light finally disappeared and he felt the barrier fall away.

As soon as he realised the barrier had disappeared Sukhoi reached out to grab David as he slumped in his arms.

"Are you ok? What happened?" He asked in concern and bewilderment, he had never seen or heard of anything like this.

David opened his eyes and smiled a thin lipped smile as he felt his strength return to him.

"It was incredible." He whispered.

Jennifer had searched everywhere for her brothers and now she was getting a little annoyed by not being able to locate them. She was tempted to try and use her telepathy, but thought her brothers may not be too happy about that, so she continued with her search. She was beginning to worry when Socata appeared before her and told her where at least one of her brothers had gone. She was escorted out of the chamber and through a maze of corridors before Socata came to a stop outside a large white door. He knocked three times and then waited.

After a few seconds the door opened and Aran Fassut appeared. Sweat was dripping down his face and his clothes were sticking to his thin frame from obvious exertion.

"Your brother is incredible." He said with a big smile and ushered the pair of them into a small passageway which lead to two large wooden doors.

"Which one? And are they ok?" She asked wondering which of her brothers was causing mischief.

"Oh, sorry, David is here, Christopher is with Braduga." Aran replied.

What was David up to now? Jennifer thought as she followed the Kavacha.

They walked the length of the passageway and then Aran opened the doors at the end to reveal an open courtyard. There were numerous men watching a spectacle that she couldn't quite see, but they were obviously enjoying the display from the smiles and clapping that was going on.

"What's happening?" Jennifer asked the Kavacha.

"Just a moment, and then you will see." He said as he escorted her to one of the sides of the courtyard where Sukhoi was standing, arms folded and smiling at something.

Sukhoi looked towards her as she approached and then motioned her to stand beside him. She then turned to face the centre of the courtyard and stared in open-mouthed shock.

David, her brother David, was standing in the centre of the courtyard surrounded by six, very large men. The men were dressed in trousers only, which were tied at the ankle. They had no other garments on and were bare footed. Each of the six men was sweating as much as Aran had been and they were all wearing a look of immense concentration as they circled her brother. Her brother was slowly turning, seemingly watching the movements of each man as they positioned themselves around him. He was also wearing nothing but trousers but he didn't appear to be sweating at all. She didn't know what was happening but from the looks of everyone watching, they were having a joyous time. Then from nowhere one of the men lunged for her brother, with his back to the attacker she knew he wouldn't have time to defend himself. She shouted a warning cry but David just turned; as if in slow motion and brought his arm round in an arc; hitting the man in the chest, and sending him backwards with a strength she didn't realise her brother had. Then, almost immediately the man was on his feet again, but this time David was ready for his opponent and moved his hand forward without touching the man and pushed him back by an invisible force, where he crashed to the floor five or six feet behind him. Jennifer was shocked at the ease in which her brother had stopped the man, but what shocked her most was that the other five remaining men were now attacking her brother together. He turned and faced his attackers as if he were dancing, moving his arms seemingly in slow motion to ward off their blows. His movements were so graceful; she couldn't believe it was even him. He spun around moving his arms in a fluid motion as his attackers tried in vain to reach him. Then two more entered the circle and began to throw knives at him.

She wanted to scream a warning; but somehow she knew he was already aware of the men. David stopped the knives before they got anywhere near close enough to do any harm. What's more, he continued to deflect the attackers who were oblivious to the two men throwing the knives.

Suddenly a bell rang, just one quick chime and then everything stopped. The two men stopped throwing, the six men stopped trying to hit her brother and David stood silently in the centre of the courtyard as the men watching began to clap their appreciation.

David then turned to each side and nodded before walking toward Sukhoi and his sister, laughing as he approached them.

David's eyes were sparkling with excitement and couldn't conceal his joy as he greeted his sister, "Did you see any of that Jen?"

"Yes," she said sternly, "what do you think you were doing, you could have got hurt out there, what possessed you to get into a fight with those men?" She continued angrily.

"Calm down Jen, we were only training."

"Calm down, calm down he says." Jennifer ranted.

"Jen, be quiet and I will explain." David said, though he was still smiling, which just seemed infuriated his sister even more.

"Go on then, explain, well, I'm waiting." She said impatiently.

"I think perhaps I should explain." Sukhoi interrupted before David could say anything.

Jennifer turned to the Kavacha, her face had gone a bright red colour and her anger wasn't abating one bit, "Well?"

Sukhoi explained that he had brought David here to teach him something of the Kavacha lore. He had shown him the training ground and had explained the rules of the "Cavan'she", a ritualistic exercise that honed the skills of the Kavacha. Then Sukhoi had shown David the scared book of the Kavacha, given to them by the Guardian himself. David touched the book and something wonderful happened.

David continued with the story from there. Once he had touched the book, it felt as if all the knowledge contained in the book had burst into his head in one amazing instant. One minute he had been touching the book, the next he felt as if he were the book. Sukhoi explained that this had never happened before, and added that the Kavacha gained their knowledge from reading the book, not touching it. It was unprecedented. This became apparent when David started to speak some of the ancient text held within the book and knew what it meant.

Sukhoi had then started to ask David some questions from the book and he could recall all the answers, and it was indeed as if he had gained all the knowledge in that one instant. No one had seen this happen except them two, but when David started to perform some of the fighting moves held within the book, one of the other Kavacha, Braito Wahtre had witnessed it. Sukhoi had convinced the Kavacha that he had taught David all of the sacred moves. Braito had been impressed by the moves and had instantly challenged David to the Cavan'she, the "Rite of Passage". Before Sukhoi could say anything David had accepted the challenge.

"Why would you do such a thing?" Jennifer interrupted flabbergasted that her brother would do that.

David smiled, "Jen, you don't understand, I had to."

"Why?" She asked.

"Because." David said sheepishly.

"Because, is not an answer David Barnes." Jennifer said clearly annoyed.

David looked at his sister and stared into her eyes, "Jen, I had to do it, I needed to do it, and if I passed the test it would mean I could be a Kavacha. It's one of the tests all the trainee Kavacha have to go through, the first really big test and it felt right somehow." He finished, but looked away from his sister as he realised how stupid that probably sounded.

Sukhoi continued with the story before Jennifer could ask anymore questions. He explained the rules of the Cavan'she, that normally one Kavacha would face three opponents. The one being tested was to knock down his opponents but not be knocked down himself for three bells. He used all the fighting moves and the Kavacha knowledge held within the pages of the book to repel his attackers. If he made it through the three bells without being knocked down he had passed the challenge.

"But there were six men in there, and two more came in throwing knives." Jennifer reminded Sukhoi.

Sukhoi explained that if the Kavacha being tested passed the first three rounds without being knocked down, he had the option to go on to the next level.

Jennifer gave David a serious scowl but didn't interrupt this time.

Each level included an extra attacker to the maximum of six. If a Kavacha reached this level, the next level included an additional attacker with a weapon of the would-be Kavacha's choice. The highest level was two additional attackers with weapons, and the six attackers without weapons.

Jennifer couldn't contain her shock and remarked. "You mean to say that David had reached the highest level of this test and he had chosen which weapons he was to be attacked with, himself?"

Sukhoi nodded, and David smiled, "Well, I am use to people throwing knives in my direction." He said haughtily, though he did have the sense to drop his smile when his sister confronted him with a scowl.

"But you could have been hurt." Jennifer admonished him.

"But I wasn't." He retaliated.

"What is more important, "Sukhoi said, "David reached the highest level of the Cavan'she, which has not been achieved for five hundred years." He finished solemnly.

"What?" David and Jennifer said together in shock.

Sukhoi nodded, "You have achieved the status of Kavacha Master."

"This is incredible." Socata said, himself shocked by the revelation.

"It was the book." David said quietly after a moment's reflection and tried to take in the enormity of what Sukhoi had just told him. "The book gave me the knowledge to defeat my opponents."

"Yes David, it did, but the book only teaches how something can be achieved, it was you that actually used that knowledge to fulfil its purpose." He reminded the boy.

"What does all this mean Sukhoi?" Jennifer asked.

"It means, that in front of thirty or so Kavacha, David has shown himself to be a Kavacha Master and now he must complete the final test, the Faran'she, the "Rite of Honour".

David physically paled as Sukhoi named the test, his smile forgotten by the thought of the test ahead.

"You ok Dave?" Jennifer asked noticing his look change.

"Yes, it's just that the book mentions the Faran'she as a test of courage and strength against your inner demons." He finished with a slight sigh.

"That is correct David, in order to conquer evil and seek the truth; you must first conquer your own demons and accept your own truth." Sukhoi acknowledged.

"Is it dangerous?" Jennifer asked in concern for her brother, as she noticed him take a deep breath and gulp in some air.

"I will not lie to you, it has some danger. If you do not face the truth and accept it, it may consume you and you will never be the same person again."

"Well, he's not doing it then." Jennifer stated matter of factly.

David sighed, "I think I have to Jen." He realised that he couldn't hide anymore, he knew he was scared, more frightened than any other time in his life, but he had to do it. If he could face his own fears and defeat them, he would be a better person for it, he knew that for certain.

"You don't have to do anything Dave." Jennifer replied.

"Yes I do, and I think I should do it now, before I change my mind." David conceded.

Sukhoi nodded with pride at the boy's words and excusing himself and Socata, they departed to make preparations for the ceremony.

Jennifer looked at her brother and placed her hand on his arm. She didn't expect the emotions emanating from him at her touch. She could feel his turmoil and the constant inner battles he was facing. She felt his need to get them all back home safely, his doubts that he had the strength and fortitude to accomplish everything he had to. She could see all his fears and weaknesses, the hole in his heart which was left by their father's death, she could feel and see it all. But she could also see a great power there also, a strength and determination that transcended everything else. What her brother could become if he only believed in himself.

"You ok Jen?" David asked concerned.

Jennifer realised that she experienced all this in a blink of an eye, and her brother wasn't aware of what had just happened.

She smiled at him, she knew he had to complete this test whether she like it or not.

"Ok Dave, you do this Faran'she." She said finally.

He smiled his thanks to her, though he couldn't understand how she had changed her mind so quickly, girls had a funny way of looking at things.

"Have you seen Chris yet?" He asked, deciding instead to change the subject.

"No, I was hoping to find you together; you don't know where he is then?" She asked.

"No need to worry about him, he's with Brad." He said smiling at the obvious relief on her face.

Socata returned then and after a brief discussion, he said he would bring their brother to them, but the ceremony was to be conducted straight away. He told them that word had already begun to circulate about Sukhoi's apprentice that had completed the highest level of the Cavan'she and was now going to face the Faran'she.

As if on cue, the room began to fill with Kavacha, eager to witness this amazing spectacle. On Sukhoi's arrival, Socata left them to get their brother.

"Are you ready David?" Sukhoi asked.

"Might as well get it over with." He said bravely, though Jennifer suspected her brother was secretly terrified of the ordeal to come.

"You know what to do?" Sukhoi asked him.

"Yes." David replied then walked into the centre of the courtyard again, and Sukhoi addressed the crowd that was still forming.

"My brothers, an unprecedented event is about to occur. David has just completed the highest level of the Cavan'she." There was a thunderous chorus of applause and Sukhoi had to wait until the crowd became quiet. "Before he can become a Master however, he must first pass the Faran'she, which has not been attempted in generations. Let the test begin!" Sukhoi shouted at the end. Then he moved back to stand beside David's very nervous sister.

The crowd didn't even murmur at this point, everyone waited for the test to begin.

Four men appeared, wearing dark robes with their hoods up and heads down so you couldn't see their faces. One of them positioned themselves at each corner of the courtyard and then the onlookers closed in for the best place to see the ceremony.

"What's going to happen?" Jennifer asked Sukhoi nervously.

"Sush, wait and you will see." He replied quietly.

There was an eerie silence as David stood perfectly still in the centre with the four men facing him from each corner. There was a chill in the air that made Jennifer shiver and then she heard what could only be described as chanting coming from the four men.

She stared in shock as a pale green mist swirled from the outstretched hands of the four robed men and snaked toward her brother.

She jumped and almost screamed when she felt a tug on her arm. Christopher had arrived with Socata and Braduga and he was trying to get her attention and find out what was happening.

She put her finger to her lips and motioned with her head toward their brother who was watching the swirling mist with undisguised dread.

"Ok, calm down David, you know what's coming and you know how to deal with it." David said silently to himself.

Even with the knowledge of the book imbued within him, he couldn't help but be scared of the strange haunting mist that moved menacingly toward him. He knew that each arm of the mist represented a test, mind, body, heart and soul. He wasn't really certain what those tests involved but once the first one struck, there was no turning back. He also knew that he could repel the mist; the book told him that, but if he tried, he would fail the test, so he stood there silently and waited for the tentacles to reach him.

He didn't have to wait long; he staggered and then almost fell to the ground as he was hit in the back by one of the arms of mist. He tried to stop himself from shouting out in pain as time after time the mist whipped his body, from his arms and legs to his back and belly. The pain was excruciating, but the realisation that it would soon be over held him in place. After what seemed to be hours; but was merely seconds the pain stopped, but the reprieve was short lived as another tentacle of mist struck him on the forehead.

It was like an electric drill trying to bore into his skull, his arms whipped up to his sides outstretched as he forced himself against the force of the attack. Images appeared in his mind, his father, his mother, his brother and sister. All trying to talk to him at the same time, but he couldn't hear the words; he couldn't hear anything as the mist searched his mind. More images appeared of hundreds; if not thousands of people that he didn't even recognise, all trying in vain to talk to him, to tell him something. He was struggling to contain the mist as it bored deeper into his mind, more and more images appeared and were discarded as the mist searched for something, he didn't know what. He didn't know how much longer he could carry on against the onslaught; he could feel his mind succumbing to the power of the mist as it continued to probe. Then the image of his father was before him; smiling, and this time he did hear the words, three words that gave him the strength to fight back against the intrusive mist, "order not chaos". His father told him.

Then the image of his father faded, but the words remained and echoed within his mind and in hearing those words, he remembered when his father had spoken them and it gave him the strength he needed to control his thoughts and push the mist from his mind.

He just managed to inhale a deep breath when it was knocked out of him. He clutched his heart as he felt an intense pain as it seared his heart and channelled through his blood to every part of his body. Through blood stained eyes he could just make out shadows dancing in the green mist surrounding him. Then the shadows began to take form and he tried desperately to blink the blood away as his father appeared before him once again. Only this time the figure before him was covered in blood and the apparition held a look of fear and pain. He tried to reach out and comfort the shadow of his father but the harder he tried to reach, the more intense the pain from the vice-like grip the mist held on his heart.

"This is your fault David!" The shadow screeched at him.

David couldn't believe what the shadow was saying to him. How could it be his fault, his father had died in a mining accident, how could it be his fault.

"You killed me; you killed me with your magic." The shadow screeched at him.

"No, you died in an accident dad." He shouted at the figure.

"No!" It shouted back. "You killed me with your magic; your magic will kill us all!" It is prophesised." The apparition told him.

"No dad!" He shouted through sobs of anguish as tears streamed down his cheeks. "You died in an accident, remember?" He said but then the figure began to fade.

"You killed me with your magic." The voice echoed as the figure disappeared.

David was distraught, how could his father even think he had anything to do with his death. He couldn't think straight, the pain in his heart had subsided, but he was so hurt from his father's words that when the next slither of mist touched him on the shoulder he jumped in shock. Then an overwhelming sense of dread and anguish consumed his very soul as he came face to face with the nightmare of his dreams. Standing where his father had been moments before, stood the dark robed figure of Nuba Driss. His head was still covered and lowered but it was rising, like it had risen in his dreams. He tried to close his eyes, he didn't want to face the demon that made him feel helpless and alone, but he couldn't, his eyes wouldn't close.

He tried to raise his hands to ward against the demon, he tried to run, he tried everything, but he couldn't move, he felt totally paralysed.

Slowly the head of the figure began to rise, slowly, ever so slowly and then David screamed a frightful howl full of fear, pain and futility. But the scream had brought forth the inner strength David had, the power that he had feared to unleash suddenly became his saviour. He embraced it, as he embraced a loved one, and he felt calmness wash over him. He could control the power; there was nothing to fear, and with that control he focused on the apparition before him and unleashed all his feelings of helplessness, of anger and pain and threw them at it. The figure staggered backwards by the intensity of the attack and then disappeared into the mist.

David had managed to close his eyes, but when he opened them again, he was standing in the middle of the courtyard, the test finally over. It had seemed an eternity and he felt utterly exhausted by his ordeal. Sweat was pouring into his eyes from his forehead and he managed to wipe it away as he looked around. Everyone was standing perfectly still and staring at him. He turned to look around him and everyone was exactly the same, perfectly still and there was an eerie silence. When he turned his head back round, he jumped in shock, because standing there before him was the dark robed figure of Nuba Driss. He still couldn't see his face but David knew it had to be him.

"You have much talent David." The figure said in a quiet melodic voice, which sounded somewhat familiar.

David could hardly contain his fear, what was the creature doing here? How could he even get there? Was he there at all or was this a continuation of the test? He just didn't know!

"What do you want with me?" He managed to ask.

"I want nothing more than to help you get home." The figure replied.

"That's all?" David asked shocked.

"Yes." He replied, "And if I help you, maybe you could do me a small service in return." The figure suggested.

"What would I have to do?" David asked suspiciously.

"Nothing beyond your reach David, I just want the Kavacha book of knowledge and your sister for a few hours."

David was shocked, Nuba Driss wanted his sister. Not him.

"What do you want with her?" David asked, though he had no intention of giving his sister to anyone, but especially not to Nuba Driss.

"I just want to use her talents to speak to the creatures of this world; she will not be harmed in anyway. I only want to read the book, they can have it back when I'm finished and then I will return you all home safe and sound. You do want to get back to Featherstone, don't you?" The figure finished.

David's eyes widened in shock, Nuba Driss knew where the children were from, and he even knew which town. He had guaranteed their safe return home and all he wanted in return was the book that he was going to give back and Jennifer's gift for a couple of hours. He had also said that Jennifer wouldn't be harmed in anyway, but although the figure sounded sincere, something troubled him. He couldn't put his finger on it, but it didn't matter anyway, there was no way he was going to even contemplate putting his sister in the hands of Nuba Driss. For one thing, he couldn't make his sister do anything she didn't want to and for another; she would crucify him for putting her into this situation in the first place.

"I'm afraid that's not possible." He said after a moment's contemplation. "I can't ask the Kavacha to give you their prize possession and I definitely can't let you use my sister for a second let alone a couple of hours." He replied.

The figure seemed to shake visibly and its head dropped further. David still hadn't seen a face, nor did he really want to, but the voice that spoke now was not the calm and melodic voice he had heard earlier. This voice was hard, dangerous and menacing, "And that is your final decision?" The figure asked in pent up rage.

"Yes." David replied weakly, fully aware of the mages anger now.

"Then you will be to blame for the deaths of everyone in the city. The pain and suffering will be on your shoulders and you will regret your hasty decision, David Barnes." It rasped at him and then the figure disappeared.

A wisp of green mist whipped at his neck as the figure disappeared and David's hand instinctively rose to rub the spot the mist had touched.

Standing there and rubbing his neck, half frightened to death by the disappearing figure he realised that the silence had been replaced by shouts of praise from the watching crowd.

Dazed and confused, David swayed as Sukhoi came to his aide and grabbed him as totally exhausted, he fell into his arms.

"It's over?" David managed to say, though whether it was a question or statement Sukhoi couldn't ask, as the boy fell unconsciously into a deep sleep.

"It is finished." Sukhoi stated proudly in response, though he knew David couldn't hear him.

Chapter Twenty Six

"Is he going to be ok?" Jennifer whispered not wanting to wake her brother before he had time to rest and recover from his ordeal.

After the trial, Sukhoi had carried David back to their room and sent for the best physicians in the city. He had explained that normally a Kavacha would be ok after a few hours rest, but admitted that in his lifetime no one had attempted the Faran'she so he wasn't sure how long their brother needed.

"He will be fine, he just needs some rest." Socata replied. He had already held a long conversation with the physician about David's condition and now tended to him in the physician's absence.

David came back to consciousness and realised immediately that he was lying on his bed and through half open eyes he could see Jennifer and Christopher talking with Sukhoi and his Ruedin.

"You should not have allowed him to take that test." Jennifer said to Sukhoi angrily.

"It was his choice Jennifer." He replied softly.

"I don't care if it was his choice or not, he could have been hurt." Jennifer said just as quietly but still angry.

"He was aware of the risks, but as you can see, he will soon be well after a little rest."

"Humph." She replied, not quite convinced.

"I'm ok Jen." David said as he pulled himself into a sitting position in his bed.

The group walked over swiftly to his bedside and smiled as David moved into a better position to see his family and friends. His colour was returning and they could see that he looked refreshed after his few hours asleep.

"You are feeling better then?" Sukhoi asked raising his eyebrow in his normal manner.

"Yes, I think so." He replied a little hoarsely.

"You gave us a fright for a minute Dave." Christopher said smiling at his brother.

"Seriously, I'm ok." He said smiling back.

"In that case," Braduga beamed at him, "may I be the first to congratulate you David, Master Kavacha." He said bowing with respect.

"What?" David replied confused.

"It's true, you have completed both tests and passed, you are now my brother." Sukhoi said smiling with pride.

David was shocked, he knew that he had to pass the Faran'she to become a Kavacha Master but he wasn't sure he had actually passed the trials and said so.

"You passed with honour all four tests and you have the mark to prove it." Sukhoi announced.

"Yes, and I don't think mam is going to be too happy about that tattoo." Jennifer stated as she moved his head to one side and touched the place where the green mist had touched him.

"I've got a tattoo?" David asked incredulously. That must have been made by the last wisp of green mist as it vanished, he thought, touching his neck where Jennifer had indicated.

"Do not worry my friend, only those with magic can see the mark." Sukhoi said as he smiled disarmingly at his sister.

David rubbed his neck again, but couldn't disguise his relief that his mother wouldn't be able to see his tattoo. He couldn't help but smile again with pride when Sukhoi told him how well he had completed the tests.

"I must admit though," he began, "when Nuba Driss turned up after the last trial, I thought I had failed." He finished, happy that wasn't the case.

"What?" Sukhoi asked in astonishment, "Nuba Driss?"

"Yes, when Nuba Driss appeared and asked me to get him the book of Kavacha knowledge to read and then hand Jen over for a few hours, and in return he would take us home, well I…" He trailed off as he saw the confused looks on everyone present.

"What's wrong?" He asked.

"We didn't see Nuba Driss Dave, we saw the four green swirls of mist attack you, saw the pain they were inflicting on you, and the green mist that marked you at the end but we didn't see Nuba Driss." Jennifer said in surprise.

"He wasn't part of the test?" David asked gulping for breath.

"No." Sukhoi replied, "Tell me everything that happened." He finished, urgently.

David related everything that had happened during the trial and his confrontation with the dark robed figure. Everyone listened in silence, stunned by both his description of the trial and more so with what Nuba Driss wanted.

"Was that supposed to happen?" Jennifer asked Sukhoi once her brother had finished his rendition.

"No, it has never happened before that I know of." He replied solemnly.

"What does it all mean?" Christopher asked.

It was David that replied, "Nuba Driss wants the power held in the book to use for his own ends. He has obviously heard about Jennifer's gift and the Dragons. Maybe the orb isn't working properly and he needs her help to make it work or at least communicate with them. With the knowledge gained from the book and control over the Dragons and other creatures, he would be invincible." David suggested.

"He would be formidable indeed, but I do not think they would help him, even if Jennifer asked." Sukhoi said.

"Maybe they wouldn't have a choice, maybe he could use the orb to compel them to do his bidding." David suggested. "I don't know, but it makes sense." David said rubbing his head. He was still exhausted and realised he needed more rest.

"We should ask the Dragons; when they return, if the orb could do that sort of thing!" Jennifer added.

"They've gone?" David asked.

"Yes, they departed a short while ago now. They are seeking my brothers, sorry, our brothers, I just hope there is enough time." Sukhoi replied.

"Yes our brothers." David said smiling at the Kavacha.

"Now you are awake, I have people to see, so I will leave you for now, " Sukhoi said and turned to face the door, "You should not worry about your ordeal too much," he said turning round to face the new Kavacha, "You deserve the title of Kavacha Master my brother, wear it with honour."

David turned bright red by the compliment and smiled in acknowledgement as Sukhoi left.

"We must leave too, but we'll return shortly." Socata announced, motioning for Braduga to follow him, they left the three children in the room by themselves.

"You really ok Dave?" Jennifer asked when they were alone.

"Fine, Jen, I think I'm still a little tired from the Faran'she." He replied, though she guessed there was more to it. "But I'm ok."

Christopher sat down on the bed and said, "You're looking a lot better than when they brought you in here." Christopher said. "We were really worried about you."

"Thanks Chris, but as you can see I'm fine now."

"Well, if you need us, we're here." She offered, as she smiled at their younger brother.

"Thanks." He replied. He wasn't exactly sure what he was feeling right now. He was still tired from his ordeal, but his mind was racing with the knowledge of the book. Images kept flashing before his eyes; problems with their solutions presenting themselves, incantations and words of magic filling his mind. He was having difficulty controlling those images, but more surprisingly, he was doing it. He was going to ask Sukhoi about it, but once the idea formed in his mind, he knew that the Kavacha hadn't experienced anything like this. The knowledge he received from the book opened his eyes to many things, and he knew he had the potential to do great things. Then he looked at his brother and sister and knew that his first priority was to get everyone back home safe and sound. He knew that they would have to leave this place, and he knew he would be sad when that day came.

"What have we got ourselves into Dave?" Jennifer said without preamble.

"What do you mean?" He replied quietly, had she somehow been reading his thoughts?

"Oh, I don't know really, maybe the fact that we find ourselves in a strange land with Dragons and other strange creatures. Or could it be the fact that we may have to confront an evil sorcerer who is sending his armies to destroy this city and the people we care about." She told him. "Or how you became a Kavacha Master and I became the Nadym Varsk and maybe the only person who can stop this madness by somehow stop this foul creature, though God only knows how. Maybe something like that for instance!" She replied sarcastically.

She had a point, David thought. What had they got themselves mixed up in?

But, it seemed right that they were there, as if it was meant to be, as if they could make a difference and help these people. If she was really the Nadym Varsk, she had to be here and she had to help, it was part of a prophecy.

"When are you going to tell them Jen?" David asked carefully, trying not to push his sister into anything she didn't want to do.

"Not sure," She replied, knowing exactly what he was referring to, "But I think there is a time and a place for me to do it, though I couldn't explain to you how I know that."

"It sounds to me Jen, that you must really be the Truth Seer." Christopher interjected.

"Yes Chris, I think I am." She replied quietly.

They talked for a while about how they were going to raise the topic to Sukhoi and the others. They really didn't have any answers at the moment, but Jennifer was adamant that when the time came she would know what to do. David could understand that having been through the Kavacha tests and let the subject drop. They continued to talk about everything else then until David stopped them and said he really did need to get some sleep. So Jennifer and Christopher watched over him as he closed his eyes and fell into a deep, trouble-free sleep.

"Good Chris, keep your arm up and hold that position." Braduga said to his pupil. They had been training constantly for the past hour and although Christopher was aching all over, he was enjoying every minute of his tutoring.

The arena was full of people training, practising and honing their skills in preparation for the inevitable battle just like Christopher. At the moment he was bare-chested and beads of sweat was running down his tired and bruised body.

"Should I not try to twist the blade aside and then come up under the guard?" He asked as he continued to maintain the position Braduga had told him to adopt.

"Try it." Braduga encouraged him. "Let's see what happens."

Christopher paused for just a second before trying the move. His timing was perfect and his aim precise, but Braduga countered the move with ease much to Christopher's disappointment.

"Good, that was well executed." Braduga praised the young novice.

"Yes, but it didn't work." Christopher replied sullenly.

"Not this time, true, but I think you have a quick mind and your skill is improving all the time. You will make a fine warrior Chris."

Christopher beamed with pride. Braduga had never before given him such praise.

"I think that is enough for today, we will practice again tomorrow at the same time, so go and get cleaned up while I tidy these away." He said as he indicated the wooden swords and the other weapons they had been using.

"Ok and Brad, thanks for the lessons." Christopher said as he collected his shirt; pulling it over his head, without undoing the buttons.

"My pleasure Chris." Braduga said as he watched his young novice walk away.

Braduga realised in that moment that it was his pleasure. The boy had a natural talent that only needed to be honed and focused. He knew he would make a formidable warrior if he continued with his training. He was a willing pupil, who constantly asked the right questions and wasn't afraid to try new techniques and take the hits if they didn't work. He realised immediately that the boy had a quick mind and his instincts were visionary at times. Yes, the boy was a natural warrior, or he would be one day.

"Indeed, my young friend." He said quietly to Christopher's back as he walked away. "My pleasure."

Smiling to himself, Braduga placed the training aides away neatly in the racks with the others and left the arena.

It had been two days since David had successfully passed the trials of the Kavacha. He recovered quickly and wasted little time as he set about honing his skills from the knowledge gained from the book. All his inhibitions about using his gifts had vanished with the trials and so had the feelings of nausea and confusion. He felt confident about using his magic and he had a thirst for trying anything and everything he could. He practiced tirelessly with Sukhoi as reports came into the city that the approaching armies were getting closer and closer. The Dragons hadn't been seen for the last few days, but the message was obviously getting through as each day brought more Kavacha and their Ruedin back to the city. They weren't the only ones however; hundreds of people had been flocking to the city from various towns and villages. The city was coping well under the strain of trying to feed and shelter everyone, and the additional manpower helped in providing a willing workforce to improve the city's defences, but the city was beginning to feel the strain of so many people.

When David returned to his room after yet another gruelling session with Sukhoi he found Christopher standing in front of a large mirror admiring himself. He was wearing identical clothing worn by the Ruedin; trousers, shirt, boots and even a turban, all matching in colour and material. The only difference David could see was on the tunic which was still on Christopher's bed. A very good likeness to Hash was emblazoned on the left hand side of it, which the warriors didn't have.

"Well, don't we look a picture, dressed like one of the Ruedin?" David said to his brother, a little enviously.

Caught by surprise, Christopher turned to see David watching him from the doorway, a slight smile on his lips as he held the door open. The two guards were still by the doorway, but were busy looking in the other direction and clearly not interested in what the boy was wearing.

"Hi Dave." He said, colour turning his cheeks a rosy red with embarrassment. "They were here when I got back, and I thought, well, they must be for me, because I couldn't see anyone else fitting in them, and as I was trying them on you walked in, and..." Christopher stammered a little self consciously.

"It's ok Chris, I agree, they were definitely made for you, and a good fit I think." David said guiltily. "I wasn't having a go."

"You think they suit me then?" Christopher asked, smiling as he turned to look at his reflection in the tall mirror to his rear.

"Absolutely." David replied smiling.

"There's some clothes for you as well, Dave, come and have a look." Christopher said as he moved towards the wardrobe to his left hand side and opened the large wooden doors. "There's some for Jen too."

David rushed over to the wardrobe, eager to see what was waiting for him. He peered into the back and saw two sets of clothes hung up. He grabbed hold of the ones that were clearly for a boy his size and build and then closed the doors behind him.

"They're almost identical to the ones worn by the Kavacha." Christopher announced.

David looked at his brother with a slight frown. "How do you know?" He asked.

"A good question," He hesitated. "I couldn't resist having a quick peak."

"It's ok; it doesn't matter, but they're identical to me." David said as he laid the clothes on his bed.

"There's a slight difference." His brother told him.

"What's that then?" He asked as he inspected the clothing.

"You have a dragon emblazoned on each side of your tunic; they look like Hash and Sak.

David unfolded the clothes and realised that Christopher was right, he did have two Dragons, and to his amazement, they did resembled Hash and Sak. It was as if the two Dragons had been shrunk and were now sitting on top of his clothes. The detail was incredible and so realistic in every detail; even the colours were bright and full of life. The clothes had clearly been created by someone who had seen the Dragons in real life and had now captured the very essence of their souls in the material.

David was just thinking about how much time it must have taken to create something so wonderful when he noticed what his brother was doing.

"Hang on a minute." He said looking at Christopher as he was strapping a sword on to his waist. "How come you have a sword, have I got one?" He asked.

"I don't think so, but you've got knives in your boots." He replied.

"Well that's ok then." His brother replied sarcastically.

"Well, let's face it Dave, you don't really need either a sword or knives now, do you?" Christopher said smiling at his brother's chagrined face.

"Yeah, but it would have been nice to have my own sword." He said a bit petulantly.

"Go on Dave, try them on." He said excitedly.

"Ok, calm down." He said smiling. "But first I think I'll have a wash, I don't want to dirty my new clothes so soon, do I?"

David walked over to the basin next to the wardrobe and started to get undressed. He then filled the basin with water from the pitcher beside it and scrubbed his hands, face and neck. As he was vigorously washing he shouted to his brother. "Have you seen Jen yet?"

"No, you?" Christopher replied.

"Not for a while." David said as he began to dry his face.

David turned to his brother as he was taking his sword from the scabbard. "But I don't think she will like the fact that you have been given a sword." He said.

"I don't care whether she likes it or not." Christopher replied with bravado. "It's mine, and it has nothing to do with her."

"Ok, but I was only saying." David said as he continued drying himself. David watched his brother swing the sword and realised that Christopher looked as if he knew what he was doing with it. Obviously seen too many films on the TV, he thought as he continued to dry himself.

"Anyway, she won't be able to complain, you should see what she's got." He said with a smile and a flourish of his sword.

"What's she got?" David asked intrigued.

"Get dressed first, and then I'll show you."

David quickly started to put on his new, clean clothes and then walked over to the mirror to admire his new look.

"Not bad actually." He said to himself. "Not bad at all."

Christopher laughed as his brother admired himself, and turned round when he heard a girly giggle come from the doorway.

"Yes, not bad at all." Jennifer laughed as she walked into the room.

"Oh, hi Jen." David said, himself blushing as his sister walked over to him and began to inspect his new clothes.

"Very nice, where did you get these from?" She asked.

"Chris said they were here when he got back, actually Chris that reminds me." David asked. "Where have you been?"

Christopher stopped smiling and looked from his brother to his sister as they both waited there for his reply. "Nowhere really." He replied. "I was just hanging round with Brad."

"I hope you're not getting in the way Chris, you know how busy everyone is." Jennifer admonished.

"I'm not getting in the way, and even if I was, I'm sure Brad would tell me so." He retorted.

"Yes, you're probably right." She relented.

"Anyway." Christopher said walking over to the wardrobe, "Don't you want to see what's waiting for you?" He said opening wide the wardrobe doors.

Jennifer's eyes widened in appreciation as she looked toward the plain white linen dress hanging within. She could tell just by looking at the dress that it would be a perfect fit, and she was excited to try it on. Beneath the dress was a pair of soft brown, knee length boots, which had a belt stuffed inside with a sheath and knife. She collected the new clothes and gently carried them over to her bed.

She brought the dress up to her shoulders and with one hand she straightened it pulling it into her body and then she peered at her reflection in the mirror to see how the dress looked.

"Why don't you two find something useful to do while I try this on." She said dismissively as she spun around in delight.

"But I've only just got back." David objected.

Jennifer just looked at her brother; it was a look that warranted no argument, a look that said, "Leave now or face the consequences", a look that made both boys turn towards the door.

"And don't go too far," She shouted toward them as they walked away. "I don't want either of you getting into any trouble without me there to look out for you."

Both David and Christopher sighed as they looked at each other in amusement. "Ok Jen, we will just wait outside for your majesty to recall us." David said as he turned to his sister with a slight smile on his face and gave her his best over exaggerated bow.

She scowled good humouredly at him as he walked out of the door but soon turned back to her dress and began to change.

They were waiting outside their room talking to the two guards on duty when Sukhoi and his Ruedin joined them a short while later.

"Well, well, who are these handsome young men?" Socata asked when he saw the two boys.

David and Christopher smiled at each other and then at the approaching men, who sidled up to them.

"What do you think?" David asked.

"Not bad, not bad at all, and an excellent fit." Braduga said appreciatively.

As the two boys were showing off their new clothes and the weapons they had been given, Sukhoi spoke quietly to the two guards on duty.

"Any trouble Grainoc?" He asked one of the guards he had known for a couple of years and had picked especially for this task.

"No Sukhoi, everything is quiet." Grainoc replied solemnly.

"Good, but remain vigilant, I am very concerned for our young friends and would not like it if anything should happen to them." Sukhoi whispered.

Sukhoi knew and trusted Guardsman Grainoc, but he was uneasy with the whole situation. He did not like the fact that one of the council elders had been subverted by Nuba Driss and this had given him cause to be worried about everyone who was in Enkan Mys at the moment.

"Where is Jennifer?" He asked pushing open the door to their room.

"Wait..." David began, but it was too late, Sukhoi had opened the door and stood transfixed as he looked at Jennifer before him.

She had already changed into her new dress and boots and was just adjusting the belt around her waist. Her hair was now braided and a leather band was wrapped around her head. The light from the sun had silhouetted her slight figure and she appeared to have a faint bright outline around her. Sukhoi could not help but smile with undisguised appreciation, as he looked at Jennifer in her new dress. It was a perfect fit, like that of the boys, and it accentuated her figure fully. He suddenly realised that he had always thought of her as a girl, but now; wearing this dress, he understood that to be a mistake, she was a young woman, and a beautiful one at that.

"You look beautiful." He said as he finally found the use of his legs, and walked into the room.

"Why thank you kind sir." She replied with a beguiling smile, but didn't notice his cheeks begin to redden as he was quickly followed into the room by Braduga, Socata and her brothers.

She suddenly laughed a full, marvellously enchanting laugh as she looked at their expressions.

"Ok everyone you can stop staring now, " She said after a moment. "Haven't you seen anyone wearing a dress before?" She said smiling.

Sukhoi recovered quickly and coughed to hide his embarrassment before stammering an apology.

David just smiled at their friends as Jennifer walked over to the mirror to admire herself. David knew that almost everyone back home found Jennifer attractive, and had often seen the same look on his friends' faces when confronted by his sister, and especially Ping, he definitely had a soft spot for his sister and she knew it. He knew she was attractive, but when you have a sister that has a foul temper, and could be one hell of a pain if she wanted to be, it didn't matter what she looked like. Knowing this made his smile brighter and bigger, thinking of the poor unfortunate souls who innocently asked his sister out on a date, only to be confronted by her temper when they didn't treat her as she expected to be treated.

Christopher was watching his sister enjoy the moment and said quietly to his brother. "Girls!" And lifted his eyebrows to emphasise the point.

David shrugged his shoulders and nodded his head in agreement.

Sukhoi shook his head as if to remove the image of Jennifer from his mind and his thoughts and announced he had news from the council. This statement had the desired effect and everyone congregated around the table in the middle of the room waiting for him to continue.

"Scouts have been sent out of the city to determine the exact location of the armies, their size and dispositions. Meanwhile, all the able bodied men and women have been making preparations for a siege."

"What sort of preparations?" Christopher asked.

"Collecting weapons, food, etc and fortifying the city against attack." Braduga replied on Sukhoi's behalf.

"Is there sufficient time?" David asked, concern etched on his face.

"I think so David, more and more people arrive everyday with news, and the city is beginning to swell with all the occupants. Many Kavacha have already returned and more are on the way, yes, I think we will be ready." Sukhoi replied. "And every person is being trained on what weapons we have available." He finished.

"Is that why we've been given these weapons?" Jennifer asked. "Because I've never used a knife on anyone and besides, what good can a knife be when being attacked by someone with a sword?" She finished brandishing her knife from the sheath on her belt and looking at it in dismay.

"Not really. I decided you needed some new clothes to fit your station as brother and sister to a Master Kavacha. As to those weapons, do not worry Jennifer, you will be well guarded at all times and will not need them. However, I thought you might feel a little better knowing you had a weapon at hand." Sukhoi added as an after thought.

"I see Christopher has a sword." David said, "I was wondering if I should have one, you know, just in case." He said, his face becoming bright red. He'd quite enjoy having a sword at his side, though he hoped he would never get the chance to use it for real.

Braduga looked first at Christopher and then at David before saying. "Chris has a sword because I have been training him, you do not need one because Sukhoi has been training you."

"Christopher has been doing what?" Jennifer asked incredulously.

Christopher's face went bright red in embarrassment, but he stood straight and tall as he faced his brother and sister. "You heard what Brad said, he has been training me to be a warrior." Before they could say anything else, he blurted. "You two have your magical gifts, and I don't have anything and I asked Brad and Socata if they would train me to be a warrior, so I could protect myself and protect you come to think of it, and well, they said yes, so that's what I've been doing." It all came out so quickly that David and Jennifer just stared at him.

"He is very good." Braduga said into the silence, trying to help.

"I agree." Socata said.

"When? What?" Jennifer began, but didn't know what to say or how to react to this new piece of information.

"We do not have time for this." Sukhoi announced. "What is done, is done."

"Yes, he's right Jen." David agreed a moment later; realising that his brother needed something to occupy his time as they had hardly spent any time with him at all recently. That explained how well he handled the sword, though. He then smiled a warm smile at his brother and added. "Let's hope we don't have to use your new skills though, eh Chris?"

Christopher gave him a weak smile, but Jennifer looked away with a shake of her head and turned to Sukhoi. "Is there anything we can do to help?" She asked, choosing to leave the conversation for a more convenient time, when she could get her brother alone to discuss his training to be a warrior.

"Let us go and speak with the council, maybe we can all find something to do." He said.

As they walked toward the door, David had a thought. "Did anyone find where Elder Awdaal disappeared to?"

"He's no longer in the city David," Braduga answered, "he left before word to stop him was raised; but it wouldn't surprise me to learn that he was with one of the armies by now."

Chapter Twenty Seven

"General Kormask," the tall, thick-set guard said as he entered the tent and saluted the even larger general who returned his salute half-heartedly, "This man wishes to speak with you on a matter of urgency." The personal guard of the general stepped aside to allow a dust stained and weary Sanag Awdaal through.

"General, I have just come from Enkan Mys and require an escort to get me to Nuba Driss." He said without preamble.

The general sighed but didn't look up, instead he continued to scrutinise the sheets of paper on the desk in front of him.

"General, are you listening to me? Do you realise who I am?" Elder Awdaal almost screeched at the big man when he didn't acknowledge his presence.

"What? Ah, yes, as you can see I am extremely busy. What did you say?" The general said absentmindedly.

"General I have to see Nuba Driss; you must provide me with an escort to him immediately." The elder ordered.

"Sorry did you give me your name? I don't recall." General Kormask said as he finally looked up into the face of the elder, after taking a moment to consider the little man. He knew perfectly well who the man was as soon as he entered the encampment. Lord Driss had told him that the Elder had contributed greatly to their cause but he had also said that the man was a pompous fool. Lord Driss was right, the elder was a fool and he took an instant dislike to him.

General Alun Kormask sometimes acted as a forgetful old soldier; many thought he was just an old man who had probably been fighting too long and should now retire. His size and bulk made him seem too old, too fat and generally look quite useless. But that's what he wanted his enemies to think and they usually did until he felt it was time to change their opinion of him. He had always been underestimated; generally because of his bulk. He was a big man, there was no doubt about it, he knew it and everyone else did too, but it was his mind that he kept sharp and effective. His mind was focused and trained to perfection on all aspects of warfare and tactics. He had read every book ever written on the subject and had studied every war and every skirmish, trying to calculate the point where battles were won.

General Kormask was one of the Imazaghan, the "Free People" and descendants of the Toureng. After five hundred years of being away from their homeland they had returned. It was his honour to lead the advance party back into Sakhalin. This great honour had been bestowed upon him by Lord Driss himself and was told to take orders from no one else but him. He had been extremely proud at that moment, but it was spoilt slightly when his Lord had told him that he couldn't take his own Regiment into battle with him. He would be given Koutla Raiders to train; though he was still able to retain some of his men to help train them to the required standard. His own troops were of the highest calibre and his pride and joy. They were renowned in the Imazaghan Army as being the best soldiers, so much so that the best of those were then chosen to be the bodyguards of Lord Driss himself. But he would do his Lord's bidding, even if it was training these "Koutlas" as they were referred to. He hadn't known what to expect when the men arrived six months earlier, he had never seen such a ragtaggle bunch in all his years in the service. As he surveyed the men, Lord Driss had arrived and told him if he could train these men as well as his own soldiers he would be rewarded beyond his wildest dreams. So in the space of only six months he had done his best. He was proud of his achievement in such a short time. They had been trained hard; without compassion and now it showed, they were ruthless and fearless warriors now; and although they weren't quite up to the standard of his own men, he knew they would hold their own in battle; well he hoped so, for their sakes if not for his.

"My name is Elder Sanag Awdaal, a personal friend of Nuba Driss." The little man screeched pompously at him.

"Ah yes, Awdaal," the General said to the Elder turning back to the map on the table. "What can I do for you?"

Sanag Awdaal could not believe how this jumped up soldier had virtually dismissed him and took a step closer. "First of all you can stop what you are doing immediately, and treat me with some respect, or shall I inform Nuba Driss of your lack of manners towards his friends." He screeched again.

General Alun Kormask did stop what he was doing and looked closely at the man before him with undisguised disgust and decadence.

"And secondly?" The General asked.

"What? What are you talking about?" Elder Awdaal replied in confusion.

"You said first of all, so, I am assuming there is a second condition?" He smiled, though if the elder had been paying attention to the general's face he would have seen that the smile didn't coincide with the dangerous look he had in his eyes.

"Yes, well, I require food and drink and some clean clothes to wear, and then I require an escort to take me to Nuba Driss." He replied as he walked over to the table and sat on the only chair available.

The general watched as the little man sat down and waited for his orders to be carried out. He had come across many such men as the elder before, who believed themselves to be more important than everyone else around them, but the general knew his own self worth and was not about to be intimidated by this self appreciating little man.

"Well!" He said as the general turned to face him in his chair.

"First of all," He replied calmly; though he could feel his anger brewing like a pot of water over a fire. "I don't answer to you, only to Lord Driss." He needed to remain calm as he still had too many plans to make that required a clear mind. "Secondly, I don't think he would like it if he heard you speak of him in that manner." The pot was definitely boiling but he was a trained soldier and had been for a great many years, he knew how to check his anger, a little anyway. "Thirdly, Lord Driss has no friends; he doesn't need any, nor care for any, and last but not least, if you don't get out of my chair this instant, I will personally run you through with my sword and leave your corpse for the buzzards." The General finished, still smiling through an evil grin; which widened and showed a mouth full of brown stained teeth from smoking too much Arakash root in his time in the service. He had remained calm but he wouldn't be calm for much longer, but the councillor finally jumped to his feet and stared at the big soldier as he placed a large hand on the pommel of his sword.

"You can not speak to me in that way." Awdaal screamed at the man, who now displayed a menacing look on his face.

Sanag Awdaal suddenly reeled from a slap across his face as the big General impossibly and with incredible speed and agility, knocked him to the ground.

"Do not try to tell me what I can and can not do in my own camp." The General spat at him venomously. "I take orders from one man and one man only, that man is not you."

General Alun Kormask turned to one of his personal guards and ordered him to take the councillor away and teach him some manners.

He watched as the elder tried to struggle out of the vice-like grip the soldier had on his arms and then turned away in disgust as the little man let out an ear-piercing scream when he was bodily dragged out of the tent.

"Who do these people think they are?" He whispered to himself in revulsion as his anger finally came to the surface. He took a few moments to regulate his breathing and control his temper, then once relaxed enough he attacked the maps on the table once more.

David was gazing out of his window as the dying sun began to set in the distance, the remains of its quietening light gently fading from the city below. The streets were still alive with activity, but the influx of people had stopped as the light diminished. He was just wondering what was going to happen to all those people when the two armies of Nuba Driss arrived when there was a knock at the door.

Christopher quickly jumped off his bed and drawing his sword he moved in front of his sister. David turned from the window and watched his brother with a slight amused smile. Since hearing that Christopher had been sneaking off to receive combat training from Braduga and Socata, David was still surprised that he hadn't noticed the change in his brother. He seemed to have grown; both physically and mentally, and David was amazed that he hadn't noticed the changes before now.

"Chris, what are you doing?" Jennifer asked him shaking her head as her brother stopped just in front of her protectively.

"It could be anyone sis, I want to be ready this time." He replied fiercely, turning toward the door and adopting a defensive stance that they had seen both Socata and Braduga using before.

Elder Srabat's head suddenly appeared round the door and looked questioningly at the three children before entering the room. "Hello, everything ok?" He asked, paying particular attention to Christopher with his sword at the ready.

"Fine thank you Elder." Christopher replied, though he kept his sword unsheathed.

"Is something the matter?" David said as he turned from the window and walked toward his brother and sister.

"I am not sure," he replied with a faint smile still on his lips as he continued to watch Christopher and walked into the room. "Sukhoi asked me to invite you all down to the common room," he said. "He couldn't get away from important matters and all the guards are busy so I volunteered to come and get you."

"For what purpose?" David asked suspiciously. David hadn't forgot the last time one of the elders had come to their room, he was not about to let anything happen to his family again.

"All your questions will be answered, if you follow me." The elder replied still smiling.

Jennifer whispered in David's ear, "I don't sense any danger here Dave." She said as if reading his thoughts.

"Beats staying in here being bored." Christopher added and finally put his sword in its scabbard.

David sighed, "Ok, please lead the way."

When they reached the common room they realised immediately that it wasn't so common after all. The were admitted through two enormous gilt crusted oak doors by a pair of large, thickset soldiers and were amazed at the sight that greeted them. They had entered a banquet hall; it had to be a banquet hall, because in the centre of the room was an extremely large wooden table with sufficient chairs to seat a hundred people, if not more. There were tapestries on the walls depicting hunting scenes and various weapons of all types were hung next to hundreds of hunting trophies. Heads of numerous beasts could be seen, from Lions and bears to creatures that the children had not seen before and probably never would see. On the left hand side of the room were a row of extremely large windows that were now being boarded up by servants. Other servants were busy lighting the numerous candles both on the walls and on the table as the daylight began to wan. The large table was actually numerous smaller tables, which were now being disassembled and placed into sections. The room was crowded with lots of soldier and advisors who were being split into smaller groups and heading towards various sections to presumably carry out some function or other.

"What's happening?" Christopher asked intrigued.

"You see before you the elite of Enkan Mys, all the generals, tacticians and Elders who are preparing for the arrival of the approaching armies. It is here that we formulate our plans and discuss our theories and propositions." He shouted over his shoulder and above the din of the various conversations which were trying to drown him out.

The three children were led to the far end of the room, zigzagging through the crowds of people towards a table that was set slightly apart from the others, with a dozen or so people standing round it, concentration etched on their faces.

David recognised Elder Hanish immediately, Sukhoi and his Ruedin were present, as were a few others that he had seen before; though he couldn't recall their names.

Sukhoi turned and smiled at their approach and the conversation stopped as everyone turned to face the new arrivals.

"Maroc!" Jennifer laughed as she rushed over to a big man as he turned to face them and placed her arms around his wide frame.

"Well met!" He boomed with laughter as all the children gathered round expressing their delight at seeing one of the first friends they had made since arriving in Sakhalin.

"What are you doing here?" Jennifer asked smiling.

Maroc's mood turned sombre, "We had no choice I'm afraid."

He quickly explained that his village had been attacked by Koutla Raiders. They managed to kill the Raiders but the Archers reported that more and more were on their way. The Archers also reported that they had seen a contingent of other soldiers appear from the mountains. On investigation, they realised that these soldiers were the Toureng, now the Imazaghan; he corrected. There were hundreds, if not thousands marching across the mountains. Realising there was no way to fight such a force, he had decided to gather everyone up and begin the journey for the city to warn the elders. He had rallied some of men from the neighbouring villages to attack the soldiers at first; to try and slow them down if possible, but after a few skirmishes they realised they were fighting a losing battle, there were just too many of them. So, they gathered everyone from all the surrounding villages to them and set off for the city. They told everyone they met en route to gather their belongings and do the same. He had met a little resistance at first; the villagers didn't want to leave their homes, but after a few smashed heads, they had decided to follow. The big man laughed at that, though the laughter didn't really touch his eyes. He had sent his sons out to the rest of the villages and towns to pass on word of the advancing army. He hadn't received any word of their progress so far and he admitted to being a little worried, but they were good strong lads and he had taught them how to look after themselves.

"Don't worry so father, "Hannah said as she approached the table with a bright smile on her face, "you know they will be ok."

"Ah there you are," Maroc boomed, his mood changing at the sight of his daughter and he gathered her up in his arms and kissed her forehead.

Hannah smiled and nodded to the children before recognising the other people in the group. She smiled warmly at everyone, but when her eyes found Sukhoi's face, the smile widened. He winked at her and she couldn't help but wink back, smiling all the time.

"I wondered where you had got to." Maroc said, "And yes you're right, they will be fine."

Sukhoi herded the group of friends and children to the corner of the room where they could chat in peace and catch up on everything that had happened since their last meeting.

Maroc found it extremely difficult to remain quiet as the details of their journey from his village to Enkan Mys unfolded, but especially when news that David was now a Kavacha Master was divulged.

He couldn't help but repeat the same words over and over. "Well, well, unbelievable."

It was when Sukhoi had just finished telling the tale with the help from Braduga, Socata and the children that the great doors opened with a heavy bang and a captain of the guard entered and banged on his shield with his sword for silence.

Without truly waiting for the noise to abate he shouted, "The army of Koutla are within sight of the city walls. The alarm bells are ringing and the soldiers are mounting the battlements."

Silence greeted him for a few seconds as everyone appeared to be in shock, and then as if turning on a tap, a cacophony of noise flowed from the crowd of people as the sound of the bells finally filtered through.

"I think we should go and take a look at this army." Maroc said above the din and with Sukhoi leading the way, the group left the room.

"Lord Driss!" Belmokhtar said as he entered his master's tent.

"What news Belmokhtar?" The man shrouded in the darkest corner of the tent intoned as the Keeper of the Kavacha Lore entered.

It was blackness in the tent, except for the weak green light emanating from the small globe in which Nuba Driss was now staring into. Even the light from the slight gap in the tent flaps could not penetrate the foul darkness. Belmokhtar was almost choking from the stench of his master's rotting flesh, but he had the good sense to keep his facial movements to a minimum. There was nothing either of them could do about the flesh eating disease that had been forced upon Nuba Driss, but the foulness of the disease was almost unbearable at times. Nuba Driss had eventually discovered a way to prolong the effects of the disease after many years of searching, but he hadn't found a cure, and the disease would ultimately kill him in the end. He had also found a way to hide the stench of decay which came with it, but he couldn't manage it for long; the effort was too much.

"Plenty my lord." Belmokhtar replied, trying in vain to gauge his master's mood.

"The boy David has taken the Kavacha tests and become a master." Belmokhtar related without hesitation. "The girl can communicate with the Dragons; as you predicted, the three children are still within the city and are awaiting my return. And as you advised, I told David that I could get them home on my return."

"Yes, I made an appearance to him while he was conducting the Faran'she." He said quietly, "I wondered if he would pass that test. He has exceeded all my expectations and more. With his power under my control the Kavacha book of knowledge will be mine."

"You believe he can break the incantation, my Lord?" Belmokhtar asked disbelievingly.

"Yes, I believe so. He doesn't realise how much power he has at his finger tips, but I know." Nuba Driss replied.

"And the girl, Jennifer?" Belmokhtar prompted.

"The girl too is impressive; by all the reports I've received and I know she can help me with this." He said caressing the orb gently.

"Have you figured out why it isn't working properly yet my Lord?" Belmokhtar asked intrigued. Ever since Nuba Driss had shown him the orb he had been hoping to get his hands on it. Not because he craved the power that it wielded, but because he thirsted for knowledge. He wanted to understand how it worked and test its limitations. But his lord and master would never allow the orb to fall in anyone's hands; not even his most trusted and loyal advisor, the orb was always with him.

"No," A slight flicker of his dark cowl indicated that he was shaking his head. "It worked perfectly well in Hal Argus, but now the power only allows me limited use. It is very frustrating, but the girl will be able to make it work as it should!" He added.

Belmokhtar looked sceptically at his master. He knew Jennifer didn't require the orb's power to communicate with the Dragons; she had proved that already, but Nuba Driss was adamant that she could make it work and he would then be able to harness its power.

"Yes, my lord." He replied quietly.

"All my plans are working out just fine Belmokhtar. Once I have their powers under my control, I will have the Book, the Dragons, and the tribes of Sakhalin will be mine for the taking." Nuba Driss rasped.

He began coughing and Belmokhtar waited patiently for the episode to finish before he asked. "What about the Guardian my Lord?"

Nuba Driss stared at the small orb held in his hands and watched the swirling gases contained within it collide with each other to produce a mesmerising display of explosions. Tearing his eyes from the spectacle he looked at Belmokhtar from beneath his dark cowl and replied. "All in good time Belmokhtar, all in good time." "Yes my lord." Belmokhtar said quietly casting a wary gaze over the orb held in his master's diseased hands until he put it back inside his robe out of sight.

"How many soldiers did the report say?" Socata said as he surveyed the camp fires in the distance, trying to gauge how many men would be sitting round them warming their hands and cooking a hot meal. They were looking out from the tower of the South gate and although they couldn't really make anything out too clearly, they could see hundreds of fires burning in the distance.

They weren't alone, it appeared that everyone else had been given the same message, and there were now hundreds of people on the battlements having a look at the army they had been warned about.

"Five thousand," Sukhoi announced, "but I must admit, if the camp fires are anything to go on, that estimate is short by a few thousand." He said thoughtfully.

"How far away are they?" Jennifer asked as she peered over the battlements.

"I would guess at least two miles, maybe three." Maroc replied.

"They'll be ready by morning." Socata announced to no one in particular.

"Will they attack then?" Christopher asked, clenching his hand over the pommel of his new sword at his side as if he was use to having it there.

"Possibly, it depends on what their intentions are. They could be here to stop anyone entering or leaving the city and wait for the main force to arrive or they may decide to attack anyway, your guess is as good as mine." Maroc said.

"When will the Imazaghan Army arrive?" Christopher asked.

"Another two or three days until they arrive." Sukhoi replied.

David looked out over the battlements and stared at the fires, he really couldn't see anything else from this distance. He couldn't help but feel responsible for everything that was happening, though he knew this war must have been brewing for the past five hundred years. One thing was for certain, the prophecy stated that when Nuba Driss attacked the three tribes again the Nadym Varsk was the only person who could defeat him. He knew that Jennifer was the Nadym Varsk and she had to be there or the tribes of Sakhalin wouldn't have a chance, though he wasn't sure if the truth of that came from within himself or from the Kavacha knowledge. The Guardian had foretold her arrival but he wasn't prepared to let her confront the demon by herself. No one seemed to know how the Nadym Varsk was going to defeat Nuba Driss but he would support her as best he could and that was why he had been training as hard as he had. There was little time as it was, but he was determined to hone his skills and protect his sister from the foulness of Nuba Driss. Then; and only then, could they finally feel free to leave this place and return home.

"You ok Dave?" Jennifer asked as she continued to look over the battlements at the enemies' campfires beyond. She could just make out the wisps of smoke as they joined with the night clouds, making them appear dark and menacing.

The crowds had come and gone throughout the night, all expecting to see something but not really seeing anything at all in the darkness. Most just filtered away, returning to their loved ones and friends with little or no news, but with an air of expectancy. The streets were still filled with many people, but the soldiers seemed to be getting everything under control; allocating rooms and then tented areas to the remaining few people who had nowhere to stay. In fact, the soldiers didn't appear to get any respite at all, as they continually rushed around the streets carrying out one order or another given by their superiors.

David was watching a soldier trying to get a screaming baby and family into an already crowded building and didn't quite catch what his sister said. "Sorry Jen, what did you say?" He asked still watching as the soldier finally managed to herd the family into the building.

"I asked if you were ok?" She replied.

"Yeah, just thinking." He replied quietly.

"Yes me too." She said just as quietly, "what's going to happen?"

David looked at his sister then and in the pale moonlight he could almost see the fear behind her troubled expression. He even thought he could smell the fear, but as he looked into her eyes he realised there was fear there, but there was something more, a strength and a sense of purpose, a determination that was battling that fear and suppressing it.

"Nuba Driss will be here soon Jen," he told her, "but I'll always be by your side and together we'll defeat him, I promise!" He said matter-of-factly, as if he had just said he would take a walk in the park.

Jennifer had noticed a power in her brother that had appeared even before he had touched the book of Kavacha Lore. He had grown in confidence and he seemed to accept everything that happened; whereas before, he had always tried to run away from it. She knew that he had idolised their father and his death had hit him the hardest. It had hit her just as bad but David had appeared more sensitive at the time, more vulnerable. Now he was telling her that, no matter what happened, he would be there, standing beside her and it gave her strength.

She knew then what she must do. "Dave, I think it's time." She said.

"For what?" He replied confused for the moment.

"For me to fulfil the prophesy." She replied.

"Jen, do you even know what to do? What you're going to say? Are you sure about this?" David asked as he contemplated what the response would be to his sister's announcement.

"This is the right time Dave; I know it is, and I think in front of the council of elders will be the right place, we need to go now." She replied and started walking away from the battlements.

Sukhoi came over to where the boys were standing and watched them watching their sister walk away.

"Everything ok David?" He asked gently, sensing some sort of tension.

"Not really," David replied turning to face the Kavacha, "Look Sukhoi, there's something I need to tell you quickly." He said. "It's Jen, she's the Nadym Varsk and she's going to announce it to the council, she's going to do it now, she says it's time to announce she's the Nadym Varsk." He finished in a hurry.

Maroc, Braduga and Socata had approached as David told Sukhoi about his sister and when he'd finished he expected some sort of outburst or questions, anything but the response he got.

"Yes, it is time." Sukhoi agreed.

"You knew?" David asked shocked at their apparent acceptance.

"I suspected, but I did not know for certain and I felt that I could not influence events." Sukhoi replied.

"I knew from the moment she touched me back in Baveystock." Maroc said quietly, a wistful look appearing on his face.

"We thought so too." Socata said as he nodded towards Braduga.

"And you said nothing." David said incredulous that no one thought to say something when the Kavacha had been searching for the Nadym Varsk for five hundred years.

"It is meant to be this way David, you more than most should understand this." Sukhoi replied cryptically.

What he understood, was that his sister had to admit to herself, that she was the one and believe it, as he had to admit to himself that he was a Kavacha. Now he had to be there for her and support her, help her in every way he could. He didn't have time to think about Sukhoi's cryptic words for the moment. He had to stand by his sister when she announced to the people of Enkan Mys that she was the Nadym Varsk.

"Let's go," He said as he rushed towards the steps, "Jen needs us, she needs all of us."

They caught up to Jennifer as she was trying to find her way through the darkened streets towards the Audience Chamber. The streets were still full even though all the taverns, houses, shops, and even storehouses were full to bursting with all the people that had arrived from the towns and villages outside the city.

"This way." Sukhoi said quietly as he took the lead and worked his way through the crowded streets.

She followed behind Sukhoi, with the rest of the party following behind. It didn't feel appropriate to say anything, so she didn't. Sensing her mood, no one deigned to speak either, so they all strode forwards in silence.

They were admitted immediately by the guards; who were acutely aware of who everyone was in the party as they approached and thought it in their best interests to let them enter without delay.

As the doors opened, Jennifer could hear the noise of people shouting over each other, and she faltered, until she realised David was at her side.

"I'll see if I can get their attention sis." He said smiling.

Closing her eyes, see tried to imagine what she was going to say to them all. She hadn't really thought about it until they had arrived and now it seemed too late. She tried to regulate her breathing and then she opened her eyes to wait for her brother to get everyone's attention.

She didn't have to wait long, David clapped his hands together and a tremendous metallic sound reverberated around the room; as if someone had just sounded a bell, but this sound was at least a hundred times louder.

Her head swivelled to look at her brother, but he just smiled weakly and shrugged his shoulders in apology. It was overdoing it slightly but when she looked back into the room she realised that she had everyone's attention now, with a hundred or more faces silently watching her.

Stealing a glance at Sukhoi; who smiled at her encouragingly, she made her way toward the Dias at the other end of the room, with the rest of the group following behind. The throng of people parted to let them through, but whispered as they passed by. They recognised Sukhoi, First of the Kavacha and his Ruedin; they knew Maroc, who was the old Master at Arms. They knew David who was the first Kavacha Master in generations and his sister who could speak with Dragons and they'd even heard of Christopher, who was being trained personally by the greatest warrior Sakhalin had ever had. So as they made their way to the Dias, they received nods and smiles from various familiar faces as well as not so familiar faces. On reaching their intended goal, Jennifer stopped and turned to face the multitude of elders, generals, lords and advisors.

Everyone seemed surprised when it was Jennifer who stepped forward from the group and opened her mouth as if to speak. No words came forth though and she turned her head to look at her brothers and her friends, they all smiled at her encouragingly. When she turned her gaze back to all the expectant faces she reached inside of her very being and listened to the thoughts that permeated through her.

It was like being caught up in a tidal wave of words, each thought crashing into her at exactly the same time. She fought for control as she tried desperately to fit a thought to a person.

Something must have shown in her face, because it was at that moment that Elder Hanish spoke. "Was there something you wanted to say Jennifer?" The old man asked as he nervously looked around the room.

"Yes Elder Hanish." She replied quietly and then coughed to clear her throat.

She realised immediately that David had done something when she began speaking because her voice boomed around the chamber when she spoke next. She looked across at him and he winked at her with a thin smile, trying to look every bit of the Kavacha Master he was.

"People of Sakhalin," she started, and then lowered her voice when she saw the effect it had on everyone, almost bursting their eardrums in fact. "There are two armies approaching the city and at their head is Nuba Driss. He is here to destroy you all and wreak havoc on the three tribes of Sakhalin. Preparations are being made to fortify the city and battle plans are being devised. The Kavacha are still searching for the Nadym Varsk, as they have for the last five hundred years. For as it was prophesied by the Guardian himself, without the Truth Seer, you can not defeat the death and destruction that Nuba Driss brings with him. I am here to tell you, that the search for the Nadym Varsk is at an end."

This piece of news could not be contained as question upon question was enthusiastically called out to the Elders. Had the Nadym Varsk been found at last one man shouted? Who was the Nadym Varsk? Where was the Nadym Varsk?

All the questions stopped when David clapped his hands once more and everyone put their hands to their ears at the sudden blast of sound.

"People of Sakhalin," Jennifer began again, "I am the Nadym Varsk and I am here to help you in your hour of need." She finished.

She looked toward Elder Hanish as she finished speaking, and he smiled at her and bowed his head. He responded to her announcement as if he already knew who she was and that surprised her, but she wasn't surprised by the response from the crowd as they began to shout again at the Elders for answers to their questions.

"Impossible, she is only a girl." One man shouted.

"No, this cannot be true." Said another.

Everyone seemed to be calling out at the same time, the noise reverberating around the room, but Jennifer just stood there and waited patiently for the noise to subsist.

"This girl, the Nadym Varsk, ludicrous." Shouted a general.

Jennifer had waited long enough and replied to the general's comment. "Is it as ludicrous as you wanting to be nothing more than a fisherman and lead a quiet life in the village in which you grew up General?" She asked the general, who went bright red but didn't reply.

"And you," She said pointing to a man in a bright red gown, "you who already has three children but wishes nothing more than to have a child of your own."

The man nodded his face sad.

"And you, Captain," She said pointing to a soldier, "you think I am just a silly girl who doesn't know what she's saying but you think I have nice legs and beautiful hair. Thank you for that, I've always thought so." She said as an afterthought.

The Captain smiled back at her and he too went bright red, but said nothing.

"I see the truth, I am the Nadym Varsk, and I am here to help you." She said, almost pleadingly.

"Rubbish, this is nothing more than some trick. You are but a girl, what can you do against Nuba Driss, how can you defeat the dark lord?" A man said from the crowd but walked to the front to be heard and recognised.

"You are right, Trefor Anthar, I am but a girl, and I don't know how I am going to defeat Nuba Driss; not yet anyway," she added, "but I am the Truth Seer and the way will be shown to me when the time is right."

Trefor Anthar was surprised that the girl knew his name, but this could also be some sort of trick and he said so.

"It could be a trick but then how would I know that your wife died two years ago from eating a poisonous mushroom and that she was..." She stopped then, she could see the pain of that memory on the face of the man before her and couldn't bring herself to finish what she was about to say, a tear came into her eye and a sad pitying smile came to her lips. "I'm so sorry." She said meekly, quietly.

Trefor Anthar regarded her silently for a few moments, the pain of the memory evident on his face, but he pushed that aside and walked over to the girl.

"My wife did die two years ago," He addressed the crowd, "but what Jennifer couldn't bring herself to tell you was that she was also pregnant, I alone knew of this and only the Nadym Varsk would know the truth of it." He finished a little quieter with his head lowered to his chest, a silent cry catching in his mouth, the pain of his loss still evidently raw.

Jennifer's heart was almost breaking, and she stepped forward to the poor man and put her hand on his heart, and whispered a few words to him as he looked into her eyes. A white light radiated from her hand onto Trefor's chest. A light that everyone in the chamber could see, and as they watched, Trefor's head tilted towards the ceiling and he closed his eyes. The light was gone a moment later but when Trefor opened his eyes, he seemed more at peace, he had embraced the pain and by doing so he had conquered it.

He gently reached out for Jennifer's hand and brought it to his lips and kissed it reverently.

"I am the Nadym Varsk, "She said again turning to the crowd, "I am here to help you all and fulfil the prophesy of the Guardian. And although I don't need your acceptance, I do need your blessing. That will be sufficient to provide me with the strength to do what I must. Together; I know, we can defeat Nuba Driss, together we can defeat his armies, and together we can rid Sakhalin of its nemesis. I need your answer now! Do I have your blessing?" A bright while light enveloped her as she finished speaking and the truth of her words reached all their hearts. Jennifer didn't feel anything herself as she was desperately trying to control her shaking body and conceal her doubts and fear of rejection from the ensemble.

It was a bit of a surprise then when Trefor fell to his knees at Jennifer's feet and even more so when he was quickly followed by many others, until at last everyone else followed as the truth was revealed to them.

Jennifer stood there amazed, with David and Christopher at her side as they watched all the Kavacha, the generals, and even the elders kneel to her.

"Let us rejoice, "Elder Hanish shouted as he began to stand, "The Nadym Varsk has been found at last, the Truth Seer has arrived."

Chapter Twenty Eight

He was walking down a brightly lit corridor; all white and clinical, an odour of rotten flesh seemed to permeate the atmosphere; the smell strong and nauseating, burning his nostrils with its putrid breath. A dense misty fog crawled along the floor and around his feet, but he wasn't interested in the fog or the smell for that matter; his gaze was focused on the obscure, indeterminate figure before him. He was walking toward that figure now; although he felt as if he was actually floating on the mist rather than walking, the dark figure watching and waiting for his arrival. Before he knew what was happening he was standing before the figure who was dressed in a monk's habit, its face obscured from view by an overlarge hood.

He knew he was shaking with fright, but he could do nothing about that, his body was no longer his own, he had no power over it anymore, the figure before him was in total control. Then he heard the footsteps behind him, faint but there nevertheless, and heading in his direction. His body began to stop shivering and he began to relax, the footsteps were getting louder as they drew closer.

Then the figure spoke, "You can not defeat me." It rasped at him as spittle dropped from the darkened hood.

"Maybe not," he agreed, "but the Nadym Varsk can!" He shouted back.

He noticed then that the footsteps had stopped and someone or something touched his arm.

He managed to glance to his side and there standing next to him was the Nadym Varsk, a bright light enveloped them both and he could feel his power and strength returning to him.

"You think you two can make a difference?" The figure laughed at them.

"Yes." They said together.

Then the figure's head began to rise and two disease ridden hands grabbed hold of the edges of its hood and pulled it down.

They both screamed!

David woke with a start and almost sprung out of his bed. It was still night, the pale moonlight casting shadows through the window. He looked across at Jennifer who seemed to be asleep, even if she was moaning weakly.

Christopher was still asleep as well, his chest rising and falling steadily as it always did.

Content that everything was ok he laid back down in his bed, pulling the covers over him and even though it was still quite mild, he shivered anyway. The dreams were coming to him every night now; the only respite he had experienced was when he had been in the Haram. He always woke at the same time he realised, always when Nuba Driss was about to reveal himself. He didn't understand why he screamed; he never saw a face, well, not that he could remember. But maybe the face beneath was so hideous that it would make anyone want to scream, he thought. He recalled then that this was the first time he hadn't had to face Nuba Driss alone. This time he had had someone by his side, this time he had the Nadym Varsk, Jennifer.

He wasn't sure why he kept dreaming the same thing over and over, but he found a kind of comfort in the fact that his sister was there with him.

He stared at the ceiling pondering the dream for quite along time when sleep finally found him once more.

"Is everything in order Major Korbatte?" General Kormask asked as he surveyed his men and looked toward the city as the sun began to rise. It was a rhetorical question, he had planned everything with precision, but it was always prudent to receive confirmation from his subordinates that all his orders had been carried out.

"Yes general." The major replied. "There are still a few people getting through our perimeter but not many." He assured the general, worried that he may query his report.

"I know Major, everything is proceeding as planned." He replied.

"Yes sir." He replied briskly, and then added, "General, a Koutla leader arrived with Elder Sanaag and wishes to speak with you." He said hesitantly.

The General sighed, "Couldn't you deal with him?" he asked, not really interested in a conversation with one of the Raiders. He had tried in vain to get along with the men, but they just irritated him. He could just about stomach the soldiers he had trained but that had taken as long as it took to train them in the first place. They just didn't have any code or honour; they would steal or murder you as soon as look at you. And he just didn't like them. The general had immediately understood why these men had been banished from their own tribes. He would have killed them there and then if he had his way.

"He doesn't want to speak to me sir," he said growing rather pale, "He wanted to speak with you."

The General had never seen the major looking so perturbed as he did now and thought this particular Raider must be quite a man to unsettle the Major so.

"Ok I'll deal with him in a moment, but as to Awdaal, what did the snivelling little fool have to say?" He asked.

"Nothing that we didn't already know, but I am sorry to report that he didn't survive our interrogation process." The major conceded with a slight smile on his lips.

"That's a shame, I'm sure that my Lord Driss won't be able to sleep tonight with thoughts of his dear friend's demise." The general chortled.

The major smiled at his senior's humour and awaited his orders.

"Ok major; let's have a look at this Koutla of yours." He said eventually.

The major shouted the order to a soldier waiting a few feet away and moments later the General watched as a large man was escorted towards him. He looked quite imposing and as he drew closer and on seeing his face, the General could understand why the Major was acting the way he was. There was a deep chilling coldness about the man; although his eyes appeared to burn with something bordering on madness, and anger barely controlled, here was a man that just seemed to exude death. He wasn't like the rest of the Koutla the General had met before, he could tell from the way he moved that he was a highly trained and skilful warrior. This man was confident in his abilities and that made him extremely dangerous, but more importantly, he realised this man knew how dangerous he was.

"General," the man greeted him formally; "I am Abdi Khouna."

The man was fierce; the general could tell, and could see that he was struggling to keep his feelings concealed. It was slightly unnerving looking at all that pent up anger, but the general had seen similar looks before in all his years of service and kept his face expressionless.

"What can I do for you?" The General asked looking directly into the Raiders eyes.

Abdi felt himself shaking but quickly controlled his body movements. He wanted something that only the General could give him and so he must try and remain calm until he got what he wanted. Then and only then could he release his anger and avenge the death of his protégés.

"I wish to be given command of the third battalion when we attack." He asked, getting straight to the point. Abdi knew this was the best way of dealing with the general. The general was a difficult man to impress, but Abdi was a seasoned warrior, he had been trained at Enkan Mys and he knew how to impress people, even generals as tough as this old soldier.

The general was shocked, though he didn't show it. The third battalion were his canon fodder; they were going to lead the attack and were surely going to get decimated when they did so. He had been contemplating who to lead those men, he didn't want to use his own officers, and now this man was volunteering for the job. It was a decision he had been deliberating for quite a while and now this man had just dropped into his lap. But, as fortuitous as this was, he couldn't just let this Koutla Leader take that responsibility without knowing why this man would sacrifice himself in this way, and so he asked him why.

Abdi didn't want to give his reasons to the General but he had to tell him something, "Old scores to settle with certain individuals in the city. I know the city will send out its soldiers when we attack and I believe these individuals will be leading them when they do. I want to greet them when they do that." He said calmly, though he didn't feel calm at all.

The general knew that the tacticians in the city would employ that tactic, so that wasn't a surprise, but this Koutla intrigued him. He wished he had more time to speak with this man, but he knew he hadn't. This Koutla had an old score to settle, well good for him! He knew this warrior would make a formidable leader of his Third Battalion and that was all he needed. He would give this warrior the opportunity he desired so much so he could end that score once and for all, and in doing so, benefit himself and the Imazaghan Army in the process. "They're yours." He said and waved his hand as he dismissed the leader.

Abdi smiled, though he didn't feel like smiling and nodding his head to the general he went to find the Third Battalion, his new command and his path for revenge.

"Was that wise General?" The Major asked as the Koutla Leader left them.

The general watched as Abdi walked out of sight and then turned to the Major, "I needed someone and he was available, he will fulfil my purpose."

The two officers then watched the soldiers preparing their breakfast; it would be the last meal some of them would ever have. The General hated this part of any campaign, the waiting, but he had no choice. He was waiting for the right time and it hadn't arrived yet.

As if the Major could read his thought, he asked, "When do we attack General?" Eagerness radiated from him. They had been waiting centuries to finally strike at their ancestor's oldest enemies and at last that opportunity had presented itself.

"Patience Major," the general replied, though he didn't feel very patient himself, "not long now." He said as he turned about and walked back to his tent.

"Good news." Socata said as he walked into the children's room.

"Oh?" David said as he finished eating his breakfast of freshly baked bread and cheese, wiping the crumbs from round his mouth with his shirt sleeve.

Jennifer tutted but didn't say anything as he did so.

"Maroc's sons have all arrived safely thankfully, although they did report that the city is now totally surrounded and they were lucky to find one weak link, which they exploited to the full." He informed them.

"I take it that link has now been reinforced!" Christopher asked as he slurped the last spoonful of porridge from his plate and put it down.

David couldn't help but smile at his brother and realised that he not only looked like one of the Ruedin now, but that he actually thought like them, almost instinctively.

"Yes it was to be expected and I do not think we will be seeing many more people entering the city after today."

"How many more Kavacha are we expecting?" David asked.

"I'm not sure; it is one of the main topics of conversation at the moment." Socata said shrugging his shoulders. "Anyway, I have to come at Sukhoi's behest; he wants to see you all now, if you're available."

Every meeting now was an invitation. The Barnes children were treated like royalty and with a reverence that they all found a little uncomfortable. David and Jennifer had tried to speak to Sukhoi and then the Council about it but the response had been the same. They were immediate celebrities and heroes to the people of the city. David; as a Kavacha Master, bewildered and inspired them, but Jennifer as the Nadym Varsk gave them hope of salvation. They would just have to live with the adoration of the people until they got use to it.

"Ok, let's find out what's going on." David agreed.

They followed the warrior until they reached a room next to the Audience Chamber and that's where they found Sukhoi talking with Maroc and his sons, staring out of a window overlooking the Koutla army.

Sukhoi greeted the children then as he noticed their arrival and then to Jennifer's surprise Maroc's three sons bowed deeply to her before greeting the two boys.

"Stop that!" Jennifer said to them embarrassed.

"Looks like you're going to have to get used to that Jen." Christopher whispered to her, "But don't for one minute think that me and Dave will be bowing to you." He said through a thin lipped smile.

"I wouldn't expect you to." She said smiling at her brother with all the reverence and grace she could muster.

"Yeah right." He whispered back, though he maintained the smile.

"Please don't do that," She said again, "you are my friends and I don't want my friends bowing and scraping to me." She said smiling at them.

They looked to their father as one, who just shrugged his massive shoulders, before they stood up and then began to ask the three children about their adventures. Everyone seemed to be talking at once, but it was Braduga's arrival that finally interrupted their narration of events as he provided everyone with an update on the current situation.

All preparations had been finalised for a siege and everyone had been detailed to perform certain tasks; from putting out fires if they happened, to tending to the wounded, which would definitely happen. Everyone in the city had been given some responsibility however small or insignificant sounding. Everyone was relieved and eager to help out as best they could. They were the three tribes and they stuck together no matter what happened to them, they would say. Even with all the preparations made and jobs allocated, the people still had one question on their lips though; it was on everyone's lips, "when were the army going to attack the city?" Braduga; like the council, the tacticians and the numerous advisors, couldn't give them the answer. Everyone had expected the army to attack straight away and use their advantage while the city was still trying to fortify the city, but they stopped when they moved into position. They seemed to be waiting for something, though no one knew what that something was, unless it was of course, the arrival of Nuba Driss. Just the thought of the evil mage made everyone shudder and the children cry.

As Braduga related all his information to Sukhoi and Maroc and discussed the intentions of the army outside the city walls, his sons continued to tell the children about their journey to the city. It transpired that this was the first time Maroc's sons had been to the city and they were just as excited about seeing all the sights as the children had been. They were also determined to see everything they could before the fun began. It was how Faran referred to the impending battle, but Thane and Bamako seemed just as excited about the prospect of facing the Imazaghan. When the conversation returned to the city, it was the men's child-like excitement and enthusiasm at seeing everything, that made the children forget their own fears of the forthcoming battle and chatter animatedly about the sights the men should experience. It was a well needed reprieve before the fun began in earnest.

Chapter Twenty Nine

Christopher was training hard trying to block the strikes offered by Socata with Braduga giving instructions at every opportunity. For some reason he couldn't quite understand, Sukhoi's Ruedin had continued to train him at every opportunity, even though they were training the hundreds of men that had arrived from the villages and town. The rest of the Kavacha's' Ruedin were doing the same, but he was surprised that they would want to give up their free time to spend it with him.

He wanted to ask them why, but he thought if he voiced the question they would change their minds and he would be left alone for most of the day. It was selfish of him; he knew, but with both David and Jennifer constantly busy with their new appointments and responsibilities, he found that they didn't have time for him any more. So he kept quiet and enjoyed the moment.

He was sweating profusely now and his muscles were straining with the constant bombardment of attacks against him, but he wouldn't stop, he wanted his friends to be proud of him, so he kept going.

It was only when Jennifer arrived, that he finally stopped, exhausted. Though he still managed to smile at his friends and thank them again for their time.

"What's up Jen?" He said as both Braduga and Socata left them to give instruction to two men who quite clearly couldn't use a sword to save their lives.

"I don't like the thought of you being taught how to use that thing." She said in disgust as she pointed to his sword that he was just putting round his waist.

He sighed, they had had this discussion a lot recently, and although he knew she didn't like it, he thought that she had come to appreciate why he had to do it.

"Is that why you came?" He asked, ready to battle with her once more about the sword.

"What? No!" She replied distractedly, "David has just sent me a message to come and find you and meet him in our room." She replied.

"We best go and meet him then, hadn't we." He said sarcastically, but when she agreed, he realised the sarcasm was lost on her. He watched her closely as they headed back to their room and realised she had changed immensely since they came to Sakhalin, but the biggest change had come when she had said she was the Nadym Varsk. She seemed to be constantly pre-occupied as if the worries of the whole world were heavy on her shoulders. Then he thought, perhaps they were. She was the Nadym Varsk, and as such, the only person that could defeat Nuba Driss, it was a great responsibility, and one she wouldn't have asked for given the choice, he knew.

It took them a good thirty minutes before they finally arrived back at their room. Christopher suddenly became alert and drew his sword, as he stepped in front of his sister defensively.

"What's wrong Chris?" She asked quietly, nervously looking around.

"There aren't any guards on duty outside our room." He whispered back. "Stay here while I check it out." He ordered.

Jennifer was about to complain, but then she saw the fierceness in his face and realised that Christopher had also changed since they had arrived in the city. He had grown in confidence and stature and if everything she heard was true, he had become very proficient in the use of the sword he carried. She remained where she was and then watched as he brother stealthily moved to the door and opened it a mere crack to peak through. He turned to her a moment later and indicated that everything was ok.

David had been pacing the room as the door opened and his brother and sister appeared. They could tell he was agitated by the severe look he had on his face.

"What took you so long?" He asked them, indicating that he wanted them to sit at the table, as he sat down next to them. His anxious face and nervous disposition made them both stare at him and each other.

"What's up Dave?" Christopher asked his brother.

"And where are the guards?" Jennifer added suspiciously.

"I've sent the guards away." He said dismissively with a wave of his hand. "But there are more important things to talk about than the guards." He said a little apprehensively.

Jennifer looked at Christopher; who shrugged his shoulders, before she returned her attention back to her other brother. "Well?" She asked, not liking the suspense her brother's uneasiness was generating.

David hesitated before announcing. "Belmokhtar has just been to see me with some very important news."

"What did the monk have to say?" Jennifer asked intrigued. For some reason she couldn't quite fathom, she didn't trust the Keeper of Kavacha Lore, but if he had something to say, she wanted to hear it. She didn't think her distrust came from her gift, but she was still trying to understand that, so maybe it did. What the source, she knew they wouldn't be there if not for him but she just couldn't bring herself to like the man.

"You're not going to like it." David replied as if trying to stall for time or for effect.

"Just get on with it will you." Jennifer told him, not inclined to prolong a conversation involving the Keeper.

David sighed before continuing, "Belmokhtar told me that the time has come for us to return home. He said that if we wanted to leave Sakhalin, it had to be in the next few hours. He couldn't guarantee when the doorway would appear again after that, if it appeared at all." He finished quickly, trying to gauge the effect it had on both of them.

He was surprised by their silence. He expected them both to shout and argue against leaving, anything but the silence that greeted him now. He at least expected his sister to say something, she was the Nadym Varsk, she had a responsibility to stay and fight Nuba Driss as only she could. She also had a responsibility to the Dragons; she was the only one that could communicate with them, without her they wouldn't be able to complete their own mission.

He had responsibilities as the only Kavacha Master; would he feel comfortable leaving the city and their friends to fight this battle by themselves? But if Belmokhtar was right and they only had a few hours to make a decision, and if they chose to stay, they may never get back home, what choice did they truly have?

They just sat there calmly looking at him, waiting. Christopher's expression was as cold as a stone wall; he didn't speak a word but continued to look at him expectantly. David realised then that they both expected him to say something more, maybe give his opinion on the matter, or even tell them what they should do.

"I know you're the Nadym Varsk," he began, "and I know you have to fulfil the prophesy of the Guardian. We also said we would help the Dragons, I know that too." He continued carefully. "We all have responsibilities now, but we need to really think about this, we must realise that this could be the only opportunity we will ever get to get back home, do we really want to waste it?" He finished. When they still didn't speak, he felt he needed to emphasise the point some more. "Belmokhtar believes this is our only chance to get back to Featherstone, the only chance to get back home and back to mum."

Still they remained silent, waiting.

He didn't like their silence; he was becoming more and more agitated. "We have to make a decision, I know that. We either stay and help our friends and take the risk of not getting back home or we go with Belmokhtar and back to where we belong." It sounded hollow even to himself, he didn't want to leave his friends like this, not now, but he needed both Jennifer and Christopher to give their honest opinion and he didn't want to bias that in any way.

"Well, what do we do?" He asked them finally, not prepared to say another word until they said something in reply.

"General! General Kormask!" Major Korbatte shouted as he entered the General's tent without permission.

"What is it Major?" He asked, letting the unprofessional action drop when he saw the excitement on the major's face.

"Griffins!" He exclaimed excitedly, "the Griffins have arrived."

General Kormask had never seen a Griffin, though he had heard stories of them as a child. He knew that Lord Driss used them extensively to do his bidding and had promised the general that he would send him some of the ferocious creatures to aid him when he attacked the city. They had arrived and now he could finally fulfil his greatest ambition, and attack the city and the people that had persecuted his ancestors so long ago. Lord Driss had related the stories of how the Toureng were cruelly and mercilessly driven from their homes and now the Imazaghan would finally avenge them and eradicate the three tribes from their ancestor's homeland.

As he contemplated his people's revenge a big smile appeared on his face.

"Major!" He called.
"Yes Sir?"
"Now!"
"Sir?" The Major replied confused.

"Now, we attack now!" He shouted enthusiastically, getting to his feet and making his way out of his tent. "Prepare the men, we go to the city of Enkan Mys and we take back our ancestor's birthright!"

"It's the alarm!" Christopher shouted. "The Koutla must be attacking the city." He rushed to the open window and could see crowds of people hurrying to their pre-arranged positions on the battlements, weapons in hand and ready for the attack to begin.

Jennifer and David joined him there within moments and as all three children watched the city come alive with people racing from one place to another David said quietly. "We don't really have a choice, do we?"

"No." Jennifer replied, "I don't think we do."

There was a knock at the door and all three turned as the door opened to reveal Sukhoi. But it was the appearance of Belmokhtar at his side that surprised the children.

"The Koutla have started their advance, all the Kavacha are required on the battlements, will you join us David?" Sukhoi asked his face devoid of all emotion.

David looked at his brother and sister for a few moments before his gaze found Belmokhtar's eyes. "I am a Kavacha Master," He said, feeling the power grow inside him as he opened himself up to its intensity, "Where else would I be; I will come."

Belmokhtar stared at him then with an almost frenzied intensity, but the look was soon gone and he merely smiled, then nodded that he understood what their decision had been.

David turned to Jennifer and Christopher and hugged them quickly and then turned back to Sukhoi. "We will all come with you Sukhoi." David said, and with nods and smiles of approval from his brother and sister, they all left the room and headed for the battlements and the imminent attack.

"There's so many of them." Jennifer said shocked, although the approaching army was still a couple of miles away, their numbers were never the less impressive from the height of the watch tower.

A single bell sounded and the gates beneath the tower began to open.

"What's happening?" Christopher asked as he saw column after column of soldiers advancing through the gates and forming ranks before the city walls.

"We will attempt to fight the army on the battlefield first. If our warriors are unsuccessful, then they will retreat behind the walls of the city." Sukhoi replied.

"Wouldn't it be safer if they stayed behind the protection of the city walls?" Jennifer asked, worried for the safety of the men as they marched through the city gates.

"Most of our soldiers are highly trained and skilful, and with the Ruedin fighting beside them to give them strength, they will be quite formidable." Sukhoi replied.

Christopher was leaning over the wall trying to get a better view when he suddenly shouted at someone below.

David and Jennifer weren't sure who he was shouting at immediately; there seemed so many warriors leaving through the gates, until they saw the crossed swords on the back of one warrior in particular.

"It's Brad!" Christopher shouted.

"Oh no!" Jennifer shouted then.

"Don't worry Jen, Brad can look after himself." David offered and then noticed where his sister was pointing.

Below; filing out of the gates, were Maroc and his sons; all heavily armed and moving swiftly to the front of the marching troops.

"Where are they going?" She asked Sukhoi.

Sukhoi looked at the children sadly and answered, "Enkan Mys needs the greatest warriors in this time of need, Maroc and his sons are amongst the finest in all of Sakhalin. They are going to do their duty and lead our soldiers against the approaching army."

"They've caught up to Brad." Christopher informed them.

"Shouldn't the Ruedin be protecting their Kavacha?" Jennifer asked looking as if she was about to be sick as her friends moved to the front of the assembled soldiers.

"They have a new role to fulfil now. The Nadym Varsk has been found and their search is over, but now they have been tasked to defend and protect the three tribes as they once protected their Kavacha. With their strength and courage the other soldiers will fight with pride and honour. They will fight beside the best warriors in Sakhalin and maybe they will be victorious in their battle against the evil of Nuba Driss." He finished solemnly as he turned to the watch his friends prepare the warriors for battle.

The children watched and listened as orders were shouted from the numerous officers to their men. Groups were reformed and realigned until the right formations were executed and then when everything was completed a quieting stillness descended on the city. It was both incredible and unbelievable at the same time. With so many soldiers paraded in front of the city in full armour; their weapons gripped in sweaty palms as they waited for their orders, not even the slightest jingle of metal on metal could permeate it. The soldiers were ready to fight; it was what they were trained to do. They watched and waited in silence, each one of them lost in their own thoughts of their loved ones and friends, as they waited for the inevitable attack to commence.

They didn't have to wait long. The leaders of the advancing army had watched incredulously as the soldiers had formed up in front of the city. They all felt it was a momentous mistake to leave the protection of the city, but they would use that to their own advantage. They gave the order to increase their marching pace to a jog. The soldiers thrust their shields forward, banging their weapons on them aggressively. Their eagerness to engage the defenders resounded in deafening clarity as they drew ever closer.

Chapter Thirty

Braduga looked impressive in his shinning battle armour as he turned his back on the advancing army of Koutla. They were inconsequential for the moment; his focus was totally concentrated on the parade of soldiers before him. With his twin swords strapped to his back as usual, he now faced his friends, his comrades, and his people. Some; quite a few in fact looked defeated already, as he glanced at their faces, they knew this was only the first army; a greater army was already en route that outsized this one four times. He had been given overall control of the defenders by the council. It was a responsibility he would rather leave to someone else, but his reputation as the greatest warrior in Sakhalin meant he had to be there. He was a living legend amongst the people and now he had to live up to his reputation, or die trying. Braduga was a great warrior, with immense skill and prowess but he was also a great leader and he knew instinctively that he had to find some words to instil courage and strength into the soldiers as they watched the advancing army approach. He wasn't comfortable speaking to large numbers of people, but his comfort wasn't the issue, the men needed some words of encouragement and they needed him to speak them. Looking down the rank and files of soldiers he spoke to them from his heart.

"Warriors of Sakhalin!" He shouted, getting their attention, and diverting it from the advancing army. "Do you know me?"

Shouts and chants of Braduga's name reverberated through the ranks of soldiers. He raised his hands for silence, which came eventually as the soldiers waited to hear what the famous warrior had to say.

"You see an army of thousands marching down on us. They come to destroy us utterly and plunder the city." He began, shouting at the men before him. "Fierce warriors, hardened men who are no doubt accustomed to fighting. But I ask you to think as you face these foes that want to kill you, think on what they are fighting for. Not families, not friends, not their homes, and not even peace. They are fighting for evil; they are fighting for Nuba Driss. It is we that are fighting for those things, but we do not fight alone. We have the Kavacha, and their sacred lore, and for the first time in five hundred years we have a Kavacha Master."

A cheer rose then and Braduga had to wait for a while for the noise to abate.

"But that is not all, " he continued, "we have found the Nadym Varsk; who has been prophesised to help us in our fight against this evil." He said pointing to the battlements and to where Jennifer was standing beside her brothers and Sukhoi.

"There before you stands the Nadym Varsk!"

The crowd turned to look to where the warrior was pointing and could see Jennifer standing tall upon the battlements, head held high. "My friends, I ask you to remain firm, stand tall and face your enemies with honour. For today we face a foul enemy, but we do not stand alone. We shall not be defeated today or any other day. We are the three tribes of Sakhalin and we will be victorious!"

A roar erupted from the men then, shouting "Sakhalin, Sakhalin", this continued up along the battlements and to within the city, as every man, woman and child, shouted the call, "Sakhalin, Sakhalin!"

Once the cries had silenced, Braduga turned to face the enemy. Maroc came to stand next to him and when Braduga nodded, he gave the order for the archers to move into position. They moved as one to the front of the ranks and adopted a well practised position beside the foot soldiers. The pike men then moved forward in front of the archers to provide an effective protective barrier around them. It wasn't long before the enemy were within range and Marco gave the order to fire. The order quickly disseminated down the ranks and as one the archers loosed their dark shafts upon the Koutla. The sky darkened momentarily over the enemy as hundreds of arrows reigned down on them.

They had obviously anticipated such an attack because they quickly stopped in their tracks and brought their shields up to cover their heads. Even so, many were too slow and the arrows found their intended targets. As the first wave of arrows left their bows the front rank went to their knees and the second rank fired, then the third. The Koutla were moving cautiously forward now, most of their earlier eagerness forgotten with the advent of thousands of arrows heading in their direction.

Noticing the change and expecting it, Maroc gave the order for the archers to fire at will and at the same time ordered the pike men and the foot soldiers to advance. The archers moved to the rear as the soldiers moved forward; first at a steady pace until they were almost upon them. A further order was shouted and the soldiers ran the remaining hundred or so yards. Screaming and shouting madly, the soldiers attacked the Koutla with vigour, but their battle cries didn't stop the archers from continuing to do their job. The front two ranks were picking their targets carefully now while the rear rank began firing their arrows towards the rear of the enemy lines. The two armies finally collided with a deafening, resounding clash of metal on metal. Battle cries were drowned out by the cries of pain as the defenders slashed and cut through the Koutla attackers.

Braduga's swords were a blur as he cut a path through the enemy, but he wasn't alone, Socata was by his side, as was Maroc's son, Thane. They were unstoppable as they brandished their weapons without mercy, without thought, as all their years of training were focused in that one place, and at that one time.

The battle was raging everywhere, the defenders appeared to have the upper hand at the moment but everyone knew that could change in a moment. With sheer determination and ferociousness they ploughed through their adversaries. They had everything to fight for they knew, they were protecting their families, friends, and their city and they wouldn't be stopped easily, they wouldn't be conquered.

It was hand to hand fighting at its worse, there wasn't much room for manoeuvre as each side tried to stab each other before they themselves were stabbed. Style and technique through months and years of training appeared to go out the window as each person tried desperately to kill the opposition without getting killed themselves.

The sounds were horrendous as metal made contact with metal and with bone. Ear-piercing screeches were mesmerising as men were cut down without thought. The stench of blood soaking the field was enough to turn the hardiest of men to retching, but it didn't stop them from fighting.

It was a fight to the death, and as the blows reigned down on each side, the noises and smells of fear and death couldn't be subdued.

From within the area of the heaviest fighting, two men found each other.

Their eyes locked for an instant, in almost recognition, as they slashed and cut with their swords at their enemies. They were lost from each others view for a moment before they found each other again and then they realised at the same instant, that they knew each other.

Their expressions couldn't have been more different though. Maroc was seeing an old friend who had disappeared from Enkan Mys at the same time as his wife and was confused by his re-appearance on the opposite side to himself. Abdi's expression was one of disbelief, then full of loathing as he identified Maroc as the focal point for where his life had led him.

Maroc saw the expression change and his brow knitted together in a frown as he tried to reason the meaning of such hatred.

They eventually found themselves face to face as the battle continued around them.

Amazingly, in the chaos of the battle they were afforded some space as they stood there looking at each other; Maroc in confusion, Abdi with expectancy, that burned with an intense hatred.

"Abdi, why are you fighting for Nuba Driss?" Maroc asked his old friend.

"I fight for myself old man, and we're friends no longer!" Abdi spat at him, though he couldn't understand how Maroc could face him so calmly.

"I don't understand, you were my friend once." Maroc said, trying to fathom the reason behind Abdi's venomous words.

Then Abdi realised, even after all these years, the Elders hadn't told Maroc that he had killed his wife. He began to laugh, a wild berserkers laugh as he watched the confused look on his old mentors face.

"What..." Maroc began, but Abdi interrupted him.

"You stupid old fool!" He spat, "They didn't tell you, did they?" He asked, though he knew the answer from the confused look on Maroc's face.

"They? Who? Tell me what?" Maroc asked, a coldness entering his heart, though he couldn't understand why Abdi's words were affecting him so.

"I killed Asmara!" Abdi yelled at him through his laughter.

It was as if a thunderbolt had struck his heart. It couldn't be true, he told himself, though he knew it must be when he looked into Abdi's eyes. Abdi had killed his wife and the Elders; for reasons he couldn't fathom, had obviously banished him from the city for his evil deed. But why hadn't they told him? He didn't understand how this could have happened. He didn't have time to think about it now though, because his wife was dead and couldn't be brought back and her killer was standing before him.

"Why?" He whispered, still in shock.

"Why? Why? Because I wanted her, why else?" He replied.

Maroc began to shake, his head lowered and his breathing became laboured as he tried to take it all in. He had not only been betrayed by his friend but by the Elders themselves. He didn't know what he had done to deserve such treatment, but he did know that he was going to kill the man responsible or be killed himself.

"Come Maroc; let me send you to her!" Abdi shouted at his old mentor.

"You have lived too long Abdi." He said quietly, controlling his rising anger.

"So have you old man." He replied just as quietly.

They both attacked at the same time, both deflecting the blows with ease gained through years of experience and hours of training. They attacked each other with a viciousness and vitality that belied their years. Their movements precise and practiced, it was more of a choreographed dance than a sword fight. Each perfectly executed movement was countered by an equally executed defensive stroke.

The battle was still raging all around them, but they were oblivious as they reined blow after blow at each other. Neither one gave the slightest indication that they were weakening, or even a hint of putting a foot wrong. They were experienced veterans, who had been trained by the best and had become the best.

It appeared they were going to fight all through the day until Maroc suddenly slipped on a bloody patch of grass. Abdi seizing the opportunity, attacked without mercy and thrust his sword towards Maroc's heart, which was now unprotected as he tried to regain his balance. He should have died there and then, he knew it and so did Abdi, but just as the killing blow was within reach, Abdi's blade was suddenly turned away.

Abdi lost his balance and rolled to the side as he was prevented from finally killing the main catalyst to all his problems.

He was on his feet in moments and turned to face the person responsible, sword pointed towards this new foe.

He couldn't believe his eyes, standing next to Maroc was the second person he was desperate to kill this day. Braduga was helping Maroc to his feet, though he was still finding it awkward in the blood drenched grass. Abdi's anger grew beyond all reason, he couldn't contain it.

"Braduga!" He screamed, "I am glad you are here, it saves me the time to come and find you once I have killed this old man." He seethed.

"You are not worthy to touch his boots Koutla." Braduga retorted turning his back on the Koutla leader with disdain.

"You will feel my blade in your heart before this day is done!" He shouted back madly.

"You must get by me first." Maroc said calmly, standing once more on solid ground in front of Braduga.

"Leave us my friend; I will deal with this one, find someone more worthy to die by your sword."

Braduga nodded after a moments hesitation, and walked away without even glancing back, to join the battle.

Hatred consumed Abdi as he charged at Maroc; swinging his sword wildly without the earlier expertise and precision he had displayed. He had let his temper get the better of him and had finally shown his weakness.

Maroc exploited that to the full and with vicious taunts he coaxed his once old friend into making mistake after mistake, until at last he made one that he could use to deliver his own killing stroke.

When Abdi overexerted himself with one particular strike, Maroc was ready and countered it with his own strike, thrusting his sword through Abdi's ribs and up into his heart.

Shock registered on Abdi's face for a moment and maybe the slightest hint of regret, whether it is regret for his deeds, or regret for not killing his old mentor will never be known, as the life finally left his eyes and he crumpled to the ground. Maroc's own anger had subsided during their battle; he remembered his children and he remembered what Jennifer had told him, and he realised that he was at peace with himself, and that's all that mattered now. Feeling nothing but the merest ounce of regret himself at the demise of his old friend, Maroc walked away and re-engaged in the battle; thoughts of his beautiful wife put aside; at least for the present.

"What are those?" Christopher asked as he pointed to hundreds of dark shapes flying from the Koutla's rear ranks and heading towards the city.

Everyone positioned along the battlements stared in wonder as the shapes began to take form. Alarm bells began to ring wildly as finally the warriors with the sharpest eyes realised what was about to descend upon them. Orders were shouted along the battlements and arrows were notched as the shapes began to attack the defenders below.

"They are Griffins Christopher; Nuba Driss's dark creatures come to menace us." Sukhoi replied with obvious disdain.

David recognised the name from a book he had read himself at school on mythical creatures, but he couldn't believe these could be the same creatures. Then a picture of one of the creatures came into his head and with it all the information held within the Kavacha book of knowledge.

"They are the same." He said out loud.

"What?" Christopher asked him.

"The Griffin, they're the same creatures as the one's I've read about back home. They're a cross between an eagle and a lion, they're normally depicted as golden in colour but these appear to be as black as coal." He said as he watched the dark creatures fly gracefully through the air. "It is written in Kavacha lore that they are immensely powerful, incredibly manoeuvrable in the air and impervious to arrows, due to their thick scaled hides."

"How can we defeat them then if not with arrows then?" Christopher asked, a little dismayed by the arrival of the creatures.

"With crossbow bolts." Sukhoi replied, pointing to a set of large wooden structures that were only now being uncovered to reveal large crossbows. "But also with a little Kavacha lore." He said smiling, though he didn't look particularly happy.

David noticed Christopher's puzzled look and explained that the Griffins were too fast for the bolts to do any damage normally, but with a little magic, the bolts could be swifter and their aim truer, which increased the possibility of hitting one of the creatures.

David looked at the crossbows and the amount of bolts they had stacked against the wooden structures and quickly calculated that there wasn't anywhere near enough to kill all the creatures that were descending on them. There must be some other way, he thought. He tried to envisage the creatures in his mind and willed the book's knowledge to help him. He wasn't sure what he was looking for, but there must be something that could help them.

The Griffins swooped down on the City's defenders; striking out with their immense claws; grabbing hold of some of the warriors and then dropping them; as if throwing a bowling ball to knock down skittles, on to the others. They swirled around the men like a dark cloud, diving, plucking, striking and clawing their way through the ranks without mercy.

The archers fired volley after volley at this new menace; but as David predicted, the arrows didn't appear to have any impact on the creatures.

The crossbow bolts; aided by the Kavacha magic brought down quite a few for a while, but they could only fire when they were in the air, as they didn't want to risk shooting at the creatures and killing their own men instead. The creatures obviously realised this as they began to circle the warriors closer to the ground.

"We must ceasefire!" One soldier yelled as one of the bolts ripped through a group of fighting men; killing many of the defenders as well as the attackers as it missed its intended target, "We will end up killing our own men if we continue."

Jennifer heard the soldier and wanted to close her eyes to the devastation the creatures were causing but couldn't. She had to do something, but what? Then it came to her, she thought about the time she had managed to get through to the Gourtak when it was attacking Braduga and opened herself up to the Griffins. She shouted at them with her mind to stop this senseless killing and leave.

She shouted and shouted with all her strength, and just when she thought they hadn't heard her, a reply came back.

"Must kill, master commands it!" Replied a Griffin.

The Griffins seemed to hover over the defenders for a moment, though David couldn't understand why. They had been ripping the defenders apart as the bolts stopped firing and David had been close to tears as he witnessed the carnage they had inflicted. He had tried to think of some way of stopping them, willing the book to help him, but as images appeared of one thing or another, he knew they wouldn't work. Now the Griffins waited.

He quickly looked over at his sister, it was obviously her doing, she was stood perfectly still with her eyes closed and her breathing laboured, concentrating on what could only be the Griffins.

Had she been able to stop the creatures? Would they leave and let men fight against men, or would they even help their cause? Could Jennifer get through to them? Everything went through David's mind as he watched his sister, and then an idea came to him. Now he had momentarily stopped thinking about the problem, the answer had revealed itself to him. He wasn't sure if it would work but if the creatures resumed their attack he would certainly give it a try, anything was better than watching them decimated their soldiers this way.

"You must stop this killing! It is wrong to kill these men. Please stop this now!" She told the Griffins.

"Master commands it; we must do what master commands or be punished." The Griffin replied in confusion and fear.

Jennifer could feel the emotions of the Griffins now, a link between the creatures and the Truth Seer had been established in some small way. She knew that all the Griffins were frightened of this master they spoke of, but she had to try and get through to them if she could.

"Stop this killing," she said to them, "and I will help you escape your master's wrath." She promised them.

She may have gotten through to the Griffins then if not for the voice she heard through the link that commanded them. "KILL THEM! KILL THEM ALL!" It commanded.

It was such a malevolent voice, full of hatred and anger, but it commanded obedience, and she knew the Griffins had to obey. The link between her and the creatures shattered then even though she tried again and again to reinstate the link.

Jennifer opened her eyes and looked at David's hopeful expression. That look died when she shook her head in dismay, "They have to kill, they are more afraid of their master than anything else, they have no choice." She cried in dismay at the creatures' plight.

David nodded and closing his eyes, he pictured the words from the book and opened himself up to them, the magic and the power consumed his thoughts. When he finally opened his eyes, he didn't really know what to expect but using his hands to direct the flows of magic he unleashed it at the Griffins.

Balls of white lightening escaped from his hands as he directed one after the other towards the Griffins. He hadn't expected balls of lightning; it wasn't how the book described the force he was to unleash, but it was working. The lightning balls hit their intended targets savagely; knocking the Griffins from the skies. It appeared to only stun the creatures, but once on the ground, the defenders attacked the creatures with vigour; slashing and stabbing them beneath their armoured scaled hides before they could regain their wits.

David could feel his strength ebb away as he created ball after ball of white lightning. He knew his strength wouldn't last long, but he had to keep going, the soldiers' lives depended on him now.

"David." Sukhoi said trying to get his attention.

"What is it Sukhoi, I'm a little busy here." He replied.

"Let the Kavacha help you." He said.

David looked at his friend then, though he continued to create the lightning balls and throw them at the Griffin. "How?" He asked.

"Open your mind to the Kavacha, seek them out and feel their presence. The Kavacha have a little magic, locate that magic and then open yourself up to it. Draw from them their magic and use it." Sukhoi offered.

David stopped making the lightning balls and concentrated on the magic in Sukhoi. Quite unexpectedly his tattoo began to throb and then suddenly his mind exploded as he felt the Kavacha magic held by his friend and the other Kavacha. His eyes burned for a brief moment and he couldn't help but close them. But when he re-opened them he could see Sukhoi's tattoo on his neck blinking like a beacon. When he looked around the battlements at the other Kavacha, he could see all their tattoos and feel their power, it was intoxicating.

"Can you sense us?" Sukhoi asked, obviously oblivious to the tattoo's power.

"Yes, I can see you all." David replied amazed at the potential power at his fingertips.

"Use what little magic we have, combine it with yours and direct that power at our enemies." Sukhoi offered again.

There was more than a "little power" he thought, but concentrated on the task at hand. He thought about the link he now had with the other Kavacha and the immensity of the power at his disposal. It was too much for one person alone to control he believed, and thought about the book of knowledge once again. Immediately the book offered a different solution in his head.

David laughed out loud as Sukhoi watched him with a worried frown on his face.

"It's ok, I'm not going mad, but I've got a better idea." He replied to Sukhoi's inquisitive face.

With that he opened himself up to the magic, and then opened up all the Kavacha to the same magic. The look on Sukhoi's face was priceless.

The book revealed that the link worked both ways, if he performed any magic used from the book, he could pass that knowledge on to the other Kavacha. They could, effectively, copy everything he did.

With this realisation, one of the Kavacha near Sukhoi suddenly created a small ball of lightning and threw it at a Griffin. Then another Kavacha did the same thing, and then another, until all the Kavacha were creating the balls and attacking the creatures.

David couldn't help but laugh as he watched the looks of wonder on the Kavacha faces as they produced the balls of lightning and then threw their creations at the foul creatures attacking their friends and family.

The onslaught was so intense that the Griffins had to retreat away from the city or pay the price, but still the lightning balls came even though they began to fizzle out before they got anywhere near the creatures.

"You can rest now Dave." He heard a whisper by his ear. Jennifer stood by his shoulder and knew that he was exhausted, even though he continued to smile at her.

"Did you see what we all did?" He asked here excitedly.

"Yes." She replied but you should rest now, let the other Kavacha do their bit.

He nodded briefly, he realised that he was exhausted, but couldn't take his eyes away from the battlefield below. Some of his friends were down there fighting for their lives; there must be something else he could do to help them.

The defenders were amazed by the balls of lightning from their battlements attacking the Griffins and sensing victory, they charged with renewed vigour, pushing back the attack. David watched them and felt that they had a chance, his attack on the Griffins and the continued attack by the Kavacha had made a difference. Maybe they could defeat this army, he was infused by hope. Unfortunately it was short lived, and he let out a deep sigh of despair as the next wave of Koutla attacked and with them hundreds more Griffins.

Maroc looked at the advancing troops and quickly assessed the situation. There were too many of them he realised, they had to continue this fight from within the city. He shouted the order to retreat, which was shouted along the line of defenders and they slowly began to withdraw, fighting as they went. The gates began to open on hearing the order with additional archers appearing to offer covering fire. They had accomplished all they could, but now they were exhausted.

Unfortunately, the attacking Koutla and Griffins had other ideas, and tried to stop them from leaving the battlefield, pushing forward and cutting down all in their way as they tried to retreat. The Kavacha on the battlements were exhausted from creating the balls of lightning and only a few managed to keep the attack going. There were hundreds more Griffins now and they just couldn't cope with that amount of the creatures, it was going to be a massacre.

"No!" David shouted in utter dismay as he saw their predicament.

There was a loud roar from the sky above him and was relieved to see that it wasn't some new menace sent to attack them, but their friends Hash and Sak. Everyone; from the warriors below, to the circling Griffins, paused what they were doing to watch the Dragons as they dominated the sky above the city. Then the Dragons screeched at the Griffins once more and began their attack. Hash and Sak were enormous compared to the Griffins and it soon became apparent that they were no match for the majestic creatures.

They ploughed into them as if they were nothing more than flies, beating them with their wings, tails, and arms as the Griffins tried to escape their fury.

Jennifer was overcome with elation at seeing her friends; they had arrived just in time to save the city's defenders as they retreated back behind the city walls.

The Griffins attacked the Dragons in groups, realising their ineffectiveness singularly. They tried to overpower them with strength of numbers alone but Hash and Sak were wise to this tactic and didn't give the Griffins the opportunity. They were larger, stronger and faster and more importantly; wiser than the Griffins and they used all these attributes to battle the creatures.

The Dragons managed to protect the last of the warriors until they were safely behind the gates to the frustration of the Griffins and the enemy archers who were shooting at them relentlessly. Once inside and safe, the Dragons roared once more at the fleeing Griffins before they too flew into the city and to the cheering inhabitants.

"You were fantastic!" Jennifer shouted at the Dragons as they descended to the ground at the foot of the battlements, where she was standing with her brothers and Sukhoi. A crowd had gathered to welcome the Dragons and people were cheering them excitedly; relief evident as they watched their battered and bloody warriors return to the safety of the city. The situation could have been much worse without the arrival of the Dragons to help their cause.

"My friends, you arrived just in time, thank you." Sukhoi said as he bowed to the Dragons.

A horn blew from beyond the walls of the city and they heard raucous shouts of elation coming from the defenders as news spread that the enemy forces were retreating rapidly from the battlefield.

Everyone physically blew a sigh of relief at the unexpected reprieve; many of the young soldiers laughing at this welcome turn of events, while the veterans merely smiled. They knew the battle was far from over. As both the young and the old soldiers; battered and bruised, filed past the Dragons, they were greeted by loved ones, family and friends, who cried unashamedly at seeing their brave soldiers return to them safe. There were plenty of women and children available to offer aide with water, ointments, bandages and food. Everyone trying to offer what assistance they could to the brave soldiers who had fought so hard.

"Braduga! Socata!" Christopher shouted excitedly, as through the crowd Sukhoi's Ruedin appeared.

They were cradling an injured Faran between them, who had a nasty gash across his left leg. Behind them came Maroc; who was supporting another of his sons; Bamako, who was bloodied and bleeding, though the cause of the injury wasn't too clear at the moment.

Two old women appeared from nowhere and began to assess the injuries, prodding and feeling with deft hands as the two men were placed on the ground. Maroc remained with his sons as Braduga and Socata walked wearily over to the group.

Everyone greeted each other fondly before Sukhoi asked the pair of warriors, "Are you injured?"

"No Sukhoi," Socata replied, "Just exhausted." He said and everyone could see the dark circles around his eyes and the gaunt look both he and Braduga had on their faces.

"Sukhoi, "Braduga said, getting the Kavacha's attention, "Where did those lightning balls come from that knocked the Griffins from the sky?" He asked in open wonder.

Sukhoi smiled before answering, "Our Kavacha Master, David." Sukhoi replied, slapping him on the back.

David looked at Sukhoi and turned bright red in embarrassment, though he didn't know why he was embarrassed about something that had obviously saved lives. "Not only me," He replied, "but all the Kavacha."

"Yes," Sukhoi said then, as if remembering, "But you opened up the link to allow all the Kavacha to copy your magic. It was from you that we knew how to create those lightning balls." Sukhoi told him.

"It seemed the best way to make the magic work." David offered.

"I am just happy that we have a Kavacha Master to show us this magic." Sukhoi added sombrely.

David was a little shocked by this revelation, "Surely you or one of the other Kavacha could have done the same thing?" He asked.

"I am the First of the Kavacha David, I did not have the knowledge to open up the link and I have never tried to create those lightning balls before." He admitted. "Only a Kavacha Master could achieve such a feat."

David was shocked but searched the book in his mind for any more references to the Kavacha Master and his abilities. There weren't many and nothing more was revealed about the link to the other Kavacha. But there were many references to creating numerous weapons of magic and was surprised by Sukhoi's admission.

"What about the spells and incantations in the book! There are lots listed." David added, shocked that the Kavacha hadn't used this knowledge before.

Sukhoi returned his shocked look with one of his own; as much as he ever looked shocked that was. "We have but there is nothing in the book about those lightning balls."

David was stunned, not in the book. He had seen the words in his mind; they must be from the book.

"You must be mistaken Sukhoi, I clearly saw the words." He said adamantly.

"You may have seen the words David, but they were not from our book." Sukhoi replied just as adamantly.

The Kavacha and the Kavacha Master stared at each other, each with their own thoughts on this strange revelation until Christopher broke the silence.

"Does it really matter? " He said. "The main thing is that it worked and you all created the lightning thingies and they helped save the day."

"Yes, you are right Christopher." Sukhoi said smiling at the boy fondly.

David nodded and offered a weak smile; he let the subject drop, though he couldn't stop thinking about the words that had appeared in his mind. The words had to be in the book, Sukhoi must have been mistaken, where else would the words come from if not from the book, he reasoned.

"I think maybe we should all get some rest," Sukhoi suggested, "They will probably resume their attack once they have re-grouped."

Jennifer had been having a conversation with the Dragons while David and Sukhoi had been talking about the lightning balls, but now she addressed everyone with some urgent news.

"There is something you should know." She said quietly, as if she wasn't sure she should say anything at all.

"What is it Jennifer?" Sukhoi asked, one raised eyebrow waiting for her to answer.

She looked at everyone then and the colour appeared to drain from her face as she answered. "Hash has just informed me that the second army has arrived." She replied.

General Kormask was fuming; he had never experienced such a defeat as this. He expected the Griffins alone to be sufficient to destroy the city's defenders. Where had those balls of lightning come from? He had never seen anything like them before, and they had helped to kill most of the first wave of the Griffins, his Lord had sent him.

Not only that, the rest of the city's defendants had escaped with the arrival of the two Dragons. He could see all his meticulous planning disintegrating before him.

He had called his troops back when he saw the gates finally close, he had to re-group and think how to recover from this set-back. He had to think of it as a setback; nothing else would be tolerated.

"How many men are still able to fight?" He asked one of the many officers he had congregated in his tent.

"About three thousand give or take a hundred, general." The man replied.

Three thousand, he thought to himself, how could this have happened, three thousand from eight, he was dumbstruck.

"And the Griffins?" He asked, "Any reports on how many are still alive?"

"We think just over two hundred General." Another answered with little enthusiasm.

It was worse than he expected, only two hundred left from over six hundred, it was inconceivable.

"General!" A lieutenant shouted as he entered the tent, breathing hard with his uniform in disarray from the battle.

"What is it?" He shouted back, trying in vain to hold his temper.

The lieutenant gulped before replying, "Lord Driss has arrived and wants a report on our progress."

"The second army are forming up directly behind the Koutla." Christopher reported to his brother and sister when he re-entered their room for the fifth time in the last couple of hours. He had been in and out of the room regularly to keep them updated on what was happening since retiring there earlier to rest. Sukhoi had insisted on both of them trying to get some rest and sleep if possible to conserve their energy. Reluctantly they had agreed; not that they had been able to get much rest, let alone sleep. The city itself was preparing now for a siege; as they couldn't very well send out what was left of their soldiers to face an army at least five times their number, even with the Dragons and the Kavacha to help them. The incessant noise from outside their window only meant that no one really was expected to get much rest. Christopher had already reported that all their friends were alive and well; if somewhat battered. Both Faran and Bamako would soon recover from their injuries and Hannah had found her brother Thane with some young women, who were extremely attentive to a few cuts and bruises he had acquired. Thane had been happy to stay with the women longer, but Hannah had almost had to drag her brother away from them bodily, to his amusement and that of his brothers when he mentioned it later. Christopher had been out among the soldiers since they arrived back behind the walls, looking to talk with Braduga and Socata and the rest of their friends, but they had been busy making preparations for the siege. David had been exhausted by linking with the other Kavacha. The effort of just holding on to the immense reserve of power had drained him more than he realised, and now he was resting, trying to recuperate before the next onslaught began, when Christopher entered the room yet again.

"Is it as large as they say?" David asked his brother when he got the opportunity to get a word in edge ways. He was sure Christopher liked the sound of his own voice, from the amount of chattering he did lately. But as he stared at his brother he didn't really need his nod to confirm his worst fears.

David looked at Jennifer with an expression bordering on defeat. "I don't know how long we can last this time?" He said. "I'm not sure we can continue to create the lightning balls for the same length of time."

"Is there something else you could use?" She asked hopefully.

"I've been searching my mind, but solutions only present themselves when I really need them. It's difficult to prepare without knowing what's available." He conceded.

"Is there nothing you can do?" She asked.

"I will have to speak to Sukhoi about it, but to be honest, if I can't think of a way; and I'm supposed to be the Master Kavacha, then I'm not sure how much help Sukhoi would be!" He replied apprehensively.

"Seems like a good idea." She offered, sensing that her brother wasn't happy that he couldn't think of anything to help them with their predicament.

"Any idea how you're suppose to defeat Nuba Driss?" David asked her changing the subject, "If you could do that soon, maybe we can put an end to all this killing."

"If I knew that." She replied indignantly, "Don't you think I would have done something by now."

"Sorry." David said abashed, he knew she would have ended this if she could.

"No, I'm sorry, this is all so crazy. Why do people have to fight all the time? It doesn't solve anything!" She finished.

"I know Jen. Especially when it's our friends that are doing the fighting out there." He agreed.

"I wish I knew what to do?" She said shaking her head in frustration.

"Well, I'm sure you'll know what to do when the time comes." David added.

"What about the Griffins?" Christopher asked, "Didn't you say, you thought you almost got through to them?"

"Hmm, maybe," She considered, "but it didn't do much good and I'm not sure I could do it again. Even if I did, Nuba Driss had such a strong hold over them that they were terrified to go against his wishes."

"Would it be worth trying to get through to them again, do you think?" David asked.

"I'll try anything Dave. If I could get them to turn against Nuba Driss, it would be one less thing to worry about." She replied.

Chapter Thirty One

They were both walking down the brightly lit corridor, devoid of all sense of feeling for their surroundings as they concentrated on the figure before them. They could feel each other shaking in fear and anticipation as they moved closer to the figure that had yet to acknowledge their presence.

It had its back to them as they quietly drew closer, and was bending slightly forward as if looking at something. They couldn't determine what it could be because the figure's body was obscuring their view.

The figure spoke, "You can not defeat me." It rasped at them finally acknowledging their presence.

"We must!" The Nadym Varsk shouted back.

"You think you two can make a difference?" The figure laughed at them.

"Yes." They said together.

The figure turned then towards them and as it did they could see what it had been looking at, there in the figure's embrace was Christopher.

They both screamed!

"Dave, Dave, wake up!" Jennifer shouted as she shook her brother. They had decided to try and get some sleep but Jennifer hadn't really expected to drop off so soon. The dream had woken her with a dreaded fear that she hadn't experienced before. Her body wouldn't stop shaking and she was drenched in sweat.

Groggily, David woke to see his sister's face wet with tears, "What? Is Chris ok?" He asked.

Shocked, she replied and asked, "Why would you say that?"

"Nothing, sorry I was just having a bad dream when you woke me." He answered.

"Was Chris in that dream?" She asked her face stricken and pale.

"Yes." He replied eventually, taking the time to look at her face this time as he heard the fear in her voice. "Did you just have a dream about Nuba Driss?" He asked her gently.

"Yes, but..." She looked into his eyes then, "You had the same dream!" She realised.

"I've been dreaming about him for weeks," he declared, "but this time it was different. This time Christopher was in the dream and he was in trouble." He said quietly.

"Was that definitely Nuba Driss? I never saw his face." She asked. She found she was still trembling, but couldn't help herself.

"I think so, I've never seen his face," David conceded, "but it must be him." He replied on reflection.

"What are we going to do?" She asked him then.

"I'm not sure, it could be just what it seems, a dream I suppose?" He suggested. All his dreams had generally been the same; the corridor, himself and Nuba Driss, now both his sister and brother had entered his dreams. He didn't know what that meant, but no one decided what they dreamed about, it just happened, didn't it?

"I don't think anything here is just what it seems, it must mean something, the only question is, what?" She asked, although it seemed she was saying it more to herself than to him.

Truth Seer Prohesy, Book One of The Legacy

David had thought originally that his dreams were some sort of warning; especially as Nuba Driss was in them, and maybe the mage had something to do with his dreams, but it was all speculation. He suggested to his sister, "Well there's nothing we can do about it now, we'll just have to keep an eye on Chris and keep him out of trouble."

Jennifer nodded, "Agreed." She replied.

"My Lord I offer no excuses." General Kormask addressed Nuba Driss in the newly constructed pavilion. It was dark inside, with the only light coming from one small candle and a faint glow coming from something his master had in his hands.

"I have read the report General," Nuba Driss rasped, "You have done well."

The general was shocked; he had done nothing of the kind and told his Lord this.

Nuba Driss sighed and explained, "You have found their strengths and weaknesses general, information that I can now use to defeat them. We know they have two Dragons and they have directed some small magic against our forces. From all the reports I've received, you could have done nothing to combat any of this, therefore you have done well."

General Kormask nodded but was surprised how his Lord could dismiss the Kavacha magic as just some small inconvenience. "My Lord, may I remind you that this "small magic" killed two thirds of the Griffins you gave me." The general said.

"Yes General, I am fully aware of that. Don't worry about their magic now, I will deal with it."

"But..." He began.

Nuba Driss interrupted him, "I will deal with it I said. If their magic had been focused and controlled as it could be, they could have destroyed all of the Griffins in one go. But even then, it would have been nothing in comparison to the magic I have at my disposal. They are nothing but weak amateurs General, weak and pathetic fools who are dabbling in things they shouldn't be." Nuba Driss explained. He didn't usually explain things to anyone but he wanted the general to know how powerful he was. He wanted him to know how inferior the Kavacha were, and more importantly he wanted him to know because he needed the general to help him destroy them.

General Kormask smiled with relief; Lord Driss wasn't holding him accountable for this defeat.

"I want you to do something for me General." Nuba Driss said after a moments pause.

"Anything my Lord." He replied soberly.

"I want you to lead my army against the city."

The general was stunned, "My Lord, that is a great honour. But surely you would want to lead the army yourself?" The general couldn't believe what the Lord Driss was offering him. If he was given command of the army, it would be the same as saying to everyone that he was the "Commanding in Chief" over the entire Imazaghan army. A title only held by Nuba Driss himself in the past.

"There is something more important that I must attend to, will you lead the army?" He asked the general.

"Yes my lord." He replied without hesitation. This was one honour he could not and would not refuse.

He couldn't think what Lord Driss would regard as more important than the assault on the city. He couldn't believe that anything was more important than attacking their oldest enemy. They had prepared for this battle for centuries. It hadn't been easy converting the Koutla Raiders to their cause, but with promises of wealth and vengeance; on the tribes that had abandoned them, they had agreed to attack the three tribes. They had sent countless spies into Sakhalin to obtain as much strategic information as possible and now here they were, facing their adversaries and exacting their own vengeance on the descendants that had banished their ancestors from their own country.

Well, he thought, if his Lord wanted to do something else and give him the glory, so be it. Who was he to argue!

"Go then." Nuba Driss demanded, "Destroy the three tribes and return our people to their birthplace."

"As you command!" General Kormask said as he saluted and left the pavilion to lead his Imazaghan army to victory.

As the tent flaps closed behind the general a figure removed itself from the shadows and approached the faint light.

"We must enter the city now my Lord Driss, before it is too late!" Belmokhtar announced.

"Yes Belmokhtar, it is time." Nuba Driss replied, "Finally it is time." He added more quietly.

The city bells began to ring as soon as the lookouts saw any indication that the immense army was moving in the city's direction.

Orders and commands were passed immediately around as everyone was given some duty or other to perform.

The three Barnes children were already on the battlements and watching the approaching army with apprehension and trepidation. They were accompanied by Sukhoi, Braduga and Socata as they watched the army; in silence, marching toward the city.

As they watched the army marching ever closer, they were each lost to their own thoughts. David was considering how to use the Kavacha knowledge to protect the city and its inhabitants. He was also trying to find some magic that could stop the Griffins; kill them even, if he couldn't stop them.

Jennifer however, had been trying to mentally prepare for another attempt at trying to speak with the Griffins, though she wasn't sure how successful she would be. If she could only re-establish the link she had before and break the hold Nuba Driss had over them. Maybe, just maybe, they would stop all this killing and leave. She knew the hold he had was strong, but she had to do something. She had felt; through the link, that they despised the evil mage but had no choice but to do as he commanded. She had felt their pain and suffering under his control and her heart wanted to cry out to them.

Christopher; standing beside his mentors, wanted nothing more than to show them how much he had learnt in such a short time. He wanted them to be proud of his abilities. He couldn't speak with Dragons like his sister, or perform magic like his brother, but he was extremely proficient with both the sword and the bow. He still had much to learn about both, but he was prepared to learn everything he could, he needed to learn everything he could. He had felt so helpless when the twin Koutla had attacked them; he had never felt so helpless and useless in his very short life, but not anymore. He may develop his own abilities in the future, but he wasn't prepared to wait on a maybe. Which was why, every waking moment was spent on honing his skills and developing new ones.

The Dragons were also watching from atop the towers, but their focus was on the Griffins and their attack, should Jennifer's attempts at breaking the link between them and Nuba Driss fail.

The approaching army had come well prepared, the small party on the battlements could see. They watched mesmerised, as the army pushed and pulled their enormous siege engines into place. They watched as they moved crossbows, catapults, trebuchets and numerous other weapons of destruction, closer and closer toward the city walls. This new army had obviously been planning and preparing for this battle for a very long time, they were here to destroy the city, here to destroy the three tribes. There was an audible sigh from the crowd of people on the battlements as each of the weapons were brought forward. They knew this was going to be a long and bloody battle, one that many of them wouldn't survive. But, they still maintained a steely look of determination in their eyes and they faced the advancing army with courage and strength of purpose. They would fight together and maybe die together, but they still had the Nadym Varsk, they still had hope.

"Do we stand a chance?" Christopher asked as he viewed the numerous contraptions and thousands of soldiers.

Braduga smiled at his young protégé, "Not much," he replied honestly, "but be steadfast Chris, with your brother and sister's help, we may yet prevail." He offered.

"The Griffins are coming!" Jennifer shouted in warning and the bells began to ring in unison at the promise of an attack.

Orders were shouted up and down the battlements to prepare for the attack. Soldiers quickly loaded the crossbows, while others collected their weapons and prepared for the siege engines to move forward. Archers were quickly summoned and they prepared their arrows so they could quickly retrieve them as needed. Then the Kavacha arrived through a chorus of cheers and adopted their pre-determined locations. Their earlier exploits against the Griffins had gained them even greater respect and reverence than they already had, with many soldiers nodding and bowing to them respectfully as they walked past. They were ready to do their duty, they were ready to link with the Kavacha Master and create whatever magic he could find to help them ensure victory.

Sukhoi turned to David, "Are you ready my friend?" He asked.

David looked toward the Kavacha as they lined the battlements and stood there silently like ghostly statues as they returned his look and waited for his magic to flow into their minds. Then he turned to the First of Kavacha and replied, "I'm ready, I will do what I can." He promised.

Sukhoi's eyes seemed to bore into his very soul, "I know." He said.

Jennifer looked away from the exchange and taking a deep breath she reached out with her mind, searching, looking for the Griffins.

It was at that moment that they heard the order to attack the city, and the Imazaghan army with the remaining Koutla charged forward with grappling hooks, wooden ladders and siege engines. The defenders were ready and prepared for the attack and the battle finally began in earnest. Archers from both sides were firing at each other without pause. It was easier for the defenders because they only had to aim at one solid impenetrable mass, but the enemy archers still managed to pick off many soldiers as they tried to stop the ladders and grappling hooks from taking hold.

The Griffins attacked the city by dropping rocks onto the defenders from above, until Hash and Sak couldn't wait any longer and attacked them with an intense fury.

Crossbow bolts fired into the air trying to catch the Dragons as they tore into the Griffins. Hash and Sak were aware of them though and easily avoided them, whilst maintaining their assault on the Griffins. David opened up the link with the Kavacha, but the only magic that came to mind was the lightning balls, which he decided to employ until something better could be thought of. Wave after wave of lightning balls were focused on the Griffins; knocking them to the ground, only for them to rise back into the air once they recovered from being stunned, to the dismay of the Kavacha and the soldiers watching.

Jennifer tried desperately to make the link once more with the Griffins as they attacked the city. She shouted at them to stop this madness. She commanded them to cease their attacks and then finally begged them to stop killing her friends.

The last gave her the opening she desperately needed. "We can not!" Came the familiar voice of the Griffin she had spoken to before. "We must obey our master!"

"I can help you!" She shouted back. "You could be free of your master."

"No one can help us, our master is too strong!" The Griffin argued.

"Can I at least try?" She asked, hoping with all her heart that the Griffins would let her.

The silence was deafening as she waited for the Griffin to respond to her request. Meanwhile, they continued with their attack on the city, and she watched in horror as they hurled rocks at the city defenders. Demolishing the walls with their throws as the rocks crashed into them, bowling soldiers off the battlements and spraying masonry into the city below.

She had just about given up on the Griffin replying as she watched the devastation unfold that she was surprised when it came. "You can try! But we must continue to attack or our master will punish us!" The Griffin replied.

Jennifer was annoyed and elated at the same time. She had hoped that if they agreed they would at least pause in their attack, but she understood the reasons whey they couldn't. She'd just have to work quickly, before more lives were lost. She maintained the link with the Griffins and searched for the same inevitable link they must have with Nuba Driss. She found it almost immediately and instinctively realised that she could break it if she put her mind to the task. Taking a deep breath she paused briefly to steady her nerve and then she opened her mind to the link; and the link with Nuba Driss. She realised that she had little time to dally and with as much force as she could muster, she blasted the link between the Griffins and Nuba Driss, screaming with the effort as she did so.

The Griffins suddenly stopped what they were doing, shocked to realise the hold their master had over them had been severed completely. The Dragons stopped their attacks on the Griffins as they felt the force of the blast generated by Jennifer. They had never experienced such a force in all their years; it was immense. The Griffins hovered above the two armies in confusion until they eventually realised that their master had no control over them any more. David noticed the change in the Griffins immediately and on hearing his sister's scream he knew she had achieved her goal. Through his link with the Kavacha he told them to stop their attacks on the Griffins and focus their efforts on the opposing army instead.

Facing his sister, he asked. "Jen, you ok?" He asked in concern as she fell to her knees.

Jennifer looked exhausted as she held her head in her hands, tears running down her cheeks. She raised her head and looked into his concerned face, but she didn't really see it was she was still concentrating on the Griffins. She had broken the link between them and Nuba Driss and now she wanted to know if they would help them against their former master.

It didn't take much persuasion. The Griffin she had established contact with was the pride leader and he was determined to enact his vengeance on his former master at the earliest opportunity.

"Master was cruel and killed our young, we will now kill master!" It pledged.

"Be careful!" Jennifer implored them; fearing that Nuba Driss could possibly re-establish the link or failing that, punish the creatures for turning against him.

"We will!" He replied and then without hesitation the Griffins turned as one on Nuba Driss's army, attacking it with more zeal than they ever had against the defenders.

They dropped the rocks they were still carrying onto the siege engines and catapults and confusion erupted. The Imazaghan soldiers were bewildered by this change in events and couldn't understand how their allies could turn their attack on them. They desperately turned their weapons on the creatures, as they were bombarded by the fiercely vengeful pride of Griffins.

The defenders; momentarily forgotten, increased their pace of attack. Volley after volley of arrows reigned down on the army as they tried to defend themselves against the creatures that now had the free will to attack whomever they chose.

"Jen we're winning, the Griffins are pushing the army back!" David shouted with joy. He was right; the Imazaghan army began to retreat away from the fierce attack of the Griffins. Control and co-ordination of the forces breaking down under the onslaught, until even the officers in charge were running away from the frenzied attack.

Nuba Driss was still speaking with Belmokhtar about their plan when he sensed the link had been severed. "Impossible!" He exclaimed.

"What is my lord?" Belmokhtar asked in incomprehension.

Nuba Driss couldn't believe it, the girl had somehow broken his hold on the Griffins and he could hear the shouts and screams coming from his own army now to confirm that the creatures had turned on him.

Retrieving the orb from within his gown he walked outside the pavilion and watched as his creatures turned their ferociousness back on his own men.

He tried to re-establish his own link, but realised immediately that it had been totally severed. Placing the orb in front of him he looked into the depths of swirling gas.

"They will pay for this." He said quietly and then began to chant. The glow from the orb intensified as Nuba Driss recited his incantation, until finally a pale green light; shot like an arrow into the sky from the orb itself.

Nuba Driss then stopped and waited. Belmokhtar looked across at his master but remained silent until he heard thunder in the sky. He looked up and was amazed to see the Griffins begin to drop from it, to plummet to the ground. Some began to rise as they recovered their senses, but when they tried to fly again he realised that they couldn't. Roars and shrieks of frustration reverberated around the battlefield as the creatures tried in vain to rise to the air. It was a pitiful sight as the warriors from both sides watched in bewildering fascination as the Griffins struggled with this enchanted affliction.

Nuba Driss watched for a few moments in satisfaction and then he turned his back on the creatures that had until recently served him so well and walked back into his pavilion.

Jennifer couldn't believe it as she watched the Griffins fall from the sky; she thought that Nuba Driss had killed them all at first. Then she heard their confused thoughts and her heart almost broke from their anguish. Nuba Driss hadn't killed them, he had done something much worse, and he had taken away their gift of flight. The Griffins would no longer feel the wind beneath their wings; they would forever be forced to stay on the ground, flightless. He may have not been able to control them any longer to do his bidding, but he had exacted his own revenge on them and taken away the only thing that made them truly happy.

"You ok Jen?" David asked, concerned by the intense look on his sister's face and the tears that were freshly falling down her cheeks.

"How could he be so cruel?" She replied.

"What? What's happened?" He asked.

"They'll never be able to fly again, the Griffins, Nuba Driss has taken away their ability to fly." She cried.

David could hardly comprehend what that meant to the Griffins, but he immediately realised the implications of such a feat of magic. If Nuba Driss had the power to take the ability to fly away from an entire species, where did his evil power end? Surely that power surpassed that of his own and the Kavacha put together, and if that were true, what hope did they have? He physically shook as he contemplated that thought.

Chapter Thirty Two

Jennifer continued to sob for the Griffins, blaming herself for their plight as her brothers and friends tried to console her.

"Maybe you should go back to your room for now and get some rest." Sukhoi suggested gently, "Socata, will you go with her?" His friend nodded, and putting his arms around her, Socata escorted Jennifer from the battlements.

"She'll be ok Dave." Christopher promised his brother, who looked quite stricken himself by the plight of the now flightless Griffins.

They watched as the creatures; now running on all fours, fled the battlefield. They weren't pursued by either side as they made their escape. They might be flightless now, but they were still ferocious and as they weren't attacking either side, nobody wanted to get in their way.

"It's just Nuba Driss and his army against the three tribes now." Braduga stated as they all watched the last of the creatures depart from sight. "Let's show them what we're made of!" He shouted.

"It is now or never," Sukhoi announced, "pass the word to the soldiers, be prepared to throw everything we have at them when I give the order." He said.

Braduga nodded in acknowledgement and left the battlements to make preparations.

"Are you feeling ok?" Socata asked for the third time as they made their way to the children's room.

Jennifer smiled weakly at his concern but merely nodded that she was. She couldn't believe what Nuba Driss had done to the Griffins, but why was she so surprised, she had heard all the stories about how evil the mage was. It just seemed so callous, he wanted to make them suffer, rather than kill them; which she was certain he could have done, had he wished it.

It took some time to get back to the room as the streets were still littered with injured soldiers; although there were plenty of people barking orders to tidy this or that thing up. Everywhere, women and children were carrying buckets of water or bandages, jars of ointments and baskets of food. If the streets weren't full of the injured, they were filled with old and young men, selecting weapons from the carts that were trundling through the streets. Every able bodied person; whether man or woman were brandishing their weapons, waiting for their orders, whilst everyone else went about some task or other that kept them busy. Sukhoi had spoken with the other Kavacha and the message had been passed on to everyone in the city. "Be ready!" If the opportunity arose, he would ask everyone to support the city's soldiers and face Nuba Driss's army.

As she walked along; almost in a dream state, she heard the odd greeting from the people passing by. When she looked up at those people she was surprised to receive the odd nod and smile from one soldier or another. Most people in the city knew who she was now, but it still brought a tear to her eye when they acknowledged her presence. After what they and their loved ones had gone through, and what they were still going to go through, they still found the time to say hello or at least smile at her, she almost cried again. She couldn't let them see her like this, snivelling like a little girl when they had just come from a battle and were preparing to battle once more. So she gathered her strength and brushed away her tears, and began to smile at them, talking to them briefly, offering encouraging comments as she made her way to her room.

It took them quite a long time to get back to their room with Jennifer wanting to stop and talk with everyone who even looked in her direction, until Socata pointed out that she needed some rest. She agreed to go reluctantly, but go she did.

"You have a knack of getting into people's hearts." Socata commented as they reached their intended goal.

"They just needed someone to tell them that what they were doing was important, that they were needed and appreciated." She replied quietly.

"I think it was the manner, in which you did it, that they appreciated." Socata said with a smile. "You were kind and caring but steadfast and resolute at the same time." He finished.

Jennifer thought about the conversations she had had with soldiers, the mothers and their children as she had made her way back to her room and said. "They need me to be strong Socata. For them I will be strong, because I am the Nadym Varsk and they need me."

The Kavacha lined the battlements once more in their allotted places, facing the remaining might of the Imazaghan army. Every so often they would look in David's direction to see if he was doing anything. He felt their eyes on him; though he could sense their feeling without having to look at them now, the link between them and himself was that strong now. He felt their tension, their fear and anxiety, but he could also sense their sense of purpose and resolve. He wanted to laugh at how he had got himself into this situation, but he didn't have the time, the strength or the inclination. His concentration was focused on the approaching army and his mind was racing with the knowledge contained within the book of Kavacha lore. His head ached with the energy he was using to find someway of defeating this army without killing anybody else. It was so frustrating, there must be some magic contained within the book that could help him out of this dilemma. As the Kavacha Master it was his responsibility to find something to save the city, but the images swirling in his mind didn't seem to be enough. He had to think of something to attack the army with, and he had to do it quickly. Because, if he didn't think of something soon, then many more people were going to die and it would be all his fault.

"No pressure then." He said to himself as he thought of the responsibility of facing Nuba Driss's army.

He looked at the hundreds of soldiers, men, women and even children on the battlements as they waited for the attack to begin. Everyone wanted to do their bit. There were hundreds of archers poised to deliver their flights of arrows. Men were joined by women as they loaded the bolts into the dozens of crossbows arranged on the battlements. Old veterans; who wouldn't be much good in a fight, were there with long staves with iron bars on the end, ready to push back any ladders that were to be used to breech the walls of the city. While inside the city itself, Braduga, Maroc and his sons had rallied all the remaining able bodied men and boys in anticipation of one last charge on the enemy. Every available weapon; whether it be a sword or a pitch fork, was gathered up by man and boy as they lined the streets. The atmosphere was intense as everyone waited for that one command, that one verbal order that would begin a tirade of devastation upon the enemy at their gates. For glory or for defeat the city was ready to fight to the last person if need be.

They waited as the army drew closer and closer, their fear of the future barely contained. Then it happened, Sukhoi shouted the order as he watched the Imazaghan army came into range of the archers. Hundreds of arrows darkened the sky once again as the archers released them on the soldiers below. Crossbow bolts were fired and re-strung and fired again without pause as they flew into the attackers, shattering shields, weapons and men as they cut through the battlefield.

The Dragons appeared from the sky and from within their great arms they threw large boulders into the ensemble of men, knocking them over like skittles and scattering them in a frenzied panic.

But the most damage came from the Kavacha themselves. They had come quite proficient in creating the lightning balls, and as they waited for David to think of something else they could use, they hurtled the balls at the enemy soldiers mercilessly.

Volley after volley struck the warriors, to explode on impact, killing everyone within the vicinity. Screams and shouts of anguish could be heard all around as many of the soldiers laid mortally wounded or dying from one attack or another.

It was then that a dark menacing cloud appeared in the sky with lightning forking down and sizzling the air. A dark figure appeared at the rear of the army and raised its arms to the sky. The lightning that had been harmlessly striking the air suddenly turned on the city and forks of white light attacked it. As it struck the wall it exploded, men and masonry fell to the ground as strike after strike hit the city wall. Then the figure was joined by another darker figure and together they both attacked the city with balls of lightning of their own making.

Cheers rose from the attackers and encouraged them to attack with vigour. As the two dark figures attacked the city relentlessly with their dark and dangerous magic, the army pushed forward, determined to take the city.

The defenders tried desperately to continue their own attack, but the two figures didn't give them the opportunity. The Kavacha were finding it difficult to concentrate as they tried to protect themselves from the projectiles blowing great chunks of rocks from the walls and the lightning that struck them from above.

David stared at the two figures in the distance; all he could see was lightning coming from their direction, but he could hear, see and feel the effects.

He searched his mind for some knowledge that could help the Kavacha, maybe protect them in some way, but although, picture after picture and word after word came into his mind, there didn't appear to be anything that could be used in this situation.

His mind raced as he dived for cover from another bolt of lightning that hit the wall a few feet from where he had been standing; blasting rock in every direction.

"I have to find something to stop those two, something that could shield us from their magic." He said quietly to himself, frustrated by their continued attack.

Then he realised that only the book itself could help him now, maybe there was some knowledge contained within its pages that hadn't divulged itself to him yet. There was only one thing for it, he would have to retrieve the book and hope it would open itself up to him once more.

With that thought in his head he left the battlements and rushed to the Kavacha building that housed the Kavacha book of knowledge.

The building was deserted when he arrived, which wasn't unexpected considering the city was under attack. He found the book unguarded and he paused deliberately to consider whether or not he was doing the right thing. He realised he had no choice; there was nothing coming into his mind that could help them at the moment, he had to do something and he needed to do it now.

He felt the spell on the book immediately, but he didn't have the time to reconsider his actions. Focusing his power on the book he concentrated on gaining as much information from it as possible. With his hands on the book he concentrated his thoughts and felt the power of it surge into him. Words and pictures swirled in his head for a brief instant and then he was flung to the other side of the room by an unseen force, the book falling from his grasp.

Dazed and confused he regained his feet and saw to his horror that the room looked as if it had been hit by a bomb. He scrambled around in the rubble until thankfully he found the book undamaged under a large piece of wood that had once been a table.

He couldn't comprehend the damage he had done, but he really didn't have time for that either, he had found what he had been looking for, but what was he suppose to do with the book now? He had no choice, the book had to go with him, he couldn't leave it behind where anyone could get their hands on it. He left the building a few seconds later after securing the book within his robes and headed back to the battlements.

"My lord, did you feel that?" Belmokhtar asked Nuba Driss.

"Oh yes, the boy has broken the spell Belmokhtar, everything is going to plan." He replied laughing as he renewed the attacks on the city with a hearty enthusiasm he hadn't had a moment before.

The two dark figures were still attacking the city with strike after strike of lightning David noticed on his return. He had to act quickly or there wouldn't be anything left of the city. Concentrating on the image he had found in the book he opened his mind to the incantation.

He could see the words of the incantation in his mind and he tried to focus on them. The incantation was for an invisible wave of energy that he could use to act as a barrier against the magic of the two figures in the distance.

He stood then and looked out over the crumbling wall of the city, with his mind concentrating on the two figures in the distance. He didn't see the figure advancing on him from over the wall, but Christopher did, and just as it was about to thrust its sword into David's heart, Christopher turned it aside. He then turned to face the attacker but one of Maroc's archers had also seen the Imazaghan soldier's attack on David and Christopher was amazed to see four arrows protruding from the offender's heart. Christopher nodded to the archer, who returned his nod before returning to the advancing soldiers.

Oblivious to everything around him, David squeezed his hands tightly together into fists and then thrust his arms forward and opened his hands, releasing the power that he had been building toward the two figures. He couldn't really see much, though he knew that he had released some powerful force. He could just about make out a distorted wave leave him and head towards the Imazaghan army and the two figures beyond. It was almost invisible, but he could see it and feel it as it rippled through the air. As the wave reached the two figures they appeared to take a momentary step backwards, but then they carried on. David realised that the distance was too great for this wave to do any real damage so he opened the link with the other Kavacha. Maybe if he could add their strength to his, the wave would do more than be an inconvenience to the two figures. He could feel the build up of the energy as he channelled the other Kavacha's magic with his own and once more he focused his power and released it at the two figures. Again he watched and waited for the wave to reach its intended goal and when it did he was amazed and relieved to see the two figures flung backwards off their feet.

Christopher had stayed protectively next to his brother; with his sword drawn and although he couldn't see or feel the wave, he could see the effects of it in the distance as the two figures were flung backward.

David wanted to shout for joy, he raised his hands in the air and the other Kavacha acknowledged it with their own hands punching the sky in jubilation and a cheer arose.

Christopher joined in with the cheering and gave his brother a big smile when he turned to look at him.

"You ok Chris?" David asked.

"Yeah, just watching your back." He replied laughing.

A groan reverberated around the battlements then as their attention was drawn back to the two figures that were now getting back to their feet. David wanted to cry in disappointment; he knew the power that he had sent through the wave was immense, but it still hadn't been strong enough to have the desired effect on the two figures, much to his disappointment.

"My Lord, what was that?" Cried Belmokhtar astonished at the force of the attack against them.

"I don't know!" Nuba Driss replied, a slight echo of something bordering on fear entering his voice, "I've never experienced anything like it before." He finished, and coughed as he pounded his chest, trying to catch his breath or at least get the dirt from his lungs.

"It can't be the Kavacha, there is nothing written in the book that could explain that." Belmokhtar replied thoughtfully.

"Maybe there is and the boy had found it." Nuba Driss considered quietly.

"You believe the boy did that?" Belmokhtar asked in shock.

"It must be the boy!" Nuba Driss reasoned. "No one else could unleash that much power unless they were linked with other Kavacha."

"You think the boy knows how to link?" Belmokhtar asked in shock.

"Yes, and it seems he has found more spells in the book than even I anticipated." Nuba Driss considered. "I need his power Belmokhtar and I aim to get it!"

"Yes my lord, but I can not believe how much he has learnt in so short a time."

"Yes, too much and too quickly for my liking." Nuba Driss agreed, "Come Belmokhtar, we must leave the battlefield for now, the army will have to fight without us while we will fight a battle of our own."

David sighed in relief as he could just make out the two figures turn away from the city and enter a large tented structure. Not relief from seeing the two figures survive his counter attack; he was surprised to realise, but relief that he had managed to stop them; at least for now. Their magic had destroyed a good portion of the city's defences, and countless lives had been lost, he would feel no regret if he had stopped them indefinitely. He took a deep breath then and realised he felt quite dizzy, the exertion of the magic he had just unleashed had taken quite a bit out of him. His head turned swiftly towards Sukhoi when his friend cried the order to "open the gates".

Sukhoi hadn't witnessed David's successful attempt at disrupting the magical onslaught; he was too engrossed in watching everything else, but once he realised the lightning has stopped, he gave the command for the warriors in the city, to charge.

With the order given and the gates finally opened the defenders emerged eager to take the fight to their enemies once more, wielding their weapons and shouting war cries as they advanced. They cut and stabbed, slashed and plunged their weapons into the Imazaghan and Koutla army, fighting for their city, for their families and for their lives.

They may have been outnumbered, but with two of Sakhalin's greatest warriors leading them; Braduga swinging his twin swords and Maroc with twin bladed axe, wielding it just as efficiently and ruthlessly, they felt invincible. The Griffins had left the battlefield and so had the two magical figures that had caused so much carnage, but they still had the two Dragons on their side and with the Kavacha as well to assist them, they attacked with a renewed belief that they would be victorious.

Maroc and his sons, Braduga and the rest of the Ruedin were all easily recognised as they pushed through the enemy soldiers. They were skilled and experienced warriors that had been trained to the highest standards and it could be seen on the battlefield now. Every cut and thrust was precisely timed and executed with a skill that bordered on its own magic. The city's defenders could only follow behind them and dispatch anyone they left in their wake. Whereas the Ruedin were stylish and skilful from their years of training, the farmers, butchers, bakers and other tradesmen were brutish in their attacks. To them there were no rules, no style or finesse as they hammered into the enemy ranks. Their only thought was about how much damage they could inflict on their enemy, before they themselves would fall. They knew they had to give their all in this battle; even if it meant their lives. To do less would be monstrous, the three tribes had become one people, one people that acted together now to fight for their freedom, their lives and the lives of their family and friends. They knew their duty and they would not live to regret any inaction they performed this day. The Imazaghan army were well trained and quite a few were a match for the Ruedin, but not many. Even the Koutla had surprised them with their viciousness at first, but now, now the Koutla were retreating, and as they did, the Imazaghan were turning also. Heartened by this the city defenders fought harder, pushing forward and striking the enemy with brutal alacrity. They couldn't let their attackers win this day, would not let them win this day.

The Imazaghan officers shouted order after order at their soldiers, forcing them to stand firm and push forward themselves, they sneered at the retreating Koutla as they ran past. They had turned out to be cowards; as everyone had originally thought. But the Imazaghan weren't cowards, they had been waiting patiently for this day, they would not turn tail from their enemies. But then the last of the Koutla finally broke, and with them some of the Imazaghan soldiers were swept back with them. The frenzied attack of the defenders continued mercilessly and the Imazaghan soldiers realised they could do nothing to stop it. Slowly the soldiers began to retreat much to the dismay of their officers in command. The officers tried to encourage their men to continue to push, to crush anyone who stood in their way; whether they were friend or foe, but their earlier eagerness was diminishing. With even the officers realising that they could not match the skill and expertise of the Ruedin, or the intense and unrelenting ferociousness of the defenders they knew what they had to do. It was too much for them, they wouldn't allow their men to endure this amount of punishment. Their men would eventually turn on them if they continued with this suicidal attack. First one officer, then many others finally gave the order to retreat. The attack on the city had failed, and now they could only think about getting as far away from the battlefield as possible. With the order given, the men wasted little time in delaying their withdrawal, but although the Koutla were already running for their lives, the Imazaghan still showed their steel. They gave one final push forward that allowed them room to manoeuvre before they slowly began to withdraw, facing the defenders with wounded pride as they retreated from the battlefield.

General Kormask watched in horror as he saw his army begin to retreat. Amongst them were his own troops that he had trained for years, they were the best, but even they couldn't stand the assaults of the three tribes. All the glory and honour he thought he would receive after this day was slowly slipping away. He had been amazed by the spectacle his Lord and the secretive Belmokhtar had displayed earlier, but had been shocked when some unseen force had knocked them both off their feet. He had thought that the Lord Driss was indestructible. He had no reason to think otherwise until this day. But now Lord Driss and Belmokhtar had returned to the pavilion, neither of them had been seen since. He had sent messengers to Lord Driss; asking him to intervene once more and use his power, but his messengers had returned, not even gaining an audience. Eventually he had left the battlefield himself and sought out his Lord's pavilion; only to find it empty. Lord Driss; it appeared, had deserted the army in their greatest hour of need and he felt numb by the realisation that he would be held responsible. So the general stood alone in his defeat, he knew instinctively that the army could never recover from this situation to mount another attack any time soon. They had waited five hundred years for this opportunity to enact revenge on their old enemies, but all their plans had come to naught. A tear came to the corner of his eye as he watched his army return demoralised from the battlefield.

Socata opened the door and walked into the room with Jennifer following just behind him. "Try and get some rest Jennifer. I will get you some Khulanha to lift your spirits." He said as he walked over to the table to retrieve the revitalising liquid.

"Khulanha, just what the doctor ordered." Said a dark shadow with a raspy voice, from beside the window.

Socata swivelled immediately; his axe expertly drawn and coming to bear in the direction of the voice.

"Stop exactly where you are Socata or the girl dies." Came another voice from behind him. The second figure had sneaked into the room and now held Jennifer firmly in his grasp with a dagger at her throat.

Socata turned his head to see Belmokhtar standing just behind Jennifer holding her tightly with a wicked half smile on his lips.

"What are you doing Belmokhtar?" He asked in shock and incomprehension.

"Belmokhtar works for me." The figure rasped again with a little chuckle.

"But he's the Keeper!" Socata said with incredulity.

"The Keeper!" Belmokhtar spat, "Holder of the Kavacha knowledge. It is nothing but child's play compared to the magic my lord has."

"Your lord?" Socata asked as he watched the figure almost glide from the window further into the room. He could hear no footsteps, as it moved closer to Jennifer and could see her eyes widen in horror as it stopped just in front of her. Socata couldn't move even if he wanted to, the figure held some power over him that he didn't recognise at first, then slowly it dawned on him. He recognised a feeling long forgotten, it was fear!

"So," the figure said quietly, "this is the great Nadym Varsk is it?"

Socata couldn't see the figure's face; but he didn't have to, he knew it now for what it was, Nuba Driss. He thought he could even smell the stench of corruption and evil emanating from him. He could also sense his own fear now that he had put a name to it. He felt it in the pit of his stomach as the hairs on the back of his neck stood on end. Whether it was a spell or not, Socata realised he couldn't move his body except his head. He glanced at Jennifer and wanted to weep at what he saw. His own fear reflected back on him, but it was this stricken face of fear that made him stamp down on his own fears and find the strength to address the creature again. Yes he was afraid, but he wasn't prepared to let his fear get the better of him, so he faced Nuba Driss and tried to relax. Hoping he could find the one opportunity that would allow him to put an end to the foul creature before him.

"What do you want?" Socata asked, trying to control his shaking body.

"Nothing now, "Nuba Driss replied, "I would have liked to have taken the boy as well, but the girl will do for now. The boy will follow eventually if he wants to see his sister alive again. But I must admit, I didn't think it would be this easy." He said sounding almost disappointed.

"What do you want them for?" Socata asked, trying to keep the evil mage busy, in the hope that help would come soon.

"I have great plans for the pair of them, but my plans don't concern you. Come Belmokhtar, it is time to leave." He ordered.

"Wait." Socata shouted. "Take me and leave the girl!" He offered.

Nuba Driss laughed. "Why would I want to do that you stupid man, it is the Nadym Varsk that I want, not you."

Socata still couldn't move, but he couldn't let them take Jennifer away, he had to do something. "So," he said, "I take it you believe the prophesy then? That says the Nadym Varsk will destroy you!" He taunted. He needed more time; he had to try and stall Nuba Driss for as long as possible, then hopefully, help would come.

"I know of the prophesy made by the Guardian!" Nuba Driss said raising his voice in anger, "But it doesn't say the Nadym Varsk will defeat me and let's face it, do you seriously believe that this little girl can defeat me? I am more powerful than you could ever imagine little man and when I combine her powers with mine, no one will be able to stop me, no one!" He cried in a crazed voice.

"I will stop you!" David said as he appeared by the door. He had entered quietly, and then closed the door behind him. "Release my sister Belmokhtar or I will kill you where you stand." He sounded more confident than he actually was, he was shaking with fear, but he was amazed that his voice sounded so clear and level that he wasn't even sure he had spoken those words himself. He had heard Jennifer's cry for help in his mind just a few minutes earlier. He wasn't sure if he had been daydreaming at first, but he wasn't about to take the chance, so he had rushed back to their room and then he had heard the voices within. He had to make a decision on what he should do next and what would be the consequences of any actions he would take. Did he have enough time to go and get help or would he have to try and do something himself. He couldn't take the chance of anything happening to his sister so he had stealthily managed to get into the room.

"I'm glad you are here David," Nuba Driss said, "It has save me the trouble of trying to find you."

David didn't say anything; he was trying to think of some way of getting his sister away from Belmokhtar.

"I believe congratulations are in order!" Nuba Driss continued.

David couldn't bring himself to say anything, so Nuba Driss continued, "Yes, you have done well my boy. Haven't been in Sakhalin two minutes and already you've earned your spurs and become a Kavacha Master, quite astonishing really."

David continued to stare at the apparition before him, he had seen this figure so many times in his dreams that he wasn't quite sure that he wasn't dreaming now.

As if Nuba Driss had read his mind, he continued, "I can see you're lost for words. I suppose it's one thing seeing me in your dreams but to actually see me in the flesh is something else, wouldn't you agree?" He asked.

David struggled to stop trembling; Nuba Driss was standing right in front of him and he was petrified of what the mage could do to him, what he could do to Jennifer. He knew he was a Kavacha Master, but Nuba Driss was a master magician that had walked the land for hundreds of years. What could David do against such a man that had the power to stop an entire species from flying again? He was also stunned when Nuba Driss mentioned his dreams, the dreams that had plagued him even before he had arrived in Sakhalin. But he was surprised that when he thought of those dreams now, he felt some semblance of control returning to his body; infused by thoughts of the corridor. He felt the power within him raging to come out and face this demon that was threatening them all. He had to think, he had to find something he could use to stop this mad man. He had absorbed the knowledge of the Kavacha, he knew magic, surely there was something in the book that could assist him now, he thought. He tried to conjure up any image, anything that could help, but nothing appeared. Here he was standing in front of the Bain of Sakhalin, the defiler of his dreams, and he could think of nothing to help. He thought about the prophesy that was also contained in the book, the same book secured within his robe, but there was nothing there to help him, only a reference to the Nadym Varsk. Jennifer was the Nadym Varsk and she was the only one that could defeat Nuba Driss. But there were no clues contained within the book in how that was to be accomplished. He turned his head to look at his sister, and he couldn't help but feel guilty for bringing her and their brother to this place. She looked back at him; he could tell that she was desperately trying to control her own fear. He smiled at her then and she managed to smile back at him.

That one small smile infused him with a little courage; he may not be able to stop Nuba Driss, but he knew he would find someway of helping his sister defeat this monster, he had to.

"Give me the book!" Nuba Driss commanded.

Again David was shocked, how did he know he had the book?

Socata turned to look at David in surprise and asked. "You've got the book of Kavacha Lore?"

Looking guiltily at Sukhoi's Ruedin he nodded in reply.

"Hand it over now or I will have Belmokhtar slit your sister's throat." Nuba Driss rasped.

Belmokhtar increased his grip on Jennifer and she cried out in pain.

"You can't give him the book David." Socata shouted outraged.

"She's my sister Socata, what choice do I have?" He replied to his friend. "Let my sister go and you can have the book." David bargained with the evil mage.

The dark figure appeared to contemplate this for a moment before giving the order to Belmokhtar to release the girl. On doing so, she rushed over to her brother as he retrieved the book from his robe and flung it to the deft hands of the Keeper.

"Why are you doing this? Why are you trying to destroy all these people? What have they ever done to you? What have we ever done to you?" He continued calmly, trying to keep his voice evenly pitched, to show that he wasn't afraid; even though he was.

Nuba Driss stood there silently, as Belmokhtar handed him the sacred book. He caressed it almost lovingly before he put it inside his robe.

As he did so, David noticed a faint green light emanating from a small round sphere inside Nuba Driss's robe. He knew immediately that the sphere was the Dragon's orb. He wanted to smile at that bit of news but he had to concentrate on the situation at hand.

"What have you done to me?" Nuba Driss finally replied. "You seriously don't know, do you?" Nuba Driss asked amazed by the realisation.

"Know what?" David replied, what didn't he know? What was he suppose to know? What was this all about?

Nuba Driss began to cackle with mirth until a coughing fit made him stop.

"I shouldn't be surprised that he didn't tell you." Nuba Driss replied a moment later.

David looked at Jennifer who had the same confused look on her face that he probably had on his, before he turned back to the figure.

Who didn't tell them what? David thought about asking but didn't want to give Nuba Driss the satisfaction, so he just waited for the mage to continue.

Unfortunately, it was at that point that Hash came crashing into the room through the window, shattering glass everywhere, with a savage cry. He was followed almost immediately by Sak. No sooner had they entered the room, than Nuba Driss disappeared, as if he had been preparing his escape all the time. He had thrown something on the floor and instantly a bright white flash blinded the occupants and a white mist obscured any view of him and anyone else for that matter.

Hash and Sak had also heard Jennifer's cry for help and quickly left the battlefield to help. It was one thing to help fight for the city, but not at the expense of helping the only person who could communicate with them and help them achieve their own quest. So they had answered her cry for help and come as fast as they could.

Sukhoi had been watching the Dragons when they had suddenly stopped attacking the Imazaghan army and had disappeared somewhere in the city. Realising that David was also missing he had gathered Christopher and they had both headed for the children's room, assuming something terrible had happened.

David wafted his arms about trying to fan the mist to see through it. He could hear cries, shouts and scuffles from various places within the room, but he couldn't see anything or anyone. He thought he heard Jennifer scream and Socata shout a warning, before hearing other voices; Sukhoi maybe, and possibly Christopher too.

Then the mist cleared as fast as it had arrived and he realised that Sukhoi had made the mist disappear with a quick incantation when he saw him standing in the doorway. Why hadn't he thought of that, he admonished himself?

When he looked around the room he saw Jennifer was on the floor; it looked as if she had been thrown to the side. Belmokhtar was firmly held by Socata. He had the Keeper's left arm behind his back; pushing it hard and high, whilst a dagger was expertly covering the traitor's throat; a few drops of blood slowly running down the blade as Socata re-enforced his grip.

Christopher was rubbing his cheek and was picking himself up from the floor while the Dragons were looking wildly around the room for signs of Nuba Driss.

"Where did he go?" David asked quickly assessing the situation and noticing that Nuba Driss was no longer in the room.

"Someone knocked me down, it must have been him." Christopher said quickly, retrieving his sword that was by his feet and sheathing it skilfully.

"After him, we must find him!" David shouted.

"It is too late my friend, he is like the wind. We will not find him now, no matter how much we search." Sukhoi said to David as he barred his way.

"No, we must find him, he has the Kavacha book of knowledge and he has the Dragon's orb." He said weakly, as everyone looked at him stunned by his words.

Jennifer ran over to her brother and held his head in her hands. "He has the orb? You saw the orb?"

"Yes it was in his robes." He confirmed.

"JENNIFER, COULD THIS BE TRUE?" Asked Hash'ar'jefar hoping above all else that it was the truth.

"Yes my friends, David has seen your orb."

"He has the book?" Sukhoi asked in shock; losing his composure for a moment.

"I'm afraid so Sukhoi." David said apologetically. "I have lost your sacred book, the Dragon's orb and I didn't get my answers." David finished defeated.

"Maybe my friend," Sukhoi suggested after a moment's consideration. "But at least we know for certain where they all are." He finished.

Chapter Thirty Three

Hannah entered the room a little apprehensively as she heard the shouting coming from behind the door before she even got within twenty feet of it. Although she entered with a winning smile on her face, she was greeted by a room full of red and angry faces.

"I've just come to tell you that they're retreating! We've managed to defeat the Imazaghan army and Koutla Raiders and they're leaving!" She said triumphantly.

They had either gone deaf or they didn't realise the significance of what she just told them because everyone was still red-faced and angry. Then she watched in unbridled shock as Socata; one of Sukhoi's Ruedin, shook the Keeper of Kavacha Lore and shouted in his face, while everyone else looked on. She didn't hear the words, but she couldn't believe what was happening.

"What are you doing you fool, let go of the Keeper!" She shouted.

"Leave it Hannah." Sukhoi said to her, his face pale and grim.

"Sukhoi, what's going on?" She asked still staring at Socata as he brought a blade up to the Keeper's throat, producing a small trickle of blood, not that anyone noticed, not even Belmokhtar himself.

"What's going on?" She said again, quite disturbed by the situation.

"We've found a traitor." Socata replied in an angry voice barely suppressed.

Shock registered for a moment on her face as she looked from Socata to the Keeper, and then to Sukhoi, who let his gaze fall from the Keeper's face to stare at hers. She noticed that her friend was close to tears, whether through anger, frustration, or something else, she wasn't sure, but she couldn't stand to look at the pain there so she looked at the floor.

"I came to find you," She said quietly, lifting her gaze to Sukhoi, "to tell you that the Imazaghan are retreating, I couldn't find you on the battlements and so I thought to find you here." She said in a whisper.

Sukhoi felt the anger dissipate as he watched the emotions on Hannah's face change from elation, through surprise to fear and to disbelief.

He sighed when he released his hold on the Keeper and moved across the room to Hannah. He took her in his arms and said quietly. "That is good news, very good news."

She put her arms around him and held him tight, resting her head on his chest she said to him. "A traitor, the Keeper of the Kavacha Lore is a traitor!"

"Why? How could you do this to your own people?" Elder Haber Bashir asked the Keeper of Kavacha Lore.

Belmokhtar continued to stare at the wall of the audience chamber in silence as he was questioned by the council of elders about Nuba Driss and his involvement with the evil mage.

Sukhoi and a handful of the surviving Kavacha had tried in vain to get some answers from the traitor, but he hadn't said a word since leaving the children's room. Now only Sukhoi of the Kavacha sat by and quietly observed as the council interrogated the Keeper. The rest of the Kavacha were trying to get the city back on its feet.

David and Jennifer were sitting quietly to one side; Christopher had accompanied Socata to the city gates to find out any word of their friends.

"Jen," David addressed his sister nervously.

She turned to look at her brother and she could tell from his apprehensive look that he was about to ask her something he didn't want to. Something she wouldn't like herself.

"You want me to try and read his thoughts, don't you?" She asked, and realised she had guessed right when David's eyebrows rose. He was behaving more and more like Sukhoi all the time, though that wasn't a bad thing, she supposed.

"I think if we can get him to talk and you listen to the truth of his words, we might actually get some answers to why we are here. He brought us here after all, or at least opened the way for us, but he's been working for Nuba Driss all along. Why would Nuba Driss want us to come here, especially with you being the one person that could stop him, it doesn't make sense." David said quickly.

"It's got to be worth a try, I suppose. Let's go and speak to Sukhoi." She replied and both children stood up and walked over to the Kavacha.

Jennifer whispered something in his ear as the elders continued to interrogate Belmokhtar. Belmokhtar frowned as he saw the children approach the Kavacha and a frightened expression passed over his face as Sukhoi approached the elders.

"David and Jennifer would like to ask the traitor some questions!" Sukhoi addressed them. Belmokhtar had been referred to as the traitor since they had captured him, no one spoke his name now, and he didn't deserve the respect a name could give him.

The council chatted quietly for a few minutes, though they couldn't really say no to the request made by a Kavacha Master and especially by the Nadym Varsk.

They quickly nodded their ascent and both David and Jennifer approached Belmokhtar cautiously.

The traitor looked up at them with a careful smile and nodded to each before whispering, "Looks like I'm in a bit of a pickle, doesn't it?" It was just loud enough for them to hear and the council couldn't see his face from where David and Jennifer were standing in front of him.

David nodded in agreement, "Why did you bring us here Belmokhtar? Why us?" David whispered back, so the council couldn't hear his reply.

Belmokhtar looked into David's eyes and then looked at Jennifer standing rigidly at his side before answering just as quietly, "Lord Driss told me to bring you here."

David glanced at Jennifer, who merely nodded that he was telling the truth.

"But why? Did he know that Jen was the Nadym Varsk?" David persisted.

Belmokhtar contemplated that question before answering. "Maybe, but I'm not sure.

Lord Driss told me to enter the door to your world and bring you into this one."

"What, all three of us?" David asked.

"Yes." He replied.

"Why?" David asked, "For what purpose?"

"He didn't tell me, only that you three were special and that you and your sister had exceptional gifts that he could use." He replied as if the question didn't really bother him one way or the other, if his lord wanted him to know, he would have told him in his own good time.

"And you didn't ask what those gifts could be used for?" David couldn't believe that the Keeper wouldn't have asked his master why he wanted them there.

"No." He replied.

"He's lying Dave, or at least he's not telling us everything." Jennifer said to her brother.

Belmokhtar looked at Jennifer and nodded to her with a smile. "Yes, there is more, but that is for my Lord to tell you."

"Why can't you tell us?" David asked, "We may not see your master again after his defeat."

"You will see him soon enough David, and maybe then you will have your answers."

"I want those answers now Belmokhtar!" David said raising his voice slightly. It was a physical effort to try and remain calm. He could feel his anger and frustration infusing his thoughts, and he could also feel his magic trying to burst through him to attack the Keeper. Containing both he asked. "Why can't you tell us? After everything we have gone through, we came because we thought you need our help!"

Belmokhtar shuffled nervously; he could sense the power building inside the boy that was a Kavacha Master, though he wasn't sure anyone else in the room could. Not even Sukhoi; First of the Kavacha, had as much skill as that. Belmokhtar was different though, he wasn't from Sakhalin. He was nowhere as strong as either Nuba Driss or David, but he did have special gifts, and it was those abilities that guaranteed his safety by Nuba Driss.

"David," he said, "I am sorry your had to be brought into this but Lord Driss is the only one that has the answers you seek, I was just a messenger asked to help you find your way here. He told me that he needed you here, but he didn't tell me why."

"Is he telling the truth Jen?" David asked his sister, suspicious that the Keeper wasn't telling him everything.

Jennifer reached out her hand and touched Belmokhtar's head. He tried to pull his head back, but once Jennifer touched him, he found it impossible to move anything, let alone his head. His eyes opened wide for a moment in shock as a white light surrounded Jennifer's hand. She was immediately shocked by the feelings raging inside the Keeper, strange and incomprehensible feelings. But she found what she was looking for straight away.

As soon as it had come the light disappeared and Jennifer said to her brother, "He feels differently to everyone else here, though I don't understand how or why? But that isn't important for now, what is important though, is that Nuba Driss is still in the city and he will attempt to rescue Belmokhtar."

"Why would Nuba Driss take the risk and rescue him." Elder Bashir stated, "Even if he is still in the city, he wouldn't take the chance against our Kavacha."

Nods and murmurs of agreement accompanied his words.

"He needs him!" Jennifer replied quietly, and then turned to her brother as everyone pondered why Nuba Driss needed the Keeper.

David stared at his sister and then back to Belmokhtar. His mind raced as he tried to figure out why Nuba Driss would need the Keeper. Words and pictures came into his mind and with them the realisation of why Belmokhtar was so important. It was why Nuba Driss needed the Keeper in the first place; he couldn't open the doorway to the corridor himself. He needed the Keeper to do it for him. Belmokhtar had already told them that he had shown them how to get there; maybe he had shown Nuba Driss the same thing. The Keeper was the key to the corridor, David realised that Nuba Driss couldn't use the corridor without him.

He also realised that if Belmokhtar could open a doorway for Nuba Driss, he could also open it for the children to get back home.

Jennifer watched silently as he brother worked everything through. She had used her gifts to see the truth, but was amazed by the speed in which her brother worked through all the facts to reveal the truth by his own methodical process.

David also realised the danger everyone was in at that moment. Nuba Driss would stop at nothing to ensure the Keeper's release. There were no guards in the audience chamber, the only Kavacha there was Sukhoi; and although some of the council of Elders were warriors, they were still probably too old to be of much use against the mage, should he show up. David realised that this would be the best possible time for Nuba Driss to mount a rescue operation. He was just about to voice his fears to Sukhoi when a raspy voice made him turn from the Keeper to where the elders were seated.

"Ah, there you are my friend." The dark and menacing figure that was Nuba Driss said as he appeared by Elder Hanish's side. A ball of lightning was sparkling in his hand as he moved around the nervous elders; who appeared to be riveted to their seats.

"Nice to see you again David, Jennifer, hope you are both well?"

Sukhoi recovered swiftly from his shock of seeing the mage and started to move towards the elders.

"Any false moves Sukhoi Mikoyan," Nuba Driss said quickly as Sukhoi took a step towards the elders, "and your elders don't get to see another sunrise." He finished, moving the lightning ball from his hand to sit atop of Elder Hanish's head.

"Now," Nuba Driss continued when Sukhoi stopped, "release Belmokhtar immediately."

No one moved.

"Kill the traitor!" Elder Hanish shouted at Sukhoi. An invisible force slammed into the elder and almost knocked him off his seat.

"I wouldn't do that." Nuba Driss returned, "I could kill you all in but a moment. Now, release the Keeper and bring the girl to me, then we will leave."

David couldn't believe that Nuba Driss thought he was going to get away with this. That they would actually release Belmokhtar and then hand over his sister, without doing anything to stop him, he must be mad, he thought. Yes, everyone was scared; he was petrified himself, but as he looked at Sukhoi, he could see the same outraged and angry face that he was probably displaying, and he knew he wasn't the only one that would try and prevent Nuba Driss accomplishing what he had come to do.

"Just like that!" David shouted angrily at the figure.

Jennifer reached out her hand to grab her brother as he took a few steps forward, but he moved beyond her reach. "Just like that, you come in here, handing out threats to everyone and you think you can take my sister away!"

Nuba Driss turned his attention on David, but didn't stop him as he continued to move towards the elders.

"Just like that David." Nuba Driss replied.

"No!" David shouted, "No, it won't be just like that at all. Not if I have anything to do with it, so think again!" He shouted as he began to shake with anger.

"You think you can stop me?" Nuba Driss chortled at him. "You, a so-called Kavacha Master think you can seriously stop the greatest mage any world has ever seen." Nuba Driss taunted.

"Somebody has to!" David said, trying desperately to control his anger and search his mind for something in the Kavacha knowledge that could help him.

Nuba Driss began to laugh, a full throaty laugh that resonated around the chamber.

The chamber then began to grow cold and the light began to fade. David noticed that everyone in the room was looking around pensively, until he realised that he couldn't see anyone else, except the dark figure of Nuba Driss.

A thick mist had obscured his view of everyone else, and he began to tremble uncontrollably. Nuba Driss appeared to glide toward him; still just a dark figure with no face, but it chilled him to his very bones as he moved closer and closer.

David couldn't move, his arms, his legs, even his head felt stiff as if someone else controlled his movements. He tried to break free, he tried to shout, but nothing happened. Then he heard footsteps behind him; quite weak at first but growing stronger with every step.

Nuba Driss was still drawing closer when he felt a warm soft hand clasp his own and strength returned to his body; he controlled it once more.

He turned his head to see Jennifer standing beside him, a frightened half smile on her lips, but with a resolute expression on her face.

He knew they would stand together and face whatever Nuba Driss threw at them. They had been in this same situation before he realised, but this was no dream, this was happening and it was happening now.

David squeezed his sister's hand and found the strength to confront the figure as it glided to a stop before them.

"Do you believe you can stand against a Kavacha Master; whose knowledge was passed down from the Guardian himself, and defeat the Nadym Varsk, who had been foretold to destroy you?" David said calmly to the dark face-less creature that was Nuba Driss.

The laughter stopped. "Yes!" He replied. "Because I have something you want!"

"What do you..." David began, but then stopped as Nuba Driss revealed a frightened and shaking Christopher by his side.

Jennifer took an involuntary intake of breath as David's throat constricted, both looking at their brother at Nuba Driss's side. The evil mage had a firm grip on their brother's shoulder and they could see the pain in his face as he squeezed it. How Christopher had been captured, they didn't know, he was supposed to be with Socata, but there was no time to ponder that now. They had to think of a way to get him back, but how?

David felt the power before he could do anything to stop it. The power seemed to act instinctively of its own free will as he felt his hand raise and a ball of lightning burst forth to hit the mage in the chest. Stunned, Nuba Driss took a step back and that gave Christopher the opportunity to break free of his grip and dove to the floor, rolling out of the way and to safety.

Nuba Driss screamed in frustration and then raised his arms and a blast of white lightning descended on David and Jennifer, Christopher forgotten as he focused on the other two Barnes children. Instinctively David raised his hand again and it was as if a shield was there to defend them against the magic. Nuba Driss howled in rage and pushed his hands forward trying to penetrate the shield, but the more he pushed, the stronger the shield became.

Suddenly the lightning stopped and David lowered his hand cautiously; prepared to raise it if required.

"You can not defeat me, don't you realise that?" Nuba Driss screeched at him.

"We can try!" replied Jennifer.

She then reached out with her mind and tried to touch Nuba Driss's thoughts. She found them immediately, she found a profound and intelligent mind, but one so full of hate and madness that she wanted to shy away from it. She found it both compelling and loathsome, but she forced her own thoughts into that mind, to try and reach any part of it that still held some small measure of compassion.

Nuba Driss screamed in fury, "Get out! Get out of there!"

Jennifer would have fallen as Nuba Driss mentally blasted her from his mind with a strength of will that stunned her, if David hadn't been there to stop her.

Nuba Driss suddenly retaliated with another burst of magic. David raised his hand, hoping the Kavacha knowledge would somehow protect them once more.

A white bright fire enveloped them; David could feel its heat and ferociousness as Nuba Driss pushed forth his attack. Again a defensive shield protected them from the fire, but David had to take an involuntary step back from the force of the blast. He could feel his brow begin to sweat as the blast continued, and he took step after step backwards, pulling his sister along with him. He tried desperately to retaliate, to push forth his own attack, but the concentration required to just maintain the shield was weakening him without trying a counter-attack of his own.

Nuba Driss began to laugh, that mad crazed laugh began again as he pushed forward; sensing victory.

David's anger grew as he desperately sought some way of defeating his nemesis, but nothing came to mind. He looked desperately at his sister and through clenched teeth he said, "I don't think I can hold on for much longer Jen!"

Jennifer nodded that she understood and tried to concentrate on Nuba Driss once more. She pushed her thoughts forward and attacked his mind with a desperateness that matched their situation. She knew David couldn't hold on much longer, but what could she do. The Kavacha told her that she was suppose to defeat Nuba Driss, but they hadn't told her how. David knew the book of Kavacha Lore inside out but he hadn't found any reference in there that could help her either. She hadn't really done anything yet, David was the one that was trying everything, while she just watched. She felt her own anger grow, she knew the strength she had, she had felt it before, but now she dug deeper, right into her very soul and called forth all the power she could. Desperate to help her brother, and desperate to defeat Nuba Driss and stop all this pain and suffering. She consumed all the energy she could find and thrust it at the still laughing creature.

An audible gasp of surprise and pain was heard as she unleashed her power and incredibly it was Nuba Driss that staggered backward. His own onslaught had been stopped and now David sensing his sister had given him a reprieve, began his own counter attack. Every thought, every magical conjuration that came to mind he used without mercy. Blasts of magic, balls of lightning, waves of force were focused on Nuba Driss, pushing the mage back with each onslaught as he tried to defend himself.

While David attacked with anger, Jennifer sought for any particle of sense or reason that remained in the mad mage. She delved deeper and deeper until she found one image, one almost forgotten image of a small boy crying as he lay on the tiled floor of a kitchen and another boy holding out his hand to help the boy to his feet.

She screamed then as she was ripped from the mind of Nuba Driss once more. She opened her eyes then and was surprised to see that Nuba Driss was lying on the floor of the chamber with Belmokhtar at his side helping him up. David was standing at her left shoulder and the room was once more free from mist. Everybody was still in the same positions they had been before, but she began to smile when she saw that they had been joined by Hash and Sak, the Dragons were standing in front of the elders with fierce looks on their faces. She saw that Braduga, Maroc and his sons had now entered the room as well.

She turned to face Nuba Driss as he was helped to his feet by the traitor. "You may have won this battle," he rasped at them, "but we will meet again!"

Belmokhtar whispered a few words and the pair of them dove for a door on their right.

Hash'ar'jefar moved like lightning but couldn't prevent the two fleeing fugitives. He managed to strike at them with his tail but made little impact; a ripping sound was heard as his tail slashed their trailing robes. The strike hadn't been in vain, the book of Kavacha knowledge fell from the tear in Nuba Driss's robe and skidded along the floor; although Nuba Driss did not appear to notice its absence as he disappeared from sight. Then before anyone could say anything, Hash'ar'jefar and his sister gave pursuit, charging into the doorway without hesitation.

David couldn't believe his eyes as he looked at the doorway. He felt the power of the corridor even before he moved into a better position to see it. He heard it calling to him, and was mesmerised by its words, its offer of power and glory. He was mesmerised by its power as it continued to call to him.

"Dave we have to follow them!" Jennifer shouted at him. "We have to help them." She insisted as her brother just continued to stare at the open doorway.

Sukhoi looked quickly towards his Ruedin and then the three of them entered the doorway on the tails of the dragons.

"Dave!" Christopher yelled pointing at their friends as they disappeared.

David suddenly became conscious of the situation and knew he needed to act. He was horrified to see his friends enter the doorway after the dragons and especially after Nuba Driss and Belmokhtar. Before he realised what he was doing, he was running to the doorway himself, shouting at Jennifer and Christopher to follow him as fast as they could.

As he reached the door he stopped and shouted at the elders. "Take care of the book!" He said, pointing to the sacred book on the floor. "Bind it again with the strongest spell the Kavacha can think of. Try and make it up with the Imazaghan, you should be the four tribes of Sakhalin, only together can you make this world a better place. I will try and protect Sakhalin from Nuba Driss and I will try and bring Sukhoi and his Ruedin back to you, but you must guard this door and the Guardian's Stone until we return."

The elders nodded in understanding and Elder Hanish managed a weak smile, "We will do as you say Kavacha Master!" He shouted as the three children entered the doorway themselves just as the doorway disappeared.

Christopher just managed to enter the corridor as the door suddenly shut firmly behind them. The three children were standing in the empty white corridor once more, all alone. Their friends and Nuba Driss were nowhere to be seen. Not only that, but all the doors in the corridor were closed, they could have entered anyone of them.

"What do we do Dave?" Jennifer asked her brother realising where they were.

David tried to think, and think quickly. He needed to stop Nuba Driss getting back into Sakhalin where he would undoubtedly wreak his havoc once more.

"I have to set some sort of protection over this door before we do anything else." He said purposefully.

"We haven't time Dave, we have to find our friends, Braduga and Socata will need our help!" Christopher shouted at him.

"Chris. I have to do this, if Nuba Driss gets back into Sakhalin, he will destroy everything and everyone!"

"Do you know what to do?" Jennifer asked him apprehensively as Christopher waited impatiently looking up and down the corridor for any signs of their friends.

Images swirled in David's mind as he sought an answer to his problem of keeping the door secure and protected. "Yes!" He shouted excitedly as the right image came to mind and he quickly invoked the incantation.

"Ok, let's go!" He said a moment later turning to the expectant gazes of his brother and sister.

"Which door?" Christopher asked, as if his brother would know the answer.

David looked up and down the corridor in dismay. "I don't know!" he conceded. "All these doors look the same and they could have entered any of them. Infact, we don't even know if they all went through the same door."

"We must find the right door Dave, what're we going to do?" Jennifer shouted anxiously.

"Jen, you're the truth seer, can't you tell which door they went through?" He offered.

Jennifer scrutinised the corridor and focused her thoughts on the doors she could see but nothing showed itself to her. "I don't sense anything." She told them disheartened.

David knew it was a long shot, but he didn't know what else to suggest.

"Right come on then, let's try the nearest door and hope it's the one they took." He said making his mind up. All thoughts of searching for their own door to take them back home never even entered their minds, so strong was their thoughts to find and help their friends.

The children ran to the nearest door; it seemed to take an age, but eventually they stood before it breathlessly and looked at each other apprehensively.

"They probably picked the nearest door as well, so this must be the one. Are we ready?" David asked them.

"We're ready." Christopher and Jennifer said together.

"Let's go!" David shouted as he opened the door.

David pushed opened the door without thought of any danger that may be lurking behind it and rushed through. He wasn't about to let Nuba Driss escape if he could help it and he wasn't about to desert his friends. He was nudged forward when Jennifer and Christopher charged into the room after him a moment later.

He turned to face them immediately, "If we want to help our friends we must turn around now, before it's too late!" He shouted urgently.

Jennifer and Christopher hardly heard him as they stood there stunned looking at the large winding slide and the hole that was just appearing which lead to their fireplace, and home.

"Jen, Chris, did you hear what I said, we must go now!" He shouted at them, waving his arms to get their attention, though he was stood right in front of them, they appeared not to see him, so he physically tried to push them back into the corridor.

"We're home." Mesmerised, Jennifer stood there as a statue with a half smile on her lips and her eyes wide open as if looking at something amazing.

David turned round to look at the slide then and watched as the hole began to get bigger. He felt the familiar tingling sensation immediately and before he could voice anything further he felt the rush as he was sucked up the slide towards the fireplace.

"Too late." Was his parting thought as he came through the fireplace to find himself sitting with his back to the sofa and looking into the fireplace with Jennifer and Christopher sat either side of him.

Incredibly they had somehow returned wearing their own clothes, and as they stared at each other and at the fireplace, they heard a familiar voice.

"You lot are up early." Annabel Barnes addressed her children as her head appeared around the living room door.

"Mum!" They said together as they scrambled to their feet and dived at their mother as she entered the room. They each put their arms around her and hugged her as she looked at them with affectionate bewilderment.

"Ok, what's going on?" She asked suspiciously as they continued to hold on to her as if she would disappear before their very eyes.

David recovered quickly from the shock of seeing his mother for the first time in months, "We've all missed you." He said, trying to keep a check on the lump in his throat and the tears that were forming in his eyes, but failing miserably.

Dumbfounded by her children's affectionate embrace, Annabel Barnes hugged her children back but replied, "I've missed you too since last night," She replied, but then she realised that she had been working a lot recently and maybe they needed a bit more attention than they were getting, "but you know why I have to work all the time, don't you?" She asked. Hoping they did realise that she was doing it for them.

"Last night?" Christopher asked, not comprehending as he looked at her face. He looked around at David and Jennifer's expressions and saw the same shocked expression that he obviously had on his.

It was Jennifer that realised first that although they appeared to have been away from home for months, to their mother they had only been away mere minutes or even seconds. She knew it to be true the minute she thought it, but as she did, she felt as if something special had just left her.

She put her finger to her lips then and looked at her brothers to make sure they had seen the signal to keep quiet; they did.

"Yes, last night. Are you ok Chris?" She asked, feeling his brow as if he was coming down with a fever.

"He's fine mam; he's just messing about as usual." David stated.

Annabel Barnes looked at her oldest son and just managed to stop herself from gasping in surprise at the fading tattoo on his neck as it disappeared.

"Right, well, thanks for the early morning love kids, but I have to get ready for work, and you lot have to get ready for school." She told them hurriedly and left the living room hastily.

They stood there bewildered for a moment but when she shouted back that she was going to make them eggy bread for breakfast but she didn't have all day, they relaxed.

"Jen, what just happened?" David asked his sister quietly as they heard their mother banging around in the kitchen.

"We're home Dave," she replied, "and it looks as if we've only been away for a few minutes, as much as I can tell." She explained.

"Quick Dave, the fireplace, we've to get back!" Christopher said hurriedly as he dove for the fireplace, searching for the hole in the back of the grate.

"I don't think you'll find anything there Chris." His brother told him.

"It has to be here. What about our friends? What are we going to do?" Christopher asked thinking of their friends chasing after Nuba Driss and the traitor Belmokhtar by themselves.

"I don't know Chris." He replied.

David stared at the fireplace, he tried to recall spells and incantations but realised he couldn't even see any images in his mind any more. All the Kavacha knowledge he had gained from the book had vanished. He could feel and sense nothing of the power he had wielded but somehow he knew it was still there buried deep within himself. He tried to open himself up to the magic of the corridor, but even that wasn't calling to him any more. He was just an ordinary boy from a small mining town once more. He was a little surprised that he missed the power, but not the burden of responsibilities that came with it. Although, he would give anything if he could get back that power to help his friends. But, the gateway to the corridor had been closed and he didn't know if it would re-open any time soon. He looked away from the fireplace then, turning his attention to his brother and sister who were standing next to him and waiting for him to speak. He didn't think anything about that until he remembered it later. Sakhalin had changed their lives and changed their personalities. As he looked at their expectant faces he knew he had to say something to them, give them some small measure of hope that they would one day return and help their friends.

"There's nothing we can do at the moment. The doorway has been closed to us, and I don't know why before you ask. But we know that the door to Sakhalin is protected and Nuba Driss won't be able to do any more damage to our friends there. We also know that Sukhoi, Brad and Socata can take of themselves. And if the dragons are with them, they will look after each other. But I promise you both now, the doorway will reopen one day and when it does we will be ready. We will find our friends and together we will destroy Nuba Driss!"

The children hugged each other then and stood silently looking at the fireplace, hoping in their hearts that they would see their friends again.

END OF BOOK ONE

Printed in the United Kingdom
by Lightning Source UK Ltd.
134721UK00001B/1-3/P